T0312344

Gold
Rush

Also by Olivia Petter

Millennial Love

Gold Rush

OLIVIA PETTER

4th ESTATE • *London*

4th Estate
An imprint of HarperCollins*Publishers*
1 London Bridge Street
London SE1 9GF

www.4thestate.co.uk

HarperCollins*Publishers*
Macken House
39/40 Mayor Street Upper
Dublin 1
D01 C9W8, Ireland

First published in Great Britain in 2024 by 4th Estate

1

A catalogue record for this book is available from the British Library

ISBN 978-0-00-860641-1 (hardback)
ISBN 978-0-00-860642-8 (trade paperback)

Typeset by Palimpsest Book Production Ltd, Falkirk, Stirlingshire

Printed and bound in the UK using 100% renewable electricity at CPI Group (UK) Ltd

This book contains FSC™ certified paper and other controlled sources to ensure responsible forest management.

For more information visit: www.harpercollins.co.uk/green

To the women who haven't been believed,
especially the ones who didn't believe themselves.

Being so caught up,
So mastered by the brute blood of the air,
Did she put on his knowledge with his power
Before the indifferent beak could let her drop?

'Leda and the Swan' W. B. Yeats

Summer 2017

When Rose opens her eyes, he has gone. The window is cracked open enough to invite a breeze, sunlight dancing in and out with the moving curtain. Her outfit is spread across the floor in all its parts: velvet flares folded into themselves in one corner, denim jacket crumpled in the other. The boots are neatly placed side by side underneath her desk as if by someone who didn't want to make a mess. She is naked.

Picking her laptop off the floor, she decides to google him. In the last twenty-four hours, six new articles have been published. One is a round-up of his greatest 'fashion hits' that must have been recently updated because the first photo is from 2012. Another claims that he is considering adopting a cocker spaniel; sources say he will name it 'Bobby'. And then there is one she has seen several versions of before that lists all the people he has dated since he was eighteen. She is familiar with most of the names on it because they're either models or daughters of Hollywood actors.

Some of the articles have comments underneath them. 'MARRY ME' reads one. 'Why has he cut his hair like that?' adds another. 'Sit on my face please, kind sir' says a third – Rose reports this comment. She goes to Twitter next and opens the first account that comes up when she clicks on the search bar. It has 850,000 followers and there are two new tweets since Rose last checked. 'Can't believe I have finally met my husband' reads one that appears to be a screengrab taken from someone's Instagram account. He is standing in between two women who look like teenagers, poorly disguised in yellow-tinted sunglasses and a baseball cap. 'He even offered to pay for our coffees' the caption continues. 'What a gem.' The other tweet shows a photograph of him walking into a bakery: 'I wish he was buying CROISSANTS for me!!' It has been liked 5,531 times. There is no point looking at his own Twitter account because he doesn't control it, so Rose scrolls through more accounts of the fans instead.

Finally, once her phone has enough battery to turn itself on, she opens Instagram. He has gained 3,235 followers overnight, bringing him up to 54.3 million in total. She swipes left, taps on his name and starts typing.

PART I

ONE

Still summer 2017
(but a little earlier than before)

The party started like all the others: strangers pretending to be best friends while looking over each other's shoulders for someone more important to talk to. The music was too loud, the volume you'd expect at the end of a wedding. Some guests looked bored because they'd seen it all before. Others were new to the scene and had taken flight, energised by the possibility of sex with a celebrity and the opportunity to snort some of their cocaine.

Rose was by the door looking at her phone. It was normal for talent to be late. He was so late, though, that it made a point. About what exactly she wasn't quite sure. But it rattled her. She had about fifteen minutes before Minnie came over to complain about how hot it was inside (even though the air conditioning was scratching at Rose's throat), a sure sign she was stressed.

The person she was waiting for was Milo Jax. He was a musician, the kind with several Twitter accounts for each of his limbs. Even Luce knew who he was, which was remarkable considering the only music Rose had ever heard coming from her room was by Craig David. At thirty-three, Milo had already won countless awards, sold more than 10 million albums, and hosted SNL twice. His music divided critics – 'charismatic bangers' versus 'tweeny-bopper pop' – but had somehow transcended negative reviews; it was hard to spend a day out and about in London without hearing at least one of his songs playing somewhere. He was classically good-looking, possessing the kind of face that was both chiselled yet cherubic, topped by a mop of tangled dark curls, and pale eyes that looked blue in some photos and green in others, depending on the light.

'It's outrageous that this is your job,' said Luce, furiously googling photos of Milo on her phone while Rose was getting ready at home. 'I had a sex dream about him when I was fourteen.'

'Fourteen?'

'Back when he was in his skinny jeans era. Best. Shag. Of. My. Life. Look at that jawline.'

Luce's phone was inches away from Rose's face; a small rectangle showing several close-up photos of Milo posing on red carpets. He did have a good jawline.

'Pretty sharp,' Rose replied, scraping out the dregs of Luce's mascara, kneeling down in front of the floor-length mirror in her bedroom. It wasn't that she didn't find him attractive, it was more the expectation that she should find him so stupendously attractive that made it hard to know whether she really did or not. Like not fancying Milo Jax made you some sort of social leper so most people wouldn't even consider the possibility.

'What are you going to do with your hair?' Luce asked, twirling her own thick blonde tresses through her fingers.

Rose stared back at herself, gathering thin, frizzy strands of hair together into a high ponytail before twisting them into a bun. She looked at Luce for confirmation.

'I think you should wear it down. You never do that.'

'It just looks so shit,' Rose replied, releasing her grip, allowing her hair to flop back down into its default position that made her look like the love child of Brian May and Hermione Granger.

'No, look. Like this.' Luce ran her hands through Rose's curls, scrunching sections up and letting them go so that they loosened. She reached for a shiny pink bottle, pumped twice into her hands and ran it through, smoothing the frizz. 'There, now you don't look like you're hiding a spider in there,' she said. 'How nervous are you?'

'I'm fine,' she replied unconvincingly.

'Don't be nervous. I reckon he's cool. You don't become that successful by being a dick to everyone.'

Rose sighed and stared silently back at her reflection. 'Can I borrow a dress?' she asked.

Rose had emailed the invitation to Milo's publicist on a whim. She knew he'd be in London that week for tour promo and figured it was worth a shot. Joss Bell was a large and loud New Yorker who had apparently once made Mick Jagger cry. A total stereotype of a music publicist, she usually had a cigarette in one hand while the other was reserved for wild gesticulations inches away from someone's face. People had written articles under pseudonyms about what it was like to work for her; one was headlined 'Stalin in stilettos'.

MJ will be there, Joss's reply stated. Walk him down the red carpet. No interviews. JB.

Minnie was thrilled when Rose told her. 'Well done, darling, I'm very proud of you,' she cooed, swooping in from a meeting at The Wolseley, the familiar jangle of gold bangles signalling her arrival.

The dress Luce had lent Rose was too small, leaving her in a constant state of tugging and wriggling whenever she moved more than an inch. It was discreet – black velvet with long sleeves – so in keeping with the dress code, but it also had an open back that scooped to the exact point where Luce had a tattoo of a butterfly, which had been done when they were at school together. Oliver would probably clock Rose's bare back and ask who she was trying to fuck; thankfully, she hadn't seen him yet.

Milo was now over an hour late. The photographers were either packing up their bags or looking around for the free sandwiches Rose had Ubered over from Pret. Joss hadn't given Rose a phone number but assured her that Milo would call her when he was close.

Rose resented that her job constantly made her feel inferior. Not just to her boss and her boss's boss because that, she reasoned, was how employment worked. But to hordes of people she didn't know, like Milo, who were simultaneously treated like gods and children everywhere they went.

It was an odd thing, having to genuflect at the altar of people who generally never did anything for themselves.

She once heard a famous comedian talking on a podcast about how funny it was that she could perform on stage in front of hundreds of people without getting nervous but had no clue how to put petrol in her car. The host admitted that he also did not know how to put petrol in his car. Both of them cackled as if this was something to be proud of, a stamp of societal superiority by dint of their own ineptitude.

Rose had little sympathy for celebrities, particularly ones like that. And so her job didn't make much sense to anyone. Least of all her. Nonetheless, this was something she consistently felt compelled to rally against. She was in a perpetual state of trying to prove her depth to the people around her. The second you tell someone your job involves famous people and parties with open bars, they write you off as someone that knows who each of the Kardashians is sleeping with but probably couldn't name the Foreign Secretary.

She checked her phone: no missed calls. Milo hadn't posted anything on social media, either. The last photo on Instagram was a blurry one of him on stage from his last tour, holding a microphone in one hand with his other outstretched towards a sea of smartphones, like he was trying to knock them all down. There was no caption, which she always found smug.

It was at this point that she started to consider he might not show up. He'd be photographed on a hike with a mystery brunette in LA, drinking kombucha and everyone would realise he was never coming at all and how adorable it was of Rose to think she could pull this off. That would be the moment she'd be told to go back to work at the private members' club. And the private members' club wouldn't take her back because she still couldn't tell the difference between non-dairy milks.

It had been almost two years and Rose still wasn't sure why Minnie had given her this job. She had applied because the members' club paid terribly and the majority of customers were rude. At best, they'd ignore her completely, grumbling orders for spicy margaritas as if they were at a drive-thru. At worst, they'd click their fingers, threaten to have her fired because their food arrived differently to how they'd asked, or offer her money to spend the night with them. Rose knew she was conventionally attractive – olive skin, dark green eyes, relatively slim – but there was nothing remarkable about the way she looked. Luce was the one with the big lips and a Victoria's Secret body she barely had to do anything to maintain. Luce had the exact right amount of beauty: enough to turn heads in a room but not so much that nobody took her seriously. This was not the case for Rose. Rose went straight up and down like an eight-year-old boy and did YouTube workouts titled 'Booty Burn'.

Minnie was one of the only regulars at the club who remembered Rose's name. One afternoon, she came in complaining that her publicity assistant had been caught stealing clothes from one of the magazine's fashion cupboards. 'I don't understand how she thought she'd get away with it,' Minnie sighed, tugging the olive out of her martini and popping it into her mouth. 'She was posting photographs of herself in a missing Dolce dress on Instagram, for fuck's sake. If you're going to pinch something, at least be smart enough not to tell the entire internet about it.'

Rose laughed. 'I guess there's no point in stealing something like that and not showing it off, though,' she replied.

'Remind me where you went to university?'

'Central Saint Martins.'

'And what did you specialise in?'

'Painting. Portraits, mostly.'

'Can I see some of your stuff?'

Rose hadn't so much as picked up her paintbrush since leaving CSM. Being surrounded by people for whom art was their entire personality had turned the thing she loved most into some sort of exclusive clique predicated on suffering and sacrifice. Blood was a new medium, masturbation was performance art. And if you thought otherwise, you were an outcast with no vision. All Rose wanted to do was paint faces.

'My phone is in the back room,' Rose replied.

'Why didn't you want to work in the art world?'

'Because I've always wanted to serve overpriced drinks to overpaid people who treat me like their personal slave.'

Minnie laughed and the two of them spent the rest of the evening sharing stories about terrible people they'd both come across at work in between impassioned conversations about artists they both loved: Francis Bacon, Egon Schiele, Jenny Saville. 'The ones that you can't look at for too long without fear of convulsing,' as Minnie put it.

Rose joined the company a week later. Arriving at

Firehouse HQ was like walking onto the set of a film you'd watch for the tenth time when you're drunk on a Saturday night. Buried in the depths of Mayfair, it was one of those enormous Regency buildings with pillars either side of the doors. Flashy enough to signify its significance, but subtle enough to pass as, say, a gallery, so as not to advertise the fact this was a place regularly frequented by the famous people whose faces fronted the magazine covers that lined each of its corridors. Firehouse published six titles in total, each appealing to a different demographic and with different circulation figures, though all were dropping annually thanks to a new thing called the internet. The most-read magazines were *MODE* and *Intel*, the company's women's and men's titles, respectively. But there was also *Veil*, a bridal magazine, *Shelf Life*, which covered interiors, and *Flight*, which focused on travel. Then there was *Hives & Dives*, a society gardening magazine whose raison d'être was the upper classes and sexual innuendos. It only had about 500 monthly readers but they were furiously loyal, which everyone had to pretend had nothing to do with the fact they were all aristocratic landowners that went to Harrow with Jasper, Firehouse's CEO and chairman. Despite the fact that Minnie was constantly trying to convince Jasper to drop the title, given its tiny readership ('It basically costs us money to keep publishing it,' she explained during Rose's interview), he was adamant about keeping it. *Hives & Dives* was Rose's favourite magazine to work on, mostly because it ran cover lines like: 'Is it Wrong to Feel Turned On by a Gargoyle?' and 'How Not to Get Lost in Your Own Garden Maze'. Her favourite, though, was: 'How to Maintain a Royal Bush', which prompted a complaint from the Buckingham Palace press office.

As publicity assistant, Rose was responsible for collating monthly press releases for each of the titles. It was straightforward, tedious work that involved reading through each upcoming issue in detail, identifying the highlights, and coming up with a strategy to get other publications to write about them. Essentially, she was just reading through the celebrity interviews, picking out the most newsworthy quotes, and emailing them to showbiz editors so that they'd publish articles about them in their own publications. But this, as Minnie told her in her interview, was the 'least interesting part' of the job.

Working in the Firehouse press office was really only about one thing: the parties, except they were supposed to call them 'events'. As print media continued to fall further out of fashion, the parties had become a financial lifeline for the company. They were the way the 'commercial girls', as Minnie referred to them, seduced luxury advertisers, convincing them that it was actually a very good idea to continue investing millions of pounds in a traditional media empire struggling to stay relevant in the digital world. It wasn't that Firehouse was doing badly, per se – people were still reading the magazines religiously, and the circulation figures were decent compared to other publishers – but the threat of irrelevance was constantly looming, like an expired dairy product you've forgotten is tucked in the back corner of your fridge.

Rose often overheard people talking about Firehouse events in the members' club: who was invited and who wasn't, which editors were seen flirting with which guests, and who had to get carried out the back door by a security guard because they'd taken too much ketamine. But just a few weeks into the job, Rose discovered that, thanks to Minnie, the real stories stayed out of the tabloids. Like when a Hollywood actress suddenly refused to turn up to a jewellery party she was hosting for *MODE* unless she received £4,000 in cash that evening, presumably to buy drugs, so an intern had to walk it over to her suite at Claridge's. Or when a major music legend in his sixties missed his cue to deliver a speech on stage at *Intel*'s 50th anniversary party because he was going down on an editor's PA in the disabled toilets.

There were around two events each month. And the press team were in charge of making sure they were well-publicised, which meant ensuring they had high-profile guests and key journalists in attendance. The most important event in the calendar was always the annual Firehouse Awards, where *MODE* and *Intel* would come together to reward various people in film, fashion and music for, well, nothing in particular. There were categories like 'Best Musician' and 'Actress of the Year' to disguise the fact that the whole thing was basically one big branding exercise for Firehouse, its sponsors, and the people they invited. The award winners were seldom chosen for any reason other than they had already planned to be in London at the time.

When Rose felt her phone vibrate in her pocket, her heart started to twist into itself. The screen read: 'NO CALLER ID'. Did people actually sell celebrity phone numbers? How much would you get for that on the black market?

'Hello,' she answered, her voice several pitches higher than normal.

'Hi. It's Milo, Joss gave me your number. Hope that's okay.'

'Of course, yes. Good evening, Milo. Are you here?'

He made a sound that resembled laughter. 'Good evening,' he replied. 'I'm just about to arrive.'

'Great, I'll meet you by the car.'

'What's your name?'

'Rose.'

'See you soon, Rose.'

Rose felt her cheeks burning as she hung up. *Good evening?* Why had she said *good evening*? She thought about what Milo might say to her when he arrived. There was the usual '*Where's the bathroom?*', '*How long does this thing go on for?*' and '*I really need to be sat next to this person and not that person so you need to make that happen*'. There were the equally common but more discreet requests, like '*What kind of champagne are they serving? I only drink Dom Perignon*' and '*How much trouble will I be in for snorting this at the table if I give you some first?*' And occasionally, there were just downright bizarre things, like the time Rose greeted a Hollywood actor and told him who he needed to thank in his speech and he kept asking why her dress looked so soft and could she send it to him later so he could take a nap on it. She managed to pass him off onto Minnie, who later told her that he was on magic mushrooms.

So far, all the celebrities Rose had expected to be lovely were monsters. And all the ones she'd expected to be monsters were lovely. With the exception of a few people, it was the ones on the precipice of fame with the biggest egos, wildest demands, and the flappiest publicists. The major stars didn't seem bothered by any of it any more, perhaps because they didn't need to be. It didn't take long for Rose to realise that fame only means as much as someone tells you it does.

She headed outside to the red carpet to meet Milo, hands not moving from the bottom of her dress. The last thing she needed was a paparazzi photograph of him arriving with her M&S knickers in the background. A Mercedes-Benz with blacked-out windows pulled up and the air around her changed instantly. It was as if something had inhaled almost all of it. Rose put one hand on her chest and tried to take a deep breath.

The crowd of teenage girls who had been lurking behind the barriers on either side of the red carpet since 5 a.m. started shrieking, their limbs shaking wildly like caged animals. There were always fans waiting for celebrity arrivals outside Firehouse events. But they were usually a mix of ages and genders, reflecting the wide-ranging clientele that usually attended the parties. Tonight though, it was almost entirely young women and their mothers.

A bodyguard emerged, seemingly from nowhere, and opened the car door facing the start of the red carpet. A man was climbing out, the shrieks growing louder and banshee-like now. Rose resisted putting her hands over her ears and stood there, smiling. Black patent loafers emerged first, then a purple trouser leg, a purple suit jacket. And then there he was. Dark curls framed angular cheekbones, full lips perched beneath a small but sharp nose, and those impossibly light eyes that scanned the scene with familiarity and detachment. He was not of this world.

Milo stopped to chat to a few fans, smiling politely when they shoved screens in front of his face. Some of them were sobbing now, gasping for breath as they clutched their hands to their chests. Rose winced when she saw one of the older women reach out from behind the gates to touch his thigh. He lightly side-stepped and moved on to another row of fans. He was good at this, giving everyone equal attention, photographs and eye contact. It wasn't just a routine he'd practised countless times. There was substance to it. He showed interest, an awareness that a single look or comment from him would metastasise into a life-affirming anecdote that would be retold and re-lived for years to come.

Eventually, he waved goodbye and blew some kisses to the crowd – 'Impregnate me!' shouted one alarmingly young voice – and started heading towards the entrance, his eyes scanning again. Rose edged towards him, feeling a thousand eyes on her. She waved at him tentatively but he didn't see.

'Hi, Milo,' she said too quietly for him to hear. She cleared her throat. 'Hi, Milo!' she shouted, surprising herself.

'Hello.' His gaze found Rose. 'Rose, I'm guessing?'

Hearing him say her name was unnerving. 'Yes. Rose. Hi. Sorry for shouting.'

'It's important to get your voice heard. Nice to meet you.' He leaned forward to kiss her on the cheek, placing his hand lightly on her arm. He smelled like the kind of lavender soap you'd buy in a French airport.

'You too. How was the journey?'

'The journey?'

Rose felt her throat clogging up again as she tried to work out from his tone of voice if he was making fun of her.

'I mean, have you come far?'

'I like your dress,' he replied.

Rose became very aware of the feeling of the hot velvet rubbing against her skin. There was sweat slipping between her thighs as she walked. 'Thanks, it's my housemate's. It's actually a bit short.' She tugged at it again. 'I like your shoes.'

'My shoes?' he said, looking down, shrugging his shoulders at the least interesting part of his outfit.

'Let's get you to the red carpet,' Rose replied, hurrying him inside.

She introduced Milo to the photographers. 'Hey, mate!' He smiled at them before getting into position in front of the step and repeat. He knew exactly what to do, posing obediently while jibing with the press, pandering to them while also maintaining that degree of separation that Rose figured was not only inevitable but necessary. Ignoring Joss's instructions after the photos were done, Milo bounded up to a trio of male journalists.

'Oh, I'm so sorry, Milo,' said Rose, sidling next to him. She hated having to do this. 'But Joss said no interviews.'

'Of course, Rose,' he said, smiling back at her. 'Thank you for keeping me in line.'

She felt her face flush. It was hard to tell if he was flirting, or if this was just how he spoke to everyone. The latter was more likely, she reassured herself.

'Who are you looking forward to meeting tonight, Milo?' attempted one of the journalists, completely ignoring what Rose had just said.

Milo turned back to face him. 'Sorry, guys. Next time!' he chimed, swinging around on his heels to face the mass of twinkling bodies impatiently awaiting his arrival. Rose mouthed 'sorry' to the journalists, who stared blankly at her like she'd just punched them in the face.

'So tell me . . .' Milo said, walking strangely slowly beside Rose.

'Tell you what?'

'What's your story?'

'My story?'

'Yes. Tell me about it.'

She laughed to hide her discomfort.

'I don't have one, I guess. Not yet, anyway.'

'And why's that?'

'We're not all global pop stars.'

'No, we certainly aren't.'

There was an awkward silence. Rose couldn't think of anything to fill it so said nothing and pulled her dress down again.

'Well, do you enjoy your job?' he asked, shaking one hand through his hair, which fell neatly back into its original position.

'It's fine.' She paused. 'I mean, whenever I describe it to other people, they tell me how glamorous it sounds.

And I can see how it would look like that. But most of the time I'm really just trying to stop people like you from telling the world about your weird foot fetish, or whatever.'

'How did you know?!'

They both laughed.

'I'm sorry Joss isn't here, by the way. But I'll be on hand for whatever you need.'

'Oh, you'll be on hand, will you?'

'Sorry. I mean . . .'

He smiled. 'I know what you mean. And I appreciate it, thank you. I'd much rather be here without Joss anyway, to be completely honest.'

'Why's that?'

'It just means I can have a bit more fun.'

Rose's cheeks flushed again and she felt an urge to end whatever conversation they were having. 'I'm going to leave you here for a bit but I'll come and find you after dinner to check in just in case they want any more photos of you with some of the other VIPs,' she said.

'VIPs. Ha,' he scoffed, finding either the concept or the acronym hilarious. 'Bye, Rose.'

'Bye.'

The next few hours were intense. Minnie was stressed because Kate Moss had taken Sienna Miller's seat so she could be next to Naomi Campbell, which meant Sienna Miller now had nowhere to sit. And Oliver was so occupied with attempting to seduce Cillian Murphy that he had forgotten to collect the key to the press room from security, which meant everyone they'd scheduled interviews for would now have to linger in the corridors until, according to Minnie, Oliver stopped 'batting his eyelashes at straight men and did his goddamn job'. Oliver was convinced that half of Hollywood was secretly gay.

The corridor was small and journalists were now conducting interviews with A-list talent while squashed together like sweaty sardines. Occasionally, on nights like this, Rose would spot guests she was excited about seeing in the flesh: actors she'd loved since she was young, or, as Minnie had promised in her interview, artists she admired. On those nights, Rose would often try to find a way of getting face time with the talent somehow, either by offering to help their publicist on the night or simply listening in on the press interviews. She had only taken one photograph with a celebrity during her entire tenure at Firehouse, which was several less than Oliver, who was constantly posting photos with guests on his Instagram.

The one occasion when Rose couldn't help herself was the night Cosima Ray came to one of *Intel*'s cocktail parties. Rose had studied Cosima's paintings at school and tried desperately to emulate them at art college. At forty-nine, she was one of the few female artists that people outside the art world had heard of. Her paintings were grotesque, horrifying things that reminded Rose of Francis Bacon's self-portraits. Except Cosima's all featured women, either their faces or specific parts of their naked bodies. The brushstrokes were bold, brash and occasionally completely nonsensical. Her work was controversial, too, like the time she painted the naked bodies of women who'd just come out of rehabilitation centres for eating disorders.

Rose had asked Minnie if it would be okay to speak to Cosima before approaching her. 'Don't be silly. Of course. I'll introduce you,' she replied. Cosima smiled politely and listened as Rose tried – and failed – to articulate how much her work meant to her, managing just a few garbled platitudes before Minnie offered to take a photo of them together on Rose's phone. It seemed like a more natural thing for Cosima to offer up; this was what most fans wanted and what most celebrities had become accustomed to giving. A photo was as easy as standing still and raising your cheeks. A conversation required effort. In the photo, Rose's eyes looked blank, her smile strained. She deleted it right away.

Tonight, though, Rose wasn't that fussed about anyone in attendance. Not unless you counted the 'Its'. The Its – or 'the tits', as Oliver called them – were a group of six women identified by Minnie as the most influential in the media industry. Always pictured in the diary pages and regularly featuring on each other's Instagram Stories, they boasted around 10 million followers between them across Instagram, Twitter and YouTube. One was a TV presenter who had written several bestselling books about self-care, another hosted one of the most popular podcasts in the country and had just launched her own line at Topshop, and a third had used her trust fund to launch a ludicrously successful fashion PR company (all of her clients were 'family friends').

It would be so easy to hate them, and a lot of people

did, including the majority of Firehouse's staff. But Rose admired them. To her, these women epitomised everything she wanted to be. Successful, confident and effortlessly gorgeous, they represented a new form of media based as much on their output as their personal brands. Products they posted about sold out, their books became bestsellers, and off-hand remarks spawned viral Twitter threads and daytime TV appearances. Rose envied them. On top of all their successes, these women were a tight-knit unit. Firm friends who looked out for one another, got drunk together, and regularly posted about each other's various achievements.

Rose was always the one fighting to defend the Its in the office when everyone tried to reduce them to vapid socialites or, worse, vapid influencers. The latter had become an increasingly common insult flung their way. Once, Minnie sent out a press release about one of the Its, Celia Bamford, coming to a launch party of *MODE*'s new biannual homewares supplement, using it as leverage to ensure the attendance of London's diary journalists. Celia had made a name for herself in fashion from a young age, having started a blog when she was sixteen. Now she was often seen in the front row at fashion weeks. Normally, the company didn't send tips ahead of time but Celia had been paid by the homewares sponsor to show up, so it was a sure thing. At least, it was supposed to be. But Celia didn't turn up. The diarists were furious, as was the sponsor, and Minnie had to graft to regain their trust. Later, everyone in the press team received an email from her publicist:

> Dear Minnie and team, we were hurt and disappointed to see CeCe referred to as an 'influencer' in your earlier press release. As you know, CeCe is a creator and writer. Very little of her income comes from sponsored posts on Instagram. We felt like this false representation of her work belittled her public persona, which is why she will not be attending any further events with you.

'But she literally is an influencer,' whined Oliver, hunched over Minnie's shoulder, chewing on a Clif Bar. 'Like, she has millions of followers, and makes money by selling things to them on social media. Her blog has been defunct since 2013. What's she writing now besides Instagram captions?'

'I know,' Minnie sighed, quickly typing a polite apology in response.

'I think there's a feeling that calling yourself an influencer implies you're a narcissist,' said Rose. 'You're profiting off your looks, your house, your Anthropologie plates . . . it's all about you and it's bullshit. I guess they know that and deep down they're embarrassed by it.'

'Oh, come off it, Rose,' Oliver scoffed, neatly folding the wrapper of his Clif Bar so it became a tiny triangle. 'Why be embarrassed when that narcissism has literally turned you into a millionaire? We'd all do it if we could.'

All of the Its, bar CeCe, were in attendance that evening but had been huddled in the smoking area since dessert had come out. Rose walked past them on her way to the loo, inhaling wafts of Marlboro Light mixed in with Jo Malone. Marissa Miller was wearing a silk scarlet gown, with a strap just about clinging onto her shoulder. Polly Jenkins was wrapped in a leopard-print mini dress that she kept hoisting up over her breasts as she puffed furiously on a cigarette. They sat close together, one telling a story while the others opened their mouths and gasped in sync. Polly's eyes met Rose for a split second; she whispered something to Marissa and they both burst into a fit of Machiavellian giggles. Rose told herself it was a coincidence and kept walking.

Back at the press room, which had now been opened thanks to Cillian Murphy introducing Oliver to his wife, things were just as manic. Minnie was on the phone asking why two *Made in Chelsea* stars had arrived. 'I told you "no",' she said firmly, presumably to their renegade publicist. 'I don't care if they promise to go home after the red carpet!'

Meanwhile, Oliver was now negotiating with a British actor Rose vaguely recognised from a *Lord of the Rings* film. Evidently, he hadn't done the red carpet and had just arrived to present the award to the best newcomer in film, which was going to a teenage girl who'd been cast in a Tarantino flick. 'Look, I'm really sorry but we can't get you from this room to the stage and off stage again without walking through some of the tables,' Oliver explained. 'It's just the way the room is organised.'

The actor, who must have been in his early forties, made an actual huffing noise and replied in a voice that sounded satirically clipped: 'Fine, but I must insist on having an escort then.'

Oliver sighed. 'We're all a little bit tied up back here but I promise no one will bother you.'

'Well, you can't guarantee that, can you? I'm calling my publicist.'

The actor stomped into the corridor, phone already to his ear. Oliver rolled his eyes and turned to face Rose.

'What do you want?' he said with such severity it was more of a statement than a question.

'Nothing, I'm just looking for Minnie to see if she needs help with the interviews.'

'You're just so bloody helpful, aren't you?' he said, squinting his eyes with disdain.

It was best to ignore him and focus on trying to find Minnie. Oliver had been fiercely competitive with Rose ever since she started at Firehouse. This was odd for a few reasons. The first was that he had been at the company for two years longer than her and had a more senior role. The second was that he was often given preferential treatment by the executives upstairs, who'd sometimes invite him to cover presentation meetings over Minnie. And the third was that at 6'5" with a bone structure to rival Cindy Crawford's, he looked like a Hollywood siren from the 1960s. Standing next to Rose should have been enough to boost his ego.

Even so, he was too obsessed with celebrities to be any good at his job, which was probably why he hadn't ever been promoted. Rose suspected he blamed this on her. The fact that she was looking after Milo tonight would have pissed him off. Oliver loved to look after talent – but the rule was you only got to do that if you were the one to book them. Still, he was often requested personally by publicists. And if Minnie didn't give in to a publicist's requests, she would risk losing the talent altogether. Rose hardly ever got to work directly with celebrity guests; it was almost always Oliver.

'It's because I'm the best,' he'd coo every time he was assigned someone.

'Or it's because you're the only man in the press office,' Minnie would reply with a heavy sigh.

'Oh, I see,' Oliver would say mockingly. 'We're spouting the age-old myth that gay men always get ahead, are we?'

Minnie would remind him that a penis is still a penis, at least to a certain circle of celebrity PRs who, in all likelihood, probably couldn't ascertain Oliver's sexuality from his email signature.

The only people Rose had walked down the red carpet were those Oliver had turned down, which so far, was just Arianna Huffington and Alan Sugar.

The party had been limping on for hours when Rose realised she hadn't eaten anything since breakfast. This was entirely accidental and would often happen on event days. She ventured over to the makeshift office they'd set up in what looked like a giant cleaning cupboard and spotted the box of sandwiches they'd bought for the photographers; there was one tuna and cucumber left, squashed up into a cardboard corner. She sat down on a fold-up chair that had been placed up against the wall on its own, looking on as Oliver laughed nervously on the phone outside the door.

'I know, I know,' he said in a far plummier accent than his own. 'My assistant just screwed up the table arrangements, I'm so sorry.' He paused. 'Yes!' he laughed. 'Yes, she's very young, you know how it is, Ruth.'

'Rose! Where the fuck is Milo fucking Jax?' boomed Liz from the corridor. Liz was the company's events manager and one of the most terrifying people at Firehouse. With a head surrounded by vermilion curls and a voice that sounded like she'd smoked fifty cigarettes, she was the one who produced the parties from start to finish and on the nights themselves was often seen juggling clipboards, walkie-talkies, and various small bags of coloured powder she'd found in the bathrooms. She once fired an intern because they wore a backless top to the office.

Quickly brushing the crumbs off her dress, Rose stood up, leaving one half of her sandwich on the chair. 'I'll just go find him now, Liz.' She asked, 'What do you need him for?'

'To make sure he's going to the afterparty,' Liz barked back. 'If he goes, so will everyone else. It won't look good for the brand if it's just us and that daft *Love Island* girl there. Make sure he has a goody bag, so the sponsors don't castrate me. Go.'

Despite trying to find Milo earlier for photos, Rose hadn't seen him since he arrived. It was easy to disappear at parties like this: there were always secret areas Liz would corner off for celebrities of his calibre so they could have a moment of respite. Firehouse events were always private – but that didn't stop various agents, publicists and plus-ones from bounding up to the most famous person in the room and asking if they'd record a video message for their sister's daughter's friend's cousin.

The tables were mostly empty by now; everyone had filtered out into the bar, leaving behind jackets and dessert. One person – Rose couldn't quite make out who – was slumped over a table, head buried in their arms. The woman next to them was talking very quickly, all dancing fingers and darting eyes, seemingly unaware that her friend could quite possibly be unconscious.

Rose went out to the smoking area, a small caged square that was the only private outdoor space at the venue. A selection of houseplants had been placed in the corner to make it look a little less like a prison cell, though it didn't make much difference. It was easy to spot Milo; he was the kind of person you instantly noticed in every room because of how other people behaved around him.

Slumped against the wall, he was enclosed by a semicircle of three women. All of the women were talking animatedly, whether it was to each other or Milo wasn't completely clear. But he wasn't saying anything and, in all honesty, looked a little bored. His eyes widened when he clocked Rose and smiled, gesturing for her to come over.

'Ah! My blooming Rose,' he said as she approached him.

The three women didn't acknowledge Rose's arrival and continued talking.

'I think they're keen to get you to the afterparty now,' Rose said over them.

'Who's they?'

'My boss.'

'Will Rose get into trouble if I don't come to the after-party?'

'Most likely,' she replied.

'Then it looks like we're going to the afterparty.'

He said his goodbyes to each of the women, kissing them all on both cheeks.

'I'll email Joss on Monday about the boots!' chirped one of them.

'Great, thank you so much!' Milo replied, giving her a thumbs-up as he walked away.

They left the building through the underground car park, where Liz had texted Rose that a car would be parked waiting for him. The lift down there was small and entirely airless, meaning Rose's body was suddenly inches away from Milo's.

'Christ,' he said, tugging at his shirt as he leaned into the corner of the lift.

'Are you okay?'

'Yeah. Just not great in small spaces.'

'Ah, yeah. This lift breaks a lot.'

'What?' His eyes were wide with panic.

'I'm kidding. Sorry.' She flushed red, annoyed at herself for making such a terrible joke. 'I've never actually been in this lift before.'

'You had me there, Rose. I'm a gullible person.'

'Here was me thinking you were someone who wouldn't scare easy.'

'And here's me thinking you would.'

Rose felt nauseous at how effortless it was for him to

flirt with her. She wasn't sure if he actually meant anything by the comment, or if he just said it for the symmetry, but she was grateful when their interlude came to a sudden halt as the lift doors opened and they stepped out into the dark, underground car park.

Milo didn't say anything and headed straight to the car door that was being held open for him by a chauffeur wearing an actual top hat. Rose realised that her time with one of the most famous pop stars in the world was coming to an end and wondered why she felt like she'd failed at something.

'Okay, it was nice to meet you,' she said. 'Would you mind taking the goody bag out at the party? Just so the photographers get a shot with the sponsor's logo.'

He nodded, taking the bag from her, his fingers brushing lightly against hers.

'Anything for you, Rose.'

'Have a lovely time this evening,' said Rose, as he climbed into the car.

'You're not coming?' he asked, buckling his seat belt with the door still open.

'Erm. No.'

'Well, that's not much fun for you, is it?'

Rose smiled weakly. 'Well, I wasn't invited. And I'm working, remember?' These were both lies: it was 11 p.m., her shift had officially finished. She could easily leave now. And any difficulty she'd have getting into the afterparty would be immediately diminished with Milo by her side.

He leaned out of the car, hand outstretched like a claw. 'I thought your job tonight was to look after me.' Looking at his dilated pupils, Rose figured he was a bit drunk. 'You should come. These things are mostly full of people being idiots and saying obnoxious things about themselves. There's sometimes free cheese, too. I think you'd find it funny.'

Not taking his hand, she took a step backwards. 'What makes you think I'd find it funny?'

'I have good instincts. And I think I know a bit about you.'

'I'll bet I know more about you.'

He smiled. 'Are you getting in or not?'

There are some moments in life when a question isn't really a question at all. And that's because the answer has already been determined by greater and more powerful external forces. Those forces could be the social norms that require you to say 'Oh, I love them!' upon receiving a hideous pair of pink pyjamas for your birthday from a distant relative. Or the pressures that compel you to say 'Go on then' when the person you fancy offers you a free tequila shot in a club even though you hate tequila. In this instance, those forces were stronger than ever, because the person asking Rose to do something was Milo Jax. And when someone like Milo Jax asks anyone to do anything, there is only ever going to be one answer.

TWO

The seats in the car were heated. Rose slipped her hands underneath her thighs to warm more of her body, not realising until now how cold she'd been. Someone at the party must have demanded that the air-con be pumped up to full whack. The leather of the seat felt sticky on her back. Milo stared out of the window as they drove, both of them sitting in silence, listening to the gentle hum of Classic FM in the background, a song with violins. She took her phone out to text Minnie.

Milo en route to afterparty. He has the goody bag. Am I okay to clock off?

Yes, darling. Enjoy yourself, she replied. Minnie knew exactly where she was. She always knew everything.

Rose tried to think of something to ask Milo that wouldn't sound too probing. In her head, she ran through various questions about the evening – '*Did you have fun?*', '*How was the food?*' and '*Any good conversations?*' – but resolved that none of them were interesting enough. Milo had the most fascinating life out of anyone she'd ever met. She had to at least pretend to be fascinating too.

'Are the seats always like this?' she asked without thinking.

'What's that?' Milo turned from the window to face her. His eyes looked lighter than they had earlier.

'The heating, I mean. My seat is warm.'

Milo laughed.

'Sorry. I'll shut up,' said Rose.

'No, no. Please. Don't stop. Tell me more about your warm arse.'

He was too good at this.

'Did you have fun tonight?' she asked in an attempt to normalise the atmosphere.

'Not really,' he sighed.

'Why not?'

'Did you have fun?'

'I always find those sorts of things quite overwhelming.'

'Well, I'd say the same.'

'Why come at all then? I was surprised Joss said yes.'

'Because she's worried I'm turning into too much of a teenage – and these are her words not mine – "heart-throb" and wants to make sure there are still some adults that listen to my music so that people take me seriously.'

'And coming to the Firehouse Awards will do that?'

'You tell me.'

'Are you asking if I take you seriously or not?'

'I am.'

'Yes, I mean, of course I do.'

'Convincing, Rose.'

'Well, what do you mean? Do I take you seriously as a musician, or a person?'

'Is the answer different for each one?'

'No, I mean, I don't know. I don't really know enough about your music to answer that. I'm sorry.'

He was smiling at her, enjoying watching her squirm. A part of her just wanted to lightly tap his arm and burst into a fit of schoolgirl giggles. The other part wanted to push a button so the seat beneath would eject her from the car and save her from embarrassing herself any further. Mostly, though, she just wanted to watch this entire interaction from above to check it was really happening.

'I try not to take myself very seriously,' he said.

'Best not to.'

He nodded.

'Didn't you have any friends there tonight? What about those women?'

'Which women?'

'The ones you were talking to outside when I came to find you.'

'Oh, right,' he said, laughing. 'No, they're not my friends. They're pretty awful, really. One of them runs this shoe brand in Mayfair and keeps trying to get me to wear a pair of her cowboy boots to an event.'

'It must be so irritating having people giving you free things all the time.'

He laughed. 'Yes, well. The boots are fine, actually. I'd probably even wear them had she not told me she'd never hire a Northerner.'

'She said that?'

'Yep.'

'Crikey. Did you ask her why?'

'I didn't have to. She just started talking about the importance of front-facing staff being from a "certain type" of background to serve a "certain type of customer". I stopped listening after that.'

'Don't blame you. There are some pretty . . . interesting people in this world,' Rose said, gesturing around herself with both hands.

'I think you're interesting.'

Rose laughed nervously and found herself looking away from Milo to face the window. It was far less stressful just to sit there in silence with him, observing drunk pedestrians swaying on the streets, wondering what they'd think if they knew who had just driven past them.

The party was in a desolate building in central London. It might have been Covent Garden or Shoreditch but it was hard to tell. They'd only really travelled from one underground car park to another and while Rose had tried to focus on where they were going, it was impossible to concentrate. When they arrived, Milo waved and nodded to a woman holding a clipboard by a large blue door, who led them into an empty room with bare white walls that smelled strongly like fresh paint.

'Sixth floor,' the woman said, pointing to a lift in the corner.

'Will you be all right?' asked Rose.

'I think I can handle it with you by my side,' Milo replied.

She scoffed.

'What?'

'You don't have to be so . . . I don't know.'

'Charming?'

'I was going to say . . . well rehearsed.'

'Maybe I'm just well rehearsed.'

'They say practice makes perfect.'

'Do they? I hadn't heard that.'

'I'm going to stop talking.'

'Please don't ever stop talking.' Despite herself, Rose felt her mouth curl into a smile. 'Have you been here before?' he asked.

'No. I know they always host the afterparties for the awards in the same venue but my boss usually discourages us from going to afterparties.' Another lie. Minnie had always encouraged Rose to go to afterparties, even offering her plus-ones. Luce was the only person she was close enough with to ask, but she feared that inviting her might reflect poorly on Rose because she would almost certainly end up being pursued by a married celebrity and cause some sort of national scandal.

'It's fun. I think you'll enjoy it.'

Rose looked down and realised Milo had left the goody bag in the car.

'Fuck,' she whispered.

'She swears?'

'Sorry. I just realised you don't have the goody bag. I had one job.'

'Just get it couriered to me in the morning. I'll post some crazy selfie with it tomorrow to keep everyone happy.'

'Really?'

Before he could reply, the lift doors opened and suddenly

they were in what felt like the middle of a dance floor. The River Thames stretched out in front of them, seen through floor-to-ceiling windows bathed in a kaleidoscope of yellow lights. Not Covent Garden or Shoreditch then. To the left was a marble bar topped with rows of what looked like pre-made espresso martinis and negronis. To the right was, as promised, a table loaded up with every variety of cheese in existence. There was music humming gently through the room; a low and steady beat that sounded as if it kept repeating itself.

She turned to Milo, who was kissing a woman on both cheeks. 'Hello, gorgeous!' beamed the woman, who was dressed head-to-toe in fuchsia leather. It was either a dress or a matching top and skirt; it was hard to tell. Her forehead was immaculately smooth, make-up professionally applied. She could have been twenty-three or forty-three. Rose stood awkwardly by Milo's side as this woman proceeded to talk about her friend's fashion brand and how she was just dying to get Milo into her designs and would he please wear something to one of his red carpet events even if it was just a pair of socks. Milo smiled and said 'Sure' in the way someone does when a distant relative asks you to get their daughter work experience. Then she started asking him about someone called Lila. This woman's eyes were fixed on him, not flinching onto Rose once. Milo didn't introduce her.

Just as they were getting onto talking about Lila's latest stint in rehab, another person bounded up to Milo.

'All right, mate?!' belched this man in his mid-forties, hitting Milo on his back in a way that made his body jolt forward a little.

This would be a good time to check out the cheese, Rose decided, walking away from the group around Milo that was gradually increasing in numbers.

The display went from one end of the room to the other and was piled up high with Brie, Camembert, Gouda and other trimmings you'd find at a Christmas buffet: grapes, crackers with rosemary and lots of the little posh breadsticks they serve in restaurants. Everything was meticulously placed, arranged to be photographed rather than consumed. Slowly, Rose cut a very small piece off each cheese and deposited it on a plate, turning around after every slice to see if she was being watched. She wasn't.

Milo, who had not seemed to realise Rose had left his side – or if he had, didn't seem to care – was now flanked by several people. It was tempting to leave. But then she'd have come here for nothing. There had to be some sort of story from tonight to relay to Luce or Minnie, even if it was just 'I went to a party and saw a few drunk actors from afar'. The story could not be: 'I went to a party, ate some free cheese that may or may not have been display-only, and then went home and finished Season 5 of *America's Next Top Model*.'

Once she'd consumed all the cheese on her plate, Rose looked around, looking for somewhere to put herself. Everyone seemed engaged in their own conversations; to interject would be to intrude. It was a good moment to find a bathroom. The ladies' toilet was tucked behind a crimson velvet curtain in one corner of the room. Unveiling the curtain revealed a small queue, including a famous model now standing right in front of Rose, leaning on the door into the actual bathroom, staring at her phone and tapping it quickly with one finger. She was wearing a purple sequin strapless gown that hugged her narrow hips; her hair was glossy. She looked much thinner than in any of the editorials Rose had seen in *MODE*. A younger-looking woman stumbled out of the toilet, knocking into the model. 'Oh m-my gosh, I'm so sorry,' she slurred in a Sloaney accent, looking up at the model. 'Hi! Oh, goodness, I'm such a fan,' she said, curling her hair around her ears, eyes wide.

'Thank you, that's kind,' the model replied in an American accent, eyes still glued to her screen. The drunk girl ignored the cue and went on talking. She was here tonight with a family friend who works at *MODE* and had just broken up with her boyfriend. She had never been to anything like this before because she was an accountant and my God wasn't it cool because she got to meet people like her and could she tell her a secret? Without waiting for a response, the girl leaned over to whisper something. The model laughed. 'Well, he sounds like an ass,' she said, eyes returning to her phone.

Delighted, the girl launched into a diatribe against men in general, repeating the words 'trash' and 'sociopathic' at least twice. 'Honestly, it's just such a relief to talk to someone who really gets it because I feel like all my friends are coupled off and I just really need more people like you in my life, so I'm just really relieved we met. I'm a Leo and I know you're an Aries so we're very compatible. What's your moon and rising?'

The model, who had managed to look up from her

phone just once without the girl noticing, finally rolled her eyes and said: 'Look, babe, I'm really sorry about the break-up. Don't get back with your ex. I have to use the toilet now. Best of luck with everything.'

The girl smiled. 'Okay! Thanks so much!' she said, waving. As the bathroom door closed, the girl turned to Rose: 'What a bitch, right?' she said. 'I hate it when celebrities are so entitled.'

Rose smiled politely and watched as the drunk girl tottered off into the night to find another audience.

Rose couldn't find Milo when she came out of the bathroom. She half-recognised a singer in the corner whose music often played on the office radio. But she seemed to be deep in conversation with another musician Rose recognised from an indie band that *Intel* had recently profiled. She did a lap around the party, hoping to find someone at Firehouse or an approachable group to speak to. She found neither and headed to the bar.

In Rose's head, a woman sitting alone at a bar was the start of something. An invitation even, for someone to start talking to her about something deeply meaningful, like the breakthroughs they'd had in therapy, or the foundations of Buddhism. It was a way of signalling your desire for human connection, even if there was really only one human you wanted to connect to. A way of telling the world you were confident and cool. That was the hope, anyway, as opposed to a clear sign you didn't fit in and sought the solace of hard liquor.

The bar was busy enough that nobody seemed to notice

Rose was on her own. It took three negronis for her to decide it was her favourite cocktail, a decision that made her feel suitably sophisticated. She had always wanted to be the kind of woman that had a go-to cocktail. At least she had achieved something that evening. Although, sitting there quietly swirling the bitter taste of Campari in her mouth and listening to the sounds of partygoers around her, she acquired enough material for at least three feature films. Everyone had a story to tell. And they were all telling it loudly and right next to Rose. There was an agent complaining about her client who was sleeping with the director of her latest film – and how it was very awkward because the director was actually married to the producer. There was the fashion designer asking her friend what people wear to pubs because she wanted to 'seem relatively normal' to the guy who had asked her on a date. Then there was the couple who famously starred together in a hit HBO TV show who were having an argument about which of them had broken the heating in the hot tub in their bedroom. Rose resolved it was him and not her because all she had done was use a sex toy in there while he had accidentally filled it with bleach on a recent acid trip. His excuse was that he thought it was a giant toilet that needed cleaning.

Rose ordered her fourth negroni when she noticed Polly Jenkins sidling up beside her, trying to get the barman's attention. Rose silently observed her, hoping for a moment of eye contact that she could use to initiate conversation. Polly didn't look at Rose. Instead, her eyes roved over and around her head in a way that seemed intentionally rude, as she waited for the barman to bring her the two glasses of champagne she'd asked for. Normally, Rose would have taken the hint and let it slide. But there's only so many negronis you can drink until integrity goes out the window.

'I love your dress,' she said, looking directly at Polly's eyes, which were flaked with white eyeshadow.

Polly remained in position, her eyes still roving. There was no way she hadn't heard her.

'I love your dress!' Rose shouted.

'Jesus Christ,' said Polly at no one in particular.

'Sorry. Where's it from?'

'Prada.'

'I love it. Really great choice. Are you having a fun night?'

Polly was actually looking at Rose now, her eyes scanning her scrupulously from the hair down. Rose tucked her hair behind her ear and smiled in the hope of unearthing some sort of humanity.

'Do you have any gear?' Polly asked her.

'Oh, erm. No, I don't. Sorry. I'm a big fan of your podcast.'

'Thank you.' Polly was fidgeting now, her fingers quickly climbing over one another as she looked around for something or someone. It struck Rose that she hadn't seen any of the other 'Its' at the afterparty.

'Who are you here with?' she asked.

'Just a few friends. Where's my champagne?' She was leaning over the bar now, trying to catch the barman's eye to no avail.

'Do you want this?' Rose asked, sliding her negroni over to Polly.

'No, thank you. Coloured alcohol makes me nauseous.'

'Yeah, same. Gross,' said Rose, feeling her face squint far more than was appropriate or necessary as she pulled her negroni back with such force it tumbled over, clattering into something behind the bar. 'So, are you recording any new episodes soon?'

Polly ignored this as the barman returned with two glasses of champagne.

'About time,' she tutted.

'Lovely to meet you!' Rose attempted.

Polly looked at Rose and smiled. 'How did you get in here?'

Rose said nothing and watched as Polly's smile turned into a giggle as she turned and walked back into the party.

This was definitely the moment to leave. But the will to do so required energy that had begun to evaporate somewhere around her second negroni. She sunk deeper into the leather stool, her body feeling heavier by the minute.

It was not clear exactly when, but at some point she felt someone tap her on the shoulder.

'Haven't seen you all night,' the voice said in her ear. This made her jump.

'Milo, hello. Cool night, right?' she replied, trying very hard not to slur her words.

'Okay! I see someone has had a few drinks.'

'You're a few drinks.'

He laughed. 'I'm pleased you're still here.'

'Why?'

'Because I wanted to hang out with you.'

'Well, I'm very busy.' She gestured around her with both hands. 'Lots going on here.'

'I can see that.'

She shuddered as the warmth of his hand rested on her bare back.

'Have you had fun?' he asked.

'I have.' Rose told him about some of the stories she'd heard. Milo laughed, particularly at the one about the fashion designer.

'I made the mistake of going on a few dates with her once.'

'Did she ask you what to wear to a pub?'

'No, but she did ask me to sign an NDA.'

'What? Seriously?' Rose had been made to write up non-disclosure agreements at work by particularly high maintenance celebrity publicists. The idea of a person forcing someone like Milo to sign one was too absurd to even contemplate unless that person was Beyoncé.

'Seriously.'

'Why?'

'I don't know, to be honest. I gave it to my lawyer, he said it was ridiculous and I didn't see her again.'

'Have you ever given anyone an NDA?'

'No. That would be fucking weird.'

'Agreed. Was she as awful as she seems?'

'She mainly spoke about herself and how much money her business was making,' he said, sighing. 'She had an actual app on her phone that pinged *ker-ching* and flashed with dollar signs every time she sold something. So yes: awful.'

'I'm not surprised.'

'How sober are you feeling then?'

'Oh, very,' said Rose, hiccupping on cue.

'How many of those have you had?' he asked, pointing to the negroni Rose had nearly finished.

'Quite a few, actually,' she hiccupped again. 'They really are delicious.'

'Come on, let's get you home.'

Rose mumbled something about not wanting to be a mystery brunette in the morning as she followed him to the lifts. Thankfully, he ignored this.

They walked out of the lift into yet another dark underground car park.

'Is this the part where you kill me?' Rose asked.

'Ha, no not quite. Don't think I'm cut out for prison.'

'Oh, I wouldn't worry about that. Your fancy lawyers would definitely get you acquitted.'

'Let's just get you home, shall we? Then we can discuss the criminal justice system as much as you like.'

His hand was on her back again.

'Hi, Ralph,' Milo said to a man in a black suit standing in front of yet another car.

'Hi, Ralph!' Rose aped.

Soon, they were strapped into seat belts and sitting side by side in a different set of warm seats. There were miniature bottles of Evian positioned in cup-holders beside each of them. Rose opened hers and finished it in seconds. Milo swiftly handed her his. She finished that one too.

'So you live in south London?' he asked.

'Yes, in a very nice flat I pay very little for that often

smells like weed,' she replied, feeling slightly more sober now that she'd consumed something non-alcoholic.

'Why does it always smell like weed?'

'My neighbours smoke it incessantly – and it's the first thing you smell whenever you open the window. You'd think I'd be more relaxed, really.'

'And you don't smoke it?'

'No, I generally avoid drugs. I used to smoke weed when I was younger but I'd get too hungry afterwards.'

'Isn't that the idea?'

'Well, yes. Maybe. I don't know. But I once smoked it with a group of boys who had no food at their house apart from frozen garlic bread. I ate the entire thing and haven't touched weed since.'

'That sounds sensible.'

'Do you like them?'

'What?'

'Drugs.'

He shrugged. 'Some are okay. But I try not to get caught up in that anymore.'

'Anymore?'

'I used to do a lot.'

'What kind of stuff?'

'Coke, MD, ketamine. The bad stuff.'

'Bet it was high quality stuff though.'

'It was actually. But my God, those comedowns aren't something I'm in a hurry to repeat. It's a cliché but when I was younger and thrust into this scene it was just all there on a platter, sometimes literally.'

'How very predictable of you.'

'Almost as predictable as a middle-class south-London girl working at Firehouse.'

'Guess I deserved that.'

'In all fairness, you don't strike me as the Firehouse type.'

'What is the Firehouse type?' she asked, knowing the answer.

'Well, they all know each other, don't they? All from the same private schools. All friends with the same people. You know people call it Nepohouse, right?'

Of course Rose knew this; Minnie was always trying to get tabloids to stop putting it in their headlines whenever something mildly unsavoury came out about the company.

'I'm not part of that,' she said.

'I can tell.'

As the journey stretched on, Rose continued regaining her ability to form clear sentences. Soon, she and Milo were chatting properly, quickly and enthusiastically in the way people do when they're in the throes of an unexpectedly great first date. They spoke about whether or not astrology is a con (Milo said it is, Rose said it can be helpful as a guide), where they both were when Trump was inaugurated (Milo was at home alone in LA, Rose was in the office, watching it on Minnie's computer screen), and why calling yourself a pescetarian is obnoxious even if it accurately describes your diet (they both agreed on this one). Conversation continued like this for twenty minutes after they arrived outside Rose's flat.

'Shall we have a drink at yours?' Milo asked.

The words repeated themselves in her head. Had he really just asked her that?

'I don't think we should, no,' she replied, suddenly feeling the urge to be alone. 'My housemate is a fan. She will probably scream and push you to the floor and lick you or something.'

'Are you a fan?'

'I'm still deciding.'

'Cool.' He paused; the silence hung between them like it wanted to ask Milo for a selfie. 'It's been fun, Rose. Until next time.'

'Right, yeah. Goodnight.'

Rose closed her front door and wondered if she'd dreamed it. It had been too surreal to be that close to him. Too strange to breathe the same air. To accept that he was a real living person who wore seat belts and listened to the radio in cars. Someone who had asked to come into her flat, a home that was lovely but still had cracks in the walls and a toilet that smelled like sewage whenever it flushed.

Of all the people that evening Milo could have chosen to direct his fame particles towards, why her? It wasn't like he needed to get into Firehouse's good books. Or anyone's good books, for that matter. Milo's reputation was pristine across the board. *Vulture* called him 'one of the music industry's good ones' in a recent profile filled with adoring quotes from people he'd worked with. One of his managers described him as 'just a really genuine, salt-of-the-earth guy'. Whatever Milo's motivation, to have his full and complete attention had kick-started some sort of adrenal reaction in Rose so that every fibre in her body had been electrified. He had chosen her, even just for a moment. And it felt like she was fizzing.

Tucking her duvet underneath her feet and burying her head deep into her pillow, Rose replayed every conversation they'd had in her head several times. She searched for something to cling onto in each exchange, scraps of evidence she could weave together to prove that it was real. There was the way he looked at her when she teased him. A soft smile, the kind you give to someone before you lean in to kiss them. The way he kept saying her name. Wasn't that something men had been told to do in order to get women to think they were into them? The way his eyes lingered on her legs every time she tugged her dress down. She agonised over her decision not to let him into her flat. If she'd said yes, would she be having sex with Milo Jax right now?

Rose had never quite mastered the art of feeling attracted to someone without letting it slip into obsession. It was a problem and it happened often. Even someone she would catch eyes with on the Tube would, within ten seconds, be the subject of an elaborate fantasy ending with them tearfully watching her walk towards them down the aisle.

Over the years, Rose had started to obsess more consciously, knowing it wasn't healthy and probably had something to do with her father, but also knowing she couldn't stop herself. It had become a part of her nightly routine. Cleanse. Moisturise. Fantasise. It wasn't just the appeal of endless possibility. There was also a sense of fulfilment in it; the men in her head did everything she wanted them to. They pushed her up against walls, crushing her ever so slightly as they lightly kissed her neck. They whispered the things they wanted to do to her, hands roving on hips before spreading legs apart. Slowly at first, and then faster, more urgent. Rose moaned, loudly because Luce would be fast asleep by now. She would be on her back, a kitchen table, maybe. More gentle kisses, this time on her thighs. Milo's hands reaching up to caress her torso, the corners of his shoulder flexing on her flesh. His skin smooth and moisturised. Rose let out a small cry as she pushed her fingers deeper inside herself. Shortly after that, she curled her toes and collapsed, weightless and limp on damp sheets.

Later, she reached for her phone and opened Instagram. @milojax followed 210 people and had 52.3 million followers. Luce followed him, as did several people she went to school with and everyone she followed at Firehouse. The people he followed were mostly musicians or models or both. There were a few names she didn't recognise. Old friends or the secret accounts of fellow celebrities, she presumed. Underneath where it said 'Followers' it said 'Message'. Rose tapped it, surprised at how easy this was. She typed:

Nice to meet you tonight. Thank you for taking me home in your big car. Suspect you won't ever see this. Okay bye.

She tapped the 'Send' icon and fell asleep.

THREE

Rose arrived at the office with bags under her eyes and two large black Americanos from the place Minnie liked over the road. She didn't feel too hungover to work, particularly not after popping two paracetamols this morning, but she didn't exactly feel fresh either. This became more apparent when she pulled her chair out from underneath her desk and spilled one of the coffees all over her keyboard. The entire press office – a small airless room with just one tiny window that barely opened – would smell like coffee beans for the rest of the day. And Rose would spend the next hour on the phone to IT getting a new keyboard.

When Minnie jangled her way into the office, she instantly clocked Rose's tired face.

'You all right, darling? Hope you didn't end up babysitting that pop star all night, did you?'

'No, no. He was fine, actually.' She paused, debating whether or not to go on. 'I went with him to the afterparty.'

'Good for you. And how was that?'

'It was all right, thank you. But not really my scene.'

'No, can't imagine it would be. There's a very limited

number of people who should feel like they belong at a party like that. Hope you managed to get some cheese. I took a Tupperware with me one year.'

'Damn, I should have done that.'

'Was Milo all right with you?'

'Yeah, he was nice actually. He surprised me.'

'In a good way?'

'In a good way.'

'Brilliant. Let me know if you need any help with the spreadsheets this morning.'

Rose nodded and returned to setting up her keyboard. The day after a major event required an inordinate amount of admin. It was Rose's job to trawl through all of the media coverage, ascribe each piece or mention a monetary value using a formula Minnie had given her, and put it all into a spreadsheet that would then be sent to Jasper and all the company's executives, editors and publishers. It would take all day and be more tedious than waiting for a kettle to boil a hundred times. But it was excellent hangover work.

She started with the best-dressed round-ups as these were usually fairly easy to find. There was an email system set-up that meant she received alerts every time anything related to Firehouse was mentioned in the press – but sometimes things went amiss, which meant she had to do a lot of manual searches too. Almost all the best-dressed articles led with Milo in the lead image. The purple suit he'd been wearing was from Louis Vuitton – he was one of the faces of their summer 2017 campaign – and the shoes were Prada. In total, the outfit cost £2,500, though the brands would have given everything to him as a gift. There were a few worst-dressed articles that Rose would not include, the reason being that they only ever featured women and often only because they'd had the audacity to wear something other than a straightforward black tie gown.

Rose actually liked the outfits on the worst-dressed list more. They had more personality. There was one pink sequin mini dress worn by a breakfast radio presenter and a neon green lace suit that, admittedly, was a bit much but the model wearing it looked fantastic. People were cruel: the caption underneath one photo of her described her as a 'sexy Kermit gone wrong'.

Next were the standard award-winner lists; some publications would just publish lists of who had won what. Dull, but it still counted as coverage, which meant Rose had to put it into the spreadsheet. Then there was the task of checking for a sponsor credit in every post. They'd send out post-event releases urging people to use the full credit so that it included the sponsor: The Firehouse Awards 2017 presented by Firehouse and Roberts. Roberts was a menswear brand that almost always sponsored the awards and dressed as many of the guests as they could. Very few publications included the sponsor, so this would then involve sending countless emails to journalists asking them to do so. They were almost always ignored but Rose still had to send them.

The only mildly interesting part of collating coverage was when it was in some way salacious. There were a few gossip pages in some of the nationals that sent journalists to afterparties to try to pick up titbits of celebrity scandal that they could write about. Rose read them all thoroughly and found several photographs of guests leaving the venue she was at last night looking 'bleary-eyed'. There was one story about the model she'd seen in the bathroom queue, who had left the party with another, much more, famous model that she was 'rumoured to be dating'. That meant her publicist had called the tabloid to tell them they were romantically involved, probably to raise her profile.

By lunch, Rose had got halfway through completing her spreadsheet and opened Instagram seventeen times, hating herself a little more as she did so. Her message to Milo had not been read. Of course, she was a fool to think of any other possibility. The man must receive thousands if not millions of DMs a day from fans trying to get his attention. Rose had been working at Firehouse long enough to know that the likelihood of Milo seeing any of them, or even managing the account himself, was low. And yet, whenever Rose looked at her message, she could not bring herself to un-send it.

It was human nature to want to get in touch with someone after you'd had a nice time together. That was what people were wired to do. To form connections – and then solidify those connections by finding them on Instagram and sending a message. She had nothing to be ashamed of and kept telling herself this as she furiously googled his name to see if anyone had written anything about him last night.

All of the articles were about his outfit apart from one,

which had gone live twenty minutes ago: 'Milo Jax spotted getting close to Polly Jenkins at Firehouse Awards after-party.' She clicked on the article. 'The revered pop sensation couldn't take his eyes off the high-flying It girl. The pair were seen talking closely in the corner all evening and sources say Milo is "quite taken" with her. Polly would be the latest in a long line of gorgeous women the superstar has bedded . . .' Rose stopped reading and went to the bathroom. She put the toilet seat down, lowered herself and waited for her heart to stop racing as the previous evening felt even further from reality.

Rose checked the message again. Still nothing. If her experience with Milo was supposed to start and end last night, then so be it. There was nothing she could do to change that. She had to trust the universe. Rose returned to her desk and continued working through the spreadsheet while mentally repeating this mantra, which she'd definitely stolen from an Instagram post.

At 4 p.m., Minnie called a team meeting. She'd just returned from a four-hour lunch with Jasper, a monthly affair after which she was usually in one of two states. The first (and most frequent) was drunk, because Jasper had plied her with vodka martinis at his latest culinary haunt in Mayfair while they traded industry gossip. The second possibility was flustered because he'd just asked her to do something very ambitious with very few resources. Today it was the latter.

'Right, I have news,' Minnie began as she, Rose, Oliver and their intern, Annabelle (her uncle was an old friend of Jasper's from Cambridge), huddled around a rectangular table in the second-floor meeting room. There was a plate of custard creams laid out in front of them and a large silver cafetière surrounded by white china teacups. As Rose poured herself a coffee, Minnie explained that Firehouse was launching a new digital-first publication. It would be called StandFirst and its target audience would be women between the ages of eighteen and thirty-five, though this was just a guideline. The company had invested a huge amount of money in it already, hoping it would boost advertising revenue – something that was now urgent given that so many of Firehouse's key advertisers were ploughing more money in social media influencers and less money in publishing companies. Firehouse needed to remind the world it was still relevant; and this was part of the wider plan to do that. But none of that mattered, really, the point was that the press team had been given the task of handling StandFirst's launch.

'Now, this campaign is going to be a little different from ones we've done in the past,' said Minnie, slowly dipping her custard cream in a mug of coffee she'd brought into the room with her. It had the word 'GIRLBOSS' stamped on the front, which meant it definitely wasn't hers and probably belonged to someone in the commercial department.

'As opposed to a regular launch party, they want us to host a reception with a fashion show afterwards,' Minnie continued.

'But it's not a fashion magazine?' asked Oliver.

'Well, the idea is that it will encompass everything that demographic is interested in. So fashion will be one of the primary sections on the website alongside beauty, travel, relationships and well-being.'

'Sounds great!' enthused Annabelle.

'Who's the sponsor?' asked Oliver, deconstructing a custard cream and laying it out on the table.

'Ah, well. This is where you're going to have to bear with me.' Minnie exhaled.

'Oh God, is it eBay or something?' Oliver looked panicked.

'Not quite. It's Jimson & James.'

'Wait. What?' His eyes widened.

'I know. But they've offered an inordinate amount of money and quite frankly we had no other options.'

'Don't they sell towels?' asked Rose.

'Yes, Rose. They sell towels and other household goods. It's hardly Chanel, I know,' Minnie sighed.

'What will the models wear?' asked Annabelle.

'Towels,' mumbled Oliver through a mouthful of custard cream.

'Well, sustainability is a huge push at the moment, so all of the clothes will be second-hand. And they want real people as the models.'

'What do you mean, real people?' asked Oliver.

'As in, not models.'

'So, like, editors? Designers?' asked Rose.

'No, more like influencers. Or, you know, "content creators" or whatever they like to be called these days,' Minnie said, using her fingers as quotation marks. 'I haven't dared tell Millicent or Simon yet – that can be Jasper's job.'

Like the majority of Firehouse's senior staff, Millicent and Simon had a severe aversion to all things to do with social media influencers. Everything influencers represented repulsed them. It wasn't that they didn't understand what they did (although Rose suspected some of the older editors still didn't know how to use Instagram), it was more the fact that flocks of them had started replacing editors as authorities in the industry, usurping the roles and appropriating the skills the editors had spent decades honing. Overnight, influencers had started popping up in the front row at fashion shows, while top editors were relegated to the second or third rows. This had led to a quiet backlash within the industry; one editor at *MODE* wrote a scathing op-ed about the rise of influencers, calling them 'vapid mannequins'. The editor was forced to issue an apology on Twitter.

'Will we try to get the Its to walk?' Rose asked.

'No,' said Minnie. 'The company wants fresh faces on the runway. I mean, we'll obviously invite the Its to the launch for coverage, but they won't walk in the show.'

'Okay,' she nodded. 'I met Polly Jenkins last night.'

'Oh, did you? Was she nice?' asked Annabelle.

'She was pretty rude, actually.'

'Shock,' said Oliver, rolling his eyes.

'I went to school with her younger sister,' added Annabelle.

'She asked me for drugs.'

'Did you give her some?' asked Oliver. 'I saw that she was hanging out with Milo at the afterparty.'

Rose felt her cheeks burning.

'Oliver, enough,' Minnie snapped. 'I'll handle logistics in terms of press and media attendance. Oliver, I want you to work with Liz on booking VIP guests, and Rose, find me influencers to pitch as models. Ideally ones the Firehouse editors don't hate, so definitely no one selling charcoal toothpaste or anything like that.'

'Can I help with the VIPs?' asked Annabelle, looking everyone in the eye to remind them she was still there.

'No,' Minnie replied quickly. 'Sorry, it's just that . . .' She took a deep breath, thinking about how to phrase her next sentence. 'The VIP publicists adore Oliver. So we need to put him front and centre.'

Oliver let out a smug giggle.

'I'll do some research on influencers,' quipped Rose.

'How's my favourite press team?' boomed a familiarly mellifluous voice from the corridor.

'Hello, Jasper,' smiled Minnie as he entered the meeting room, right arm swanning out to one side as if he'd just stepped onto a stage. Famed for his colourful tailoring – always bright, always bespoke – he was dressed head-to-toe in a crimson three-piece suit, sunlight from the nearby windows bouncing off his bald head. His cheeks were flushed, probably from sinking six martinis at lunch.

Rose and the rest of the team smiled and said hello. Oliver grinned in the corner, knowing what was coming.

'And how's my favourite press officer?' Jasper beamed at him, illuminating Oliver's face like a literal spotlight. The bizarre bromance he had somehow established with Jasper was nauseating. Minnie always assured Rose it was just because of the celebrity PR teams. Oliver's relationship with them meant he was the person bringing big names to the company parties, which in turn meant he was ultimately the person convincing advertisers to spend more of their money on Firehouse brands.

'I've just been telling everyone about StandFirst,' said Minnie.

'Ah, yes. Our new little project to keep the kiddos interested in us old fogeys! Splendid stuff. Splendid.'

'Have you seen all of the coverage from last night?' asked Oliver.

'Oh yes,' he replied. 'Excellent work, Oliver. And everyone else, too. That Milo is such a charmer, isn't he? I had a wonderful chat with him about my vegetable patch. He knows an awful lot about allotments and things. How did you manage that, dear?' Jasper was looking at Oliver like he was a six-year-old boy.

'That one was actually all thanks to Rose,' said Minnie, nodding towards her. Rose could practically feel the heat of anger radiating off Oliver, who had passive-aggressively lifted up one of the ears of his headphones and pointedly inserted it. She had never spoken directly to Jasper but presumed and hoped he knew who she was because of her regular coverage emails – and the fact that she worked with Minnie.

'Wonderful work, Roisin,' he said, nodding at her.

'Thank you,' she replied. 'It's Rose actually.'

'Hm.' Jasper paused to consider this. 'Delightful. Annabelle darling, how are you getting on?' he asked, his voice softer now.

'Very good, thank you. Everyone is being very kind to me,' Annabelle replied, smiling gratefully.

'Splendid. Just splendid. Minnie, let's have another catch-up in a few days.'

'Of course, Jasper. Speak then.'

'Oh, and Oliver?'

'Yes?'

'Remind me to drop you a line about next weekend? Aggie is desperate to have you round again.'

Minnie rolled her eyes. Agatha was Jasper's wife; the pair of them had been obsessed with Oliver ever since he managed to get Kylie to host the Firehouse Awards in 2016. They regularly invited him to their Chelsea townhouse for dinner parties, or 'salons', as Oliver would call them.

'Toodles all!' and the ringmaster was off.

'Right, off to work, everyone,' said Minnie, walking briskly out of the room with Annabelle's heels clacking behind her.

Oliver, still seated, turned to Rose.

'Did you have fun last night?' he asked.

'Yeah, bit tired.'

'Ha. Yeah, well, that's what happens when you leave a party with a major pop star.'

'What?'

'I heard you left the party with him.'

'What? From who?'

'I never reveal my sources,' he replied, zipping his mouth together with his fingers.

'He just dropped me home, that was it.'

'Oh, don't be a dick, Rose. He shags everyone. I know at least four women in syndication who he's fucked.'

'Nothing happened,' she replied sternly.

Oliver scoffed: 'Right, of course not. You'd just be the only human on the planet to turn Milo Jax down.'

Rose plugged in her headphones and walked out.

Firehouse used to have a red list of talent that was banned from working with the company in any capacity under any circumstances. It had been created by a former editor of *MODE* – Mabel Marbles – who had an ongoing booking at the Priory so the company could send her there whenever her drinking went over the line, which it often did. Mabel had created the list after someone invited the male model she'd been having an affair with to a Cartier party she was hosting. When he arrived, he tried to kiss her in front of everyone. Mabel's husband left shortly after.

Over time, though, whisperings about the list, who was on it and why, started to get a little too loud around the building. Eventually, part of it was published in *Private Eye*. Rose wasn't working at Firehouse at the time – but Minnie had come into the private members' club that afternoon and told her about it after her third martini.

After that, the list had to go. At least in written form; everyone who worked at Firehouse could probably still recite the names. And Minnie kept a secret handwritten version in her desk drawer just in case anyone needed to know who was banned from Firehouse events. Very few people knew about the handwritten list outside of the press office. In fact, it was probably just Jasper, who would often barge in to have a peek at it from time to time, the two of them gossiping about any new additions.

Reasons for going on the list varied. They could range from arriving at an event hungover to throwing a tantrum because of being served instant coffee on set instead of freshly ground. Rose considered it a little ironic since members of Firehouse staff did both of these things regularly. Back in the day, the list was mostly made up of actors and musicians. Now, it was heavily populated by influencers.

Someone had been put on the list after she threw up on a Miu Miu sample dress mid-blow dry – her publicist claimed she had an intolerance to hot air (specifically when it was near her face) despite the fact she'd already admitted to going out the night before. Another red-lister went into a K-hole at a black-tie dinner to celebrate the June issue of *Intel*. She had been escorted out through the kitchen so as to avoid the paparazzi at the front but one snapper managed to get a shot of her passed out in the arms of her bodyguard. Her team relentlessly badgered Minnie into telling the press she was just jet-lagged.

Rose reviewed Minnie's handwritten list at her desk (no one was allowed to take it outside the press office). Having memorised a few of the names, she started to browse articles with headlines like 'Fashion Influencers to Follow Now' and 'Influencers You Need to Know About'. She wrote down the names of everyone featured who was under the age of 35, had over 500,000 followers and wasn't already on the red list. She reviewed the remaining accounts, checking for anything Minnie would deem off-brand, which, in addition to selling charcoal toothpaste, included promoting fast-fashion sponsorships, reality TV stints and grammatical errors in captions. People who were constantly posting about 'something exciting' they couldn't talk about yet and started every video by saying 'hey guys' in the exact same intonation also had to go.

'Rose, can you get me those names by the end of the day, please?' asked Minnie from behind her computer, which was diagonally across from hers.

'Yep, sure, I'm just printing it off now. It's a bit short.'

'That's fine. We only need to pitch a few people. Commercial will get the rest. Have you listed that @cosmoclara one?'

Rose checked her screen. 'Yep, she's on there.'

'Great, Jasper mentioned her at lunch. His daughter is a big fan and she's got millions of followers. Apparently charges £10,000 for a sponsored post. Obviously, we can't afford that. So do what you can.'

'I'll get her, don't worry.'

'I know you will. You got us Milo Jax, you can definitely get us someone whose name starts with a symbol.'

At home, Luce was lying on the sofa, fast asleep, body curled into the foetal position. A box of tissues was on its side next to her. *The Holiday* was playing on the TV, which had been put on mute.

Rose shuffled in next to her, gently touching her forehead. Luce stirred and made a moaning sound.

'Hey. What happened?' asked Rose.

'It's over,' Luce mumbled. 'We ended it this morning.'

'Oh, babe, I'm so sorry.'

'Thanks,' she replied, sitting up and rubbing her eyes, which were red and swollen. 'I can't believe we lasted three years, to be honest.'

'Yeah, I mean, me neither,' Rose replied, wrapping herself around her housemate.

George and Luce had always had a volatile relationship. They'd both cheated on each other (Luce with a colleague, George with an ex-girlfriend). Luce came clean when it happened, George continued to lie until Luce found naked photos of the ex on his phone. At first, he denied it. Called her 'crazy' and insisted the photos were old. Then the ex-girlfriend drunkenly rang Luce on a night out and told her how George had fucked her over his dining-room table at least four times during their relationship.

Somehow, they managed to stick it out for a few months after that, though Luce never really forgave him. The next break-up happened after a blow-out argument when they were in Sicily. George flew home two days early and Luce had a brief fling with an Italian man named Marco who may or may not have been in the Mafia. They got back together again a few weeks later.

Rose always took news of Luce and George's break-ups with a pinch of salt.

'Do you want to talk about it?' Rose asked, stroking Luce's hair.

'Not really. I've been on the phone to my mum all day,

I think she's going to pick me up this weekend. I want to go home for a while.'

Rose always envied people who could 'go home'. Unlike Rose, Luce's home was not a two-bedroom flat in Clapham, where wine bottles doubled up as candlesticks and the radiator was always lined with knickers. Luce's home was a countryside pile, where cashmere blankets were folded onto sofas and bottomless PG Tips lived in a silver polished pot labelled 'Tea'.

'Going home sounds like a good idea,' said Rose.

Luce snuffled, wiping her eyes. 'Distract me. What happened with Milo Jax?'

'Oh, nothing. He was a bit annoying.'

'How come?'

'It doesn't matter. Let me make you some pasta.'

'You're being weird.'

'I'm just hungry,' she replied, walking to the kitchen.

Rose poured an entire box of penne pasta into a saucepan and filled it with boiling water from the kettle. She reached for a jar of tomato sauce and placed it beside the pot. Her phone had no notifications, showing just the time and her background: a stock image of Budapest she mistakenly thought she'd taken herself, then decided to keep it because it made her laugh when she realised she hadn't.

She opened Instagram. Her finger automatically slid left and tapped on the conversation at the top of her DMs. Her message to Milo had the word 'Seen' beneath it. 'Fuck,' she whispered to herself. There was no way of knowing when he had read the message. It could have been hours, minutes or seconds ago. For all she knew, he could be staring at the exact same screen as she was right now. If it had been hours, then the 'Seen' was confirmation that Milo had chosen to ignore her message. That he was just going to read it, knowing full well Rose would see he'd read it, and not reply. That would be a power play, wouldn't it? Or would it just mean that he was too busy? Or that he had opened her message whilst in bed with a supermodel – and possibly also Polly Jenkins – and they had laughed about that silly little PR girl with the frizzy hair who kept following Milo around all night. That wasn't what had happened. Rose knew that. But Milo would frame it that way to make the supermodel laugh before she gave him another blow job.

She paused for a moment of rational thought. Why would Milo open her message while in bed with a supermodel? And were his messages actually opened by him, or a member of his team?

A sharp pang of heat hit her right foot.

'Shit!' she yelped.

The water had boiled over and was now frothing all over the kitchen counter, where it had dripped onto the floor and over Rose's toes.

'You okay?' shouted Luce.

'Yeah, all good. Sorry.'

There was now water spilling over her phone screen.

'Fuck's sake,' she muttered, grabbing a tea towel that had some patchy red wine stains on it to wipe the screen, shaking the phone until drips of water started to come out from the bottom.

The theme tune of *America's Next Top Model* was now blaring loudly into the kitchen.

She managed to unlock her phone, bringing the conversation with Milo back onto the screen. Underneath where it had said 'Seen' was now the word 'Typing . . .'.

Rose watched it silently and was certain no one had ever been this still. Her breath was neither rising nor falling because she wasn't actually breathing at all. Then the word disappeared. Now, her message was just 'Seen' again. She let out a sigh and laughed at herself. When she looked back over at her screen, 'Typing . . .' had returned. Seconds later, it was gone again.

The agony was too much. Rose put her phone on flight mode and shut it away in the cutlery drawer with a loud thud.

She put both hands on the kitchen counter to steady herself, closed her eyes, and tried to inhale and exhale. Inhale and exhale. Inhale and exhale.

Rose and Luce ate their pasta side by side on the sofa, watching a twenty-three-year-old model from Texas crying because all her hair had been chopped off.

'She really does look so much better now,' said Luce.

'Yeah, must be hard to have no choice in the matter though.'

'I don't know. I'd love someone to just tell me what I need to do in order to be beautiful.'

'I guess that would be nice.'

'Yeah, like, hey if you wear these clothes, change your hair to this colour and use this exact shade of lipstick, everyone will find you irresistible.'

'Most people already find you irresistible, Luce.'

'Oh, sod off.'

It was true. Luce always had someone after her even when they were at school together. And when she was in a relationship there was always a long line of men and women waiting for news of her to be single again. She would date both, often at the same time, but so far her only serious relationships had been with men.

'What if someone told you that the thing that would make you irresistible was going bald and gaining two dress sizes?' asked Rose, digging out a particularly cheesy piece of pasta from her bowl.

'Well, they wouldn't say that, would they?'

'But what if they did?'

'Maybe I'll get a fringe.'

'It would suit you.'

'Yeah, I think so,' Luce replied. 'I just want someone to tell me what I need to do to nail life. Like, not just about how I look. But how I should do everything. What I should eat. Who I should date. How I should dress. It would be such a load off.'

'I would love for someone to tell me who to date.'

'I mean, that would be good so you don't waste another eight months chasing after total self-obsessed wankers like Billy.'

'Can we not talk about Billy?'

'You can't still be into him.'

'I'm not. I just don't need to talk about the man I wasted years thinking I was in love with when I was a teenager.'

'He's got a receding hairline now.'

'Who?'

'Billy. He posted a photo on Instagram the other day of himself on a beach in Costa Rica and I reckon he'll be bald in a year or two. So that should make you feel a little better.'

Rose hated that it did make her feel a little better.

'I haven't spoken to him in a long time.'

'Keep it that way. What about Dick Stick?'

Dick Stick was Luce's less than socially acceptable nickname for Ed, Rose's sort-of ex. They'd met at Luce's twenty-fourth birthday party – he'd tagged along with one of her colleagues. With almond-shaped eyes and full kiss-me lips, he was beautiful to look at. A living, breathing work of art, as she often told him. And for whatever reason, that night he'd decided to ignore Luce and her tall lawyer friends and pursue Rose. Things between them moved fast, and after just two weeks Ed asked Rose to be his girlfriend, like the way eleven-year-olds ask each other to hold hands for a week. The following month, he told her he was falling in love. By month three, they were planning their Italian wedding together. Then he began to withdraw – and that's when the arguments started. Soon, Ed, who called himself an actor despite the fact he'd never been cast in anything and didn't actually have to work because he came from a family of retail tycoons, was putting her down all the time. He said she had no real ambition of her own and just absorbed those of other people, and called her superficial several times. Luce hated him. Still, Rose never stopped seeking his approval. Even when he ended things, she couldn't help but ask if it was because he thought she was vapid. 'No, of course not,' he replied, lightly putting his hand on her arm as if she were a dying relative. 'You're fit and funny. I just don't think we're very compatible.'

'I haven't spoken to Ed in a long time, either,' replied Rose.

'Good. Proud of you. Do you have any other fun parties coming up this week? I feel like it would be good for me to get out. Find someone spicy to sink my teeth into.'

'Already?'

'God, not for a relationship. No, no. Love is obviously a lie. I just think some attention would be good for me.'

'*Intel* has some whisky brand party happening on Wednesday. I wasn't going to go but if you fancy it I could ask Minnie?'

'Will there be hot people there?'

'I don't know but I can guarantee there'll be several people who will want to sleep with you.'

'Okay, but, like, on a scale of, say, George to Milo Jax.'

'We don't think George is attractive anymore?'

'Absolutely not. He gives me the ick.'

'Maybe we should send you on *Love Island*.'

'I would like to come on Wednesday, please,' said Luce, ignoring the *Love Island* pitch as she scooped her finger around her bowl, licking off the remaining tomato sauce. 'Then I can go home on Thursday, happily hungover and suitably shagged.'

'Okay, I'll ask Minnie tomorrow.'

'Thank you.'

* * *

Later, Rose was lying in bed drafting boilerplate pitches to influencers on her laptop for the launch of StandFirst. They followed a similar format, one structured by Minnie. Every pitch email had to do the following: detail the event and how many posts or photographs would be required, outline any freebies or gifted items on offer, and clearly state exactly how long they'd be needed for and if there was any available fee, which there never was. Hence the importance of the perks.

The most important thing, though, was to massage the person's ego. Usually that person was not the person you wanted to come to the event. It was their publicist – and their ego was often larger than that of the talent they represented. But a surprising number of influencers didn't have publicists per se. They had assistants, and because you never really knew who would be reading your email, it was best to pander to the influencers themselves.

Rose spent seven minutes drafting a pitch. Then, feeling tired, she closed her laptop, and went into the kitchen. It had been two hours since she put her phone in the cutlery drawer. She had turned off her notifications for Instagram several weeks ago in the hope of reducing the amount of time she spent on the app. The idea was that she would then have to open it in order to receive messages from it, making her usage more of a conscious choice as opposed to a passive one incited by a notification. That was the theory, anyway. But most of the time she found herself just opening the app even more frequently than before, looking for notifications.

There was a red circle next to the arrow in the top right-hand corner of the app. She had one new message.

A swipe of her thumb to the left and there he was. @milojax. The top line of his message in bold: *Oh, hello. How nice to he . . .*

The message had been sent an hour ago. She tapped it.

Oh, hello. How nice to hear from you, Rose. How are you?

Her phone slipped out of her hands and made a loud thud as it smacked the floor.

She quickly picked it up, ignoring the white cracks that were now splintered across her screen, moving as quickly and quietly as she could to her bedroom.

Tucked underneath the warmth of her duvet, Rose opened her phone and stared at the screen. Okay, so he had replied. It must be someone on his team who had seen Rose worked for Firehouse and was therefore being friendly to maintain good relations. It was business.

Rose opened her Notes app and began drafting a reply she knew she would probably never send. Nonetheless, she wanted to have it ready before she went to sleep. Otherwise she'd just spend all night crafting it in her head anyway.

Oh hi. I'm good thanks. You?

Way too boring. Also, don't copy him. He'll clock that immediately.

Hey

Too American.

Hey man

Seriously?

Hiya

Too chirpy.

Oh hello

Stop copying him.

Oh hi

For fuck's sake.

Maybe longer messages were better.

I'm great, thank you. Just waiting for another pop star to invite me to a party with a fully-loaded cheese board.

Sounds like you're referencing a porn film.

I'm good, thank you. Just waiting for another pop star to bring me to a fully-loaded cheese board.

He might not even like cheese.

I'm okay, thanks. Just looking for another fully-loaded cheese board.

Definitely a porn film.

I'm fine.

Something is wrong.

Hi Milo. I'm fucking confused about what you want from me and why I can't write this piece of cunt message.

'Piece of cunt' is a fun turn of phrase and you should be proud of your creativity but it's not a real one and you cannot use it.

Rose closed the app again, threw her phone across the bed and let out a silent scream into her pillow.

It was 00:05, according to the light on the alarm clock she'd bought when she moved in and still hadn't worked out how to use as an actual alarm. She opened her laptop and typed, 'most dramatic ANTM makeovers' into Google. There was a gallery of 152 images on *Cosmopolitan*. She started to click through. By 31 – the buzzcuts section – she had fallen asleep.

Rose decided to reopen the message to Milo on her way to work, somewhere in between Pimlico and Green

Park. She carefully positioned her reusable coffee cup in between her 30-denier swaddled thighs, checking to see if there was a man sitting in front of her. There wasn't; the seat was filled by a woman in her mid-thirties reading a copy of *Tess of the d'Urbervilles*, a book Rose had loved until someone told her it was referenced in *Fifty Shades of Grey*.

All good, thanks, she typed, directly into the response box, with the new confidence of someone who'd had a seven-hour sleep. *Just waiting for another pop star to lead me to a pimped-out cheese board.*

She tapped 'Send' and locked her phone, zipping it away in the front pocket of her backpack.

The woman in her mid-thirties got off at the next stop, and Rose resumed drinking her coffee with her legs tightly closed.

In the morning meeting, Rose found herself continually finding an excuse to look at her phone. She repeatedly opened up the email app and swiped up to check for any new messages. Then she opened her call history, which was interchanged between Luce and Uber drivers. She started looking through her camera roll and then her online banking app.

'Rose, do you agree?' Minnie asked, eyes looking down at her phone.

She looked up. 'Sorry, um, yes, I do.'

'What was I asking about, Rose?'

'Sorry, Minnie. I'm a little tired today.'

'Do you agree that we should have @cosmoclara open the show?'

'Yes, that sounds like a plan to me.'

'Great. Have you pitched to her yet?'

'No, not yet. I was going to send the email today.'

'Let me know how you get on. Upstairs are very keen.'

'Of course.'

They continued talking about the event. Oliver started rattling off the guest list he'd drafted, prompting Minnie to nod in approval. Rose looked back at her phone and opened Instagram to search for @cosmoclara. She had a new message.

'Rose, Jesus Christ, get off your phone,' snapped Minnie.

'Sorry,' she said, quickly turning it off. 'My housemate just broke up with her boyfriend, she keeps messaging me.'

Her body burned with the lie. Luce hadn't sent her a text since this morning (to ask if she had a lighter so she could burn old birthday cards from George).

'Oh, poor her,' Minnie replied, fumbling around in a drawer underneath her desk and pulling out an empty make-up bag covered in Clinique logos. 'Here, go to the beauty cupboard and fill this with bits for her.'

'That's really kind of you, Minnie. Thank you. Also, I was wondering if it might be possible to come to *Intel*'s event on Wednesday with her? I'd be happy to help with any work things on the night if you need it, too.'

'Absolutely. Oliver is working on that one with Annabelle so he'll make sure your names are on the list.'

'Thank you so much.'

'Sure. Now go write that email,' she said, snapping back into authority mode.

The only way to research @cosmoclara on Instagram

without being distracted by the new message, which may or may not be from Milo Jax, was to not open Instagram. So Rose typed @cosmoclara into Google and, thankfully, numerous articles came up. There were interviews with various online websites, including one that described her as the 'millennial influencer that's rewriting everything you hate about millennials'. There were videos on YouTube, ones where she took you around her roof terrace – she'd recently had a garden designer do it up – ones where she showed you her wardrobe, which she'd converted from the spare bedroom, and ones where she talked you through her 'go-to date night beauty look'.

Then there were interviews about her diet – vegetarian – and clips documenting everything she ate in a day. There were multiple podcasts, too, with some focused on life advice while others were about Clara's favourite restaurants. There was, apparently, nothing this woman kept to herself. No sign of a partner, though, which would surely be something she'd at least mention in one of these interviews. If not to share this vital part of her life then at least to commodify it somehow. She must be single.

Rose began crafting her email, being sure to quote her in interviews and mention how many of the company's key editors would be in attendance – face time with them was always a huge pull. Then she attached a few articles that had been published after previous launch events to illustrate how widely covered the event would be. In terms of freebies and gifted items, these would be minimal. The sponsor would be providing everyone with their own personalised, hand-embroidered towels. But that was hardly a draw for someone like Clara, who was probably getting sent personalised handbags from Dior every other week. Hand-embroidered or not, at the end of the day, a towel was still just something that lived on a rail in your bathroom.

Given how much the company had invested in the publication itself, the remaining budget for the launch was relatively low. Still, the prestige, exposure and numerous Getty photographers sent to attend would be enough to get @cosmoclara on board. Rose sent the email and spent the rest of the day watching YouTube videos documenting Ryan Reynolds's relationship history. Oliver had taken Annabelle to meet a group of journalists from the *Telegraph*. Minnie was out to lunch with the PR team at Louis Vuitton. By 5 p.m., no one had returned.

The beauty cupboard was located on the fifth floor of the building next to the offices belonging to *MODE*. Anyone could pay a visit so long as they had written permission from a senior member of staff (Minnie had given Rose a note) and made a donation for every item they took – different charities were chosen every month. Usually cleared out by entitled editors and wily interns, the cupboard was surprisingly full today. There were endless rows of products stretching back almost two metres, including everything from lipsticks and mascaras to candles and bath oils.

All of it was ludicrously expensive: Jo Malone, Liz Earle, Crème de la Mer. Entire shelves dedicated to face moisturisers that contained SPF, categorised into their varying amounts. There was a whole section dedicated to plumping lip glosses. Another for contouring sticks. And one for night oils. These were products that Rose – and most of her colleagues – couldn't possibly afford on their salaries. Rose had a hard enough time paying the minimal rent Luce's family asked for each month.

After picking up things she knew Luce would like – Lancôme mascara, Bobbi Brown eye kits, YSL red lipstick – she started to add bits for herself. A bronzer from a French brand she recognised, a primer from one she didn't. And an eyeshadow palette with four sparkly shades. Rose rarely wore make-up but the idea of it always appealed, like a mask she'd been waiting to grow into. Mascara and lipstick was all she ever really dabbled in. Maybe now she would become a woman who wears eyeshadow.

On her way out, Rose unlocked her phone and sent Luce a WhatsApp, noticing she was online.

Coming home now. Minnie has said yes to Wednesday and gave me a free pass to the beauty cupboard so have picked up some bits.

That's so sweet re beauty bits ! Thank you. Would love some red lippie. And YES to Wednesday! Let's cause chaos xxxx

Rose replied with a heart emoji and opened Instagram. Milo's message had been sent three hours ago.

I feel so used. What are you up to this week?

On impulse, Rose double-tapped the message, producing a small red heart underneath, and replied: *Aside from looking for cheese, I'm mostly working and looking after my broken-hearted housemate. How about you?* before locking her phone and zipping it in the front of her backpack.

Rose stood still and tried to breathe but all she could

manage were a few quick shallow gasps. She put her hand on her heart and felt it thumping angrily. What the fuck was happening?

*

'You promised there would be men here,' sighed Luce, sucking on the olive from her martini like it was a lollipop.

'There are! Look around,' said Rose, gesturing around the dimly lit restaurant they'd been tightly packed into. The room was, indeed, mostly filled by men, as was usual for parties hosted by *Intel.*

'They are all gay.'

'They are not all gay.'

'Maybe I should sleep with a gay man.'

'I'm not sure that's how it works.'

Luce turned to Rose and raised an eyebrow. The YSL red lipstick somehow had made her full lips look even more pouted, ripe and ready for action. Her skin was glowing and clear; she looked far too good for someone who had stayed up all night alternating between sobbing over her ex-boyfriend and re-downloading every dating app in existence.

'What about him?' Rose asked, pointing towards a tall blond man leaning against the bar, smouldering at the camera as the Getty photographer fawned over him, snapping away.

'Too pretty for me.'

'How about him?' she ventured, nodding over at a man lingering on his own by the fireplace in a black Trilby hat, drinking from a champagne flute.

'You're not being serious.'

'Let's try the smoking area?'

Luce sighed and pulled her tights up. 'Maybe I should just go home. This was a stupid idea.'

'No! Come on, we'll find you someone.'

'Can we get another drink first?'

'Sure. Let's go to the bar.'

'I'm going to pee. But I'll meet you in the smoking area?'

'Sounds like a plan.'

At the bar, Rose checked Instagram. Milo hadn't opened her last message. It felt strange keeping something so monumental from Luce. Although, at this point it might still not be monumental at all. For all Rose knew, Milo did this kind of thing every week, sweeping unsuspecting women off their feet with the odd DM here and there for the sake of the high it gave them – and subsequently him. Nonetheless, the idea of telling anyone felt fundamentally wrong. Like she'd be breaking the spell.

The drinks menu was almost entirely made up of whisky-based cocktails. They'd been given glasses of champagne on arrival but apparently these were not being served behind the bar. Rose didn't dare risk a negroni and instead ordered two gin and tonics. Everything was free.

'He's here. Fuck,' a female voice whispered loudly to Rose's left. She turned to see two women she recognised from *Intel.* They were among the few women in the editorial team there. Rose had never spoken to either of them directly but had seen them around the office, almost always together. Both of them were, like most of the Firehouse women, tall and statuesque, all high cheekbones and skin courtesy of a celebrity facialist's cream that was rumoured to have been made from foreskin.

To her right, Rose overheard two men. 'Why do you love it so much?' one asked the other.

'I just think the word "pussy" really rolls off the tongue,' he responded, smirking. 'Say it with me . . . "poo . . . ssea".'

Rose shifted herself closer to the two women so their voices drowned out the men.

'We can just avoid him,' the other woman was saying. 'He's the one that should feel embarrassed, not you.'

'I hate my life.'

'Could I get two of the whisky cocktails please? Thanks. Look, you haven't done anything wrong here.'

It was a widely accepted Firehouse fact that the editors at *Intel* were badly behaved. The publication had a hard time shaking the 'boys will be boys' reputation it had acquired under the editorship of Steven Stone, who was said to have had sex on every floor of Firehouse HQ with a famous British model when they were dating in the early 1990s. He used to leave bags of cocaine on his favourite writers' desks on Friday afternoons. Sometimes he'd also leave phone numbers. The few women who dared to work there were walking targets. None lasted longer than a year.

This behaviour was not only tolerated but encouraged; it made you more of a man and therefore better suited to influence other men at the magazine. Simon had done his best to eradicate the culture Steven had left behind. It sounded like he needed to try a little harder.

'It's time,' said the woman's friend. 'You need to report it.'

'Don't be ridiculous.'

'I'll come with you. We can tell Jasper together.'

'Jasper is the one who hired him. Their families play golf together or some shit.'

'Still. He has an obligation here.'

'What am I supposed to say when they ask for proof?'

The girl put her head in her hands and started to breathe heavily.

'Come on, let's just go home. This isn't worth it.'

As they left, Rose's drinks arrived. She was walking towards the smoking area and, distracted by what she'd just overheard, she bumped directly into someone walking towards her.

'Oh gosh, I'm so sorry,' she said, gin and tonic spilling down her hands.

'Watch where you're going,' said Oliver, towering above her.

'Oliver, please,' she sighed. 'Not tonight, okay?'

'Milo isn't here, if that's who you're looking for.'

'I'm not. I'm here with my housemate.'

'Yes, you enjoy yourself. Don't worry about me, I'll be here slaving away by the door.'

Rose sighed, knowing Oliver found nothing about his job 'slaving'. Being by the door and greeting everyone with air kisses as they came in was literally his dream way to spend an evening, particularly because it also gave him the power to turn people away.

'I can help if you like?'

'No. Please don't. I'll keep all of the credit for tonight, thank you very much.'

'You'd get that anyway, Oliver.'

He scoffed.

'Do you know anything about an incident at *Intel*?'

'You're going to have to be a little more specific.'

'I overheard the two women in editorial talking. It sounded like one of the editors had been . . . I don't know exactly what. But one of the women . . . she seemed pretty upset.'

'Yes, I know what that's about.'

'What?'

Oliver rolled his eyes. 'It's improper to gossip, Rose.'

'Was it one of the senior editors?'

'What do you think?'

'If you know something, why aren't you doing anything about it?'

'Because I like having a job. Have a fabulous evening, Rose,' he quipped before strutting away.

Upstairs, Rose spotted Luce right away. The glint of her silver dress was peeking through a mass of long black suits.

'Hey,' Rose said, approaching the group but looking exclusively at Luce, glass in her outstretched hand.

'Oh, thank you!' Luce replied before turning to no one in particular and booming: 'This is my gorgeous housemate, Rose. She works at Firehouse.' One of the men turned to look at Rose, his eyes surveying like an airport scanner before returning to Luce.

'Where do you work?' asked a different man, his eyes firmly fixed on her friend.

'I'm a very boring lawyer,' she replied.

'You don't look very boring to me,' said another of the men, whose body was inching closer towards Luce's, the satin of his suit almost touching that of her dress. It was all so predictable. There were five men positioned around her now, each one of them engaging in a black-tie pissing contest for her attention.

Rose stood silently near Luce, observing each of the men who, given the combination of their height and bone structure, could only have been models.

They had moved on to discussing a photoshoot one of the men had just done with Gucci when Rose started to zone out, her mind drifting back to Milo. He wouldn't be here tonight, of course. She'd already googled him earlier that day: he was performing in Paris. Rose had managed to go forty-five minutes without checking if he'd seen her last message. She decided that was long enough and told Luce she was going to the bathroom.

There was no toilet roll but she did have a new message on Instagram: *I'm abroad at the moment but I'll be back in London this weekend if you're around?*

Rose stared at the word 'around' until it started to go fuzzy. Around for what? Drinks? Dinner? Sex? All three? And in what order? She understood that unpicking ambiguity was often a necessity when it came to communicating with someone you are attracted to. But with Milo, the possibilities of what he could want from her were as endless as they were unfathomable. All she really wanted from him was clarity. And yet, she knew this was probably the one thing he was incapable of giving anyone, especially not in writing, where it was only ever a few screenshots away from making headline news.

She resisted the urge to reply right away and returned to the smoking area, where she found Luce making out with one of the male models. There was no point in interrupting, so Rose headed back downstairs in search of another reason to stay at the party.

Dancing had overtaken the bar area; the lighting had been turned down so low Rose could barely distinguish one gently bopping body from another. In one corner, a group of people seemed to be cheering. Rose watched as they helped a woman up so that she was now standing on top of the bar, barefoot and holding a bottle of champagne. She tossed her head back and drank from the bottle as the small crowd cheered. It was only when Rose moved closer that she saw the woman was a famous model who had supposedly been sober for ten years.

The only other room in the venue was now occupied by small groups of people either drinking or taking photographs. Rose didn't recognise anyone but decided to do a lap. She wanted to give it a little longer in case Luce decided against going home with the model in favour of crying on the sofa and watching reality TV. Finding no one and nothing, Rose settled into an empty corner table next to two attractive actors she recognised. Both of them were the stars of a new crime drama that everyone had become so obsessed with it had put her off watching it completely.

One of them looked up as she sat down and smiled at her in a way that made Rose think it was okay to say hello. So, she did.

Both men introduced themselves and one, the taller one, asked why she was alone. Rose explained what had happened with Luce and George – and her housemate's newfound mission to get laid.

'Classic,' the actor who smiled at her said. 'I'm Leo.' He reached out to shake her hand and introduced his friend, Michael.

'What do you do?' she asked Leo, aware he'd know she already knew the answer.

'I'm an actor. So is Mike.'

'Oh, cool. I work at Firehouse.'

'Do you now?' his eyes lit up. 'Are you an editor at *Intel*?'

'No, I work in the press office.' She watched as his expression switched from intrigue to indifference. 'How come you guys weren't at the awards last weekend?' she asked, knowing both had been invited.

'I was filming in Utah,' said Michael. 'How was it? Saw Milo Jax was there. He's such a hero.'

'Yeah I was gutted to miss out actually after I saw he was there,' added Leo.

Rose tried hard not to allow herself to go red. But Leo appeared to have clocked it.

'Do you know him?' he asked, intrigue returning.

'No. Not really.' She paused. 'I mean, we hung out a bit at the awards.'

'Oh, did you now? Check you out. Hanging with the most desirable man on the planet. He's quite the charmer, isn't he?'

Rose scratched her arm just to have something to do with her hands.

'Did you go to the afterparty with him?' asked Michael. 'I've heard so many stories about those afterparties. And about Milo actually.' Both of the men chuckled.

'I did, yeah,' Rose replied.

'So coy!' said Leo, his body closer to hers now. 'What did you say your name was again?'

'Sorry, I've got to go.' Rose stood up, realising sweat had started pooling above her top lip. 'My colleague needs me by the door.'

Before the men could say anything else, she was gone.

Wherere did you gooooo????

Helloooo?

Rose??

Rose.

Gone to Harrison's house. Told him my ex was called George. George Harrison! Lollololol. Back in am.

Rose felt a wave of guilt wash over her. It was unusual of her to leave Luce without saying goodbye.

I'm so sorry, she wrote, replying to Luce on WhatsApp. *Met some weird actors downstairs and then just felt exhausted and bolted. How was it? Are you home?*

Luce instantly appeared online and started typing. *I squirted.* She added several water droplet emojis.

Congratulations, Rose replied. *I didn't know you could do that.*

Neither did I! Was great. Although a bit like having a small wee.

In a good way?

Oh, in a very, very good way.

I wouldn't know.

We need to find you a Squirter Gun.

A what?

That's what I'm calling men who make women squirt.

Hahaha okay. Not sure I've got that in me though.

We ALL have it in us! Just need to find the right Squirter Gun.

Are you going home?

Oh, I'm already home. I came in at 5 a.m., packed up all my bits and got the first train out. Wanted to recover from my hangover in a big hot bath.

Fair enough. And you feel okay?

I'm great. George never made me squirt. Harrison did. I've basically fucked the Beatles. This is a special day. Did you have fun?

Rose told Luce about the two women at *Intel* she'd overheard.

Do you think I should tell Minnie? she asked.

No. You have no idea what even happened. It's none of your business.

I know but what if someone did something . . . you know.

This is why I love you, my little Rosebud. You're too gentle for this world.

What do you mean?

Trust me. If those women are sleeping with the editors at Intel, they're getting something out of it.

You think so?

Yes. Also, I follow lots of the Intel editors on Instagram. And they are DILFs.

You hear so many gross stories about them.

I would fuck at least four of them.

It wasn't until after work that Rose replied to Milo. She had kept her notifications off in fear of his name popping up on her screen while she was in the office. Whatever was happening, Rose knew it was only going to keep happening if she kept it a secret. Positioning herself comfortably at the kitchen table with a cup of peppermint tea in front of her, she composed her message.

I'm around. Don't tell the press.

She felt a jolt of pride at the joke. Milo opened her reply instantly and began typing.

Good, he wrote. *Fancy coming to mine?*

Rose gulped. As forward as such an invitation would seem in regular circumstances, in this one it made sense. Of course Milo wanted to meet at his house; anywhere else and they'd be photographed together. It didn't mean they were going to sleep together. Nonetheless, when a woman goes to a man's home for the first time, there is always a slight sense of unease. No matter how attractive the man is, how safe he may make you feel, how polite he is to waiters, the unease is there. Spawning all kinds of anxieties and worst-case scenarios. It may fade, of course, depending on how long you've known the man. Rose had known Milo for five days.

Sure. When? she replied, instantly wondering if she should have been more assertive. He had chosen the place. Shouldn't she have chosen the time?

The word 'Seen' appeared immediately. Seconds later: 'Typing . . .'.

How about tonight? 8pm?

Sounds good.

It was already 6.15 p.m., which left her with alarmingly little time to get ready. She was about to jump in the shower when she realised that she didn't know where Milo Jax lived. Did he expect her to find it online?

She opened her messages again.

Are you just going to guess my address then? he'd replied.

I could probably google it.

'Seen' immediately, again. Her heart beat violently as the next three minutes passed. There was no reply. She had taken the joke too far. He was the one feeling uneasy now. He'd never reply. In fact, he'd probably gone back to bed with the supermodel. She should've just asked him for his address like a normal person. She turned her phone off and opened her laptop.

'Where does Milo Jax live?' was the first thing that Google suggested after she'd typed out the first two letters of his name. The first result was on TMZ: 'Milo Jax home: The £9.3 million estate purchased by the music sensation'. There was a photograph of a vast townhouse overlooking Regent's Park that Milo was said to have bought earlier that year. It must have had seven floors. The pictures from the inside made it look like a forgotten palace, all Renaissance artwork and patterned furniture. It was lavish in a strangely old-fashioned way that is rarely associated with mega-famous pop stars in their thirties. But perhaps Milo was a strangely old-fashioned man. The article noted how this was his second UK home; his first was a modest four-bedroom home in Suffolk near the village where he'd grown up. According to the article, Milo also had homes in LA, New York and the south of France.

Next, she searched his name on YouTube. The first result was a video of him performing at the Grammys last year in a white three-piece suit with garish pink lapels. The second was from when he was fifteen – MILO JAX FIRST EVER YOUTUBE VIDEO (FULL VERSION) – the clip that had made him famous. Rose watched as an even more cherubic Milo played the guitar, wide earnest eyes looking longingly into the camera as he sang 'Wonderwall' by Oasis. It was from there, Rose had now learned, that Milo had been contacted by an executive at Sony, who encouraged him to go to a prestigious performing arts school when he turned sixteen. By seventeen, he was signed. By eighteen, he had the number one single in the country.

Rose opened Spotify next. He had 60,400,232 million monthly listeners and the top track was that first number one single. 'The Way You Are' was a paean to one woman ('I love nothing more than when your make-up is on the floor') and had been streamed more than one billion times. Like anyone with taste, Rose did not like this song; it was too jangly and irritating because it had been played everywhere when it first came out in 2012. Also, the lyrics were, quite clearly, dreadful and barely sensical. She had never really listened to Milo's discography beyond that because of this. Listening now, some of his recent stuff was more tolerable. There was one song called 'Brush It Off' that had more of a rock influence behind it, harsher drums and a steady beat; Rose added it to her running playlist. Milo was currently on tour promoting his fourth album, *Ministry of Hearts*, which sounded almost identical to the first, possibly in a bid to create similar sales figures. She concluded that they were the kind of songs you could enjoy listening to, possibly in a stranger's living room after a night out, when they could fade into the background in between bursts of ABBA and Fleetwood Mac, but wouldn't voluntarily listen to.

Rose turned her phone on and immediately opened Instagram. It was now 6.45 p.m.

Hey, so sorry, began the reply from Milo. *I fell asleep. Long day. Come to the Brampton Gate Mews near Camden. It's number 5.*

That's okay. I can be there around 8.30pm ish?

Perfect. Have you eaten?

Did Milo Jax want to cook for her? Perhaps he had a private chef who was in the process of making his dinner and needed advance notice if they were going to cook for a second person. Maybe there were already other women at his house, and Rose was being called up for the next shift. Did this mean she was going on a date? And if there was no chef and Milo couldn't cook, would they order a takeaway? How would that even work? She took a deep breath.

I always have inordinate amounts of pasta on the go at home and was about to tuck in. I can bring some if you like?

A chef among us! Don't worry about me. See you soon.
There was definitely a private chef.

Rose had shaved everything from the eyebrows down. As she walked up the escalator at Camden Town station, she felt an urge to scratch herself, which meant she had probably missed a patch, or had already started to get an ingrown hair on the journey.

She folded her arms, tucking her phone in her left pocket as she felt the rush of Underground wind swoop up her sleeves. After walking a suitable distance away from the station and its crowds, Rose opened Citymapper, which told her that Brampton Gate Mews was another six minutes away by foot. On the way, she looked around for signs of celebrity life. A cafe that only sold matcha lattes, perhaps, or an Italian deli that sold jars of pesto for £7. All she saw, though, was a pub, an off-licence and a post office.

She was wearing her favourite pair of velvet flared trousers. They had a zip down one side and two pockets on the front that made her hips and waist look smaller. On top, she'd chosen one of Luce's designer slogan T-shirts that she'd borrowed for a party months ago and forgotten to return. Luckily, Luce also seemed to have forgotten about it. It was white, oversized and read: 'Women are Wonders' in cartoonish red writing. She'd tucked it into her flares.

On her feet, Rose wore her white boots with the square toe because they made her 5'6" legs look like 5'7" legs. Finally, she wore an oversized vintage denim jacket Lola had given her three years ago when she was clearing out her cupboards. It had gold zips and large pockets in unexpected places. She was also wearing the only proper bra she owned – her breasts were too small to require underwire – and a matching lacey black thong. Just in case.

She could see the entrance to his street now; it was just opposite a Co-op. Given that it had only just turned 8.30 p.m. and she was thirsty, going inside felt like the right thing to do to kill some time. It would be weirdly enthusiastic for her to turn up at the exact time they'd agreed, anyway. There was also the simple fact that arriving at someone's house empty-handed was rude, even if that someone could probably afford to buy the entire contents of a supermarket three or four times over. So, she bought a bag of pitta chips and a bottle of Merlot; the total was £8.90.

The road Milo lived on was so inconspicuous most people would walk straight past it without the faintest idea. Tucked behind another row of much larger houses overlooking Regent's Park, it wasn't even gated. Just a narrow, cobbled street with a few garages and doors. To the right of door number 5, though, was one giveaway: a small camera and a keypad, and, unlike the other houses, no letterbox or doorbell. Rose spent a few seconds thinking about where his post went and then realised if she lingered too long, it might alert some sort of alarm system and then she'd get arrested for stalking. She opened Instagram and sent him a message: *Outside*.

Seconds later, the door buzzed and opened slightly. The first thing Rose saw when she pushed it open was a garage with two cars parked side by side. She didn't know enough about cars to name the models – Luce would know – but one was a large SUV, the other a smaller sports car. Both were black and had regular number plates. There was a narrow staircase directly in front of her.

'Hello!' came Milo's voice from somewhere upstairs. She walked up slowly, not allowing the inconspicuous entrance to dampen the expectation that she was stepping into a once-in-a-lifetime property.

Milo emerged, standing at the top of the staircase.

'Half-expected you to have a butler waiting for me,' she said.

'It's his day off,' Milo replied, reaching his arms out to her.

His body felt warm and damp, and Rose noticed how much larger he was than her. Almost a foot taller, she suspected, his torso taut against her chest in the way being famous must mandate. Clad in a baggy pair of tracksuit bottoms and a white T-shirt, he looked like he'd just stepped out of the shower. He pulled away from hugging her and Rose noticed that his hair was wet, so perhaps he had. The dress codes they'd each privately established for the evening were wildly out of sync. She looked like she was going on a date and trying very hard not to look like she tried very hard. He looked like he was about to watch a film and masturbate.

'Come inside then,' he said, ushering her in.

'I'm not a vampire,' she quipped.

'What?'

'Never mind. Sorry.'

His home couldn't have been further from the typical

celebrity abode. In Rose's head, people like Milo lived in museums with bare walls, spiral staircases and coffee machines like the ones you get in coffee shops. Or ostentatious rooms like the ones she'd seen in the article. This was just a few rungs above student digs.

There was a door directly in front of her, presumably for a bathroom, and what looked like a bedroom and kitchen on the right. Milo led her into the room to the left: a small living area populated by nothing but an antique-looking coffee table, a burgundy velvet sofa, and a piano. The walls were bare apart from a giant *Pulp Fiction* poster. There was a rattan rug on the floor and a Diptyque candle on the coffee table. A box of cereal lay horizontal – and empty – in one corner of the sofa, a pile of papers in the other. Rose looked closer and identified the cereal as Frosties.

Nothing about this room or the flat made sense, except for the dying cheese plant on the windowsill because Milo definitely was not the kind of person that would make time to water his own plants. And it didn't seem like hired help had anything to do with this place.

'Is this for me?' he said, pointing to the bottle of wine tucked under Rose's arm.

'No, I just tend to bring my own bottle of wine to people's houses in case they only have Echo Falls,' she quipped.

'Ha, I see. I'll open it,' he said, as Rose passed him the bottle. 'So how are you?' The question reminded her that she had absolutely nothing to talk about with this man.

'I'm fine, thank you. How are you?'

'Did you manage to get into work okay the next day? Not too hungover?'

'Oh yeah, it was okay. I mean, I felt like crap, obviously. But so did 80 per cent of the office.'

'Did you have fun, at least?'

'Those events aren't really my thing.'

'No?'

'I used to love them when I started the job. There was something . . .' She stopped herself. 'It's going to sound weird saying this to you. But it was like being in those rooms made me feel like I was a part of something. Something very few people get to be a part of. And even though I was just an observer, there was something . . . I guess . . . special about that. It made me feel like I mattered in a world that is constantly trying to make people feel the opposite. I've never had that feeling before.'

'I can understand that.'

Rose scoffed. 'Can you?'

'Yes, of course,' he said.

'Do you enjoy it?'

'What do you mean?'

'This life,' she said, holding her fingers up in quotation marks.

'I think we need some wine first before we start asking the hard questions.'

He led her into the kitchen, which was the size of her bathroom at home. There were a few more dying house-plants on the counter and several water bottles with his name on them by the sink. The shelves were lined with vitamin jars, most of which looked empty.

'Why do you live here?' she found herself asking.

'What?' He looked shocked, popping the cork out of the bottle of wine.

'Sorry, I didn't mean . . .' she trailed off.

'It's okay. I know it's a dive. This is actually just the mews flat. The main house is across the courtyard over there . . .' He pointed through the window.

All Rose could see was the back of a very tall, very cream building that must have been the house from the article. There were French windows throughout. It was hard to make out anything inside except for a few ladders and some paintings in ornate gold frames.

'Picasso,' said Milo from over her shoulder.

'You're kidding.'

'Yes, Rose. I'm kidding.'

'I paint, you know.' She instantly regretted saying this.

'Do you?'

'I mean, I used to. I went to art college.'

'You continue to surprise me, Rose.'

'I could say the same about you,' she replied, gesturing around his student digs.

'Look, Sasspot, I only just bought the place. It's one of those old draughty Victorian townhouses where everything could be beautiful if it wasn't falling apart.'

'Sure,' replied Rose, still peering through the window, trying to get a sense of the actual place where this man lived, or would one day live.

'I'm getting a lot of work done to it. Stripping floors, redoing the ceiling, new fireplaces. All that sort of stuff.

So for now, when I'm in London, which is hardly ever at the moment, I'm here, in the mews.'

'How's that?'

'Charming,' he said lightly in a way that made it impossible to ascertain if he was being serious or not.

'Show me around then.'

'Why with pleasure, m'lady.'

In truth, there wasn't much to see. Aside from the kitchen and living room, the only other spaces in the mews were the bathroom, which had paint peeling off the walls and a bath that looked like it hadn't been used (or cleaned) in weeks, and his bedroom. It was the only space in the entire flat that had been paid some attention.

The walls were a dark olive green, the kind you often get in countryside hotels that serve complimentary afternoon tea, and the bed looked king-size, which meant it took up most of the available space. On the walls were two black and white photographs of the Rolling Stones Rose had never seen before. She looked closer and realised they were both personally signed.

'What do you think?' he asked, leaning against the wall outside his bedroom, taking a long sip from his wine.

'Charming,' she replied, smiling.

They drifted back into the living room and settled on either side of the velvet sofa. At some point, music started playing from somewhere. A soft, quiet beat that you might expect to hear in the lift at a museum.

Milo asked about her painting. She found herself divulging everything she hated about art college – the pretentious professors, the superiority of the students, and the way she was constantly pushed to work with new materials when all she wanted to do was paint people's faces.

He asked about her previous jobs, her family, her daily routine at Firehouse. Rose answered everything in detail as it became clearer that Milo had no interest in talking about himself, either because he was fed up with having to do so or because information about him had capital in a way it didn't for Rose, and he might not trust her yet.

She quickly realised that asking him direct questions only ever resulted in opaque answers; it was best to let him offer up personal information on his own terms. And he did begin to open up as they moved on to a second bottle of wine from Milo's cupboard. It was from 1982. So, he had expensive wine, and it tasted like a completely different drink compared to the bottle Rose had bought. That was one learning. Another was that he was more of a dog person than a cat person. And that he did have control over his own Instagram but had turned off all notifications and swore to never really look at them. How, then, did he see her message?

'I might have looked you up on Instagram after that night,' he confessed.

'Really?'

'Yes, really.'

'Oh.' Rose sifted through her entire Instagram profile in her head, trying to see what Milo had seen. 'Why would you do that?'

'You intrigue me,' he added.

'And yet, you didn't follow me.'

He laughed in a way that made Rose feel like he was well aware there were entire gossip forums dedicated to analysing the people he followed on social media. Every new person on his follower list was practically its own news story.

At one point, after Rose's insistence, Milo showed her his fridge. He asked if she used to watch *MTV Cribs* as a kid, and she assured him that, like any sensible millennial woman, of course she had. Because what better way is there to understand a person than by seeing what food and drink they choose to store and, crucially, how they chose to store it? Inside Milo's fridge was a carton of unsweetened soy milk, a takeaway box that looked like it had a half-eaten portion of noodles inside, three lime-green unlabelled bottles left over from a juice cleanse he did last week, an unopened block of butter and three bottles of Veuve Clicquot.

'It all makes sense now,' she said nodding.

'Look, I'm never here. Especially not now while I'm touring.'

'Of course.'

'What's in your fridge?'

'Oh, I couldn't possibly tell you. Privacy is very important to me.'

He smiled and lightly placed his hand on her arm.

It was easy to flirt with Milo. But it was harder to go beyond that, to find any kind of depth in their conversations. That didn't matter, Rose thought. If this was all he was going to give her, it would still be an experience worth having, a story worth telling.

They'd been chatting for two hours when Rose felt a desperate urge to pee. This often happened when she was distracted. The calling signs from her bladder would go unnoticed until she was literally about to urinate on the floor.

'Sorry, do you have a toilet?' she asked, interrupting his story about the marble fireplace he was getting imported from Italy.

'No, you have to go outside.'

'Of course, you have a toilet. You've even shown me the bathroom. Sorry. I'm feeling a bit drunk now.'

'Funnily enough, we keep the toilet in the bathroom. Go forth,' he gestured his hand towards the living-room door.

Sitting on the toilet, Rose allowed her upper body to flop onto her lap so that her head was dangling in between her legs. The room was spinning and this was definitely making it worse but she couldn't energise herself to lift her head up again. She wondered if there was a moment when she was supposed to leave and how that moment would be communicated. Would Milo start clearing up? Or would he say he was tired? Maybe he'd just tell her it was time for her to go. It was impossible to tell whether or not he was enjoying talking to her. What if he tried to kiss her? Should she try to kiss him? That might set off some sort of alarm system again.

She returned from using the bathroom after what felt like five hours to find Milo leaning against the fridge, watching her. They both smiled as she sidled next to him, neither of them uttering a word as their arms brushed against each other. Maybe he did want to kiss her.

'Have you ever been in love?' Rose asked.

'On to the harder questions now, are we?'

'I don't think it's a particularly hard question. If you have, I think you'll know.'

'There have been times when I've definitely felt like I was in love, I think. But that's often the case.'

'What do you mean?'

'Well, when you first hook up with someone you really like who likes you too, there's that instant attraction, isn't there? An intensity that sort of wakes you up. A rush.'

She nodded, trying not to blush.

'It's like, you want to spend every second of your time just being with that person to see what happens next. Like, even being in their presence makes you . . . better, I suppose. As if everything was black and white before and now it's in technicolour.'

'And you've felt that?' she asked, wondering which romcom he'd plagiarised that metaphor from.

'Yes. That I've felt. Many times. But I'm not sure that's love.'

'Why not?'

'Because I think love is supposed to feel different.'

'Safe,' she countered.

'Yes, exactly,' he smiled, turning to face her directly. 'Whereas part of the fun of that first bit is that you don't feel completely safe. You have no idea what's to come – and that can be terrifying. But it's also a turn-on. The real question, Rose, is have you ever been in love?'

'No. Never.'

'But you've had relationships?'

'Sort of.' She decided not to tell him about Ed.

'Good ones?'

'I feel like you're interviewing me.'

'Maybe I am. It's quite nice being on the other side of the table.'

'Can I ask you some questions now?'

He sighed and walked over to a half-drunk bottle of gin and topped up his glass without offering to top up Rose's. 'What do you want to know?'

'What are your parents like?'

'Fine and low-key.'

'You get on with both of them?'

'My mum, yes. We've always been very close. My dad not so much.'

'Daddy issues?'

He laughed. 'You could say that. Are you close with your dad?'

Rose felt her chest tighten. 'No. I – I don't actually know him.'

'What do you mean?'

'He left when I was a kid. Just walked out the door and never came back. It's such a cliché.'

'Oh, wow.'

'I got over it a long time ago. He had some high-flying city job and left us with plenty of money so I can't complain too much.'

'Sure, but not having a dad isn't exactly ideal.'

'I do have a dad. I just don't know him.'

'Well, judging by his behaviour it sounds like it's best you don't.'

Rose fidgeted with her hands.

'I'm sorry,' Milo said, leaning closer to her.

'Don't be.' She decided to change the subject. 'Do you enjoy being famous?'

Milo laughed and rolled his eyes. 'That's your next question? I was expecting something a little more exciting.'

'That's my next question,' Rose said.

'Would you like to be famous?'

'Don't politician me. Answer the question.'

'Look, there are obviously parts of it that I enjoy.'

'Like?'

'The parts that anyone would enjoy.'

'You don't have to be so embarrassed to admit that you like drinking ludicrously expensive wine and getting to skip queues at airports,' she replied, waving her hand in the direction of the 1982 bottle they'd long ago finished before moving on to gin and tonics.

'Those are the highlights, to be honest.'

'Come on. Tell me.'

'It's not that I'm embarrassed. But I don't know. It's not something I created, wanted, or even thought about. And it's not real,' he sighed and took a big gulp from his drink. 'I just wanted to make music.'

There are certain things in this life you're not supposed to admit that you want. If you're a woman, for example, you aren't supposed to admit that you would like to be a little bit thinner, even though Rose and every woman she knew wanted this. The rules about wanting were more lenient for men for obvious reasons. But whatever your gender, there is one thing no one is supposed to admit to coveting. And that is fame.

You could admit to wanting wealth, success and all the paraphernalia that comes with it. But wanting fame itself, craving that obscene level of attention, admiration and analysis, no one was supposed to want that because it would make you sound like an arsehole. Milo couldn't even bring himself to say the word let alone admit that it was something that applied to him. It was hard to tell if this was out of modesty or something else that was evidently harder for Rose to understand.

Nonetheless, he continued to talk about the downsides of whatever level of special attention he was willing to admit that he had, a ritual she suspected all famous people performed to non-famous people on a regular basis. The 'I'm just like you' dance, as Minnie called it. Rose listened intently as Milo rattled off the downsides of touring – how he'd never really been able to enjoy travelling because there wasn't enough time to explore the cities, and if he ever tried, he'd either be swarmed by fans or would have to arrive at sightseeing spots before opening hours, which made the whole experience feel austere and inauthentic.

Then there were all of the friends he'd lost over the years because so many of them tried to get something out of him, whether it was performing at their relative's wedding or promoting someone's sister's new fashion brand on Instagram. Some had been offered inordinate amounts of money to talk to the tabloids about him – and he was shocked by how many did. The paparazzi thing was an obvious nightmare, too. He had to fire one of his managers because he was colluding with paps every time he went out in public.

The hardest thing, of course, was dating; he never mentioned anyone by name, or divulged any information that was too detailed, instead speaking in generalisations and opaque references. But it was the most he'd offered about himself so far. He explained how quickly relationships were ruined when they got into the press, how awkward it would be when someone was referred to as his 'girlfriend' before they'd been on a single date, and how it would be even more awkward when he found out that person had been the one to leak the news themselves.

Then there were the women who just wanted fame by proxy. Sometimes they'd even steal items of clothing he'd worn in public recently and wear them to events to confirm they'd been sleeping together. The sad thing was that it often worked. Those photos would appear in a tabloid and then the women would be interviewed, ostensibly to promote their own 'projects' but really to unearth more gossip on Milo. They'd complain about the unwanted attention they'd received on social media before talking avidly about the brand they were about to launch and where you could find them on social media.

Rose could recall a few of these interviews; they reflected a corner of the internet Oliver often talked about in the office. There was one woman Milo had dated who had a full-page feature in a national newspaper all about her fledgling wellness empire after she'd been seen outside a pub with him. She spoke ad nauseum about building her brand and how difficult it was to be taken seriously as a business owner with all the sudden attention she was getting. When asked about the rumours surrounding Milo, she replied: 'Oh, I can't talk about that.' Neither a denial nor a confirmation. The papers all reported the quote as confirmation of their romance the next day.

The actual dates themselves were also a nightmare, he added, often involving endless logistics that made the whole thing feel more like a conference than a date. Like finding a restaurant where photography was banned. And entering into the venues separately or through back doors to avoid the paparazzi. And hoping that the women he went on dates with wouldn't secretly call the paparazzi themselves.

'So, do you just not trust anyone then?' Rose asked him.

'I trust everyone until they give me a reason to prove otherwise.'

'That sounds risky.'

'It is. But I have to be able to live my life.'

There was a long pause that Rose decided to fill with an obvious question. 'What's it like for the women?'

'What do you mean?'

'Well, I've noticed what some of your fans can be like when you start dating someone. They aren't exactly very nice.'

Rose had seen how fans would launch online attacks on any woman Milo was seen with, filling their Instagram accounts with hate. Many of them were young women themselves, incandescent with rage because the man of their dreams had been taken from them.

'Oh, right. Yeah,' he sighed. 'I really hate that they have to go through that. One or two people I've dated have spoken to me about it. But, sadly, there's not much I can do.'

'Isn't there?'

'I can't control every person on the internet, Rose.'

'No, but they're your fans, aren't they? Surely that gives you some degree of control.'

He smiled. 'Yes, they are. But I'm not responsible for them. Just as you're not responsible for . . . I don't know . . . anything awful your colleagues have ever done.'

'I'm not sure that's the same.'

'Okay, look. Yes, I hate it. Yes, I know how horrible it must be to go out with me. But what am I supposed to do? Hide away and devote my life to celibacy?'

'I don't know,' she shrugged, aware that the more she challenged him, the sooner she'd be shown the door.

He laughed and took both her hands, his body the closest to hers it had been all evening.

'Rose. Can I tell you something?' he asked.

Unable to say anything with him standing so close, she simply nodded.

'You are so much more beautiful than you realise.'

She exhaled the only air that was left between them. 'How many people have you said that to?'

'Not as many as you'd think.'

If there was a moment that Rose was supposed to have left, they'd long passed it by now. But if there was a moment that Milo was going to kiss her, they were in it right now. She had fantasised about this. Dreamed of it. Longed for it. It was strange, then, what she did next.

'I'd love another gin and tonic please,' Rose said, moving over towards the bottle.

Milo had run out of gin and handed her a glass of

something brown that tasted like whisky. Her mouth wrinkled at the flavour of it as it burned her throat.

'Do you have any mixer?'

'Sure,' he replied, grabbing a bottle of tonic water and topping up her glass by a centimetre.

He held up his own glass to hers. 'A toast,' he said.

'To what?'

'To a great night – and the beginning of a beautiful friendship.'

She laughed. 'God, you're lame. Cheers.'

The next time Rose looked at her phone, it was 1.03 a.m. She had two missed calls from Luce. Not unlocking it, she turned her phone off and put it back in her jacket pocket. Milo was in the bathroom, or getting more drinks, she couldn't remember. She was sitting on the sofa staring at Uma Thurman's fringe.

There was no way of knowing how many drinks they had each had, or how many hours they'd spent talking, or even what they'd talked about. Something about exes. Something about *Cribs* again. Did she start asking him about those rumours surrounding Leonardo DiCaprio? Rose had been talking for a while before he got up to pee. And she had definitely spoken about Ed and let slip that he had dumped her. Or had she said she'd dumped him? All she knew was that things started to happen around her in slow motion. Like they were happening to someone else and she was watching the action unfold.

Milo came back from the bathroom and the music somehow got louder. He extended his hand to Rose, inviting her to dance. He pulled her body into his, raising her hands above her head and moving her hips in sync. He rolled her out and Rose twirled, noticing the ease with which he flung her out and brought her in again, bending her back so that her head almost grazed the carpet before quickly pulling her close to him so their lips almost touched. He spun her round and round until she collapsed onto the sofa, giggling in a drunken dizzy daze.

Soon, they were taking turns choosing songs. He played a song she pretended to know; she played 'Wannabe' by the Spice Girls. They moved together and apart: her with a glass of something resembling nail varnish remover in hand and a pair of his sunglasses perched on top of her head, him empty-handed, eyes hungrily fixed on her swaying limbs.

'If I ever get married, this is a song I'd dance to at my wedding,' announced Milo, tapping at something on his phone. 'There,' he said, as a gentle guitar riff started to play to the backdrop of some piano. The introduction of a growling vocal. It was beautiful. 'You like it?' he asked her, smiling.

'Who is it?'

He didn't answer and instead moved around the living room, slowly rotating his hips.

She closed her eyes and listened, wanting to take it all in. The voice transported her somewhere else. She wasn't in that room any more. She wasn't even on solid ground. She was floating, her limbs gliding in the direction of the current.

* * *

It wasn't clear when or how she and Milo started kissing, or who kissed whom. But the second she felt his tongue inside her mouth, everything suddenly shifted into a moment of clarity. A sense of hyper-awareness of what was happening. Senses enlivened by his touch, Rose could tell it was a good kiss. The kind you replay over and over until the memory of it becomes the thing you remember rather than the kiss itself, which only makes it better. His tongue was soft and gentle. She moaned as his hands moved through her hair and then she felt them on her hips, pushing her back against the wall, his erection firmly pressed into her.

They reached out for more of each other, their limbs twining around one another like growing branches, finding new parts to touch and grip tightly. His body guided her to the bedroom, mouth not moving from hers as he tugged at her flares, managing to peel her out of them by the time she fell back onto his bed. Rose gasped as he pushed his tongue inside her, hands roving her hips. She arched her back, fingernails digging into his duvet.

By the time he was thrusting himself into her, the clarity Rose had acquired earlier began to dissipate. She caught herself studying Milo's face. Entirely unfamiliar, it was contorted in the way it is when someone has sex but somehow worse than she had seen before. His mouth had curled up into some sort of snarl, nose wrinkled and angry. He was groaning loudly, saying words that made her wince, words that made her want to close up into a compact, airless shell.

He turned onto his back so that she straddled him. She relaxed a little when she was on top, the drunken haze taking her elsewhere. Closing her eyes helped, too. She pushed her palms into his shoulders and moved herself to a rhythm that felt steady and full. It felt better, like she could go through with it. At least in a way that would make him feel like she'd enjoyed herself. It was the least she could do.

When it was over, Milo offered to get a car to take her home. She agreed and didn't question why he came in the car with her, nursing a bottle of tequila they both drank from in the back seat. The alcohol slipped down more easily now, a quick potent burn that warmed every part of her. She could tolerate it.

PART II

ONE

Did you drop me home? Rose sent the message and gently lifted the weight of her limbs out of bed. Her entire body had a pulse. She held on to the walls for stability as she ventured towards the bathroom. But it wasn't until she sat on the toilet that she noticed the pain. It was unbearable: a shooting, sharp sensation that plunged through her like a dagger. On instinct, she looked down. 'Oh my God,' she whispered to herself.

Rose had bled from sex before. Certainly after the first few times with Ed. But not like this. This blood was bright, look-at-me, red. The kind you get from a paper cut rather than a period. And there was a lot of it, enough to fill a shot glass at the very least. She tried to stand up but quickly sat back down, wincing as the drops dribbled down her thigh, forming a faded crimson patch right around her kneecap. Some made it all the way to the floorboards, staining the wood.

Rose sat on the toilet for several minutes, holding a scrunched-up ball of toilet roll against herself until her hand felt damp. Every time she tried to stand up, the dagger seemed to push itself deeper inside her. Clutching her stomach tightly with her back hunched over, she managed to lift herself up just enough so that she could open the cupboard underneath the sink where they usually kept ibuprofen. There were endless empty packets that Luce had inexplicably chosen not to throw away. Eventually, Rose found two packets that had one tablet left in each of them and swallowed them both, using the little saliva she had to wash them down.

She needed to lie horizontally. The bedroom was too far, so she got into the bath. Her body unfurled and she placed both hands on her stomach, rubbing them in circles like Lola used to do whenever she was sick as a child. She turned both taps on and let the water fill up the tub around her until there was just a centimetre between where the water stopped and the lip of the bath. The glugging sound from the drain told Rose off for filling the bath so much. So she tilted her head back and allowed herself to go fully under where there were no sounds at all. The need for breath came faster than she expected. She let it linger for a moment too long and emerged, gasping madly.

Wrapped tightly in a towel, Rose slowly made her way back into the bedroom. There was a small array of scarlet stains halfway down the bed. On impulse, she ripped the duvet cover and sheets off, stuffed them into a black bin bag and buried them in the wheelie bin outside the front door. It was as far away as she could feasibly get them in her current state. Burning the bin bag was tempting, too. But the last thing she needed was her neighbours thinking she was a pyromaniac.

Back underneath her duvet, Rose checked her phone. It was 7.49 a.m. Fear of being caught out for lying or exaggerating had always stopped her from taking a sick day. Today, there was no other option. Unsure of how many details to offer, Rose drafted potential messages to Minnie in her Notes app.

Hi Minnie, so sorry. I'm not feeling very well today so won't be coming in. Did that sound too authoritative? Was 'won't' a bit extreme?

Hi Minnie. I'm not feeling very well today. Sorry.

Why was she apologising? It's not someone's fault if they're unwell.

Hi Minnie. I'm not feeling well enough to work today. See you Monday hopefully.

Should she outline some symptoms? People work through illness all the time. What warrants a sick day?

Hi Minnie, I'm not feeling well enough to work today. I have a really bad headache and a fever.

She'll tell you to take some Lemsip. No, she wouldn't do that. Although with the stress around StandFirst, she might?

Hi Minnie, I had food poisoning last night. Not well enough to work. Hope that's okay.

Rose ran out of patience. She copied and pasted the food poisoning message and sent it to Minnie, turned her phone off and closed her eyes. Hours later, she was woken up by the pain returning. It was now 11.30 a.m. – the ibuprofen must have been wearing off. She turned on her phone and, ignoring the reply from Minnie, went onto Deliveroo to order some more from the local Co-op. The delivery was £3 more than the actual ibuprofen. Rose sighed and thumped her phone down on the bed.

Feeling more awake now, she tried to piece together the night. It was hard for her to get her key in the front door; she could vaguely recall Milo eventually taking it from her and opening it himself. Beyond that, though, nothing was clear.

Fragments of memories floated like giant bubbles in and around her head. Milo helping her up the stairs. Milo making a comment about the wallpaper in her bedroom. Milo's weight next to hers on the bed. They were all there, bouncing within reach, taunting her. But every time she tried to get close to one, the bubble popped. Its shiny surface instantly dissolved, leaving behind nothing but sour, sticky residue.

Her phone rang and she hated that for a split second, she thought it might have been him. It was Lola.

'Hi, Mum,' Rose croaked, immediately burrowing herself back under the duvet, which felt scratchy and harsh on her skin.

'Hi, darling, how are you?'

'I don't actually feel that great. Can we talk later?'

'Why? What's happened?'

If Rose told her mother anything about Milo, she would tell the receptionist at her gym. And then her hairdresser. And then the woman who waxes her legs and all of her other friends. Rose mumbled something about having stomach cramps. Lola made sympathetic noises and suggested painkillers, before launching into an unsolicited review of Zara's latest collection. Everything in there was *gorgeous* at the moment apparently, including a pair of high-waisted culottes that would go really well with a cropped sparkly jumper she wasn't young enough to get away with but might help her pass for forty-two. Eventually she reached her conclusion and, apparently forgetting that Rose was supposed to be at work, asked if she would like to meet for a walk.

The pain was still there, but she thought it had eased enough for her to get dressed and go out to buy more ibuprofen. Luce wouldn't be back until next week. It probably wasn't a good idea for Rose to stay at home all day on her own, anyway. She suggested her favourite spot on the Heath, right behind the men's swimming pond. Lola agreed and said she'd be there as soon as she'd asked the 'lovely lady at the till if culottes were still in season'.

Realising she hadn't worn enough layers, Rose sat on a clean patch of grass across from the pond, pulled her knees up to her chest and hugged her legs tightly. For whatever reason, the pain had subsided, at least enough for her to push it towards a forgotten corner of her mind for now. It was one of those perfect late spring mornings. The kind you always see in adverts for Center Parcs: clear blue skies, fledgling blossom inching its way up trees, and people walking dogs in loafers and trench coats.

Lola was running late and had sent Rose two voice notes on WhatsApp informing her as such. The first: '*Hi Rose. It's Lola. It's two o'clock. Oh bugger, is this recording? I'm not sure if this is recording, hang on.*' And the second: '*Right, I think it probably is recording. Hi, darling. It's Lola. It's a few minutes past two o'clock. I should arrive in about ten minutes. Sorry, darling. See you soon.'*

Rose silently observed the scene for a few minutes. She observed the pace of her breathing and realised how tired she was, closed her eyes. And there he was. In his kitchen, smiling at her. In a bed – which one? – his body on top of hers. His mouth smothering her from the inside out. She shivered, shaking her arms and shoulders. 'Fuck's sake,' she muttered under her breath, opening her eyes and reaching for her phone. She opened Instagram; there were no notifications. And her message to Milo still lacked the word 'Seen' beneath it.

Rose looked up and saw a woman wearing head-to-toe leopard print walking towards her, waving frantically. When she was just a few feet away, she tripped and fell forward over nothing in particular.

'Oh, bugger,' she said, quickly pulling herself upright.

'Are you okay?' Rose asked, embracing her mother and helping her up.

'Yes, yes. Absolutely fine. Just a little tired. You know I fall over when I'm tired. How are you, Bitsy?'

'I wish you'd stop calling me that.'

'Why?'

'Because it sounds ridiculous in public. Like I'm on a posh hockey team or something.'

Ignoring her, Lola continued: 'You know the phrase, you laid your bed and now you have to lie in it.'

'I think it's "made your bed".'

'Ah, yes, of course.'

'Why?'

'No, nothing. Don't worry. Let's walk.'

Rose and Lola had the kind of uniquely intimate relationship that exists between a single mother and daughter. It elicits a different kind of dependency whereby each needs the other equally, although in very different ways. Theirs was a living situation that had seen all sorts of iterations, from a three-bedroom home in Highgate where they had home-cooked family dinners every night, to a studio flat in Tufnell Park that may or may not have also been home to a family of mice (Lola used to tell Rose fairies lived inside the walls).

It wasn't until Rose turned eighteen that Lola offered up any information about Rose's father. She had given up asking long before then, as her mother would only ever repeatedly refuse and make references to *Gilmore Girls*. Lola met Richard on a beach in India when she was twenty. She had gone backpacking with a group of school friends; he had gone with some friends from university. The two groups collided one evening at a shack in Goa that was famous for its sunsets. She was at the bar, waiting to order another round of Kingfisher beers, when a tall man with long hair down to his shoulders sidled up next to her. She was just about to move away in anticipation of a cheesy pick-up line when he started talking about turtles. They were his favourite animal. He had come to Goa primarily to see them nesting on the beach. And had she seen any yet?

Lola was pregnant two months later. For a while, they played happy families quite convincingly.

But by the time Rose was six, he was gone. Lola picked her up from school and explained that daddy had decided to go away for a bit. Rose asked when he was coming home every day for the next two years until someone at school mentioned the word 'divorce' and Lola was forced to explain to her inquisitive daughter that her father was, in all likelihood, never coming back.

Richard's absence only strengthened the connection between Lola and Rose. Even now, one of them could usually sense when something was wrong with the other. Today, though, Lola didn't seem to pick up on Rose's cues. Or if she did, she didn't say anything about it, which, on this occasion, was a relief. Because if Lola did ask Rose what was wrong, she would cry without any reasonable explanation or understanding as to why. All she knew was that the bleeding had stopped for now, as had the pain, and it would be easiest to write both off as some sort of menstrual quirk.

They walked for two hours, ambling through sunlight and shade as they crossed through the Heath's wooded areas. Lola made the odd remark about everyone they passed on their way.

'That person looks a bit like my mother,' Lola said, pointing to an older woman wearing oval sunglasses underneath a large wide-brimmed hat. She was dressed head to toe in black. Lola hated her own mother; they'd been estranged since the divorce. Rose had always suspected it was one of the reasons why Lola had been so devoted to her.

'Little bit,' she replied.

'Very gaunt face. Like someone who had all the life sucked out of their cheeks when they were young.'

'I'd quite like someone to suck the life out of my cheeks.'

'Oh, don't be daft, Bitsy.'

'I have a moon face.'

'You're beautiful. Don't you dare.'

A loud ping went off from somewhere inside Lola's trousers, prompting her body to jolt forwards comically far.

'Oh, bugger,' she said, surveying her phone.

'What's wrong?'

'When is forty-eight hours?'

'What?'

'Don't judge me, Bitsy. From Wednesday: when is forty-eight hours?'

Rose sighed. 'Friday.'

'Shit.'

'What's wrong?'

'No, nothing, it just means I have to watch a film I rented in the next six hours.'

Rose let out a gentle laugh. 'Which film?'

'*Superbad*.'

Lola had several eccentricities, though she hated it whenever someone described them as that. With an endless canon of nonsensical epithets and a peculiar penchant for bro comedies, she was always good at distracting Rose, whether it was with stories about people she despised for no apparent reason, or consistently getting her idioms mixed up ('remember, Rose, it takes two to toss' etc.). Then there were tales of her latest hobbies, all of which would become obsessions for several months at a time. A few years ago, Lola went through an axe-throwing phase, suggested by a man in her gym. Then there was the salsa-dancing phase, a different man from the same gym. And more recently, a duck-racing phase. Rose wasn't sure who suggested that one.

Today's phase was life drawing.

'This lovely woman in my building told me about it and, honestly, it is the best three hours you'll ever have,' Lola said.

Obviously Rose had done plenty of life drawing at art college; it had never interested her. She didn't have the patience for drawing anything, least of all a stranger's penis. A woman wouldn't have been quite so bad, but the life models were always men. The thought of her mother doing this made her shudder.

'The model we had this morning was very handsome,' Lola added.

'How old was he?'

'I didn't ask, actually. But I did find out that he's currently studying for a master's in physiotherapy at UCL. I told him I had a daughter.'

'Why?'

'Well, I'm probably too old to go out with him. But you—'

'Jesus, Mum.' She started to picture Lola chatting away to this poor naked man about his degree and her single daughter.

'There was another one I thought of for you, actually,'

Lola continued. 'Although it was rather strange because all the other women in the class were wearing wedding paraphernalia and I was the only one who wasn't.'

'It was a hen do?'

'Yes. Anyway, this darling girl, Sophie, was getting married and her maid of honour had arranged this life drawing class for the hen. She must have been about your age. The model was a friend of theirs. Jack, I think was his name. He looked a bit like that famous singer, Milo . . . what is it. Twix? Wax? Anyway, apparently Sophie is a huge fan, which was why they booked him . . .'

Even if Rose wanted to keep listening, she couldn't. The sound of his name had switched something off in her brain. All she could hear was the birds and the sound of them splashing down into the ponds that were now stretched out on either side. She turned to her left to look at them while Lola continued talking. One by one, they dived head-first into the water, their wings pulled right back so as to streamline their slim bodies. They went under only briefly, subsumed by the darkness of the water momentarily before emerging triumphantly, flying up, up, up. Then they were back, soaring towards clouds with the enthusiasm of newborn children.

On the Tube home, Rose checked her work email. It stopped her thinking about how little space there was between the edge of the Tube and the tunnel. This was a reality that had never stopped bothering her, no matter how many times she'd taken the Tube. There was always something suffocating about it that made her feel like she had to try harder to find the air she needed.

Most of the emails were from Minnie. The subjects, as usual, were all in caps. Thankfully, none of them were addressed only to her, which meant they could wait until the morning.

GUEST LIST//VIPS UPDATES//OLIVER CONTACTS????
DO WE STILL CARE ABOUT SHANIA TWAIN?
ANYONE SEEN THE SKIMMED MILK?

These aggressive epithets were interspersed with pitches from celebrity publicists about up and coming 'talent' they wanted to get along to Firehouse events. Most people were reality TV stars. The words 'dynamic', 'innovative', 'fresh' and 'young' were repeated at least twice in all of the subject lines.

There was still no reply from @cosmoclara, though, which was really the only email Rose had been hoping to see when she opened her phone. That and anything along the lines of 'FREEBIE ROOM NEEDS EMPTYING' in it. The freebie room was a small, empty office that had become a dumping ground for miscellaneous unwanted items that had either been sent to editors or left over from photoshoots. You'd be just as likely to find a four-pack of toilet roll as an Yves Saint Laurent handbag. Hence why, unlike the beauty cupboard, it usually stayed locked. But every so often the room became overwhelmed with items. Even if you hadn't seen the email, you'd know it had gone out purely by looking at the state of Firehouse's stairwell: a cacophonous herd of stilettos furiously clacking on marble floors. It was heartening to see that no matter how much prestige the editors at Firehouse obtained, nobody was immune to the excitement of free stuff.

The Tube stopped without warning in between the next two stations. Rose looked around to see if anyone else in the carriage had noticed. There was an older man sleeping in one seat and a couple, also basically on one seat, snuggling together. They hadn't flinched. Rose shuffled in her seat, looking at her phone screen and trying to ignore her racing heart. *The Tube would move soon*, she repeated to herself. *The Tube would move soon.*

She opened WhatsApp and tapped on Luce's name.

Hey honey. Sorry I missed you last night. You okay? It would send when she next had Wi-Fi. Rose closed her eyes and tried to picture something to calm her down. An empty beach. It was always a beach. There was a vast bank of white sand and crystal-clear turquoise ocean before her. She took a deep breath and the Tube shuddered forward. She connected to Wi-Fi at the next stop. Luce's reply was instant:

Yeah I'm all right thanks, not really sleeping but have been chatting to a really hot vegan butcher from Tottenham I found on Hinge.

Sounds like a catfish.

He's 6' 5"!

What happened to the Squirt Gun/Beatle?

We tried to have phone sex last night and it was pretty hot until he started calling me 'mummy' in a baby voice.

Luce hadn't been single for longer than a month since Rose had known her. She would break up with someone, usually after a few years together, and go home for a while. Then she'd be back on the apps and have a few one-night stands with tall bearded men who live in east London or petite brunette women that describe themselves as 'creatives'. Then there'd be a comedown period where she'd tip into solipsism and have at least two existential crises. Finally, there would be the self-love phase, aka a commitment to being single fuelled by Kelly Clarkson and Carrie Underwood songs. And then a month or so later, Luce would be in another relationship.

Come home soon xx, Rose replied, stepping off the Tube at Clapham Common. Halfway up the escalator she saw a poster for Milo Jax's tour. Then she saw another. They were lining the entire wall. His face stretching itself into different expressions with a list of dates below. The next few gigs were all over Europe. Then he'd venture to the US before heading to Mexico, Singapore, Thailand, Japan and Australia. Some of the posters featured quotes from journalists. Many featured five small stars, too. 'THE POP STAR OF THE CENTURY' – *Rolling Stone*, read one.

Rose's chest tightened as she approached the top of the escalator. She clenched her fists as she tried to take a breath. The inhalation began but it didn't go deep enough. Rose put one hand on her chest and the other on the moving escalator handrail. She tried again. When she couldn't draw breath, she started to panic. She kept trying, gasping, inhaling. A sound came out of her mouth but not one loud enough to alert anyone to what was happening. Something pushed her forward and everything went dark.

TWO

There was a spot forming beneath Rose's eyebrow. Inflamed, angry and globular but not quite ready to pop. Its bump had changed the shape of her brow line so that it looked like she was frowning. There was red elsewhere, too, like around her nostrils, where she often got black-heads, and on her chin. Places where you didn't want your face to be red. Rose held her arm outstretched and looked at herself in more detail, her phone screen reflecting back all of her imperfections. She didn't take a photograph; this was not something she wanted a record of. But lying there, back on her bed, phone in front of her, she just observed. It was 10.39 a.m. on Monday morning and she had taken the day off work again.

This time it wasn't by choice. Rose would have much preferred to go back to work immediately and get on with plans for the launch. Falling behind would only mean things would pile up – and Oliver would delight in giving her extra work. Her GP had just given her a letter recommending two days off work following the panic attack – that's what he'd called it. Rose had binned the letter and told Minnie she had a stomach bug.

When Rose had opened her eyes that Friday afternoon after seeing Lola, she was horizontal, the floor of Clapham Common station cooling the space on her back between her T-shirt and jeans. Two people in high-vis jackets hovered over her, asking questions and touching her wrists. Rose nodded to indicate that she was okay. Yes, she could hear them. No, she didn't think she had a concussion. Yes, she felt a bit dizzy. Two fingers. Rose Martin. Rose Martin. Rose Martin. They hadn't heard her the first or second time.

She turned sideways in an attempt to get up and watched as hordes of people emerged from the escalator and headed straight towards the exit without so much as even acknowledging the girl on the floor. Not one person met her gaze, not one came over to check she was okay.

After a few perfunctory obligations, like signing a form to say she wasn't dying and would go and see a doctor, Rose was allowed to go home. One of the men in high-vis jackets asked if she'd like a lift and because of the way his eyes lingered over her body when he did this, she said 'absolutely not'.

As for the panic attack, Rose couldn't tell Lola, who would probably rush her straight to A&E and demand an MRI scan or something equally melodramatic. Luce didn't need the extra stress – she'd explained in her last voice note that she still hadn't been sleeping at all. And Rose didn't need anyone else asking questions she wasn't ready to answer, although the GP had made a good go of it.

Sitting unusually close together in a small, airless room at 8 a.m., he asked if Rose had had any difficult experiences recently. This man, Dr Smith, was new at the practice. She could tell by the way he carried himself, like an expelled bully who'd just arrived at his next school. He had an unpleasantly long salt-and-pepper beard and breath that smelt like whisky and chewing gum. One bristle appeared slightly yellow, which Rose suspected was egg yolk from his breakfast.

'No,' she replied, shaking her head. 'It was nothing. I just feel a bit funny on the Tube sometimes.'

'Why's that then?' He looked down at his clipboard. 'Miss Martin, is it?'

'I don't like when it stops,' said Rose, eyes fixed on the twiddling fingers in her lap.

'Isn't that what the Tube does?'

She looked up; he was smirking at her.

'Look, I really don't think I need to be here. Can I just leave now?' Her forehead was starting to feel hot.

'Of course. Here, take this.'

Dr Smith handed her a piece of paper with the words 'Mindfulness Exercises' at the top.

'These are some breathing exercises you can try the next time you have a panic attack.'

She bristled at his use of 'the next time'.

'Thank you.'

'Goodbye, Miss Martin.'

Attempting to shake the feeling that she needed to take a shower, Rose had walked home as quickly as she could and made herself a peppermint tea before getting into her still sheetless bed. She hated doctors, especially ones who ate with the entirety of their face. There was something animalistic about it. Milo had still not seen Rose's message.

He had, however, posted several Stories about his European tour that Rose had now watched so many times she'd inadvertently memorised the entirety of his schedule. The next night was in Budapest.

10.45 a.m. There was still so much day left ahead of her. And all she could do was stare at herself in the screen of her phone, going over all the potential reasons why Milo hadn't read her message. And at that moment in time, all of them had to do with her face. The spot, the redness and also her nose. It had a distinct ridge in the centre. If you looked at it from a certain angle, it was a Disney villain nose. From other angles, it looked fine. Not pretty, exactly, but fine. It was the kind of nose celebrities would fix as soon as they arrived in LA.

Rose locked her phone: 10.47 a.m. She had around eleven hours to get through before reaching a somewhat reasonable bedtime for a twenty-six-year-old woman. There were a lot of things she could achieve in that time, like launching a website. Or baking banana bread. Twice. She could learn to juggle, or speak French. She could read an entire book from start to finish, something she'd feel too embarrassed to take out in public. Like *Politics for Dummies* – did they even make one? – or one of the Twilights. She could learn about taxes. Pensions. Credit ratings. All the things she should have probably learned about before becoming an adult. She could volunteer. Make soup for the day at a homeless shelter. Talk to people in her local old people's home. Walk someone's dog. Talk to someone's dog.

First, Rose had to shower; she could still feel Dr Smith's

breath lingering on her clothes. No one was going to let her walk their dog if she smelled like a pub basement. When she returned to her bedroom, hair just about held together on top of her head in another towel, the one that had been wrapped tightly around her fell to the floor, revealing her naked body in the standing mirror by her desk. There she was, all oddly proportioned limbs. Her arms dangled limply either side of her torso, which was too short and shapely in the wrong places. Usually, Rose felt indifferent to her body. It wasn't something she hated nor was it something she adored and cherished in the way people on social media told her she should. It was just there, existing. Today, though, at that moment, she found herself completely fixated on it. Stepping closer to the mirror, Rose pivoted so that she was facing it front-on. She gently touched parts of herself, observing the way her skin reddened when she pushed too hard, or pinched for too long. Something about it felt foreign to her. Like the flesh was no longer hers. She looked at other areas of her body, pushing both hands against herself as she moved up her legs and on to her thighs. She grabbed at the meat of them, digging her nails in. Feeling nothing, she dug in harder, waiting for something to happen. A signal of ownership. She waited a little longer until her skin was vibrating with pain. But Rose ignored the alarm and continued to push until eventually her fingers couldn't bear the pressure anymore and they collapsed onto her legs, her breath expelling in a single, forceful exhale that brought her to the floor.

THREE

It seemed like as good a time as any to go for a run. Rose was hardly athletic but she had always been a runner of sorts. Not the kind that ran quickly, of course – her legs were not long enough to move at a rapid pace without making her feel like she'd punctured an internal organ – but she would regularly do a few laps around Wandsworth Common, pausing to stretch, absorb the beauty of the natural-ish world and look at her phone. She had made some key edits to her soundtrack, removing Milo's song, 'Brush It Off', feeling a sense of achievement as she tapped 'remove from this playlist'.

It was also when she was running that Rose found she had her clearest thoughts. She would depart with questions and return with answers. This time, though, as she darted around dogs and padded past pedestrians, she couldn't find the right path. There were too many obstacles filling her head, each one of them a different anamorphic version of Milo's face. Sometimes it resembled someone familiar and cheery, like the first time she saw him. Other times, his face was beneath her, an unrecognisable thing with alien features. It was when the face appeared above her, though, that stirred the most unease. Rose turned the volume up on her iPhone, the sounds of Robyn's 'Dancing On My Own' now reverberating through every neuron in her brain. This was objectively a very happy, very good song. Nothing bad could happen to Rose as long as she was listening to this song. The second it finished, she dragged the timebar back to the start to play it again. Then she played it again and again for the twenty minutes it took her to get home.

Later that afternoon, after several naps and telling Netflix that yes, she was still watching *America's Next Top Model*, Rose decided to delete her conversation with Milo. He still hadn't read her message, and now even the sight of his name in her inbox made her want to vomit. Like she needed to expel the words entirely from her body and mind. There would be no memories to recall if she never had any memories in the first place. It was easier just to erase it all.

Rose deleted the conversation with a firm swipe and tap of her thumb. Once his name had gone, she went onto his profile and unfollowed him. Another firm tap, this time with her index finger. Blocking him would give him the satisfaction of knowing he'd affected her. So she refrained. Then Rose opened her laptop, went to her search history, typed 'Milo', and deleted all 337 results, grimacing. It was confronting to see how much time she'd spent googling him. Now, though, all of it had vanished. Rose had been digitally and spiritually cleansed. There was a newfound feeling of lightness. She was in total control. This was easy.

It was at that moment Rose decided to download a dating app. She'd never used one before, apart from briefly signing up to Tinder at uni because all her housemates had done it and, well, she was curious. But she'd deleted it after waking up to seven photographs of a flaccid penis. Her friends told her this was abnormal; the penis was supposed to be erect.

Thankfully, most dating apps had since deleted the picture feature. Rose recalled overhearing some of the *MODE* staff talking about an app called Mix in the Firehouse cafe; it was marketing itself as an empowering feminist platform. The idea was that women had to be the ones to message the men they matched with first: a reversal of traditional power dynamics. Rose concluded that the good men would be on an app like this. The kind of men that read novels and called their mothers every Sunday. A good man would help. It would be validating to feel wanted by someone. And it would distract her, though from what she still wasn't sure. How hard could it be? She had just slept with one of the most famous men on the planet, hadn't she? That meant she was on a par with all of the other women he'd been with, logically speaking. Women who were at the upper echelons of attractiveness. Supermodels. Actresses. Heiresses. Rose now knew the list off by heart; looking at it several times a day had become a strange source of comfort and reassurance. Technically, she belonged there too.

For her profile, Rose could choose six photographs. She decided to upload three. There was one of her and Luce at a fashion and film party for *MODE* that Rose had got

Luce into – Luce went home with a Radio 1 DJ that night – where they were arm in arm and smiling at the camera. Rose couldn't remember who took the photo but it was taken far enough away from her face to reduce the villainy of her nose. Then there was a picture Lola had taken of her rifling through rails at a stall in Portobello Market. It must have been summer; she was wearing a yellow linen sundress and a wide-brimmed straw hat. Again, you could hardly see her because it had been taken from across the road. Finally, Rose chose a selfie she'd taken at her first red carpet event with her earpiece visible. Minnie had sent her to get a blow-dry that morning.

The written prompts were trickier. Rose knew she wasn't supposed to answer these earnestly. But trying too hard to poke fun at them was equally embarrassing, like you were somehow above it all. She tried to keep things light. 'Dating me is like . . . going to the supermarket. Mildly thrilling' was her first one. 'I'm a regular at . . . my supermarket' was the second, and for the third, she went for 'a fact that surprises people about me' and put something about being obsessed with sharks because it's a widely known fact that all straight men love sharks.

The 'Virtues' section was trickier. The app wanted definitive short answers to things Rose had spent years trying to ascertain, like her religious beliefs (none) and her politics (too uninformed to be armed with anything she'd feel comfortable discussing on dates). On top of that, there were questions about her family plans and her views on having children. Major life choices and views had been reduced to a matter of ticking one box over another. Rose declined to answer them all, doing the same for the 'Vices' section, which asked for her habits around drinking, smoking and drugs. Potential dates didn't need to know about any of that before they'd even met her; they could work it out along the way.

Once her profile was complete, Rose went to the bathroom and sat on the toilet, swiping through her options. It was astonishing to her how many men got this so terribly wrong. There was an inordinate number of the kind of people Luce would fawn over – i.e. indie hipsters who won't eat meat because it's bad for the environment but happily inhale dangerous amounts of cocaine at the weekend. They weren't even ashamed about it either, literally calling themselves vegans on their profiles and then putting a 'yes' next to the pill symbol to indicate they did, in fact, consume narcotics.

Everyone else was either far too earnest, declaring their love for travel, wine and animals as if that made them unique, or making way too much of an effort to show they weren't taking it seriously ('I hate it here'), which only made it seem like they were the ones taking it very seriously.

Rose swiped left on the majority of profiles, getting through fifty or so in the first few minutes alone. There were a handful that she swiped right for. One, Mick, twenty-nine, was because he had green eyes and worked in advertising, which had become a sexy industry thanks to *Mad Men*. Another, Jimmy, twenty-six, was because he was 6'3" and had a cat in the back of one of his photos ('cat people are good people,' Lola always said). And another because he was a filmmaker with long dark hair, and Rose liked the idea of dating a filmmaker with long dark hair. She decided he'd be the kind of man that used a Nokia 3210 and spent Sunday afternoons in a darkroom developing photos he'd taken on a vintage Nikon camera.

Just downloaded a dating app, Rose told Luce over WhatsApp.

About time, she replied immediately.

Are people always this awful?

If they're men, generally, yes.

Luce always said the sex she'd had was better with women and yet still only ever seemed to turn to men for relationships. Rose found her own vagina intimidating enough, let alone anyone else's.

Her first time was with a boy at Central Saint Martins who was in her first-year sculpture seminars. Timmy Gray. They were friends first and would often end up watching Marvel films together in bed at 4 a.m. after nights out, sharing bowls of pasta they'd miraculously cooked in the microwave and smothered in cheddar.

Things went on like this for a while until one night Rose stumbled back to Timmy's room at 2 a.m. and crawled into bed with him. He stirred and turned around, holding her against his warm bare chest, which smelled like expensive fabric softener. The sex was as good as you'd expect given the circumstances. Rose was mortified when he asked halfway through if she was 'a virgin'. Obviously, she said that she wasn't. But this was a bad lie to tell: Timmy had to literally guide her hips down onto him because she hadn't quite worked out the physical logistics required to have sex. The whole thing was so humiliating Rose stopped going to the sculpture seminars altogether.

The second man was Ed. Sex with Ed always felt like she was doing him a favour. Sure, he went down on her and attempted to pleasure her in the way most men are told they ought to by older brothers or boys in the year above. But after a while, it became clear that this wasn't something he was doing for her. Not once did he ask if what he was doing felt good, or what she wanted him to do to make it feel better. And because he didn't, Rose never felt comfortable enough to direct him. To this day, the only person that had ever made her orgasm was herself. It was lazy to fake it, sure, and probably terrible for feminism. But she'd long ago accepted that it was also easier and less time consuming for all involved.

The third man was Milo.

How are you holding up? Rose typed out to Luce.

Not good.

Luce's name immediately flashed up on Rose's phone.

'Hey,' she whispered.

'Hey.'

'Are you okay?'

'I miss George. I can't sleep. And when I do sleep all that happens is I have sex dreams about George.'

Rose sighed and listened as Luce continued to regurgitate the same statements she returned to after every George break-up. Yes, they've both been awful to each other. But they both still loved each other. Can love be enough? It's enough for Posh and Becks. Isn't it supposed to be enough? He's the only man that is good at sex. Squirter Gun was good but he had the baby voice. Why do men use baby voices in bed? Do they think we want to mother them while they fuck us? God, George is so good. But Luce could never trust him. And how can you have a relationship without trust? But God, the sex.

Usually, Rose had the patience for it. Tonight, she wanted to get back on the dating app.

'Can we plan a girls' night soon?' asked Luce, her voice all pleading whines like it was when she'd ask her mum to make them chicken nuggets as kids. 'Just you and me like we used to before I met stupid George.'

'That sounds great,' Rose replied. They set a date in a few weeks' time when Luce would be back home.

Within seconds of hanging up, Rose had returned to swiping through strangers. Seven people had liked her and there was one match: Jake, twenty-seven. He was 6'1", had a sandy blond mop of curls, and worked in accounting. Looking at his profile now, Rose couldn't remember why she'd liked him. He was attractive enough, but the photographs were fairly standard: in a pub with some friends, a team football photo and one marginally pretentious shot of him sitting on a balcony covered in expensive-looking plants, gazing pensively down towards the floor in the way people do when their friends yell, 'Give us a candid one!' Still, he had a good face – and she could just about make out his abs through the football shirt, which was damp and clinging to his body. Mystery solved.

She scrolled down to look at the rest of his profile. Liberal views, sure. Occasionally takes drugs, of course.

Agnostic, whatever you say. Rather than just liking her, though, Jake had gone to the extra effort of replying to one of Rose's prompts. Of course, it was the one about sharks. *Did you also know there are nine different types of hammerheads? Wild*, he wrote.

Rose shuffled herself down, deeper under the covers. She'd got so used to the feeling of having no sheets on her bed now, it was as if she'd never slept with sheets on her bed at all. While googling 'fun shark facts' on her phone, Rose opened a page titled '12 Shark Facts That May Surprise You' that had been created specifically for *Shark Week* in 2016. She could tell Jake how sharks have no bones, or how the earliest species date back to roughly 450 million years ago. But that probably wasn't going to turn him on.

Ever seen one in real life? she replied. Jake messaged back within minutes to inform her that, yes, he had seen a shark in real life. A hammerhead, no less. Even if it was a lie, Rose didn't care. He had replied quickly, which was an excellent sign, she thought, considering how Luce was always lamenting how long people took to reply on apps.

Conversation moved from sharks to other 'beasts of the sea', as he called them, to places they wanted to travel to and films they'd enjoyed. Rose avoided any subjects surrounding music; it wasn't worth taking the risk. They chatted without stopping until 2 a.m., flirting in the manner that only strangers can, exchanging bits of banal information that somehow become tantalising in those early stages, when things like 'rank your favourite supermarket sandwiches' and 'what posters did you have in your childhood bedroom' can feel thrillingly erotic. *Sleep well, Rose*, Jake wrote, when they had both resigned to their mutual exhaustion.

You too, she replied, too nervous to add anything else in case it put him off somehow.

The next morning Rose decided she was ready to go back to work because if she took another day off, all she'd do was spend it on her phone or mentally list everything that was wrong with her or look at Milo's Instagram Stories on the Instagram account (@artgirl809) she'd created at 4 a.m. after waking up at 2.30 a.m. and unsuccessfully trying to get back to sleep. He'd played in Vienna last night.

'Hi, Minnie, feeling much better. Coming in today,' she emailed as she was getting ready, slipping on a pair of Luce's furry loafers that looked almost identical to the Gucci ones she'd seen all over Instagram.

For the first time since she started working for Minnie, Rose decided to put make-up on for work, balancing her coffee cup in between her thighs as she applied mascara on the Tube, using her phone screen as a mirror.

Minnie seemed relieved when Rose walked into the office.

'Thank God you're back,' she said, rifling through papers on her desk.

'Why, what happened?'

'Jimson & James isn't happy with Shania Twain as the performer.'

'What? That makes no sense,' said Rose.

Oliver grunted in the corner. 'My one chance to dance to "Man! I Feel Like a Woman!" in front of Shania herself . . .' he mused, staring out of the window.

'Apparently the CEO just saw her concert in Las Vegas and wants someone he hasn't seen before.'

'That seems a bit ridiculous.'

Minnie shot her a look as if to remind her that ridiculousness was the nature of this job.

'Anyway, I'm about to meet Janet at MilkyWay to try to convince them to give us a name. Oliver, I want you to come with me.'

'With pleasure,' he replied, smiling at Rose as he stood up from his desk.

MilkyWay represented Milo. It was the agency Joss ran from the US; Janet was her deputy who worked in London. Rose took a deep breath that turned into an awkward yawn.

'Tell her about the VIPs too,' said Oliver.

'Yes. So, Jimson & James are also concerned that there aren't enough VIPs coming to the launch and are threatening to cancel.'

'Cancel? Can they even do that?' asked Annabelle. The party was in three weeks.

'Oh yes,' Minnie replied. 'It's not like Firehouse has the budget to fund these sorts of things any more.'

'Right . . .' Rose firmly put both hands on her desk, shifting into action mode. 'What can I do?'

'Did you ever hear back from Clara's Martinis, or whatever her name is? It would be a big help if she said yes.'

'Let me have a look in my email.'

Rose had been avoiding her email since the panic attack, if she could even call it that. She typed 'Clara' into the search bar and saw only the email she had sent.

'Sorry, nothing yet,' she told Minnie. 'I'm going to follow up now.'

'Thank you, darling. And how are you feeling?'

'All fine, thank you,' Rose replied, ignoring Oliver's giggles from the corner, where he was tapping furiously on his phone. 'Bad Deliveroo order.'

'Poor you,' Minnie said before putting on her coat. 'Right, I'm popping to the bathroom. Oliver, meet me downstairs in five. And, Rose, look after yourself. Stomach bugs are the worst.'

'Especially ones you get from pop stars,' Oliver cackled as the door closed behind Minnie, eyes and fingers still magnetically attached to his phone screen.

'For fuck's sake,' Rose muttered under her breath.

'Oh, come on,' said Oliver, finally looking up. 'You're not getting any sympathy from me because the rock star gave you chlamydia.'

'Grow up,' she replied, realising her hand was shaking as she snatched her phone off the desk and walked out.

'You could probably sell your swabs on eBay for £100!' he shouted behind her.

Everything was throbbing as Rose steadied herself against the corridor's wall. She closed her eyes and tried to picture the beach. But it was just Milo's face again, a collection of moving features and shapes. All of it twisting something inside her and producing a screeching sound, like a live lobster that had just been dunked into boiling water, gasping for breath.

'Nice to have you back,' chimed a soft voice to her left.

Rose jumped, opening her eyes to see Annabelle smiling sweetly at her.

'Thanks, Annabelle, sorry,' she replied, feeling her face flush red.

'It's okay. Hope you're all right. Let me know if you need me to help with Clara.'

'Thank you. Yeah, I'm fine. See you tomorrow.'

*

The next morning, Rose avoided all eye contact and direct communication with Oliver. Luckily, Minnie was in the office all day, which made it easier. He tended to toe the line a little whenever she was around.

Today, he was mostly listening to music and snacking while trawling through the August issues with intermittent commentary about Botox.

Rose was surreptitiously reading an old *Vanity Fair* interview with Milo when she saw the email from Clara pop up.

> Hi babe,
> So sorry I missed your first email – I rarely check this inbox tbh. This sounds awesome. Just looping in my chief operating officer, Fraser, who can discuss the fee.
> CC xx

'She replied!' Rose exclaimed.

'Who?' asked Oliver, pulling his headphones off.

'Clara?' asked Minnie.

'Yes, but it looks like she's asking for a fee.'

'Bugger. Of course they are. Well, we don't have the budget for a fee. Jimson has put all of the money towards a performer we have yet to book. At this point, I'm half expecting them to ask Oliver to sing.'

'You sing, Oliver?' Annabelle asked him.

'Oh, just a little,' he said, faux blushing. 'I was a chorister at school. Jasper and I have that in common. He was a chorister too. At Harrow, of course.'

Annabelle looked at him carefully.

'Liz must be loving all this,' Oliver said.

'Oh yes,' tutted Minnie. 'She has taken the day off today to go to Soho Farmhouse to decompress.'

'Firehouse is paying for that?!' he retorted.

'I think Jimson is paying. Buttering her up so she does whatever they want her to,' said Minnie, sighing.

'I want to be buttered up,' Oliver replied.

Maybe you should give Jasper a call? Rose heard herself whisper in her head, wishing she had the guts to say it out loud. 'Clara has looped me in with her chief operating officer, so I'll try and negotiate with him,' she said.

Oliver let out a haughty cackle. 'Chief operating officer! God. Like she's running Google.'

'Brilliant, thank you,' said Minnie. 'I've got to go and meet Jasper quickly.'

'Why? Has something happened?' asked Rose.

'Oh, you know. Just another Hollywood publicist threatening *Intel* with libel if we PR some quotes from her client's interview.'

'It's a big 'un,' said Oliver, smug that he knew something the rest of the team didn't.

'Who's the interview with?' asked Annabelle.

Minnie said the name and the room gasped in unison. 'I know. It's brilliant they landed him on the cover in the first place. But he got drunk in the interview and said something slightly questionable about his much younger female co-star. So . . . we're in discussions with lawyers.'

'At least he didn't say he wanted to grab her by the pussy,' Oliver sniggered.

Rose's body clenched at the word.

'No,' sighed Minnie. 'Nothing quite as vile as the current leader of the free world, thankfully.'

'I just don't understand how he got elected after that,' said Annabelle.

'Oh, please,' Oliver scoffed. 'As if middle America gives a crap about a little sexual harassment. London certainly doesn't.'

'Keep this to yourselves, everyone. Okay?' added Minnie, halfway out the door.

They all nodded.

Clara's chief operating officer Fraser replied to Rose's next email.

> Hey babes, thanks for this. So attendance is £3,000, depending on what you need from Clara. £10,000 if you want her to walk in the show. Let me know.
> Thanks,
> Fraser.

Rose wrote back:

> Hi Fraser,
> Thanks for this. Any chance of bringing this down slightly? All we'd ask is that Clara share a few posts on her Stories and ideally one on her grid on the night. Can of course send cars for pick up and drop off.
> Thanks,
> Rose
> ----
> Rose, Clara would love to meet you for coffee to discuss. Are you free today at 12.30pm? She'll meet you at The Wolseley.

It was 11.20. Rose replied *yes* immediately.

'Got a meeting with Clara,' she said, loud enough so that Oliver would hear through his headphones.

'Oh great! Well done,' said Annabelle.

'How much?' asked Minnie, swanning back into the room to grab her coat.

'They want £10,000 for her to walk in the show. £3,000 for attendance. But I'm going to try and negotiate with her in person.'

'You'd think this woman was Lady sodding Gaga,' Oliver laughed, who had either turned the volume right down or had only ever been pretending to listen to music. 'Don't get your hopes up, sweetheart.'

'Make sure you talk her through the social media strategy,' said Minnie, handing Rose a scarlet file with the words FIREHOUSE X STANDFIRST SOCIAL STRATEGY splashed across it.

'Will do. So she'll come for the reception, take photos for Getty, and then we'll give her a front-row seat in the show. Is there anything else I need to know?'

'No hotel room. We're saving those for the performer and their crew. Ask about dietary requirements, too. The reception is going to be seafood canapés.'

'Seafood canapés?'

'Yes, don't ask,' Minnie sighed. 'Another demand from Jimson's CEO. Apparently he's on some sort of seafood-only diet.'

'Okay, no problem.'

Rose had been to The Wolseley once for a leaving lunch Minnie threw for an old intern. All she could remember from the visit was wondering why so many people could afford to get blow dries and drink champagne in the middle of the day. It was just as busy today, a cacophony of clinking silverware and corporate gossip filling the room.

By 2.15 p.m., Clara had still not arrived. The jug of tap water someone had brought over to Rose's table had long been empty and she'd gone through almost all of Clara's Instagram posts since 2014. That day alone, she had posted twelve Stories. The first one showed her getting a facial at a new clinic in Belgravia. *Best start to the day, thanks so much #gift*, she wrote over the top, tagging a brand Rose remembered as being the place where Kim Kardashian had something called a vampire facial. Then Clara had posted a selfie outside of Cecconi's. *Lunch meetings made better with Italian food :)*, she wrote before uploading a photograph of what looked like a plate of *Cacio e pepe*. Rose's mouth started to water. She had briefly stopped at Pret on the way to The Wolseley to grab a tuna sandwich. Even though she was going to expense the meal, Clara struck Rose as someone with expensive taste. And she wasn't going to risk expensing a £300 bill by ordering a proper meal herself too. Equally, she couldn't exactly tell Clara not to order whatever she wanted considering this was, evidently, what she was accustomed to doing. Hence the safety sandwich.

At 2.27 p.m., the swoop of a door pushed too hard and a clanging of jewellery indicated the arrival of someone in a fluster.

'Sorry, miss, you can't use your phone here,' the host said to the woman.

'Oh yes, of course, sorry,' she replied, holding her phone to her ear.

'Right, Fraser, I'll call you after. Okay. Yes, I will do. Yep. Okay. Bye. Bye.'

Clara looked almost identical to her photographs. Her cheeks were just as high, her eyes wide and deer-like. Her skin looked like it had been smothered in expensive serums and lifted by something clever and non-surgical. She was wearing a beige linen trouser suit over a crisp white shirt. All of it appeared immaculately cleaned and steamed, as if it had all been freshly unboxed that morning. It probably had.

Clara followed the host to Rose's table, eyes fixed on her phone.

'So sorry I'm late,' Clara said, standing behind her chair, eyes still on her phone, fingers tapping furiously.

'Don't worry at all,' Rose replied, pulling her hand away slowly when Clara's didn't move to meet it.

'Okay,' she said, putting her phone on the table with the screen up, and then sitting down, neglecting to thank the host who pulled the chair out for her. 'Let's talk about the event! Remind me what it is?'

Rose dived straight into talking Clara through StandFirst and their plans, outlining the reception, the runway show and the performer they had yet to confirm. She explained how she'd need to arrive around ten minutes after the start of the event, take some photographs for Getty and then a few on her phone for social media. Ideally, she'd take a few videos too, filming herself at the event and posting it live while she's there, tagging Firehouse and the new StandFirst handles.

Clara sat and listened quietly while her phone lit up every twenty seconds. Rose was trying hard not to look down at it but the constant flashing was distracting. It looked as if the same name was messaging her on WhatsApp.

Rose had started to explain the seafood canapés when Clara's phone rang.

'God, I'm so sorry,' said Clara, her face flushed and

agitated. 'Do you mind if I answer this? It's my boyfriend. If I don't answer, he'll just keep calling until I do.'

'Of course, don't worry.'

Clara looked relieved, her eyes furrowed in the way they do when the person is embarrassed. Mouthing the words 'so sorry', she picked up her phone and walked back towards the entrance and then outside.

Rose continued to flick through Clara's Instagram. It made sense for her to hide a relationship from her followers. Even if her boyfriend was on social media, it would be an infringement of his privacy to put him on hers. Maybe he didn't want that, which was fair enough.

Rose tried to imagine what it must feel like to have 1.2 million people watching your every move on social media, piling you with praise and criticism in equal measure. Rose had 526 followers on Instagram, which was quite a lot for a regular person. She suspected this was due to the fact that she worked at Firehouse. People either wanted to see photos from the parties or be featured in the magazines. After she got the job, Rose posted a selfie outside the famous Firehouse HQ sign and swiftly received a text from a boy she'd gone to school with asking if she could get his girlfriend an interview at *MODE*.

When Clara returned, her eyes were red and swollen.

'Sorry,' she said, her voice soft and uncertain. 'Right, where were we?'

Rose wanted to ask if Clara was okay, to give her an opportunity to explain that she clearly wasn't. But this was a meeting, one that her job possibly depended on. Clara's relationship was none of her business. So she asked if Clara preferred oysters or lobster.

Clara nodded as Rose spoke about the menu, glassy eyes fixed on her knees. By the time Rose had got onto talking about shellfish allergies, it had become impossible not to ask. Clara was as close to tears as any person could be without actually crying.

'I'm sorry, Clara, are you all right? We can do this another time if you prefer.'

'Yeah, I'm fine, God, I'm so sorry . . .' She looked up at Rose now. 'It's just things with my boyfriend. They are, erm, tough, I guess.'

'Don't be silly, it's okay,' Rose replied.

'Do you have a boyfriend?'

Milo's face instantly sprung into her head, and suddenly her whole body had tensed. Rose shivered, shaking her head and shoulders to erase the image.

'No,' she mustered. 'But I've had some . . .' She paused, unsure what she was trying to say. 'I know that men can be disappointing.'

'God, tell me about it.'

'How long have you been with your boyfriend?' Rose needed to shift the attention away from her.

'Four years. It's been pretty rocky for a while. If I'm being completely honest, we probably should have broken up after a month.'

'I'm sorry to hear that,' said Rose, instantly regretting the formality of her words.

'He told me to get out of the house this morning, called me a narcissist . . . all of the usual insults he flings my way when he's angry. So I'm just trying to figure out my next move.'

'Is it his house?'

'No. I'm the primary earner, which he loves just as much as you can imagine.'

'Do you have somewhere else to go?'

'I can go to my mum's. It's just complicated. And now he's apologising and begging me to come back to the house, promising he won't ever say that to me again, telling me I'm the love of his life and he wants to marry me,' she sighed. 'It's just exhausting.'

Rose sat and listened as Clara talked about all of the times her boyfriend had made her feel small, criticised her career and pulled her away from friends. The arguments were dramatic and frequent. The apologies, long and heartfelt. He'd had a difficult childhood, she explained, and took things out on her without meaning to. She loved him a lot. They'd been to couples counselling a few times and the counsellor explained all the necessary steps they needed to take in order to make it work. She had to prioritise him over her work, he had to cut down his drinking. But none of that seemed to work, leaving them trapped in this endless cycle.

'He thinks I need to go to the Priory for depression,' she said.

'Do you think you're depressed?'

'No. Don't get me wrong, I have my moments. But he's the one opening a bottle of wine at 2 p.m. on a Tuesday and doing a line of coke on his own just because he found some in his bedside drawer. And somehow I'm the one that needs help.'

Clara went into detail about more of their arguments, how he'd compare her unfavourably to his exes, how he'd make snide remarks about what his friends thought of her. But he could also be so loving towards her, showering her with gifts, planning trips away and making her feel adored. Clara was still crying. And Rose noticed that the waiters had been avoiding their table for the past twenty minutes.

'Come on, let's get you to the bathroom,' whispered Rose, taking Clara's arm.

Rose waited outside the cubicle as Clara sniffled and blew her nose.

After a few minutes she emerged, all shallow gasps and flushed cheeks.

'God, I'm so sorry. Thank you so much,' she said, steadying herself on the sink as she took a packet of make-up wipes out of her Gucci tote bag and began to erase the smudges under her eyes. Then she took a large Burberry pouch out of the bag and, pulling out an eyeliner and mascara, started to reapply.

'I know you won't,' she said, holding one eyelid out so she could carefully put her liner on, 'but I just have to ask for my own peace of mind . . .'

'I won't tell anyone, Clara. Don't worry.'

She turned to face Rose and smiled. 'Thank you.'

'Can I ask, is that why you don't post about him? Because you're not happy?'

Clara scoffed. 'I post about a lot of things that don't make me happy,' she replied, flicking her eyeliner with the ease of a conductor.

'In all honesty, it's just a bit embarrassing,' Clara

continued. 'He's always told me that what I do doesn't matter.'

'What does he do?'

'He works in insurance. For superyachts.'

Rose couldn't help but laugh.

'I know,' Clara replied. 'Anyway, he hates the idea of me sharing our relationship online. To him, the idea of telling strangers about your holiday is like telling your family which STDs you've had. He's never liked that this is my job. So I keep him out of it.'

'Would you ever leave him?'

'Yes. And I have, many times. And for about two days I have this incredible freeing feeling, like I've just climbed a mountain or something. Everything feels lighter. But then he gets in touch again. He apologises. He sends presents. He tells me everything I want to hear. And after a while, it just . . . starts to sink in.'

'You start to miss him?'

'I know that probably sounds ridiculous. But in spite of it all, I really do love him so much. And a part of me thinks, well, love isn't supposed to be easy, is it?'

Clara explained how they met. She was a naive twenty-three-year-old model for Topshop; he was a cocky thirty-five-year-old accountant. They crossed paths at a nightclub in central London. She hated him at first, writing him off as an arrogant city bloke. But, after much insistence, she reluctantly gave him her phone number. He soon charmed her with his self-deprecating sense of humour, his culinary prowess and his childlike obsession with cartoon-covered socks. Also, he was kind to her. The first man to tell her she was beautiful and really make her feel like she was. The first man to say he was in love with her and make her feel like it was true.

'In those first four months, I honestly felt like I was living in a Disney fantasy world,' said Clara. 'Everything happened so quickly. We moved in together and that's when he started to turn.'

'You don't have to justify it to me, I get it. Those earlier moments with him keep you clinging onto hope. So every time he does or says anything cruel, you remember this is the man you fell in love with. And you just wait for him to return.'

'Exactly. It keeps you going back.'

Two women in their mid-forties burst into the bathroom.

'Vodka martinis just flood through me!' yelled one in a shrill voice, rushing into a cubicle.

'God, yes, me too,' barked the other, turning to look at Rose and Clara. 'Oh, hang on a minute, aren't you that Instagram woman?'

Clara smiled and stretched her hand out. 'Hello. My name is Clara.'

'That's right! Cara's Cosmic!' the woman replied, ignoring Clara's lingering hand. 'Oh, my daughter adores you. Can I please take a selfie for her?'

Clara quickly looked at herself in the mirror and then at Rose; she hadn't finished applying her make-up and, frankly, her eyes still looked like they'd just been weeping.

'Actually . . .'

'She's not doing photos right now. Sorry,' said Rose,

sticking her hand out to her. 'Hi, I'm Rose Martin, Clara's publicist.'

'Oh, right,' the woman snorted, limply shaking Rose's hand. 'You lot have publicists now, do you? What a shame.'

'You didn't have to do that,' Clara whispered when the two women finally walked out.

'It's okay. She didn't even know your name. Hardly a fan,' she replied.

'Thank you, Rose.'

'You're welcome.'

An hour after they said their goodbyes, Rose received an email from Fraser.

All in for £3,000. Deal?

Sent from my iPhone. Please excuse typos.

Minnie managed to get the extra budget from Commercial. When she asked Rose how she managed to negotiate the fee down, she explained they had a lot in common, which made her realise it was true. Rose started following @cosmoclara when she got home.

Later that evening, Rose sat on the sofa with a bowl of buttery pasta and opened the dating app. She smiled when she saw Jake had replied to her last message with several long ones. They had moved on from favourite films and meals to which family members they liked the most and which they liked the least. Jake had sent her a paragraph about his great uncle Geoffrey's penchant for full fat cream and how he secretly put it in his cornflakes every morning when his wife wasn't looking.

It was a distraction. But it wasn't enough to stop Rose from regularly checking up on Milo's Instagram through her new account, which had clearly sent some kind of alert to Silicon Valley because the entire Explore page was filled with photos and videos of him from fan pages, which posted daily updates based on sightings. Occasionally they shared old red carpet photos, fawning over his boyish grin and poorly judged outfits. Mostly, though, they were blurry photos that people had presumably taken surreptitiously, in which he was usually either exercising, eating, or walking with a friend. They could not be less interesting. Rose was aware of this – and still, she had become addicted to checking them several times a day, inhaling every detail she could.

Of course, when Milo wasn't on her phone, he was singing a song on the radio in the corner shop, fronting a billboard as she crossed the road on her way to work, or being furiously discussed by a group of teenage girls on the bus. Milo was everywhere and nowhere all at the same time. And the more of him Rose absorbed, the further away her memory of that night felt. Had it not been for the fact that her bed still had no sheets on it, she'd wonder if it even happened at all.

There was a big difference, Rose had learned, between voluntarily looking for information about Milo, and stumbling across it unsolicited. When she was looking at fan accounts, the content fed something in her, regardless of how banal it was. And when she discovered something new, she could feel it spike her adrenaline. Her appetite for all of it was insatiable. When she came across Milo without expecting to, though, it elicited something else entirely. Rose had got better at controlling her breath and stopping herself from hyperventilating, mostly because she didn't want to have another panic attack in public. But it required conscious effort. Like she was having to rewire something in her brain to prevent it from going down a certain neural pathway. One that made her want to run into an empty field and scream into the wind until every organ split open.

When Jake suggested they meet for a drink, Rose sighed with relief. She proposed the World's End pub in Camden. It was on the Northern Line – easy for both her and Jake, who would be coming from East Finchley. A pub was always a safe bet on a first date. Sometimes there were even candles in wine bottles on the tables, which Rose always thought was romantic in a kitsch Richard Curtis kind of way.

After confirming a time with Jake – 7.30 p.m. – Rose put her phone on Airplane mode and tried to nap. She plaited her hair so that it wouldn't frizz, applied some lip balm, wriggled herself underneath the duvet and closed her eyes. It would have been a great time to meditate if this was something Rose knew how to do. Instead, she lay there and allowed her mind to slowly drift herself into a deep, but efficient, sleep. It worked for around ninety seconds. She tried to stay still a little longer but she kept returning to the empty beach. It was the same as always, except this time she was walking towards the water. She stepped into it, feeling the damp sand squelching in between her toes as she moved deeper until every part of her was underneath the waves. There was a lightness to her new underwater form that, defying gravity, was still standing upright. She found peace, succumbing to the stillness of it all, the way that her body was no longer something in her control. It wasn't hers or anyone else's. At that moment, it belonged to the sea. After a few seconds, she tried to swim back up to the surface. But suddenly a weight was holding her down. She kicked harder and faster, reaching with her arms as the little air she had escaped. Everything in her body tightened with panic as she moved more frantically, the water filling her body until it wasn't a body at all but a dark solid mass, indistinguishable from everything else. Then the scene turned into something different. She was with Milo. The memories of their night together playing out scene by scene. His body pressed against hers, the water of the ocean now compressed onto a single tongue, wet and slippery as it slithered up and down her neck. Slowly at first, then so quickly it felt as if her entire body was drowning in his.

When Rose woke up, she was hyperventilating, her body soaked with sweat. She clutched the mattress and closed her eyes until she could take a full breath without gasping.

It was 6 p.m. by the time Rose had calmed down enough to start getting ready for the date. She didn't want to wear anything that would remind her of Milo, which meant no flares and no slogan T-shirts. So she opted for a T-shirt dress she'd bought in a Free People sale that skimmed her thighs, her favourite pair of chunky loafers, and the polka-dot black tights that Lola bought her last year for her birthday. Then, to balance out the proportions, an oversized black leather jacket on top.

Make-up took the longest, mostly because Rose hardly ever wore it and, as a result, didn't really know how to apply it. But it felt like something she should try tonight. Jake would appreciate it; it was also an opportunity to try out that four-part eyeshadow palette she'd brought home from the beauty cupboard.

With no brush, Rose used the pad of her ring finger to smudge some of the burnt orange shade across one eyelid. She stared at her reflection, looking back at the type of woman she could be. A woman who wore such ostentatious eyeshadow sent a clear message to the world about who she was. A woman louder, bolder and braver than Rose. Someone who wore matching underwear and had sex so loudly she regularly received complaints from neighbours through her letterbox. She wiped it off with a make-up wipe and tried another shade: a deep purple that looked like a blend between a glass of Merlot and a moonlit sky in the summer. This colour reminded her of Lola. On the surface, it was pure, unadulterated drama. But if you look at anything for long enough you'll often find something entirely different hiding beneath the surface. In this case, it was subtle shades of brown and black flecks of delicate glitter. A woman wearing this eyeshadow kept secrets, not just from others but also from herself. Another make-up wipe.

Blue next. This one reminded Rose of her childhood, when she and Luce would cover themselves in neon pots of eyeshadow they'd picked up in Claire's Accessories. She still hadn't replied to Luce's voice note from last week, though surely nine minutes was more of a podcast. She made a mental note to reply tomorrow morning after the date.

This blue wasn't quite as bright as the shade they would smear across their faces as teenagers. It was softer, as though the person wearing it didn't have to try too hard. This woman was cool and therefore probably also European. Make-up wipe.

The fourth shade on the palette was gold. She had intentionally saved it until last, anticipating some sort of poetry to this being her final choice. Rose cleaned her finger with the wipe this time so as not to mix it with any of the previous shades. It was richer than the others, more velvety to the touch when she rubbed it onto her finger. She dabbled it across her eyelid slowly, noticing how bits of glitter fluttered down past her eye, settling onto her cheek with every pat. It looked even better on the second eye. Like her green eyes now appeared greener, her expression instantly enlivened. Whoever this woman was, she possessed an effortless confidence that Rose did not. But it was one she felt fit to try on for tonight. It was always good to try new things.

On the Tube, Rose tried to calm her nerves by opening a news app on her phone. This was, as it turned out, a very bad idea. The first four stories were all about the Grenfell

Tower fire; the death toll had now reached fifty-two. The next stories were either follow-ups about the London Bridge terror attacks, or the Manchester Arena bombing that happened last month during an Ariana Grande concert – the terror threat had been 'critical' ever since. And the rest were about Brexit. The country was, quite literally, bursting into flames.

After clicking on the 'Fashion and Lifestyle' section, Rose found an article about '20 Feminist Slogan T-shirts to Buy Now'. The majority were variations of that famous Dior one ('We Should All Be Feminists') that, by now, had been praised just as much as it had been criticised. But a few political ones stood out, like the one that read: 'THIS PUSSY GRABS BACK'. Rose saw it cost £150 and put her phone down. When the Tube reached Euston, she turned to see a woman step on board holding Milo's face. It was taking up the entire back page of the *Evening Standard*. Tour promo.

The pub was busier than Rose had imagined whenever she'd thought about how the evening might play out. It would be hard to find any table, let alone one in the corner that looked romcom worthy. The lighting was also a little harsher than she'd have liked, meaning the spot she'd furiously covered up with three-year-old concealer would probably be visible under the glare of fluorescent lighting.

There was one seat free at the bar. Rose wriggled out of her leather jacket and hung it on the back of the high-top, mustard-yellow chair. She ordered herself a gin and tonic and told the barman she was just going to the bathroom. By some miracle, her make-up hadn't faded at all during the journey. But even so, Rose decided to dampen a piece of toilet paper and dab underneath her eyes to make sure there were no mascara smudges. She blinked back at herself in the mirror a couple of times, pleased with the look she'd created. The gold eyeshadow really did bring out the green of her eyes.

It was now 7.27 p.m. Rose's drink was waiting for her when she returned to her seat. She decided to wait another five minutes before messaging Jake. Perusing the pub, she saw that most people were in large groups. There were the indie-looking twentysomethings in black jeans and band T-shirts, talking enthusiastically about whichever act they were about to see that evening. There were the beer-belly dad types sneaking in a few pints before they went home. And there were a few corporate blokes in suits that looked wildly out of place. Rose was struck by the fact that the pub was almost entirely filled by men. Nothing anyone said was distinguishable, their booms overlapping one another as everyone talked over each other, forming one sound.

Hey, just arrived, Rose typed in a WhatsApp message to Jake. *No seats annoyingly but have found a small spot at the bar. See you soon.*

According to Jake's WhatsApp status, he'd last been online at 7.24 p.m. This was a good sign. He was probably still on the Tube, she assumed, watching his name to see if he was about to come online. After a few seconds, she decided this was a bit weird and locked her phone, taking her first sip of the gin and tonic.

Rose continued to look around the pub, trying to work

out if anyone else was waiting for a dating app date. When the thought of Jake standing her up entered her mind, she pushed it to one side. That was not happening tonight, she assured herself.

She noticed one couple on a table to her left who looked like they'd just arrived, piling their jackets behind them on a hook. He was in his mid-thirties, all floppy blond hair and checked shirt. He wore drainpipe jeans and Dr Marten boots. She was wearing a plain black T-shirt and grey skinny jeans that showed off her impossibly thin legs. Her hair hung loose around her shoulders, caramel tresses that looked as if they hadn't been trimmed for six months or so. She wasn't wearing any make-up.

The way he touched her when she hung up her coat indicated an intimacy and familiarity, the kind you have with someone you've already slept with. They wouldn't have met on an app, Rose reasoned. They'd be the kind of people that looked down on dating apps, telling their friends they preferred to meet people 'the organic way' because it was 'more authentic'. She watched as they settled into their evening, arms resting on the table, folding over one another.

7.42 p.m. Jake was a bit late now. Rose reopened their WhatsApp conversation. The first thing she noticed was that the 'Last Seen' bit had disappeared underneath his name: 'Jake Hinge'. His profile picture – a shot of him wearing a snorkel in Mauritius – had also gone. He had read her last message, though, because it had two blue ticks next to it. Rose's mouth went dry.

Hey, are you okay? she wrote, aware of the futility as she tapped 'Send', prompting a single grey tick to pop up next to her message. She waited, staring at her phone screen until it went dark and locked itself. When she felt tears rolling down her cheeks, she wiped them off, looking around the pub to check no one had noticed. It must have been obvious what had happened. Even if no one was looking, the humiliation was overwhelming. She gulped down what was left in the gin and tonic, threw her jacket over her shoulders and left.

Rose knew what she was supposed to do now; the script had been written endless times. She was supposed to go into another bar with better lighting, flirt with the barman and tell him what had happened while he plied her with free shots of vodka. Then she'd hear all about the ex-girlfriend who cheated on him with his best mate and they'd tumble into his warehouse flat in Stoke Newington together at 2 a.m., messily trying to undress one another. Against all odds, they'd have incredible sex and Rose would come three times just from foreplay.

But she did not have the energy to chase that fantasy. Not tonight. Instead, she crossed the road to buy a packet of Marlboro Golds at the off-licence. As she stood outside digging through her bag for her wallet, a homeless woman wrapped in a red blanket asked her for money. Rose fished out her wallet and handed her the £10 note she had withdrawn that afternoon to buy lunch in the food market near the office on Monday.

'Thank you, love,' she whispered.

'You're welcome.'

'Why are you crying?'

'Oh,' Rose laughed, rubbing the tears away from her face. 'Sorry. I just got stood up.'

'Oh, my girl. Men are awful.'

'Yes, ha. Yes, they are.'

'Do you have any pills?'

'Oh, erm, no. So sorry.'

Rose walked inside the off-licence, where 'The Way You Are' by Milo Jax was playing on the radio.

FOUR

'Hey, I really miss you too. I'm so sorry it's taken me a while to reply. Are you still not sleeping? Have you tried those Nytol things? Don't bother with the herbal ones. How's home? When are you coming back? Oh, sorry, yes, yes just one flat white for me please. Oh, er, don't worry. Soy milk is fine, yes. Thanks so much. God, sorry, Lu, I'm getting Minnie a coffee. Give me a ring when you can – I've deleted the dating app. Will explain why when we talk. Had a bit of a . . . Oh, brilliant, thank you. Yes please, more foam on that one would be great. Okay. Erm, anyway, yes, give me a ring. Love you so much.'

Rose's phone made a satisfying *whoosh* as the voice note delivered. The ticks turned blue immediately: a pang of guilt; Luce only ever opened messages instantly when she was in the deep depression stage of her break-ups. Something to deal with later.

'Actually, do you mind just holding on to these while I go to the loo?' Rose asked the barista in Starbucks.

'Of course, miss.'

'Thank you!'

There was a man in front of her in the queue. He was tall, gangly and fidgety, as if he'd been up all night snorting something. The second the bathroom was free, a couple exited together with their child, whose nappy they'd just presumably changed.

'So sorry,' the mother said to the slowly forming queue of people.

'No worries,' Rose smiled back.

The man ignored her and walked straight into the bathroom, bringing the door to a close with a loud thud.

A few seconds later he emerged, still irate about something. Rose went inside. Sitting on the toilet, she realised there was no toilet roll and that this was probably what the man had gone to collect.

As she was wriggling back into her knickers, someone started knocking furiously on the door.

'Sorry! I'm just in here,' Rose whimpered.

The knocking turned to banging and the door was shaking. 'Get the fuck out!' a voice boomed.

Rose quickly pulled herself up and opened the door.

The man who'd gone to get toilet roll was standing in front of her, fists clenched, brow furrowed.

'What the fuck do you think you're doing?' the man screamed at her, his face inches away from Rose's.

Even if she wanted to speak, she couldn't. Her body was trembling too much. She managed to take a step to the right to get out of this man's way.

'How dare you. Stupid bitch!' he shouted, slamming the bathroom door so loudly even the baristas were looking over.

Rose stood there silently for a while, unsure what to do. She started shaking.

There were three people in the queue now, silently observing her to see what she would do next. One woman and two men. Rose was staring at the floor when the woman came over to check she was okay.

'Yes, yes, I'm fine. Thank you.'

'What a bellend,' was about all she could make out from what this woman said.

Back at work, things were busy. She was grateful for the distraction. It was something to do: getting on the Tube, picking up the coffees and then coming home and breathing a sigh of relief because the day was almost over. Rose couldn't remember the last time she'd slept through the night, often waking up at 1 or 2 a.m., looking at her phone and then lying there for hours, waiting for it to get light outside, or hearing the sound of her neighbours' water running upstairs. It was only after she had some sign of life, or reassurance that she wasn't the only person awake, that she was able to fall back asleep.

Rose had blocked Milo on Instagram during one of her 4 a.m. scrolling sessions last night. She had gone past the point of caring if he noticed. And even if he did, it was her only way of communicating something to him. Still, Rose found herself continuing to check her DM requests in the blind hope she might still have a message from him, who, noticing she had now blocked him, would be so desperate to contact her that he'd reach out on one of his secret accounts. But there was never anything there aside from bots saying they loved her style and wanted brand ambassadors to represent their fake athleisure companies.

'Okay, we cannot seat the buyer at Net-a-Porter next to the buyer at Selfridges, Annabelle,' said Minnie, firmly.

'Oh right, yes, sorry,' Annabelle replied in her plummy voice, quickly shuffling the name cards out of the plan and ousting them to the corner along with the rest of the names they hadn't yet found seats for.

'No, Alexa Chung is there,' said Liz, pointing to the spot where Annabelle had just moved the buyer at Selfridges.

'Right, okay,' said Annabelle. 'How about here?'

'Tucci,' replied Liz, rolling her eyes.

'Who?'

'Stanley Tucci,' she said, her voice raised now.

The pressure from upstairs had clearly started to sink in. Either that or Liz was due another company-funded spa day. Even Minnie, who quickly rearranged the seating plan, seemed stressed. You could always tell what sort of mood she was in depending on her outfit.

On a normal day, Minnie would glide into the office in one of her floor-length patterned kaftans. Her wardrobe was teeming with them, and she wore them even in the bleakest months of winter. Often loaded up with her trademark gold costume jewellery. The bangles were usually paired with chokers, drop earrings, the lot. Today, though, she had stripped this aesthetic right back. Just one gold bracelet, and a pair of simple gold studs. The dress was purple and patterned, grazing the floor as she walked.

But it lacked all the tassels and bobbles that defined her usual style.

This was the first time Rose had worked on an event's seating plan. It wasn't really her job to be there today – and the September issue press releases needed doing – but Minnie had wanted her involved with the entire process of the event this time.

'Who do you think Clara's strawberry daquiris will want to sit next to?' Liz asked, thumbing her place card pensively. She had got into the habit of naming Clara after a different drink every time she mentioned her.

'You know it's Cosmo Clara, Liz,' said Minnie, rolling her eyes.

'No self-respecting adult should ever have to say those words earnestly,' Liz replied.

'I think someone who isn't famous, actually,' said Rose.

'Oh really? Thought she would have loved to be rubbing shoulders against celebs,' Oliver guffawed.

'Pretending she's one of them, you know,' agreed Liz.

'I don't think she's like that,' said Rose.

'They are always like that,' said Oliver.

'And yet you adore them,' replied Liz.

'I do not,' he snapped back.

Rose stayed silent. She didn't have the energy to go up against another man today.

'I really liked that pink leotard she posted about the other day,' said Annabelle, quietly.

Oliver shot her a look and just let out a huff of smug laughter. He was incredibly selective about which celebrities were worth lauding and which were worthy of derision.

'I'll put her next to Billy Kilmson, that daytime producer from ITV,' said Minnie.

'Wait, why is he coming?' asked Liz.

'They give us good coverage on the morning shows,' said Minnie.

'I don't think we need to seat him. Let's move him to standing. Save the seats for the ones who will make a fuss.'

'You say that like it isn't everyone,' said Minnie.

'Do you have anyone who needs his front-row seat?' asked Rose.

'Potentially,' replied Liz, looking over at Oliver.

'Ah, yes, of course,' nodded Minnie.

Oliver shot them both a look. 'I haven't sorted it yet. Bear with me. I'm still talking to Joss.'

'Is it Milo Jax?' asked Annabelle, her voice irritatingly high-pitched.

'Nothing is confirmed at this stage,' replied Liz.

'As soon as I know something, I will tell you all,' said Minnie, nodding gently at Rose, who managed half a smile in return as she tried to dull the paroxysm of thoughts that had suddenly rushed into her brain.

After work, Rose decided to walk. Not all the way back to Clapham – that would take roughly two hours and twenty-seven minutes, according to iPhone maps. But her office was right by Oxford Circus, just twenty minutes away from Hyde Park. She could walk through the park, past the Palace, and then head towards Victoria and get on the next train to Clapham Junction. She could walk the rest of the way from there. That should still leave her with enough time to get to the dinner.

Luna's dinners felt like more of an obligation than an invitation. 'Dinner Party' was always the name of the WhatsApp group next to an emoji. This time it was a firework. Menus were decided weeks in advance – allergies and dietary requirements taken into account, of course. And everyone always had to 'pitch' an idea for an after-dinner game; Luna would then choose the one she liked best.

The bit Rose hated the most, though, was that there were always seating plans, the politics of which she'd long tired of at Firehouse. Of course, there was often a strategy behind Luna's table placements. Last time, Rose had been seated next to Luna's cousin, Joseph, who worked for his dad's investment fund and spent the entire dinner talking about how funny it was that he had a serious job and still managed to go on 7 a.m. benders twice a week. Luna thought they'd be a good match, which, naturally, Rose found deeply insulting. The time before that, Rose had been seated next to a woman named Martina who worked at Mast, Firehouse's biggest competitor. Luna probably suspected they'd trade tales and gossip about various awful people that worked at their respective companies. But Martina mostly talked about which parts of her face she wanted to get plastic surgery on.

'What do you think I can do to these bits?' she asked Rose, pulling at the loose skin on her eyelids.

But before Rose could attempt an explanation at why people, generally speaking, need to keep the skin on their eyelids, someone down the table shouted: 'Stop snorting coke, babe!'

'Never!' Martina cackled back.

Rose dreaded to think who she'd be put next to this time. Luna and Rose had met at art college; they were in the same seminar for a Renaissance art history unit and bonded over a mutual dislike of everyone else in their group. 'Are we the only ones who don't love the sound of their own voice?' Luna had turned to her at the end of their first week.

'Apart from Robin over there, I think so,' replied Rose, pointing at a boy in a hooded sweatshirt leaning against the wall in the corner. He was asleep.

'Oh, my flatmate shagged him last week,' she replied. 'He definitely loves the sound of his own voice. Could hear him through the walls.'

It was true, everyone else in their seminar talked a lot, especially Sophie Matthews. She had read every text on the reading list and used every opportunity she could to brag about it. The professor eventually banned her from speaking in seminars so that other people had an opportunity to talk.

Luna had a close-knit group from her elite boarding school in Hertfordshire and, bar one or two, they were all fairly awful and would often act as if they'd never met Rose despite having met her several times. It was impossible to know if they were doing this to feign superiority or if they genuinely didn't recognise her. Maybe it was just a posh thing, like saying 'loo' instead of 'toilet' (*Hives & Dives* was always publishing lists of 'dos' and 'don'ts' like this).

'I don't know why they do that,' Luna would assure her each time. 'They're the most insecure people I know. So, I wouldn't let it bother you.'

At first, Rose would be polite and introduce herself. But that trick got old by the third time, and she eventually started calling people out on it. Soon, Luna stopped inviting Rose to dinners with people she'd already met. It seemed that the circle of her friendship group was far-reaching enough for her to choose different people every time. Most of the guests worked in either recruitment or property.

Rose wasn't ever entirely sure what Luna did for work, or if she even worked at all. She knew that her family had money and that, after graduating, Luna's dad gave her £5,000 to start her own vintage scarf business. Whenever Rose saw her after they left art college, Luna would only ever talk about who she was sleeping with, her most recent holiday, and where she was going on holiday next. She was often pictured in the party pages when she went out – Minnie had even invited her to a few of their events. The scarf business had yet to surface.

'You're here! Hi, gorge, so good to see you,' Luna said, opening her front door, bottle of Laurent-Perrier dangling from one hand. She was barefoot and wearing a tiny black sheath of sheer fabric that had been tightly wrapped around her slim torso, the material clinging to the middle of her thighs. You could quite clearly see she was wearing a pair of tight boxer-short knickers and a matching black lace bra underneath. Her curtain of golden blonde hair had been dyed lighter and was styled neatly into a plait that sat comfortably on her left side. She was wearing a light coat of mascara and a smudge of pink lip gloss that made her bee-stung lips look somehow even more divinely swollen.

'So good to see you, too,' Rose replied, her hands wrapping around Luna's slim back.

'Do you like it?' Luna said, twirling around in her hallway.

'The dress? Yeah, it's lovely, where is it from?'

'I made it, babe! New business. Scarves out, sheer mini dresses in!'

'Will clogs be next, Lu?' muttered a low voice from inside.

Luna spun around as Rose walked in and closed the door behind her.

'Funny!' she scoffed, her head tilting to the side, mockingly. 'Rose, this is Ben. He's a family friend.'

'We grew up in neighbouring villages,' Ben clarified, leaning forward to give Rose a kiss on the cheek.

He was wearing a navy-blue corduroy shirt tucked into a pair of brown tweed trousers. He looked remarkably smarter than the two other men in the room who were sitting on the sofa behind him.

'That's Paul and over there is Marco, who I think you must have met at another one of these,' said Luna, pointing to the corner of the living room, where both men were cradling cans of Budweiser and looked deep in conversation. They turned to smile at Rose and waved before turning back to face each other; the last time she'd seen Marco was outside a club in Leicester Square when he was asking to borrow her phone so he could ring his dealer. She told him it had run out of battery.

'And that's May and Flouff,' Luna added, gesturing at two girls huddled together on a navy-blue chesterfield sofa.

'Flouff?' Rose whispered.

'Short for Florence,' Luna whispered back. 'Her dad is the duke of some shire or other, I can't remember which.' She pulled away as if to make an announcement to the room. 'Right, I just need to check on the vol-au-vent canapés. Mingle amongst yourselves.'

'So how do you know our precious moon girl?' Ben asked Rose.

'We were at art college together.'

'How lovely. So are you an artist too?'

'What's that supposed to mean?' She paused. 'Sorry, that was defensive.'

'That's quite all right. I didn't mean to touch a nerve. You just look like the kind of person who would call themselves an artist.'

'I see. Which art college did you go to then?'

'Ha, I didn't go to university, actually.'

'That's unusual for Luna's group of friends.'

'Ah yes, well, you see she didn't exactly choose to be friends with me. It just so happened that our parents liked the same tiny pocket of Somerset and decided to raise their families there.'

'Why didn't you go?'

'Couldn't decide what to study, wanted to travel, so I did. Then I came back and got an internship at my uncle's ad agency. Now I'm an account manager there.'

'You make it sound so simple.'

'The benefits of being a straight white man with connections.'

Rose laughed. Ben had a pleasing face, the kind that was angular in all the places that made him universally attractive, but soft in parts, too, which made him seem more approachable. His hair was dirty blond, his eyes so light they almost looked grey. He wasn't characteristically good-looking in the way someone like Milo was. But for a regular person, and by the more lenient standard that accompanied that, this was someone a lot of women would call 'hot'.

The irony of Luna's regular dinner parties was that she couldn't cook. But she was always so generous, probably spending upwards of £200 on preparing inedible three-course meals for everyone, providing copious amounts of wine and not letting anyone go near the dishwasher (Rose had discovered this was because Luna always hired someone to clean the house the day after), so people kept coming.

It was also probably because of this that no one had ever told Luna that she couldn't cook. Even though the meal was often soggy and tasted a bit like water that had been left in a plastic bottle for too long, people would smile politely, make *mmm* sounds, telling her she should write her own cookbook.

Her home was also excellent for parties. With five storeys, it was a palatial townhouse tucked behind the King's Road that had originally been purchased by Luna's family as their 'London base'. But all of Luna's siblings were still at school, and her parents (both retired investment bankers) were constantly travelling the world. So, she almost always had the place to herself and whatever bevvy of friends and lovers she was into at any given moment. People mostly came to socialise or talk about themselves, politics or sex. This time it was the latter.

'I couldn't even wrap my hand around it,' said Flouff, puffing furiously on one of the Marlboro Touch cigarettes she had just ordered to the house via Deliveroo, tapping the ash into an empty wine glass to her left – Luna also let people smoke inside her house, another draw.

'It wasn't erect at all?' enquired Luna, eyes wide in dismay.

'Nope,' Flouff replied, inhaling deeply. 'Barely the size of my little finger and it dangled slightly to the left like it was looking for somewhere to hide. Honestly it's a good thing because had we actually managed to have sex, it would've been dreadfully embarrassing trying to pretend I could feel a thing.'

The whole table erupted into laughter.

'Poor guy,' muttered Ben, who Rose was pleased to find had been placed next to her in the seating plan.

'I know. He's probably pretty insecure about it.'

'Oh, God, not that. I mean, poor guy for having to try and pretend you're getting turned on by that,' he replied, nodding towards Flouff, who was now holding the cigarette in her mouth and gesticulating with both hands about another sexual encounter she'd had.

Rose laughed.

'How come I've never seen you at one of Luna's lovely soirées before, then?' Ben asked, twirling spaghetti around his fork and setting it back down on his plate. It was meant to be some sort of *pomodoro* dish but Luna had clearly failed to fully drain the pasta after it had cooked.

The dish in front of them was more of a red, watery soup with bits of pasta in it. Rose took one bite and didn't bother with the rest, strategically moving it around enough on her plate so it looked like she'd made several attempts before giving up.

'I haven't been to one for a while actually. I usually have work events in the evenings.'

'Oh yeah? What do you do?'

'I do PR for a publishing company that makes magazines,' Rose replied, knowing what would come next.

'That sounds very glamorous. Which magazines? Not Firehouse?'

'Yes. Firehouse.'

'Very cool. My godfather went to school with the man who runs the place. Jasper something, right?'

'Yes. And of course he did.'

'Ha. I like you, Rose.'

'Why?'

'Tell me more about yourself.'

'That feels like something you'd ask in a job interview.'

'What do you like to do in your free time?'

'Now you're making it sound like a Spanish oral exam.'

'It's a bit early to mention oral but I'll let that slide. Go on, tell me.'

Rose could feel herself starting to sweat.

'I don't really know how to answer that,' she replied.

'Well, do you read? Play golf? Watch birds?'

'Yes, no, and absolutely not.'

'Pleased we established that.'

'What do you do with your free time?'

'Oh, I don't have any free time,' he replied, winking before gathering his and Rose's plates and taking them into the kitchen.

With Ben gone, Rose looked around the table for a conversation to join. To her left, Paul and May were having a heated debate about Brexit. It wasn't completely clear but from what she heard it sounded as if Paul had made a xenophobic remark and May had been chastising him for it. But Paul, who was rolling his eyes – and a cigarette – didn't seem too bothered and was now listing all of the political predictions made in *The Simpsons*.

To her right, Flouff was telling Marco about the non-surgical treatments each of the Kardashians had had done, how much they cost, and where you could get them in London.

Rose decided now would be a good time to use the bathroom. Washing her hands, she looked at her reflection and hated how tired she looked. Her eyes were sunken in a manner reminiscent of celebrity mugshots. It was hard to remember the last time she'd had a full night's sleep. Just below her left eye, she noticed an eyelash. She dabbed it onto her finger and held it out in front of her. Closing her eyes, she thought about what to wish for. All she saw was Milo. Whenever she pictured him now, his face would appear and then morph into someone completely unrecognisable with outsized features. This time, what she saw barely looked like a face at all. It had become something entirely alien, almost like it had been painted, except the brushstrokes had blurred so the colours were muddied and indistinguishable from one another. The cheeks bulged outwards alongside what used to be an eye so that the face became a kaleidoscope of spherical objects arranged in a way that was comparable only to a Francis Bacon portrait: horrifying, violent, mutilated. She opened her eyes; the eyelash had gone.

Luce had called Rose three times that evening. She sighed and called her back.

'Hey, you okay?'

'You told me to ring you back,' Luce tutted. 'You're impossible to get hold of.'

This was ironic seeing as Luce was usually the one who was impossible to get hold of.

'Sorry, I'm just at Luna's for one of her ridiculous dinner parties.'

'Okay, I just wanted to talk details for our girls' night. I was looking at a list for places to meet men in London and there's this rooftop bar that's supposed to be great but we need to book and—'

'Sounds great, book it.'

'Are you sure? I need to put down a deposit.'

'Yes. I'm sorry I've got to get back to the table. Are you okay?'

'It doesn't really sound like you have time for me to answer that.'

'I'm sorry. Promise we can chat properly when I see you, okay? Love you.'

'Okay. Love you.'

When Rose returned to the dinner table, Luna was distributing pieces of paper and pens.

'Right, three names everyone! And please for the love

of God don't put any bloody *Harry Potter* characters in there. That joke is very much over,' she said.

'Oh, come on, Lovegood. Give us a spell!' shouted Paul, winking at Marco.

'Fuck off, Paul,' Luna snapped.

Of course, they were going to play the hat game. The games at Luna's were hit and miss and often went on for hours, depending on the Oxbridge headcount. You couldn't leave until they had finished; that was the rule. At one dinner party a few years ago, Rose fell asleep at the table. The games had been going on since 10 p.m. and they must have played at least four by midnight. When she woke up, she was told off by one of Luna's family friends because she was supposed to be his partner for the T-shirt race, which was when you had to take a T-shirt out of the freezer and put it on as quickly as possible. He demanded a do-over with a new partner 'for the sake of fairness'. Rose went home just as Luna started rummaging around the spare freezer for more T-shirts.

The hat game was fairly mild by comparison; Rose was relieved. You each had to choose three recognisable people, put all the names into a hat, and then go through as many as you could in forty-five seconds by describing them to your team. You could use any words and actions so long as you didn't name the actual person. Once you'd been through all the names, you had to do it again in a second round, only this time you could only use one word to describe them. Then, for the third round, you could either act out the name, sort of like charades, or you could make a sound. By that point, though, everyone was generally too drunk to care. Once, someone put Luna's mother in the hat. It was all going well until the sound round, when one of the guests described her by making sex noises. He was not invited back.

Rose usually tried to play it safe by putting cartoon characters as her names. Two of those and then someone completely inoffensive, like Tom Hanks. No one ever had anything controversial to say about Tom Hanks. Milo had never been a name in the hat before, at least not in any of the games she'd played at Luna's, though Rose knew it was a possibility. Whether this was something she wanted or not, she couldn't quite work out. She looked around the dining table, imagining everyone's reactions if she told them about her night with Milo Jax. Luna would be jealous and probe her for information about his house, May would pretend not to care and probably say one of her mates had shagged him too, and Paul would probably respond by trying to sleep with Rose just so he could tell people that he had fucked the same person as a celebrity. Flouff would ask about his penis.

'Right, everyone ready?' cooed Luna, shaking the hat so that every little folded piece of paper was suitably jumbled.

'Ready as we'll ever be,' replied Ben, topping up Rose's water glass with white wine.

'Thank you,' she mouthed, smiling.

Inside the hat was the usual mix of world leaders (Trump), dictators (Stalin), celebrities (Katy Perry) and dinner party guests (Paul). Luna delivered a masterful impression of Daffy Duck, waddling around the dining room with her hands clasped together forming a beak in front of her face. Marco was surprisingly good at doing Naomi Campbell, strutting into the kitchen and then taking a tumble like she famously did in a Vivienne Westwood show, and Ben did a solid Tom Hanks, singing 'You've Got a Friend in Me' and later telling everyone that yes, he did sing a solo in his school play and no, he would not be taking any requests. Then it was Rose's turn.

By this point, there were only a handful of names left. All the usual contenders had come and gone. Rose took the hat and started scrambling around.

'Stand up, love!' boomed Marco.

'Don't call her that,' Luna shouted back. 'You know her name is Rose, for fuck's sake, Marco.'

Ignoring him, Rose stood up.

'Kate Moss' had been written on the first card in tiny neat writing. Rose hesitated for a moment while she decided how best to handle this. She pouted her lips and pretended to pose in front of a camera.

'A model!' shouted Ben. 'Erm, ah fuck, I don't know any models.'

'You're so full of shit, mate,' muttered Paul.

'Gisele!' yelled Flouff.

Rose shook her head and continued scrunching her lips together so hard they started to ache.

'Kendall! Hailey!' Flouff tried again.

Rose bent down, put one finger on her right nostril and pretended to sniff from the table.

'KATE MOSS!' shouted Flouff, triumphantly.

Rose took another name out of the hat, aware she only had about ten seconds left before the timer ran out.

'Milo Jax' – she stared at the name blankly, looking closer to make sure it was really there.

'Who is it?' asked Marco.

'Come on, Rose, we're running out of time!' chimed Flouff.

Rose tried to open her mouth to say something but nothing came out. She looked back down at the piece of paper, which somehow slipped through her fingers and fell to the floor.

'TIME!' shouted May, triumphant at her team's win.

'Who was that, babe?' asked Flouff, picking up the piece of paper from the floor.

'Sorry,' replied Rose, quietly. 'I didn't know who he was.'

Flouff giggled. 'Milo Jax! You didn't know who Milo Jax was? Oh, get fucked. Don't you work in celebrity PR or something?'

The rest of the table laughed.

Rose said nothing and sat back down, quickly finishing the rest of her glass of white wine and then promptly pouring herself more.

'The things I would do to fuck Milo Jax,' said Flouff, lighting another cigarette, the smoke blowing directly in Rose's face.

'I'd fuck him,' added Marco.

'I bet you would,' conceded Paul.

'I feel like he'd be the kind of guy that goes down on you immediately and makes you come five times in a night,' mused Luna, who was sitting on Paul's lap and drinking directly from a bottle of red wine.

'Do you ever watch those clips of him on his latest tour?'

asked May. 'He's so cute with fans, wishes them happy birthday and stuff. Someone I know went to see him once in Paris, she was in the VIP section because of her job.'

'Who was it?' asked Luna.

'Oh, I really can't say,' she replied, smirking. 'Anyway, he spotted her from the stage and sent over one of his bodyguards to ask if she'd like to meet him after the show. Obviously, she went. And they slept together in his dressing room. Imagine! No idea how they keep that kind of thing out of the press.'

'Wow,' said Flouff. 'What does the girl look like?'

'No, I already said I can't tell you who she is,' replied May.

'He's not fucking Santa Claus,' said Ben, who must have noticed Rose staying silent.

'Ah yes, that inherent sex god Santa Claus,' May laughed.

'Can we stop fangirling a popstar and get on with the game please?' said Ben, sternly.

Rose was grateful not to get Milo again in the next round, when everyone had to say one word for the names. Instead, Paul got him. 'Rose!' he yelled, gleefully pointing at her when he pulled his name out of the hat. 'Milo Jax!' yelped Luna, flapping her hands with excitement.

By the time they'd finished round two, everyone was mercifully too drunk to carry on. The group had splintered: Flouff was now chain-smoking outside with Paul. May and Marco had gone to pick up more coke – it transpired they'd been doing it since the start of the night. And Luna was upstairs on FaceTime to her new Brazilian boyfriend.

Rose and Ben were still at the table. They had been discussing death row meals – Ben's was a roast dinner: 'diabolically dull'. Rose said buttery pasta with tuna.

'Pasta with tuna?' Ben asked, genuinely aghast.

'I know. It's hardly Michelin stuff,' she replied. 'My mum used to make it for me.'

'Cute. To be honest, a Michelin-star meal might bloat you. No one wants to arrive at heaven's pearly gates with a bloated belly.'

Rose smiled and yawned, noticing the clock on the wall that informed her it was nearing 1 a.m.

Ben topped up her wine again. 'Rose, can I ask you something?'

'Sure.'

'Did you really not know who Milo Jax was?' he asked.

Rose stayed silent.

'I just find it hard to believe, given your job,' he continued. 'Isn't he in the magazines all the time? He was at one of your parties the other day, right?'

'Yes, he came to the Firehouse Awards,' she replied, her tone sturdier.

'Right. So, what happened? You know him, or something?'

'Kind of.' Rose hoped this would be enough for Ben to stop asking questions. This, she quickly realised, was naive.

'Stop. Don't tell me you . . . and him?'

Rose looked down and said nothing.

'You are full of surprises, Rose.'

'What's that supposed to mean?' she snapped.

'Oh,' said Ben, caught off-guard by her frostiness. 'I didn't mean . . . I just. I don't know. Sleeping with someone like that. It's a pretty big deal, I guess. I don't know anyone famous. I'd scream it from the rooftops.'

There were many things Rose wanted to say in response to this. She wanted to tell Ben that his last sentence alone highlighted just how little he understood what had happened to her. And how warped his view of the world must be to think that sleeping with someone famous will elevate your life in any meaningful way. She wanted to tell him that people like him are the reason men like Milo get away with behaving the way they do. That people like him are the problem.

She wanted to lecture him about the value society places on fame. And how it makes no sense that these are the people we've decided matter more than others. Fundamentally, she wanted to tell Ben that she judged him for being impressed by the fact she'd slept with Milo. What was it that made it impressive? Why did that change his opinion of her? Did it raise her sexual stock value?

But she also desperately wanted to confide in Ben. She wanted to tell him that he was the first person she had allowed to know the truth. And that she still couldn't remember what the truth really was. That she was starting to see his face everywhere and it was morphing into a Francis Bacon painting and she was worried she was going slightly mad. That she may never find out what really happened because Milo had been ignoring Rose ever since it happened. And she was too terrified to try getting in touch with him because of what he might tell her. And how every time Rose thought about any of this her lips trembled just a little and she stopped being able to breathe for a few seconds.

But Rose decided not to say any of this to Ben. Instead, she kissed him.

Ben's lips were soft and full. He was a good kisser, pulling Rose's body towards him with one hand on her arm, running his fingers along her neck with the other. They must have been kissing for several seconds, maybe even minutes, when they heard Luna's voice.

'I knew you two would get along!' she chimed, audibly delighted.

Ben pulled away and glared at Luna like she'd just stepped on his foot in one of her feathered stilettos.

'All right, all right, I'll leave you to it,' she replied before leaning into both of them: 'You can use my bedroom if you like. I just found my brother's stash of K,' she winked and skipped off into the garden.

Ben looked at Rose. 'Do you want to?'

'Sure,' she said by default.

Upstairs, they fell onto the bed together, entangled in each other's bodies.

Ben tugged at Rose's T-shirt. She sat up and wriggled out of it before doing the same to Ben.

His lips curled into a smile as he looked at her body.

'You're beautiful, Rose,' he whispered, leaning back in towards her. And for a brief moment, she felt like she might be.

Within seconds, Ben had disposed of Rose's jeans, his mouth was roaming around her knickers before tugging them off with his teeth and thrusting his tongue deep inside her.

She tried to enjoy it. Her eyes were closed and she was able to imagine it feeling pleasurable, she even managed a few moans and fist clenches. But in that moment, her body became something she was no longer in possession of. It wasn't that she had lost control of it, or that she couldn't move. It was a body that didn't belong to her any more. Perhaps it was the alcohol. Rose was looking down at herself from above. Her face and body were obscured, a series of geometrical shapes knocked together in the colour of milky flesh. Ben was just about visible, a blond mass of hair and limbs. Rose felt something sharp and the scene before her went black. Then she heard herself screaming.

*

'Hey Lu. Sorry I couldn't chat properly last night. Is everything okay? Would love to FaceTime soon. Sorry, things are a bit crazy at the moment. But yes, am super excited about our girls' night. That rooftop place sounds great. Call me about timings and stuff later? We can dress up and – oh, sorry no it was oat milk not soya milk. Yeah. Thanks. Anyway, tell me how things are at home? The flat feels so empty without you. Pasta doesn't taste the same. Are you sleeping better? Call me when you can and we will plan the best girls' night ever. Lots of love. Okay, okay bye.'

Rose was mid-yawn when the coffees arrived; she hadn't slept a full night in as long as she could remember. Recently, she kept waking up at 3 a.m. It was almost always on the dot, which spooked her a little more each time. After ten minutes of lying still with her eyes closed trying not to look at her phone, she would relent, going into 'Settings', finding the list of people she'd blocked (mostly random men and people asking her to buy followers), unblocking Milo, tapping 'Message' and staring for a little while (she'd stopped logging into the fake account because it made her feel like a crazed fan).

There were now long lists in her Notes of potential messages she could send him. These included:

How are you?
Hi.
Did you die?
Hey you. How's it going? Been a while.
You should try to get a better PR team. Haven't heard anything about the tour.
Hiya.
Hey Milo, I'm sorry to get in touch so out of the blue but I really need to speak to you about what happened that night.
Drink soon?

Minnie was pacing the office holding her phone to her ear when Rose walked in, smiling up at her when she handed her the coffee. Oliver was eating a bag of particularly crunchy roasted peanuts. 'Thanks,' he just about managed as she put the coffee on his desk.

'Sorry, Annabelle, I wasn't sure what you'd want.' Rose

turned to her. Annabelle was always overdressed for work, although perhaps that was inevitable when your entire wardrobe consisted of designer clothing, courtesy of your parents. Today, she was in a black silk pleated dress that grazed the floor. Her make-up was immaculately applied, her hair perfectly smooth and brushed. Half of it was pulled back off her face in a Chanel hair clip.

'Oh, don't be silly,' she replied. 'It's fine. I don't actually drink coffee, I prefer matcha.'

'Noted,' Rose nodded. 'What's going on?' she asked, pointing over towards Minnie.

'It's Clara. Her manager emailed Minnie late last night to say she is pulling out of the party.'

'What? Did he say why?'

'Nope. Something about "personal circumstances".'

Rose sighed, sat at her desk and logged onto her computer, waiting for Minnie to get off the phone.

'Goddammit,' Minnie said as she hung up.

'Any luck?' asked Annabelle in a tone that was far brighter than was appropriate.

'No. No luck, Annabelle,' she snapped back, eyes fixed on her phone. 'Fraser still won't tell us why she's pulled out. He's just insisting that she can't come any more and now he is trying to plug one of his other C-list clients who I've never heard of but is apparently huge in the clean eating world, which is a phrase I don't understand or particularly care for. And I know the men upstairs won't either.'

'Because they all prefer to eat something dirtier?' grumbled Oliver through a mouthful of peanuts.

'I think I might be able to help,' said Rose softly.

'Oh yes, you went for lunch with her, didn't you?' Minnie's eyes lit up.

Rose nodded.

'And she liked you. You were essentially the reason she signed up in the first place, right?'

'I think so. I mean, it's hard to tell but I think we definitely connected.'

Minnie rummaged around her handbag: a tired leather Mulberry satchel that looked about twenty-five years old.

'Here, take this,' she said, handing Rose a black debit card with the words FIREHOUSE embossed across the top in silver lettering. 'Take her to Cecconi's. Or Scott's. Or literally wherever it is she wants to go. Convince her to come. Please.'

'I will do my best,' she said, taking the card. 'I'll see if she wants to meet for breakfast.'

'Yes, perfect. Thank you.'

In the lift, Annabelle caught up with Rose. 'Rose!'

'Hey,' she said, holding the lift door.

'Sorry to bug you. I just wanted to ask you something quickly.'

'Sure.'

'I know you brought Milo to the party last time. I was wondering if I could do something to help get him here this time to perform. I know Minnie and Oliver have been trying but I'm not sure anything's been confirmed yet. I wanted to see if you had any tips?'

Rose felt her stomach lurch.

'I'm not sure I do,' she replied sternly. 'He's on tour at the moment.'

'Yes, I know, but there's a gap in his schedule – we could fly him from Berlin to London and back to Amsterdam the next day and it would be fine.'

'I don't think it's a good idea, Annabelle.'

'Why not?'

Rose paused to consider the prospect for the first time. If Milo did come to the StandFirst launch, she could confront him. Or, at least, talk to him and try to piece together the compilation of sounds, images and feelings that had been hopelessly roaming around her head since that night, looking for something solid to cling to.

'You can try emailing Joss directly,' said Rose, firmly. 'Tell her about the reach of StandFirst among younger people. Correlate that with his fanbase. Send her all the positive coverage from when Milo attended the awards. Tell her about all the other talent we have lined up so far. And work out the highest possible fee you can with Liz. He won't do it again for free.'

'Thank you so much, Rose,' she replied, delighted. 'I still can't believe you met him. I'm such a Jaxer!'

Rose pressed the button to close the lift.

'Was he, like, flirty with you when you saw him?' Annabelle asked, her hand now in between the lift doors.

'No.'

'Does he have a girlfriend?'

'I don't know, Annabelle. Google it.'

'But did it seem like he had a girlfriend when he spoke to you?'

Before Rose could stop herself she was shouting: 'For

fuck's sake, Annabelle! What the fuck are you getting so obsessive about?'

Annabelle took a step back, her expression a mix of terror and intrigue.

'Sorry, Annabelle. I'm sorry,' said Rose, her cheeks piping hot.

'No worries,' she replied quietly.

'I have to go.'

The lift doors closed before Annabelle could intercept again.

There was a bench bathing in the morning sun just across from the office; Rose sat there and took a deep breath. She would have to apologise to Annabelle properly tomorrow. The last thing she needed was reports to Jasper that 'Roisin' in PR had screamed in her face.

Clara hadn't posted anything on Instagram that day – and there was nothing on her Stories. Her most recent grid post was from three days ago and was a reel of selfies taken in what appeared to be the bathroom of a lavish hotel suite. She was holding up different lip glosses in each of the photos, her lips pouted and glistening like they'd just been dipped in lacquer. *Loving my new @LivLipKits*, she captioned the post. *Perfect for a date night ;) #ad #spon.*

Hey Clara, Rose began in the DM. *Just heard the news from Minnie. I know this might sound odd but I just wanted to check in. I'd love to chat to know if you're okay?*

She tapped 'Send'. The word 'Seen' instantly appeared underneath.

Clara started typing. Then she stopped. She started again.

Rose's eyes were fixed on her screen. This routine continued for three minutes. Finally, a small block of text appeared.

Hey Rose. I really appreciate you getting in touch. Kind of you. I'm okay, thank you. I'm so, so sorry about the event. Really wishing you well. Maybe next time. MM x.

Rose sighed and started typing back. *That's okay. I wanted to talk to you, actually. Nothing to do with the event. Are you free for breakfast? I have Minnie's company card. We could go anywhere you like?*

Typing. Not typing. Typing again. Not typing.

I love the avocado toast at Cecconi's. I saw you posted a pic of it the other day, Rose wrote.

I can be there in 35 minutes. Ordering an Uber.

Great! See you soon x.

X

Rose texted Minnie: *Meeting Clara now at Cecconi's. Will sort.* She wanted to prove to Minnie that she could do this. That she wasn't 'the girl who got Milo Jax'. She wanted her name to be as disconnected from his as much as possible. She'd be 'the girl that got one of the biggest social media influencers in the UK to walk in the fashion show for the StandFirst launch party'. She would be 'the person who saved the fucking day'.

Fantastic, darling! Keep me posted.

Will do x.

Rose decided to walk straight to Cecconi's from the office to get one of the good tables. It was one of those rare restaurants close to the office that opened for breakfast and stayed so for the rest of the day.

Minnie would always sit in one of the corner tables whenever she went, the same table often occupied by Firehouse editors and publishers, and sometimes the cover stars too. It was the perfectly positioned spot for people watching while face-down in a bowl of pasta.

Today, though, it wasn't busy. There were a few tables of stiff men in even stiffer suits circled around teacups filled with espresso that looked like toys in front of their wide frames. One woman in her mid-thirties was sitting alone at one table, drinking a black coffee and reading a magazine. Rose looked closer and noticed the font of the interiors title at the top. It was the current issue, August, which featured an interview with a couple in their mid-forties whose names Rose couldn't remember. But she could vividly picture their home: decked out in mid-century antiques and rugs the wife had flown in from India, it was the kind of flat Rose had always fantasised about living in. The walls were a range of shades, light greens and sapphire blues. The furniture was leather, corduroy and plaid. None of it made sense and yet, somehow, piled all together, it worked. Calm among chaos.

Rose had spent all of yesterday trying to shake off what happened over the weekend with Ben. The whole thing was mortifying. She'd explained she was just too drunk and needed to get home. He looked absolutely terrified but nonetheless asked for no further explanation, got dressed, and helped her order an Uber. It was a measured response considering she'd screeched like a wild animal the second he put his tongue inside her. When they got downstairs, Paul and Marco were dancing in the living room to

'Blurred Lines' of all things, the others must have been taking ketamine in the bathroom. Thankfully, it didn't seem like anyone had heard Rose.

She quickly said goodbye to Ben, kissing him on the cheek and saying 'See you soon' knowing she would never see him again. When she woke up on Sunday morning, all she felt was shame and regret. She had a long, hot bath, and threw everything she'd worn last night into the washing machine. She sent a thank-you message to Luna, who was one of those people that always had fifty unread messages on WhatsApp and didn't reply to anything within one month. When she did reply, it would probably be with another invitation to another dinner party that Rose would politely decline.

It had been particularly difficult getting out of bed that morning. Hence why Minnie's instruction to spend the day with Clara was a welcome ask. The alternative would have been sitting at her desk pretending to write a press release for the September issue of *MODE* and watching videos from Milo's tour. They had become impossible to avoid; she was always seeing stories about him during her morning research rounds. Half of the articles were about dramatic things that had happened at the gigs, like a couple getting engaged, or someone fainting in the crowd. The rest were about who Milo was rumoured to be dating. Apparently, he'd recently been 'getting to know' a twenty-four-year-old Spanish model with legs the size of Rose's arms.

Clara arrived hunched underneath a white silk blazer, which she wore over a pair of white flared jeans and a white poloneck jumper through which you could see a cream lace bra – La Perla, presumably. It was the kind of outfit Rose would never even consider wearing, mostly because of how dreadful she was at washing white clothes. One drawer in her bedroom had become a graveyard of pale pink and purple clothes that had once been white. Whenever she wore lipstick, which was not as often as she'd like, it would wind up staining something somewhere.

Two of the waiters were nudging each other in the corner; Clara didn't seem to notice. Though it was hard to tell where she was looking, underneath a pair of huge rectangular sunglasses with interlocking gold Gs on either side. She smiled at Rose, flashing her even white teeth as her glossy lips curved into an almost smile.

Rose noticed the smell of cigarettes that had been masked with sweet perfume lingering on Clara's shoulders when she leaned in to hug her.

'It's so good to see you,' Clara said as she shuffled into the seat opposite Rose, putting her hands underneath her thighs.

'You too,' she replied.

'I hope you know I really wanted to do the show,' she said, sunglasses firmly staying put.

'I know you did,' Rose replied. 'But we don't have to talk about that now. Let's just have a chat and eat something delicious.'

Clara smiled. 'That would be great.'

Conversation with Clara was remarkably easy so long as Rose only spoke about herself. She was far more inquisitive this time than the last, quizzing her on art college, her relationship with Minnie, and how she landed her job at Firehouse. She asked about the flat, Luce, her mother, her father. All of it. Every time Rose tried to turn the subject onto Clara, she'd bat it away, somehow managing to bring the subject back to Rose, like a Tory MP being asked about the single market on the *Today* programme.

There was a stiffness surrounding Clara that morning. Every inch of her body was covered by clothing or accessories; all Rose could see was her mouth and nose. Her sunglasses were so oversized she couldn't even see her eyebrows.

'Are you dating anyone at the moment?' Clara asked, taking a sip from her second soy cappuccino. Her fingers were trembling.

'No, I'm not dating anyone,' she replied. Rose had not told anyone about Ben or Jake. It made it easier to pretend nothing had happened at all.

'How are things with your boyfriend?' Rose asked.

Clara took a short breath and let out a small noise that sounded like an attempt at laughter. But it came out as more of a whimper. She lifted her hand and wiped something away underneath her sunglasses. Her wrists were small and delicate, like a child's. Rose noticed that Clara wasn't wearing any jewellery, her bare fingers and neck suddenly starkly different to how they appeared on Instagram, often dripping in various jewels she had been paid to promote.

'Is everything okay?' asked Rose softly, leaning in towards Clara.

'Sorry,' replied Clara. 'I find it really hard to talk about him. I also haven't slept in a while.'

Rose desperately wanted to tell her that she had also not slept, to confide in someone about what had been going on. But that would only raise further questions – and, frankly, today was about Clara.

'That's okay. We don't have to talk about him if you don't want to.'

'No, it's fine. I'm actually fine. Gosh, sorry. I'm so embarrassed,' she said, tossing her head as if to shake off the moment of vulnerability.

Rose waited for Clara to ask her something else, not wanting to probe any further. But Clara allowed the silence between them to linger, re-positioning her sunglasses and taking a few shallow breaths.

'I don't think it is fine, Clara,' said Rose finally.

Whether it was having her experience validated by a stranger, or something about the way Rose acknowledged what was so obviously happening right in front of her, this prompted something in Clara.

She took her sunglasses off, revealing porcelain skin and glassy eyes, and took a deep breath. 'I know I need to leave him,' she began. 'I know that things are bad. Actually, I think they're very bad. I know that now. I do.' Her tone was flat and monosyllabic in the way it is when someone reads aloud from a piece of paper. 'But sometimes, Rose. Ugh, God, sometimes they are also wonderful. When things are going well with us, it feels as if I'm living this stupidly perfect life. I have this man who adores me, showers me with compliments and gifts and all the love I could ever want.'

Rose nodded. 'I understand.'

'I have everything!' Clara said, eyes wide now and looking directly at Rose's. Her pitch was higher, louder, manic. 'Do you know that I can snap my fingers and get any designer bag I want in a few hours?' she said. 'I can't remember the last time I bought an item of clothing. Or a pair of shoes. Or a tin of sodding lip balm. I can't remember the last time I went to a restaurant I wanted to go to. Or a holiday I didn't have to post on social media about. All of it is just . . . given to me. For no reason other than a number next to a ridiculous username I made up after a night out in my early twenties.'

Her arms moved furiously as she spoke, illustrating her every word with a different physical flourish. Rose steadied her hands on the table just to make sure she didn't knock something off it.

'It's the dream life,' she continued. 'I don't deserve it. No one does. And Mark . . . he just . . .' She paused. 'You know he asked me to marry him?'

'Really? When?'

'Last year. Technically, we're engaged. And when he asked me, I swear to God it was the most romantic thing anyone has ever done.'

'Where were you?'

'Paris. At the Hotel George V. Roses, champagne, the whole thing. It was a total stock image proposal but I absolutely adored it. Then later that night, we had an argument. I can't even remember what it was about. But eventually he grabbed my hand, yanked the engagement ring off my finger, called me a "dumb cow" and walked out.'

'Do you talk to your friends about any of this?' asked Rose.

'No. None of them even know we got engaged. I couldn't tell anyone; it was too humiliating.' She took another deep breath and leaned in towards Rose. 'You have to understand, I really don't talk to anyone about this.'

'Why not?'

'Because I can't, Rose. My team has been putting pressure on me to end it the minute I told them Mark wouldn't let me post about him. And my friends are just so bored with it all, obviously. But none of them know the extent of what's been happening. They think the fact that I keep going back to him means I'm choosing this. Like I have a victim complex that means I want to stay miserable. But it's just not that simple. I honestly sometimes wish it was. Mark can be kind, generous and really thoughtful. It would be so much easier if he was a monster the entire time. This is going to sound like a ridiculous example but a few months ago I came home after a long shoot and he'd made me a full roast dinner with a vegetarian wellington and everything.'

'That's nice of him.'

'It was. But then we sat down to watch a film later and this actor I used to hook up with appeared on screen. Mark lost it and started accusing me of choosing that film because this guy was in it. I swear I didn't even know he was in it. But Mark didn't believe me. And then . . .' Her eyes started to water again.

'Fuck's sake, I'm sorry, Rose.'

Rose put her hand on Clara's arm. 'It's okay, Clara. You can tell me.'

Clara sighed through pursed lips.

'I am fine, I promise. And he didn't hit me or anything,' she said, looking down at her feet.

'Right.'

'But he went into a kind of wild rage. He does this quite a lot when he gets upset – and more so when he's drunk, which he was. I later found out he'd spent the day at the pub and had then come home and drunk a bottle of red wine while he was cooking. He has never hit me. I promise he has never hit me.'

She was speaking faster now, vomiting every sentence.

'Anyway, then he accused me of cheating on him,' she continued. 'He was shouting a lot, pacing around the living room, screaming at me, "You fucked him. I know you fucked him." Then he asked me about the size of this actor's penis, asking me how it tasted in my mouth. God, it all sounds so childish when you say it out loud.'

'No, it doesn't,' said Rose.

'Things went on like this for a while and then he eventually picked up one of the wine glasses on the table and threw it across the room. The shards went everywhere. So did the wine, leaving these enormous blotches all over the floor. The stains are still there, hiding underneath a rug he bought me the following week.'

Clara had lost the ability to hold back her tears. She was panting now, her hand clutching her chest. 'I know it sounds ridiculous because it's just a wine glass and it didn't even touch me. I don't even think he threw it directly at me. But it was still so . . . violent. The act of it. The look in his eyes when he threw that glass, it was just . . .' She trailed off, trying to calm herself down. 'I couldn't see him, Rose. That person was a stranger. And I felt scared for the first time. I felt that this man, this person I love . . . That he had vanished. And this new person who was here, in my home, could really hurt me.'

Rose nodded as one of the waiters approached their table and, on seeing Clara sobbing, swiftly turned around. She was a different person to him now too: a glossy veneer splintering right in front of him, losing its shine.

Clara took a large gulp of water and continued. 'Afterwards, he rushed over to check I was okay and apologised. He was practically on his knees, begging I forgive him.' She put her head in her hands and took a few deep breaths. 'I told him I wanted to stay somewhere else that night, so he booked me into a suite at the Dorchester for two days. Listen to me, some sob story, right?' she said, laughing.

'Shall we go somewhere else?' Rose asked, nodding at the waiter for the bill.

'Yeah, okay,' Clara nodded, rubbing her eyes before putting her sunglasses back on.

They left the restaurant and walked towards Hyde Park, which was mostly empty aside from a few young mothers pushing prams in matching athleisure sets. Clara was telling Rose about more arguments she'd had with Mark. There was one occasion when she had surprised him with a trip to the Lake District for his birthday. But when he discovered that the trip had been gifted to her by the hotel PR, meaning she had to post about it on Instagram, he lost it. By the time they'd arrived at the hotel, Mark had already booked another hotel room nearby and insisted he would get the train home the following morning. Clara had managed to assuage his anger over dinner and they'd had sex all night. They wound up extending the trip by another week.

'It is the best sex I've ever had,' Clara said, adding how, before meeting Mark, she'd never really enjoyed sex at all. 'It always felt like something I was performing,' she said. 'Sort of like my social media. Maybe that's why I'm so good at it,' she laughed.

Rose nodded, hoping not to be asked about her own sex life.

'Don't your followers ask you about your love life?' she asked.

'Oh, all the time,' Clara replied. 'I get hundreds of DMs a day, and so many of them are from women asking if I have a boyfriend. Of course, they all assume I'm straight, which I am. But still. That bothers me.'

'Do you ever reply to any of them?'

'Never. I used to when I started out. The whole thing was so novel; I couldn't believe anyone wanted to speak to me about my life. So I'd have all of these conversations with them as if we were friends. Then it started to get a bit weird.'

'What do you mean?'

'Well, one guy worked out where I lived and started delivering flowers to my door each week. It was harmless at first but then he started leaving notes too . . . I ended up reporting it to the police but they said they couldn't do anything unless he actually broke into the house or physically attacked me.'

'I see. And now?'

Clara stopped and turned to face her. 'Now, they're all just looking for a reason to hate me.'

She told Rose about the online hate forums that post about her. There were thousands. Not just on Reddit but on dedicated blogs and websites where people would go to dissect and dismantle her every online and offline move. There were certain threads she could quote word for word, entire paragraphs people had written tearing her apart. Some were by total strangers. Others were by followers she'd briefly met or spoken to. And some were just people who'd worked in restaurants and hotels she'd been to, accusing her of being rude.

'There is an entire thread dedicated to a dinner I hosted on behalf of a skincare brand where they were serving beef burgers. One half of the group called me a cheapskate and the other accused me of being a liar. I didn't even eat them!'

'Why would that matter?'

'Because I post so much about vegetarianism and yada yada yada. So the second I'm associated with anything animal-based I'm labelled a hypocrite for going against my values. My team is constantly telling me not to get sucked in to the negativity but it's impossible not to. I don't know who has that kind of strength.'

This, Clara explained, was another reason why she had never posted about Mark.

'Imagine having your relationship subjected to that kind of scrutiny,' she said.

After a pause Clara went on: 'It's just exhausting.'

'What is?'

'Pretending I wanted this. Pretending I enjoy it. All the lies we tell ourselves.'

They continued walking around the park until, eventually, Rose asked if they could sit somewhere because her back was starting to hurt. They rested on a park bench overlooking the Serpentine, sitting silently for several minutes.

'See that couple?' asked Clara, pointing towards an elderly couple walking past them. She was using a walking frame, he had his hand on her upper back. They must have been in their eighties.

'I always thought I wanted that. As I get older, I think how much easier it would be to just be alone. To never have met Mark. To never have had this career, and gone into hairdressing or something.'

'You could still do that?'

She laughed. 'Don't be daft. This is my life now. And in a few decades, that will be me and Mark,' she sighed. 'To the outside world, we'll look like a sweet, happy couple who still make each other cups of tea in the morning and hold hands when we're sitting on the sofa at home. He'll probably even believe that we are that couple. I will play my part so it looks like I'm happy. But on the inside, I will be burning.'

They spent the rest of the day together, ambling around Hyde Park, buying coffees at various pit stops along the way. At some point, Clara suggested they get a drink. Before Rose could think about it, she had hailed a black cab, told the driver an address and opened the car door. The pub they went to was one of Clara's favourites, she said. She hadn't been there in years because her manager told her it was too 'lowbrow' for her to be seen there.

'But it's, like, 3.30 p.m. on a Monday so I'm sure it will be empty anyway,' she told Rose.

As predicted, the pub was deserted aside from two tables, one where a man in his mid-fifties sat alone, nursing a pint of Guinness, and another where two women who looked like they belonged in an A-Level maths class sat drinking from cans of Coca-Cola, huddled over a phone.

Clara asked the barman for his most expensive bottle of white wine. 'For two very expensive ladies,' she said, winking at him. She pointed to a table in the corner and went to the bathroom, giving Rose an opportunity to check her phone. There were five missed calls from Luce and a text from Minnie.

She wrote out a message to Luce first.

Sorry, just with an influencer for work, she wrote. *Going to be here a little longer but will aim to meet you at that bar at 9ish? xxx.*

The message from Minnie read: *Any luck?*

Not yet, she's in a bit of a bad way so I'm trying to bond with her a little. I'll get there, Rose replied.

Do whatever you need to, said Minnie. *Within reason*, she added a second later.

It was reassuring to work for an older woman who had no interest in competing with Rose or putting her down in the way she'd heard so many women did at other workplaces. Luce had endless stories of female colleagues going up against one another at her law firm. Rose felt lucky not to have to deal with any of that at Firehouse. Sure, Oliver was always antagonising her, and Annabelle seemed to serve no real purpose other than using the office as her own personal catwalk. But Minnie was always in her corner, which made all the other stuff bearable.

Rose had been waiting for an opportunity to mention the party. It seemed ridiculous now to even bring it up given everything they'd discussed.

Clara came back from the bathroom and sat opposite Rose, pouring both of their glasses to the top.

'Clara . . .' she began.

'Cheers!' she said smiling. It was the first genuine smile she'd seen from Clara all day.

'Cheers,' Rose replied, tilting her glass forward.

They'd almost finished the bottle by the time Clara started talking about how a recent sponsorship deal with a designer in Milan had fallen through. This was Rose's moment.

'Clara, I wonder if we . . .'

'Shall we get some cigarettes?' Clara interjected before Rose could say anything else, wide-eyed and scanning the room, as if looking for a levitating packet of Marlboro Lights.

'Sure,' she replied.

Clara waved over at the barman, mouthing 'we'll be right back', to which he looked bemused considering the music was very quiet and had she spoken the words he would've almost certainly heard her.

'Can't believe how expensive these are now,' Clara said as she unwrapped the clear film of her newly purchased cigarette packet and threw it on the ground. She was visibly drunk now. Rose was holding it together, though she felt a little light-headed.

Either the drinking, the process of talking about her relationship with Mark, or possibly the cigarette had stirred something in Clara. Because, illuminated by the golden glow of summer's early evening light, she had settled down; it was as if something in her had been released. It was strange seeing the shift in real time. Rose wasn't sure exactly how or when it happened. But the woman in front of her was not the same as the one crying into her bone-china plate at Cecconi's. This woman was front-facing and ready to present this version of herself to the night.

Rose nodded, taking a cigarette into her hand as they walked back towards the bar. 'I didn't realise you smoked.'

Clara laughed. 'Only on special occasions.'

She grabbed Rose's hand, cigarette dangling out of her mouth and started walking more quickly. 'And this is one of them. Come on!' she shouted as Rose trailed behind. 'We're going to finish that bottle of wine and then we are going out.'

FIVE

Rose's ears were ringing. 'Do you think they have earplugs anywhere?' she shouted into Clara's ear.

'What?' she shouted back.

'Do you think they have earplugs?' Rose tried again, feeling the tug of her vocal cords.

'I can't hear you!' Clara shouted back.

'Earplugs!' she pointed to her ears.

Clara shrugged and continued dancing.

They'd ended up at a private gig somewhere in east London. The definition of the private part wasn't clear. Earlier on in the evening, Clara had taken Rose to the launch party of some new Italian restaurant in Mayfair. It had a wall of red roses with a gold throne perched in front of it designed specifically for people to take photographs. The chair was an antique that had been designed in the Baroque period. Somehow, none of it looked cheap. It just looked ridiculous.

At the launch party, a man wearing a blindingly bright blue suit approached Clara from behind, putting his hand on the small of her back to kiss her as he said hello. Rose observed the conversation for several minutes before Clara introduced her. He worked at a production company and he wanted Clara to post some Instagram Stories for his new feminist film about zombies.

'They've all come back from the dead to kill the men that wronged them,' he said.

'Wow,' said Rose, mockingly.

'I know!' the man replied, completely earnestly.

Clara was apparently too drunk to pick up on any of this.

A second man who looked exactly like the first started flirting with Clara. He introduced himself as 'Joe, just Joe' and explained he was the manager of this 'hot new boyband' who just happened to be playing a gig tonight and did they want to come along and sit in the VIP area? The words 'hot', 'VIP' and 'boyband' were enough to convince Clara. So, there they were. Rose to Clara's left, trying to resist putting her hands over her ears while Clara bumped up against 'Joe, just Joe', whose hands roved frantically around her hips.

They were standing at the front of a box overlooking the right of the stage, giving them a perfect view of four indie boys wearing drainpipe jeans and holding guitars. Only one of them seemed to be playing his instrument. The other three were mostly bopping around, singing a mix of pop-that-wants-to-be-rock songs you could easily imagine a group of teenagers wailing along to in a karaoke booth at 4 a.m. There must have been at least 20,000 people in the venue; Rose had heard of the boyband before and dismissed them as basic. So far, they hadn't surpassed her expectations. Clearly a lot of other people disagreed, the little lights from their smartphones pointed towards the stage as they sang their lyrics back to them in total synchrony. Even Clara seemed to be attempting to sing along to some of them, too, her mouth moving in the slobbery way it does when someone is drunk and hoping that what comes out will resemble words.

As the next song came to an end, one of the men who hadn't been playing the guitar started to riff with the audience, making jokes about Theresa May: 'What's the naughtiest thing you lot did today?' he asked, all cheeky chappy like a boy in the year above everyone always has a crush on. The crowd shouted back various indistinguishable things. 'Bet none of you were quite as naughty as little Miss Theresa though. Those fields of wheat, am I right?' he added to rapturous applause.

It was 8.15 p.m. and Rose already had four missed calls from Luce. Now was the time to leave; progress hardly looked promising with Clara. The rooftop bar was only twenty minutes away by Tube. She could call Luce on her way to the station.

'Anyway, I wanted to have a little word with you because firstly, I have to say thank you for coming out here tonight,' the singer continued. 'It's our first proper London show and it's a real honour to be here with all of you. Now, to mark the occasion, we thought it would only be fair if we brought a friend to celebrate it with us.'

The volume of the room had now been turned to its max, shrill screams echoing from below. Rose turned to Clara, who was still dancing. 'Joe, just Joe' caught Rose's eye and smirked. 'Wait for it,' he mouthed at her.

'Without further ado, please, everybody, welcome to the stage the brilliant man who has kindly taken time out of his sold-out world tour to join us. It's none other than Mr Milo Jax!'

It was hard to establish the order of what happened next. Milo's arm wrapped around the man with the microphone. A story about how they'd been at school together. Something about getting kicked off an art trip interspersed with laughter and pats on the back. Then more music. His hands squeezing the microphone. His voice. Him. And the deafening screams of 20,000 people reverberating around Rose, dulling her senses and reaching for her throat.

'I can't actually believe they brought Milo Jax on,' said Clara as they stood in the line for the bathroom. 'Joe, just Joe' had given them a pair of gold wristbands to get them into the afterparty.

'Are you into his music?'

'Oh no, not really. I just think he's the sexiest man alive. Even the way he was singing on stage, moving his hips like that. You just know that man fucks with a capital F.'

Rose nodded, pulling at the neckline of her shirt. 'Do you think he'll be at the afterparty?'

'I hope so,' Clara replied, in between gulps from the bottle of water Rose had bought for her. 'Joe said they're all old friends. He flew in from Munich just to do the gig with them.'

'I see.'

'Apparently he's a total dreamboat. God, I can't wait to meet him.'

'I sort of know him,' Rose said before she could stop herself, regretting it instantly.

'What? You do?'

'He came to the Firehouse Awards and I had to walk him down the red carpet.' Her heart was racing.

'Oh my God, what was he like?'

'He was fine.'

Clara raised an eyebrow. 'Fine? Seriously?'

And because Rose didn't want to talk about Milo further, and because she knew there was only one thing she could say to satisfy Clara, she said: 'He's just so hot, isn't he?'

'Thatta girl,' she smiled and skipped off into the cubicle that had just opened.

The afterparty wasn't as much an afterparty as it was a poorly lit room behind the stage with a bar. The room was filled with mostly record label executives and other gold wristband peripherals. No one in the band had arrived yet. Nor had Milo, who had presumably hopped straight onto his private jet and gone back to whatever European city he was playing in the next evening (Prague). Rose was sipping on a warm beer while Joe and Clara giggled and touched each other as much as people could get away with in public. She was half-listening to their conversation about Joe's trip to Spain, which he kept referring to as 'España', when she heard Clara say her name.

'You know him?' asked Joe, turning to face Rose.

'Who?' Rose replied.

'Milo!' jumped in Clara. 'I was just telling Joe how you guys were friends.'

'We're not friends,' said Rose, feeling her cheeks burning. 'I just meant that we'd met at the Firehouse Awards.'

'Were you nominated for something?' Joe asked.

Clara burst into a fit of giggles.

'No, I work there,' said Rose. 'In the press office.'

'Oh cool,' he replied politely. 'Well, you can say hello to him yourself now if you like.'

She heard his laugh first. That familiar yet entirely alien sound, one that had initially elicited a thrilling tingle as if to signal the start of some transcendental, magical connection. Now, hearing it made her feel like someone was stamping on her chest.

As he moved deeper into the room, Rose caught a glimpse of a silver pair of boots, their glaring shine reflecting everything back. She stepped to the side in an attempt to jolt her body into breathing, a move that brought the back of his head into view. His hair looked longer up close, shaggier, like it hadn't been washed for weeks. The sight of his hand ruffling through it made her shudder, and yet she found herself fixated, observing the minutiae of every movement as if to be sure it was happening. That after everything he was right there, just a few feet away.

'I'm just going to the loo,' Rose whispered to Clara, her pulse thumping loudly.

She had three choices. To leave immediately, apologise to Minnie and wish Clara the best. To stay and dart around Milo until she could convince Clara to leave. Or to forget about Firehouse, her dignity and all social norms, and kick him in the balls.

Washing her hands, Rose stared at her reflection in the mirror, looking for instructions. Her cheeks were puffy, probably from the beer, and her eyes were just glassy enough to pass as tired. The concealer she'd dabbed onto the spots around her mouth had started to fade. She quickly reapplied it, digging around in her make-up bag for whatever else she could find.

'I love your outfit,' said a soft voice to her left.

Rose turned to see a pretty petite blonde, wearing a white vest, white skinny jeans and pumps with the Chanel logo on them. On her arm was a Louis Vuitton tote bag.

'Thank you, I like yours too,' she lied. Rose was still in her work clothes, which consisted of the usual mix of a loose-fitting shirt over a short denim skirt and black boots. There was nothing special about her outfit.

'It's so interesting,' the woman added.

'It's what?'

'You just look so cool,' she quipped, smiling sweetly.

'Thank you.'

Rose didn't understand the compliment, and was fairly certain it was an insult coming from someone dressed like Harrods had thrown up over her, but the brief interjection was enough to stabilise the situation. Rose would go back into the party and tell Clara she was going home; she couldn't afford to piss her off by pulling a French exit.

She waded through the crowd, which had grown so significantly it was now impossible to get through it without her arms bumping into others. 'Sorry, sorry,' she kept muttering with every bash of flesh, keeping her eyes firmly fixed on the floor in case one of those arms belonged to Milo.

Finally, she could hear Clara and looked up to see her gesticulating at someone. But by the time he'd come into her field of vision, it was too late.

'Milo, you know Rose. From Firehouse?' Clara said, smiling as the man now standing inches away from Rose turned around to face her.

'Hello, Rose from Firehouse,' he said, smiling.

She stared back at him silently, searching his face for recognition. But there was none. Just those pale eyes looking into hers like they were doing her a favour. Rose said nothing and continued to watch his expression, waiting for it to do something to signal her existence. But after a few seconds, she couldn't really see his face any more. The picture had gone blurry, like she'd taken out her contact lenses. It was just that familiar series of shapes again, something that might have resembled a nose but instead had become an oblong weapon pointing directly at her. It was next to a spherical object, the curvature of which was now grazing against her cheek, pushing into it harder and harder.

'Rose, get in. My followers will lose their minds,' Clara's voice said in slo-mo.

'Of course,' said Milo, his laugh morphing into a grumbled roar that filled the room. And then his hand was on her back, warm and damp through her shirt, pulling her in next to him. She could smell his sweat. Someone somewhere shouted 'Smile!' And then all she saw were the rough outlines of bodies, circling around her, looking, shouting, vying to be coloured in.

Rose knew what was about to happen. She could feel her balance tipping over. He was standing right next to her. No. No. No.

The last thing she remembered was the camera flash piercing behind her eyes.

When Rose woke up, she was outside a hotel room, slumped against the wall and next to a pool of vomit that could only have been her own.

'Are you all right?' an unfamiliar male voice asked.

Rose turned her head as much as she could, her vision blurred by tears. When she saw it wasn't Milo, she turned back towards the pool of vomit and, feeling a pang in her throat, leaned over further as yellow bile spilled out in front of her.

'Oh, God, poor you,' the voice continued. 'Don't worry about that, I'll call someone to clean it up. Do you want me to order you a taxi home?'

Rose's stomach twisted; she had been sick so rarely in her life that it wasn't a feeling she'd ever been able to get used to. The fact that it was happening now, in what looked like a very expensive hotel and in front of a stranger that may or may not be friends with Milo Jax, was a lot. She could vaguely remember Clara saying something about going to another afterparty nearby hosted by someone called Robbie or Bobby. Judging from the booming sounds of 'Despacito' trilling from behind her, Rose assumed this was that party. And Clara had somehow managed to get her here. Given the circumstances, it was looking likely that she'd lasted a few minutes before trying to take herself home and winding up in the corridor. At least they weren't playing Milo's music.

Rose needed to go home. But as the raw physical pain of vomiting started to ease in between purges, a different impulse fought through. Milo had seen her and said her name, even if he acted like it was the first time he'd ever heard it. She had not imagined that night and she certainly had not imagined seeing him just now. He knew her. It happened. And Milo wasn't going to get away with pretending that it hadn't.

But Milo was not the one outside the hotel room with her, checking to see if she was all right after she'd presumably fainted and started spontaneously being sick. This man had. Perhaps he was Robbie or Bobby. It felt rude to ask.

If Rose went home now, it would only send the message to Milo that he had had an effect on her. That he had the power to hurt her. Rose could not allow that to happen.

'No, I don't want a taxi. I just drank too much but it's all gone now. Thank you,' she finally replied once she was sure there was no vomit left to expel.

'All right then. You want to come back inside? Someone called Clara was flapping around earlier, asking if Rose had gone home. I'm guessing that's you.'

'Yes. That is me. I think,' said Rose, picking herself up off the floor and standing to face Robbie or Bobby.

'Oh, well, she has been talking very highly of you,' he replied, looking at Rose in the way she wished Milo had.

'Yeah, well, she's probably very high.'

He laughed. 'Come on, I've already called housekeeping to sort out this mess. Let's go back inside.'

There must have been forty people in the room, which soon turned out to be a suite comprising three bedrooms, two bathrooms and a capacious living space. The traditional Regency decor that lined the walls jarred with the scene that was taking place within it. Cliques of three or four people were dotted around, some smoking out of windows, others sitting snug on mid-century sofas, touching, kissing and entertaining whoever was looking.

Clara was thrilled when she saw Rose. 'If I'd known you were such a lightweight I wouldn't have given you a drop!' she exclaimed, wrapping her arms around her tightly. 'Oh,' she said pulling away, her nose wrinkling. 'You smell a little bit like vomit, my love.'

Rose lifted up the bottom of her shirt, which she had only just seen was now stained with smudges of orange and brown.

'Right, come here,' said Clara, ushering Rose into one of the bathrooms and promptly spraying her with various fragrances that were lining a sunken tub that had a TV screen embedded into the wall next to it. Clara's nose was covered with white specks. Rose flicked them off as Clara scrubbed at her shirt with damp toilet roll that was flaking onto the floor. Unfortunately, the stains were not removable. So, without asking, Clara tugged Rose's shirt off, leaving her exposed in the grey and white Calvin Klein sports bra she'd bought three years ago.

'Right, remind me to take you lingerie shopping,' said Clara, throwing the shirt in the bin and giving her the white blazer she'd been wearing earlier in the night. 'Don't you dare vomit on this,' she said, sliding Rose's arms through it. 'It's Dolce.'

Rose nodded. 'Did you buy it?'

'Don't be ridiculous,' she replied. 'There,' she added, buttoning up the blazer and stepping back to admire her work. 'Oh, yes. Now we're ready.'

At art college, one of the things painters are taught about at length is triptychs. Comprising three pieces or panels, a triptych forms one larger painting. Sometimes each of the panels is created so they can stand alone; then the others are viewed as complementary pieces. Occasionally, though, the panels rely heavily on one another to create one comprehensive narrative. There are other forms, such as diptychs and quadriptychs, where there are two or four panels, respectively. But the triptych, Rose was taught, was at the upper echelons of multi-faceted artwork because of how it pertains to the power of three. There is a clear beginning, middle and end, with each new painting bringing depth to its predecessor and allowing it to be seen in an entirely new light. Some of Francis Bacon's most famous paintings are triptychs. The most horrifying is generally considered to be *Three Studies for Figures at the Base of a Crucifixion*. Set against a harsh orange background, the work features three anthropomorphic creatures, each more tortured than the next. In the first, the creature is severely distorted; you can just about make out its snarl. In the second, you can see a mouth baring its teeth aggressively towards the viewer, like an animal identifying its prey. The third creature is the most violent, its mouth open beyond the constraints of human capability, teeth visible alongside a single ear. Look long enough and you'll hear its scream.

There had been many interpretations of the piece since it was first exhibited in 1945. Some scholars linked it to the Holocaust, while others claimed it illustrated the fear of nuclear weapons. But Bacon himself said the creatures represented the Furies from Greek mythology, Goddesses of vengeance that punished men who disrupted the natural order. It was Rose's favourite painting.

Spending time with Clara was like looking at a triptych: she was someone whose self had been splintered into three parts. In the first panel, you'd see her Instagram profile. The identity anyone could see if they looked her up online. Rose would use swathes of gorgeous yellow shades to represent this. Something you'd look at and find it hard to tear yourself away from because of how attractive it was. In the second, you'd see something similar but with a bit of bite, brushstrokes of darker colours edging closely to the light. This was the side of Clara that Rose had seen over breakfast. Someone who was struggling to maintain the flawless facade she'd spent years creating. In this panel, Rose thought, you'd also see a mouth, somehow, like Bacon's anamorphic creature. If you looked from far away, the expression would appear as a smile. When you got closer, it would turn into a snarl.

Then the final panel. This was a side Rose would never see, she reasoned, because of how deep within Clara it resided. In this painting, Rose would use every colour available to her. But she would blend them all together, flagrantly and messily, so that they merged into some sort of dark brown sludgy shade that appeared almost black. The only part of the painting that would appear light would be the mouth, which, like Bacon's, would be stretched open.

The line was long. It stretched from one corner of the Testino book to the other, right from Kate Moss's eyebrow to her lower lip. Rose watched in silence as Clara giggled, squatting down on the floor and inhaling the entire white powdered substance in less than three seconds.

'I don't think I've ever seen a woman do a fat line like that before,' said the man standing behind Rose.

'Neither have I,' she replied, still staring at Clara.

When Clara flicked her hair upwards, her eyes met Rose's. Beads of sweat speckled down her smooth forehead. Her lips were glossed and full, her cheekbones protruding more noticeably. Her pupils were enormous.

'Want one?' she asked Rose, waving the bag of powder in front of her face. Rose had done coke once before at Glastonbury Festival with Luce, who had assured her it was 'just like taking a really strong espresso'. It kept her awake all night. Rose had spent two hours hyperventilating in her tent alone, freezing cold and with Luce's sleeping bag on top of hers. Luce crawled back to the tent at 10.30 a.m. after having fallen asleep at Stone Circle. With all this in mind, there were many reasons for Rose to turn down the drugs. She ran through all of them as she bent her body forward, placed one finger over her left nostril, and breathed in as hard and fast as she could.

It was 2.43 a.m. when Rose finally checked her phone. There were too many notifications to scroll through; a lot of messages that might have been from Luce. But all she could focus on was that none of them were from Milo, so she turned it off and put it back in her jacket pocket. The night had faded into a series of indistinguishable monologues from strangers, bathroom whisper sessions with new friendships formed over nothing in particular, and more visits to the Testino book. Rose's heart had never pulsated so fiercely; it was angry with her. She dulled the guilt with whisky because it was the only alcohol she could find. She'd been pretending to like it for so many hours now the way it singed the back of her throat had become almost enjoyable.

Clara had barely come up for air. She had been stationed in one of the bedrooms for most of the night, reclined on a king-size bed with her legs propped up against its plush pink velvet headboard, entertaining any and all who visited her. Rose had overheard her speaking to a director about a film based on her life. Clara would play herself, she suggested, because she had once played Tallulah in *Bugsy Malone* at school. This was enough to convince the director, who immediately broke into a wobbly rendition of 'My Name is Tallulah'. Rose had not heard her mention Mark once, and whenever someone at the party asked if Clara had a boyfriend, she'd quickly assure them that she was single and ask if they had any single men for her.

Rose had long ago given up trying to talk to her about StandFirst. But she had not given up on looking for Milo, even though it was far easier to keep looking for more cocaine. 'Very fat lines!' as the man racking them up kept announcing each time, like he was introducing a lion tamer. She didn't know for certain if Milo was even here, which was probably the point. With the sheer volume of people squashed into this hotel suite, and all its various dimly lit rooms and corners, it was the perfect place for hide-and-seek. Rose figured it was a good time to play.

Milo wasn't in any of the bedrooms. After discovering two women having sex in one of the bathrooms, Rose headed to the second, shushing the sound of her heartbeat. Her fingertips fizzed at the prospect of finding him. She felt more energised than ever: armed with enough substances to fight whatever battle was waiting for her.

Rose could hear muffled men's voices inside as she approached the door of the bathroom, and swiftly pushed it open with such force she fell forward.

'F-fuck,' she stuttered, suddenly feeling the effect of all that she'd consumed. She steadied herself, hands pressed firmly against a cold marble floor.

'Rose?' asked a man's voice.

It took her a couple of seconds to realise she'd won whatever game she'd set out to play. She looked up, body on all fours, her face so close to his it was tempting to try and bite some of it off.

There were two other men in the bathroom, both sitting in a sunken tub, passing a plump joint between them, the smell of weed suddenly entering Rose's system, blending with everything else inside her.

'Are you okay?' asked one of the men in the bathtub.

'I'm fine,' said Rose, swatting his hand away and hoisting herself up. 'I need to talk to you,' she said, pointing at Milo, who was sitting cross-legged on the floor.

'Right, sure. What's up?' he asked, smiling.

Rose shot a look at the two others. They took the hint and left.

'Good luck, mate,' one of them chirped as he shut the door behind him.

'Do you know who I am?'

'Sorry?'

'Answer the fucking question.'

'I said your name, didn't I? Rose.'

She resisted the urge to stamp her foot.

'Why have you been ignoring me?' she said, feeling her throat clogging up.

'What?'

'On Instagram.'

'I don't remember seeing a message from you. It might have been someone on my team that opened it if you sent me one.'

'Someone on your team?' Rose held her hands up to mock quotation marks as she repeated his words.

'Yes, Rose. Someone on my team,' Milo parroted.

'Stop calling me that.'

'Isn't it your name?'

'You tell me.'

'Are you okay? Do you need me to get you a car home?'

Rose made a sound that didn't quite pass as anything capable of coming from human vocal cords; it was a cross between a wail and a howl.

Milo laughed. 'It's good to see you,' he said, standing up with an air of finality and heading towards the door.

'What happened that night?' Rose heard herself ask.

He turned around, a flash of intrigue. 'What's that supposed to mean?'

'There are parts that I can't remember.'

'I think they call that being drunk, Rose.'

The fizzing intensified. 'Stop saying my fucking name.'

'Whoa. Relax.' He was now holding up both hands at her, like she was pointing a gun to his head.

'No. You fucking relax,' she said louder than intended. It was hard to stop now. 'I . . . I . . . do you have any idea what you've done to me?'

'Okay, time to leave I think,' Milo said, chuckling as he opened the bathroom door, letting himself out. The men from the bathtub were waiting outside like bodyguards – perhaps they were. Rose stayed still, staring back at them. They patted Milo on the back and walked off, laughing.

SIX

There were fifteen missed calls when Rose woke up. Three of them from Minnie. The rest were from Luce. Fuck: *girls' night.* An instant wave of nausea hit her, like someone was dancing on her gag reflex. She ran through all the excuses she could offer up. It was a work thing. She had to convince Clara to come to the event or she'd lose her job. Her phone temporarily glitched. She fell down one of those giant unexplained holes in the street and lost all sense of time and space for the exact amount of time they were meant to be having their girls' night. Rose sighed. There were no excuses. There was just Milo.

Flashbacks of him in the bathroom played out like a mental tableau. The dancing turned to stamping. Rose groaned and muffled her face into the pillow, trying to work out a plan of action. Luce first. The best thing to do was ring her. FaceTime would work well; it was harder to be angry over FaceTime. Rose's face filled the screen; she looked haggard, all sunken eyes and grey skin. She would eat something green after the call.

Luce answered on the second ring and Rose's face shrunk to the right-hand corner.

'What the actual fuck?'

Even in her anxious, post-break-up state, Luce still looked like she'd just returned from a two-week holiday in Barbados. Her skin was so poreless and clear that it shone; her lips pink and pouted.

'Luce, please. I'm so sorry.'

Rose put her fingers to her forehead, pausing for a few seconds.

'I don't even know where to start. Can I just explain please?'

Luce scoffed. 'Try me.'

'It was a work thing, okay?'

Silence.

Rose started from the beginning, clear and clinically, as if pitching to an investor. StandFirst. Firehouse's flailing readership figures. The importance of social media influencer marketing. Clara.

'All I'm hearing is that you ditched me to hang out with some hashtag hoe.'

'Minnie asked me to try and convince her to come to this launch, it wasn't like that. I promise.'

'Yeah? Why do you look so hungover then? And why were you online on WhatsApp at two a.m.?'

'What were you doing up at two a.m.?'

'Rereading old messages to George.'

'Luce, you really should stop—'

'You are in absolutely no position to lecture me right now.'

'You're right. I'm really sorry.'

'Are you going to tell me the truth?'

Rose's throat went dry. There was no way that Luce knew about Milo.

'What do you mean?'

'Oh, come off it, Rose. I know Milo was there.'

'What?'

'Are you dating him? Is that what this is about?'

'Of course not.' Rose could feel her eyes watering.

'I saw pap photos of him leaving some hotel last night. And according to Clara's Instagram Stories, she was also at that hotel. It's all over the *Daily Mail*. They think they're dating.'

'Oh God.'

'I knew this would happen.'

'Luce, look, this isn't what you think.'

'Whatever. I didn't end up coming to London after you ignored all of my calls so I'm going to be at home for a bit longer. I'll see you when I see you.'

'I really miss—' but before Rose could finish her sentence, Luce was gone and she was staring at the ghost of herself again.

She still had another hour before she could get away with making something up about a broken boiler and working from home. The only thing to do now was turn her phone off, set an alarm for 9.29 a.m., and go back to sleep.

When the alarm went off, Rose could only see Milo's face. He was grinning, looming over her like a demonic clown. And the laughter. God, the laughter; it ran around her head like a siren. Rose shook her head and closed her eyes until it all dissolved. Everything was thudding steadily, her throat raspy from the cigarettes she must have chain-smoked at some point. She replied to Minnie, who'd left several concerned messages.

Any luck re Clara? read one.

Rose? All okay?

Rose, I'm worried. Please call me back.

Rose closed her eyes and tried to remember if she had spoken to Clara about the party. They seemed to have spoken about absolutely everything else, like how she was going to leave Mark and become a hatha yoga teacher in Ubud. And how she would make that film about her life with the terrible singer as the director. And she would cast Tara Reid as her best friend to rehabilitate her image.

Rose couldn't recall talking to her about Milo, which meant she probably had not.

She could remember that Clara was the one who had found her on the bathroom floor. And after that, which could have been minutes or hours later, they had somehow ended up in a kebab shop stuffing cheesy chips into their mouths faster than they could breathe. Clara kept calling her a lightweight – did she say something about a drinking problem? It was probably one of the only times in Rose's life she'd be grateful someone assumed she was an alcoholic.

She decided to text Clara.

Hey. Last night was fun and strange. Thank you for taking care of me.

Clara replied immediately: *Of course! Excited to see you at the launch.*

Okay. So she wasn't a completely useless person. Perhaps she'd raised the question of the launch in between mouthfuls of cheesy chips. Or in between drags of cigarettes – that was it! They'd found a full packet of Marlboro Lights on the floor as they left the party and smoked them one after the other on the way to the kebab shop that Clara was adamant they visit. She said something about being in disguise, which might have explained why she was wearing a baseball cap that definitely wasn't hers. Rose decided it was best not to ask questions about how or why she'd managed to get her to agree to come to the launch and just accept that she'd done her job, albeit in a slightly unconventional way.

Looking forward to seeing you then, she replied.

Rose called Minnie back but there was no answer.

Yes, all good. Clara is in, Rose wrote on WhatsApp. *Sorry for being out of comms all day yesterday. I'm going to work from home today if that's all right. We have someone coming round to look at the boiler.*

Great! Well done. Fine by me, Minnie replied.

Later, Rose tapped through Clara's Instagram Stories. The photos from the hotel had been deleted, presumably because of the *Daily Mail* article. All that remained was a picture of her smooth, scarlet gel manicure posted this morning that surely must have been old. *Thank you so much @NailsByFlo for this gorgeous shellac mani*, read the caption.

Rose typed Luce's name into the search bar. She scrolled through Luce's profile until she reached her very first posts (this didn't take long seeing as Luce barely used Instagram except to look at photos of sausage dogs and baby goats). At the very bottom, she recognised three overly saturated snaps of sunsets from their trip to Luce's family's holiday home in the south of France. There was a picture of the two of them together that Rose could remember Luce's mum taking. They were sitting on a bench perched on top of the mountain their house was on, arm in arm, facing out towards a pink and orange sky.

I'm so sorry. I miss you. Rose sent the message within seconds and stared at her screen, waiting for the tick to go blue. But this time, it stayed grey.

There was an obvious solution to all this: tell Luce the truth about Milo. Rose wasn't sure why she still felt compelled to keep it a secret. It wasn't as if she owed him anything, or that telling her was going to somehow make its way back to him. Still, every time she felt the urge to be upfront with Luce about it, something would stop her, a voice in the back of her head that was particularly loud today. Sometimes it would tell her she was only obsessing over Milo because he was famous, or that no one forced her to go to his house. Other times it called her a whore. The worst was when it said she'd made the whole thing up.

Are you still going then? Luce's reply flashed up on her phone.

Rose gasped with relief. *To what?*

OMG. The hen, Rose?

Oh fuck.

Rose had archived the 'Give her a shot, she's tying the knot' group months ago because the notifications had become incessant. Pippa's hen do seemed a lifetime away then; why did she need to vote on which penis game was the most family friendly for Pippa's mum six months in advance? Or at all? Rose had not seen Pippa Ver de Veux in two years. They were part of the same friendship group at school, in so much as they sat around the same tables at lunch and went to the same parties on weekends. But they would struggle to get through any kind of meeting if it was just the two of them. It wasn't that Rose didn't like Pippa; she was fine. She was just very different from Rose. Loud, crude and always in a never-ending cycle of sexual escapades, she was the group's unofficial ringleader. She was certainly the most sexually adventurous, having famously had a threesome with two boys when they were in the sixth form. Hence the irony that, out of everyone, she was the one getting married first.

Pippa had met her fiancé, Mike, at Glastonbury. Rose had only met him once. An insurance broker with a permanently ruddy face and protruding belly, he was hardly in line with the bevvy of models and actors Pippa had bedded over the years. But maybe that was a good thing. And it wasn't like she needed to marry for money; Pippa came from a legal dynasty. Ver de Veux & Partners was a magic circle firm that had been in her family for decades. Whenever she told anyone she'd gone to school with a Ver de Veux, they were impressed.

They were 'pure-bred old money', as Luce would say. Pippa wasn't too obnoxious about it. Of course, there was the lack of self-awareness people have when they come from money like that – whenever they went shopping for clothes as teenagers in charity shops, Pippa would wait outside because she didn't like 'the smell of old clothes'. But, generally, she was kind and warm, if a little ignorant.

Did you forget about it? asked Luce.

Maybe.

You've been in your celebrity bubble for too long. Come back to the real world. Those notifications have been driving me mad.

Rose told herself that Luce had every right to be rude to her given the context; she was just grateful for the communication.

I might have archived the chat.

I'm not coming. Have fun.

Wait, what? Why can't you come?

Because my mum is hosting a garden fair here and I'm helping her out.

You're going to tell Jessie that you're trading a hen do for a garden fair?

No, obviously not. I'm going to tell her someone has died.

Isn't that bad karma?

Lol. Whatever's going to happen to me here can't be worse than what would happen at that hen do.

Luce and Pippa had a fractious relationship; it was surprising she'd even been invited to the wedding, let alone the hen. They'd been close growing up in the way wealthy families always are. But in year ten they had both fancied the same boy and things started to turn sour. They fell out for good when Pippa caught Luce giving him a blow job in the school theatre.

I don't know how I'll cope without you, said Rose.

You'll be fine.

When are you home? Rose asked.

Depends how long work lets me off for compassionate leave.

They gave you that because of the break-up?

No, I told them someone died.

I think you should probably stop doing that.

Rose was hoping for a laughter-face emoji. But nothing came. The ticks turned blue and Luce went offline.

They had only ever had one argument. It was when she'd just been dumped by Ed, and Luce was spending every night in the flat with George. Rose had politely mentioned a couple of times that she found it hard being around the two of them all the time but, as Luce eventually pointed out mid-argument, this was her flat and she could bring anyone she wanted to it. Things between them blew up one night when Rose came home crying because she had found out that Ed had a new girlfriend, and Luce asked her to spend the evening in her room because George was coming round to celebrate their anniversary. It turned into a vicious argument, with Rose accusing Luce of prioritising her relationship over their friendship and Luce accusing Rose of being self-absorbed.

Rose tried to point out that she paid rent to live there and it was her space, too, but after a while she couldn't even bother arguing. It was ultimately Luce's flat. And she was lucky she only charged her £500 a month (around half of what the room was worth). The fact they hadn't argued since was less about neither of them doing anything to piss the other off, it was more that the power dynamic between them had silenced Rose into submission whenever an issue arose. If Luce did or said something that annoyed her, it was easier to let it slide. And when roles were reversed, Rose would just apologise first and all would be resolved. This time felt like an exception.

Rose took a deep breath and un-archived the 'Give her a shot, she's tying the knot' group, scrolling for what felt like ten minutes until she reached the first message.

HEY GALS, thought I'd get this started finally. As you know, our darling Pips is getting married in September, and as Maid of Honour/Chief Bridesmaid, I've been tasked with arranging her HEN! THAT'S RIGHT, OUR FIRST HEN IS UPON US!

Save 15th July in your diaries immediately. Location is Pippy's mum's place aka 'the chat-veux'. Will be overnight. Personalised PJs.

Please let me know ASAP if you can't come so I can fill your spot. And transfer £250 to me by Monday so I can start organising food etc.

LOTS OF LOVE,
JD xxxxxx

The first bolt of anxiety came when Rose realised she hadn't paid. The second came when she saw Jessie had named and shamed her for this. The third came when she saw Jessie had done so again. Rose quickly started tapping out a message.

So sorry guys, have missed a lot. Yes, I'll be there. Paying you now, Jessie. Let me know what else I can bring.

Jessie started typing and a link to a Google spreadsheet appeared. Rose opened it on her phone, there were multiple tabs: FRIDAY, SATURDAY, SUNDAY, MISCELLANEOUS, PACKING LIST, GROUP RULES. Rose looked at as much of it as she could without accidentally typing something erroneous into one of the cells. The level of detail was impressive. Jessie had planned every moment, even down to appetite maintenance (SATURDAY: 12.45–13.45/MAX 14.00: A LIGHT LUNCH BUT DON'T EAT TOO MUCH BECAUSE WE HAVE TEA! SUGGESTED TO EAT AT 60% CAPACITY).

Thanks guys, she replied. *Can't wait.*

Rose flicked her thumb up and right to close WhatsApp. She tapped on Instagram. The app opened on a new post from Milo: a photograph of a plant in black and white that she recognised from the apartment last night. She must have unblocked and followed him when she got home last night, either to send an angry message or passive aggressively like all his posts.

Thankfully, she'd done neither of those things.

'For fuck's sake,' she whispered to herself.

Her finger hovered over the 'Message' button. She knew contacting Milo now would only make her feel worse. She knew that he would almost certainly not read it, let alone reply. And then Rose would turn her phone off, dig out the pasta that had been in the fridge for the better part of a week, and eat it while googling ways to work off the calories in pasta in thirty minutes.

But still she found herself writing the message, unable

to stop her fingers as she typed. *Hey, nice/weird to see you last night. Sorry, I was a bit drunk. How are you?*

Sent. Rose deleted the conversation from her inbox so that she could not un-send the message. She put her phone on Airplane mode and walked over to the fridge.

Rose only ever thought about her father when she was tired. Mostly, it happened on days like this, when she'd been out late the night before and had too much to drink. In this case, there was the added bonus of the large quantity of cocaine working its way through her system, which was slowly attacking every last blip of serotonin she possessed. Now she'd finished work and distraction was harder to come by, it wasn't Milo she was thinking about, it was the handful of memories she'd retained about Richard. Scenes projected themselves in her head, with different faces taking the role of her father each time. Sometimes he was a scruffy short man in need of a shave, his eyes dilated and elsewhere. Other times, he was a tall, suited business executive who talked with his hands. He'd left them at an odd time. No six-year-old knows who they'll become as an adult. But their development will be starting, personalities and traits taking form despite still being, quite objectively, a very small and helpless human, an innocent flimsy thing that needs and depends upon both of its parents. Lola had destroyed every last piece of evidence of Richard's existence after he'd left, leaving Rose to fill in the blanks with her imagination. She didn't even know his last name.

Lola had once invited a group of friends around to

vandalise the clothes he'd left behind. Rose could remember sucking on a strawberry Frube on the toilet seat while her mother and three other women poured red wine onto white shirts they'd piled up in the bath. There was one suit she could remember Lola saying Richard loved. Something about it being from Armani and belonging to his father. Rose recalled seeing one of her mother's friends hacking at it with a pair of gardening scissors, gleefully distributing pieces among the other women who swiftly threw them out of the bedroom window. And so they disposed of her father, blithely waving goodbye to all of his parts, leaving each piece of fabric to flutter aimlessly around London until it found somewhere to settle.

Rose was well-versed in all the clichés – women whose fathers had abandoned them were forever plagued by feelings of low self-worth and replicated that abandonment in their romantic relationships yada yada yada – and she hated that it all applied to her. She also hated that she couldn't watch *Mrs. Doubtfire* without hysterically sobbing. And that *The Parent Trap* was out of the question. Even *Taken* was a bit much.

All Lola had ever told Rose about Richard, besides how they met, was that he'd left the country. And that he'd probably moved somewhere with turtles because of his 'stupid childish obsession with fucking turtles'. To this day, if Lola saw anything turtle-related on TV or otherwise, she'd immediately launch into some sort of nonsensical diatribe against them: 'Cowards of the animal kingdom!' was one phrase she often returned to.

Whenever Rose tried to push for more information

about Richard, Lola would change the subject or find an excuse to leave the room. She had become an expert in the practice of avoiding all things Richard in the way one probably has to when someone shatters your entire world. It was for these reasons that Rose had never told Lola about the time she thought she'd seen him. It couldn't have been him, of course, because not only are there no turtles in London, or presumably rather few, but Rose could barely remember what Richard even looked like – any photos had been lost to Lola's coven. There was just something about the man's face. It must have been 2014. She was waiting outside a Pret near Luce's office to meet her for lunch when she noticed a man across the road with his arm wrapped around a much younger woman. His head was rolling back as he laughed and puffed on a cigarette with his free hand. It wasn't that his face looked familiar, although there was a slight ridge on his nose exactly where Rose had hers. It was the moment he turned to kiss the woman and then just as quickly turned away, his expression changing from one of elation to exasperation. It was as though the joy Rose had just seen left him all at once, if only for a moment. It was only a flash. Because seconds later, the woman said something that made him laugh again. But Rose recognised it immediately. It was a routine she had performed many times.

The most fully formed memory she had of her father didn't really involve him at all; his absence was integral to what happened. It was just before he left for good.

Lola had gone to Ibiza on a yoga retreat for the week, so it had been Rose and Richard at home. He would try to tie her hair into a high ponytail for school. But it would be so messy, with bits poking out everywhere, that Rose would untie it when she got out of the car and do it again herself. She never had the heart to tell him he had done it wrong.

That week, Rose remembered feeling like more of a thing on Richard's to-do list than his daughter. They'd walk the supermarket aisles for ready meals that she could microwave herself for dinner while he went out. There was macaroni cheese and hamburger and chips. But Rose's favourite was the tuna bake. It was the easiest one not to burn in the microwave.

Richard had gone out for the evening, leaving Rose and her tuna bake alone for a few hours. It was 9 p.m. and Richard was supposed to be home at 8.30 p.m. Rose tried to call him on the house phone but couldn't work out how to use it. She sat on the sofa and waited. Her mind started to race, wondering where her dad had gone. She worried that he might have been run over. How would Mum cope? How would she cope? Would this mean she would have to leave school? How would she tell people that her father had died? And then it became difficult to breathe. The air around her felt more dense, too thick to inhale. She felt desperate. The more she tried, the harder it became to catch her breath. She started to make sounds. Not shouting, because that didn't quite work. What came out was a sort of quiet yelp. Rose had dug her fingernails into the sofa either side of her legs, closed her eyes and prepared to die. Then she had felt someone grab her by the shoulders and she was in her father's arms, his heart beating against her cheek. Her breath returned and Rose opened her eyes.

'What happened?' she asked Richard.

'I don't know. I just came home and found you like this. Are you okay?'

'I think so,' she replied. 'It felt like I was dying.'

'You're not dying,' Richard said, his breath a mix of spirits and cigarettes. 'It will be all right. I'm here.'

And he was. For another week.

The comedown lasted for days. Rose would force herself out of bed, sit at her desk in silence for eight hours, pausing only to use the toilet or heat up some soup, and then come home, stare at her phone for a few hours on the sofa, and then do the same from bed. She tried ordering new bedsheets online but whenever she got to the payment part she always managed to talk herself out of spending the money. She'd tried calling Luce a few times but there was no answer. The only thing she achieved in those few days was racking up a dangerous number of hours of screen time, many of which were spent staring at her Instagram inbox. No, he hadn't messaged her.

By Friday evening, she was in urgent need of company. So she rang Lola.

'Hello, darling!'

'Hey, Mum.'

'How lovely to hear from you. How are you?'

'I'm fine. Are you around this evening?'

'I've got a spinning class. Would you like to come?'

'Oh, erm. When is it? I'm not sure I'd be up to that today.'

'No problem. We could do hot yoga instead?'

Hot yoga might help, Rose thought. She probably still had plenty of toxins left in her body that could be sweated out.

'Sure, hot yoga. I'll meet you there. Text me the details.'

'Great! See you then. Love you.'

'Love you.'

Rose lasted twenty minutes in the class. Lola was right, it was hot. Too hot. The second she walked through those doors into the candlelit studio, it felt suffocating. They were midway through something called the dancer's pose when Rose felt her limbs collapse beneath her and she tumbled into a sinewy woman to her right.

'Shh!' the woman snapped as Lola turned around and helped her daughter up.

The class only got harder from there. Watching Lola helped; her mother was dreadful at yoga. She was surprisingly flexible for a fifty-six-year-old, stretching her limbs out and moving into the splits with ease. But she seemed incapable of following instructions, elegantly gesturing her arms into the air like she was performing on stage while everyone else was tilted down to the floor in triangle pose.

They were in the middle of another complicated pose when Rose heard a moaning sound coming from the corner of the room. Relieved it wasn't Lola, she looked closer to see a young woman in a pink sports bra panting with pleasure. Was she . . .? Could she be . . .?

'Congratulations, darling!' cooed Lola, prompting the room to burst into a fit of girlish giggles.

'Mum!' Rose shushed.

'What?' Lola whispered back. 'It's quite common! Why do you think I started doing hot yoga?'

Later, they sat on wooden benches in the reception area drinking complimentary herbal tea that the receptionist assured Lola had been brewed on site.

'I'm not having any pesticides this week, that's all,' her mother smiled back as she took a glass for herself and Rose.

'I don't think there are ever any pesticides in herbal tea, Mum,' said Rose.

'You never know, Bitsy.'

Lola was halfway through a story about her hairdresser's dog who had befriended the neighbourhood rabbit when Rose found herself interrupting.

'Can we talk about Dad?'

Unease stretched across Lola's face. She took a large sip of tea.

'Bitsy,' she paused. 'Really?'

'Please.'

'What do you want to know now?'

'Where is he?'

'I don't know,' Lola replied, eyes fixed on the tea in front of her.

'You must have some idea. Surely there's information on

the bank statements from the money he sends? A country? A tropical island? Literally anything.'

'There is information on the bank statements, yes.'

'Well? Where is he then?'

'Please don't go looking for him.'

'He's my dad!'

'Do you know how hard I have worked to protect you from him?'

Rose softened, leaning back in her chair to offer up some space as her mother hardened.

'How much I had to sacrifice?' she continued. 'Why would you want to go running to him when all he's ever done is abandon you? He left you,' she paused. 'He left us. But I'm here. And I'm not going anywhere.'

'I know,' replied Rose.

'Isn't that enough?'

'Maybe, I don't know. Don't daughters need fathers?'

'No, Rose,' Lola replied, firmer and more resolute now. 'There are some fathers they need to be kept away from.'

*

The office felt busier than usual when Rose returned to work. This often happened when an important event was coming up: eager freelancers and interns would fill the Firehouse halls, clipboards in tow, keen to impress the bosses in the hope they'd be hired full time. They almost never were unless they were related to an editor or publisher.

Rose had not spoken to Clara since she'd texted to say she'd be at the launch. But Fraser had emailed Minnie to confirm her attendance. So she had obviously done something right.

'Good work, Rose,' she had said when the email came through.

And though Rose wasn't entirely sure what work she had done, unless you counted getting drunk and taking drugs with a VIP guest, she accepted the praise and bought herself the expensive hummus and a bouquet of red roses on the way home that day.

Lola had always filled the flat with them when she was growing up. 'Roses for my Rose,' she would chirp on Saturday afternoons, lining the kitchen with jugs of whatever bunch she'd picked up on the way home from her shift at the gift shop.

Rose was still glowing from her professional success when she walked into the team meeting the next morning.

'Now that we know Clara is coming, we need to refine the guest list and we need to confirm our performer,' Minnie said as everyone settled around the table.

'I've been working on Milo Jax,' Annabelle chimed.

'What?' Rose had managed to momentarily erase this information from her brain. 'To the launch, you mean?'

'Yes! I told you, remember?' Annabelle replied with a knowing smile.

'Yes, sorry.' She'd completely forgotten about screaming in poor Annabelle's face.

'Don't worry, I'm overseeing it all,' added Oliver.

'We got close to confirming it the other day but it's proving difficult to organise transport,' added Annabelle.

'I see, I see,' tutted Minnie.

'He's in London right now,' said Rose, without thinking. 'I mean, he was, last week.'

'How do you know that?' asked Oliver.

'I must have seen a pap picture in one of the tabloids. I don't know.'

He scoffed. 'Sure.'

'As you guys seem to be close, Rose, I would really appreciate your help on this one,' said Annabelle.

'Yes, why don't you help Annabelle, Rose?' said Oliver, smiling.

'We are not close,' Rose said firmly. 'Of course, Annabelle. What do you need?'

'Joss Bell has been ignoring my last few emails. Would you mind just following up for me? I can loop you in with my thread so far.'

'Okay, no problem.'

'I could just do it—' said Oliver.

'No,' snapped Minnie. 'She hasn't been replying to you either. Let them handle this please.'

Oliver let out an irritable sigh.

'Brilliant! Thank you.' Annabelle practically leapt out of her seat, quickly tousling her fingers through her hair and flipping it all onto one side like a posh jack-in-the-box.

Talk turned to the seafood buffet. There would be calamari, of course. Prawn cocktail, because it photographed well and the pink would match the decor.

'Are we sure about the seafood thing?' asked Oliver. 'I mean, I don't eat it because I'm allergic but even so I'm sure there will be other people who are allergic. And also . . . it's a fashion show. Do we really want it to be so . . . fishy?'

'I have pushed back on the sodding seafood reception every goddamn day,' sighed Liz, her head in her hands.

'As have I,' said Minnie, smiling. 'Jasper is convinced it's time to reinvent the prawn cocktail. What was it he called it?' She turned to Liz.

'The kitten heel of the canapé world.'

'Right, yes, that was it.'

'Jesus Christ,' said Oliver, rolling his eyes.

'Clara will take some good photos of it, won't she?' added Annabelle.

'Yes,' Rose replied. 'She can make anything look good.'

'Right, let's discuss our high-risk aversion strategies,' said Minnie.

This was always a highlight of pre-event planning meetings. The team would go through all the various things that could go wrong before, during and after the event, each one more absurd than the next. Then they would come up with tactics on how to avoid and deal with them. For StandFirst's launch, the risks were heightened because it wasn't just a cocktail reception, it was also a fashion show. That meant there would be more people involved and therefore more high-risk scenarios. Minnie read through the standard list, which included key people not showing up, key people being disorderly (drunk or on drugs), and key people making impossible demands they could not fulfil.

'Sorry, who exactly are the non-key people?' asked Annabelle earnestly.

'Oh, no one gives a toss about them,' said Oliver.

'The majority of attendees, to be honest,' clarified Minnie. 'Basically anyone we don't put on the tip sheet. So managers, publicists, plus-ones . . . you know.'

Annabelle nodded and scribbled something down on a notepad.

Then came concerns about the sponsor, which basically amounted to how to avoid pissing them off. The range of things in this category were vast and largely depended on the individual sponsor, how much money they'd spent on the event, and if anyone working for the company was friends with anyone at Firehouse. No one at Jimson & James was in any way associated with anyone at Firehouse, which was one of the reasons why everyone was so vexed they'd been chosen as the sponsor at all.

The truth was that the luxury labels more commonly associated with Firehouse (the Pradas and Guccis of the world) didn't want to spend their money on publishing companies anymore. All of the budget they had was being invested in influencers. This was what made StandFirst's launch so vital. It was a way of modernising Firehouse and showing advertisers that it and, crucially, its magazines were still relevant in the digital age. That all of it still mattered.

Then there were the more detailed and specific risks. Rose had never worked on an event with a fashion show before. But Minnie used to work in-house for a major Italian designer so this was her wheelhouse.

'Sometimes models don't show up,' she began. 'That shouldn't happen this time seeing as we're paying them from a commercial budget as opposed to an editorial one. But still, you never know.'

'What were the fashion models like?' asked Annabelle.

Minnie raised an eyebrow. 'Hungry.'

'Didn't one of them faint backstage at a show once?' asked Oliver.

'Actually there were two of them. And that happened more than once. But the less we say about that the better.'

'Is the cotton wool and orange juice thing true?' Annabelle asked.

'I remember the first time I saw a model in real life,' said Oliver wistfully as he leaned back in his chair twirling a custard cream between two fingers. 'It was at London Fashion Week and I'd snuck into a show with a friend. I swear to God, those women. Beautiful but my God. They are bones and air.'

'It will never change,' sighed Minnie. 'Hopefully, we shouldn't have any issues like that this time because the models we've employed are not models,' she said.

'No, they're definitely not,' scoffed Oliver.

Liz read out the line-up of the not-models. There were twelve in total, and each would be styling themselves, arriving in an outfit that was entirely second-hand, either sourced from vintage shops or hand-me-downs.

'Are we getting approval of the outfits beforehand?' asked Minnie.

'Yes, I've asked them all to send photos,' confirmed Liz.

'God, yeah, imagine if one of them turned up in a mesh bikini or something,' said Oliver.

'Jimson will need to approve what they're wearing too,' added Minnie.

'Of course. Do you think Izabel will want to see them too?' asked Liz.

'Oh yes, absolutely,' Minnie nodded.

Izabel DuPont was a senior editor at *MODE* who had been appointed editor of StandFirst. She was responsible for collating the editorial for the website and had been chosen by Jasper to head up the launch. Rose had never met her. But she had stood next to her in a lift once and because it was such a small space, and it seemed odd not to, Rose said hello. Izabel must not have heard her. She was one of the most notoriously terrifying women in the company. With long blonde hair that fell to her waist and a razor-sharp fringe, she always looked more like someone who belonged in the magazine's pages as opposed to its offices. Her outfits were usually a mix of loose-fitting collared shirts in either blue or white, structured rigid denim jeans or tailored trousers and a black tailored blazer. All of it would usually be from Celine, as Rose had gleaned from Izabel's Instagram (50,000 followers) and was often accessorised with a small Chanel handbag. She was very beautiful. She was very thin. She was French.

'Has Izabel sent over the editorial for the launch yet?' asked Oliver.

'No, she hasn't actually, let me see if we can get that sent over,' replied Minnie.

'How are we supposed to PR a website when we have no idea what's even going to be on it yet?' he added, now building a small tower out of clementine peel.

'They've given us a general brief, which is that its content is geared towards young millennials and Generation Z.'

'But what does that even mean?' he asked.

'Your guess is as good as mine. But I think it will be

more like political commentary, fashion op-eds, a bit of pop culture . . . that kind of thing. Also, Rose, Fraser has asked if Clara can be profiled for the website as part of her fee.'

'Sure. That makes sense.'

'I have passed Fraser onto Izabel's team. So they can deal with that.'

'What about responsibilities on the night?' asked Oliver.

'I was just about to get to that,' replied Minnie firmly. 'Oliver, you'll be handling the red carpet arrivals.'

'Of course. Who else?' he said smugly.

'I don't know what you're so pleased about,' said Liz. 'The talent is extremely meagre.'

'Still,' he smiled. 'Great for networking.'

'Yes,' said Minnie. 'But we don't have any super VIPs. Unless we get Milo, of course. Annabelle and Rose, you'll look after the performer, whoever he, or she, is.'

They both nodded.

'If it's Milo, don't you think it would make more sense for me to take care of him?' asked Oliver.

'That would be absolutely fine with me,' said Rose.

'Nope,' replied Minnie. 'This is Rose's opportunity, Oliver. Not yours. Besides, Joss seems to be the only publicist that doesn't favour you over everyone else.'

'Fine, whatever,' he said, continuing to fiddle with his notepad.

'Do we have a backup in case we can't get Milo?' asked Rose.

'Not yet. But I'm sure if we can't get him we'll just rope someone else in at the last minute. There's always some desperate D-list musician hanging around in the wings,' said Liz. 'I have a list on my phone.'

'For the love of God, please do not share that list with anyone,' said Minnie.

'Yes, yes, I know,' nodded Liz.

'We also need to set up a meeting with Izabel,' said Minnie. 'And then another one with Michael.'

Michael was the publisher of *MODE* and had also been given the job of publisher for StandFirst, which was bizarre given that he was in his mid-fifties and a raging alcoholic. Minnie often excluded him from meetings, staging fake ones with just him, her and Oliver, so that he wouldn't realise he wasn't being included in the real meetings, which he never did because he was always too drunk to notice.

Izabel had refused to have meetings with him anymore because she claimed they always made her clothes smell of vodka. 'The leather that Celine uses really holds on to the smell of alcohol,' she once told Minnie in an email.

The meeting concluded and Annabelle cornered Rose.

'I really appreciate you helping me,' she said, smiling sweetly.

'You're welcome,' Rose replied. 'And I'm sorry about the other day. I get weird when I'm tired.'

'Don't worry about it,' Annabelle replied. 'For what it's worth, I think you guys would make a great couple.'

'What?'

'Oh nothing, I just mean . . . I don't know what I meant. Sorry. I'm just so excited!'

'Annabelle. I really need to get back to this. I'll send that email, okay?'

'Amazing, thank you!'

Rose sat down at her desk and plugged in her headphones hoping everyone would leave her alone.

She opened Joss's last email to her and felt her insides contorting as she typed.

Hi Joss,
Hope all is well. Getting in touch because I'd love to know if Milo might be available to perform at the launch of our new supplement, StandFirst, on 20 July. Appreciate it's very last minute but we've spotted a gap in his tour schedule and wondered if we might be able to make something work.
Let me know if you might be interested and I can pass on further details.
Kindest,
Rose.

After work that day, Rose left the press office without a word and went straight into the second-floor bathroom, heading for the last cubicle at the end of the row. She sat with the toilet seat down, closed her eyes and pictured herself standing alone in an empty field. She opened her mouth and let it out, imagining a sound louder than any human could possibly make. Her fingers curled, digging into her legs, her face contorted until it hurt, every single fibre in her body fired up to amplify the scream. She let it continue until hot, globular tears were rolling down her cheeks and her breathing resumed.

When Rose opened her eyes, she saw there was a small

sliver of blood on her thigh. Panicked, she quickly scanned the cubicle for the source of the cut she'd developed. A rogue piece of glass? An unexpected sharp corner somewhere on her way in? Only when she reached for toilet roll to clear it up did she see the blood on the nail of her index finger.

PART III

ONE

It was the night before the hen do and Rose could no longer avoid the 'Give her a shot, she's tying the knot' group. She had managed, so far, to get away with quietly observing the conversations from a safe distance: skimming past chatter about the 'Legs Bums and Tums' classes the hens had been going to together (Jessie: *Omg my thighs are literally THROBBING like hams after that*) but fulfilling any financial or logistical obligations when asked.

Since she'd last checked in, and duly paid the £250 as requested, without knowing what she was paying for because the bridesmaids had been 'sworn to secrecy', conversation had run from where you could find the cheapest feather boas to estimated salaries of each of the single men coming to the wedding. For a group of women with so much of their own money (mostly family wealth), they were also weirdly obsessed by how much, or how little, other people had.

The start time (9 a.m.) had also been fervently discussed.

Fran: *Hang on, 9am in Salisbury?*

Grace: *Lol are you sure?*

Jessie: *Yes – the bridesmaids are all staying in the *mystery* location the night before.*

Fran: *But the rest of us aren't . . .*

Jessie: *I know – sorry, babe. Just drive up early and stock up on caffeine! Or there's a 6.30am train from Waterloo.*

Rose could tell this exchange would have triggered a splinter WhatsApp group with Fran and a few others bitching about the early start.

Meanwhile, she still hadn't sorted a lift. The train would work but she'd be doing herself no favours by isolating herself from the group even more so early on. It would be something that was talked about, possibly in the splinter group.

Rose: *Sorry I've missed a bunch of messages. Does anyone have space in the car tomorrow from London?*

Jessie is typing.

Multiple people are typing.

No message came through. Rose sighed and put her phone back in her front pocket and walked home.

She plugged in her headphones and browsed through Spotify, looking for something happy and harmless, settling on a playlist titled '#FeelGoodFriday' compiled by someone called SmileySam that kicked off with 'Dog Days Are Over' by Florence + the Machine.

Three songs in came 'The Way You Are' by Milo Jax. She should have guessed. Normally, Rose would have quickly scrambled around for her phone to move on to the next song. But this time, she didn't skip it. She wanted to remember how she felt whenever she'd heard this song before, to listen to it as someone else, someone who'd never met Milo Jax, or even ever imagined meeting him. Someone to whom Milo Jax was, ultimately, a total stranger beyond the character he chose to present to the world. That person would probably enjoy this song. Rose found herself pressing next after the first chorus.

It would have been so much better if Luce were coming to the hen. She was her ally in that group. Since they'd left school, Rose had made as much of an effort as she could to distance herself from them, politely declining birthday parties and group dinner invitations. But weddings are, similar to funerals, among those rare sort of life events where it's generally accepted that you will invite people you no longer like or speak to. Rose didn't realise this rule also applied to hen dos.

She arrived home, walked straight to her bedroom and flopped onto her bed, allowing herself to lie still for several minutes before reaching for her phone.

Fran: *I have one space.*

Rose: *Oh really? That would be amazing. Thank you.*

Fran: *Meet outside Archway at 6am.*

Rose: *Ha, very early! Yes I will be there, coffee in hand.*

Fran: *Don't be late.*

Rose sent a thumbs up emoji.

Rose: *Do we need to bring anything?*

Jessie: *Packing list is in the doc!*

Rose searched for the document in her WhatsApp search bar and after wading through several colour-coded tabs found one titled PACKING LIST <3.

CLOTHING
Fancy black dress for dinner
Costume in the style of your allocated 'drunk Pippa'
Jeans suitable for chilling
Yoga pants/leggings for walking
Swimming costume (no bikinis please)
Warm socks or slippers
*Sleepwear will be provided

TECHNOLOGY
iPhone charger – please bring your own so no one has to borrow anyone's ;)
Portable speaker – in case ours dies!
Headphones – for your own leisure

TOILETRIES
Toothbrush
Toothpaste
Deodorant
Shampoo/conditioner
Make-up remover
Tweezers
Razor
Hair dryer
Hairbrush
Tampons
*Towels will be provided

ACCESSORIES
Anything remotely phallic you have in your house, including bananas but no brown ones please.

Rose: *What's my allocated drunk Pippa? Sorry, just catching up.*

Jessie: *In the doc!*

Rose returned to the document and, in the 'DRUNK PIPPA' tab found her name next to the words: 'Freshers' Week'.

Pippa had gone to Liverpool. Rose's allocation was surprisingly poor organisation from Jessie, who would have surely thought to give this role to one of Pippa's uni friends. It was impossible for Rose to know what Pippa was like during Freshers' Week; she had been set up for failure. She guessed Pippa would have gone to one of those awful traffic light parties during Freshers' Week. The ones where single people have to wear green, people in couples wear red, and those with so-called 'complicated situations' wear orange. It was a tiresome university ritual. Rose packed a green T-shirt and a green bobble hat Lola had given her.

The rest of the packing took all evening and by 11 p.m. Rose had sunk half a bottle of white wine she'd found in the fridge, trying hard to ignore the flavour of vinegar.

When she was done, she set her alarm for 5.30 a.m., wincing at the thought. She closed her eyes and tried to feel optimistic about the weekend.

What could have been ten minutes or ten seconds later, she opened her eyes and found herself opening Instagram. It was an unconscious habit by now. The message she had sent to Milo after that night with Clara was still not 'Seen'. Rose grunted.

She hated herself for googling him again, even more so

when his name was predicted the second she opened Safari on her phone. Still, she tapped it.

There was a new US chat show appearance, presumably conducted to promote the upcoming US leg of his tour, which would start next month in Chicago.

Rose watched the full clip on YouTube, recoiling and lusting in equal measure as she saw this man play up to the role he had long ago established for himself. He was reclining on a black leather sofa, sipping from a branded mug as the sycophantic host asked a set of pre-approved questions designed to make him look good.

Host: 'Now, Milo, obviously you are one of the hottest pop stars in the world right now.'

Audience whoops and cheers loudly.

'But it wasn't always that way, was it?'

'Oh, I know where you're going with this one,' Milo grinned, eyes lighting up at the prospect of making himself seem relatable.

'Go on, tell us about the school talent contest.'

He laughed and ran his fingers through his hair in the way men are told to do in order to flash their bicep.

Female audience members swoon.

'I can't believe you're making me tell this story.'

'So, you auditioned, right?'

'Yes. I was eleven and was a little bit obsessed with Madonna.'

Female audience members swoon louder.

'Who you've met several times by now, surely, right?'

'Yes, I've been lucky enough to meet her, yeah. Oh God, I hope she doesn't watch this.'

Audience laughter.

'Anyway, I decided to sing "Vogue" at the audition.'

Louder audience laughter.

'Suffice to say, I did not get into the talent show.'

The host could barely control his laughter. 'Wait, wait. What did they say to you when you finished?'

'They suggested I try out for the tennis team instead.'

Both Milo and the host were now in hysterics.

This was the difference between actors and musicians. Actors are supposed to play a part; the line between who they are and who they pretend to be is explicitly clear. But musicians are supposed to play themselves, which makes that line blurrier. After all, they are still offering some sort of identity, one that is often misconstrued as their own.

'Cunts,' Rose said out loud, surprising herself. She opened Twitter and despite never having tweeted anything since she created her account in 2016 found her thumb hovering over the icon to draft a tweet. Milo's name was trending – it was always trending. She wondered what would happen if she tweeted the words 'I fucked Milo Jax. I don't remember what happened. Then I woke up bleeding.' She tapped the icon and typed out those exact words just to see how it felt to have them there in front of her, written out on a public platform. All she had to do was tap 'tweet' and the world would know. It was a strangely satisfying feeling. Because seeing those words there, realising that her experience could be validated in writing, even if just for her own eyes and even if just for a few seconds, it gave her a feeling of something she hadn't had in a long time. For once, Milo's name did not mean confusion, frustration or fear. It meant she had power.

Feeling emboldened, she closed Twitter and opened Instagram, armed to confront Milo. She did not expect to find the word 'Seen' underneath her last message to him. But there it was. Staring back at her, waiting for her to do something about it.

Then, without the words 'Typing', another word appeared in front of her.

Hello.

His message came out of nowhere, like he'd written it in his Notes and copied and pasted it to her. This, she rationed, was unlikely because it was just one word. Five letters.

'Cunt,' Rose said aloud again, enjoying it this time, giving extra emphasis to the finality of the 't'.

Saying 'hello' was worse than saying nothing. Milo was rubbing her face in both his disinterest and her insignificance. A greeting. A fucking greeting? 'Fucking. Stupid. *Cunttttt*,' she continued. 'Fuck. Fuck Fuck!' She was shouting now, burying her face in the pillow so as not to annoy her neighbours. When Rose was satisfied, she went into the bathroom, splashed some cold water on her face, got back into bed and fell into a listless sleep.

The next time she opened her eyes, it was dark outside: 2.04 a.m., according to her phone. The message from Milo was still there, waiting for her inside a pink icon on her phone. It was important that she didn't reply. Rose never wanted to think about that man again, let alone speak to him.

She started to draft replies.

I'm fine. Why did you . . .

I'm fine thanks. Why did you ignore . . .

Hi.

She stared at the two letters and tapped 'Send', then realised he might not reply to that.

How are you? she added.

Rose let out a groan and went back to sleep.

In the dream he is there. Maybe a little taller than she remembered. He takes up more space. The hair, however, is the same. The corners of his arms just as honed and muscular. They are on a bus and he is sitting in front of her. She is on her way to school. But she's not a child. Neither is he. Both of them appear as they are. It's strange. Next to her is a woman she likes but it isn't Luce.

Milo has turned around to talk to her. He is smiling and asking her about something. She is smiling too, giggling now as well. He is looking at her with familiarity and warmth. He brushes her arm when she says something funny. It's affectionate. Then he turns back to face the front. She waits for him to turn back to her again. She waits the whole journey, ignoring the woman next to her, who is talking about nothing in particular. Rose keeps waiting for Milo to turn back to her. But she can't speak to him. She tries, opening her mouth to say something. Nothing comes out except air.

They arrive at school and Rose waits. A little later, it happens. He gets up, turns to look at her and reaches out his hand. There is a marshmallow inside it. 'Here, have this,' he says, smiling. Rose takes the marshmallow but before she can thank him, he has gone again. As has the marshmallow, a sweet, sugared figment of her imagination.

When Rose rolled over to switch off her alarm, it was 6.41 a.m. For a millisecond she tried to get back to sleep, forgetting why she'd woken up so early. Then she opened her eyes properly and saw the missed calls. Fifteen to be precise, mostly from Fran. Rose called her immediately.

'What the fuck, Rose?'

'Fran, I'm so sorry I must have overslept. Where are you? Is it too late?'

'We've left,' she replied, gum smacking between her lips.

'Shit, okay,' Rose sighed.

'Tight schedule. I waited for ten minutes but we had to leave,' said Fran.

'Is there any way I could come and meet you?'

'Um, I dunno. I can probably pick you up from a station or something if it's on my way.'

'That would be amazing, thank you! I'll have a look at the route and text you.'

'Fine. Bye.'

'Bye.'

Rose could feel her heart beating all over her body. It would have been so easy to not go now. All she had to do was send a message to the group saying she wasn't feeling well and didn't want to get anyone else sick. She hadn't slept properly and wouldn't be fun anyway. It was tempting.

But something stopped her. Maybe it was the thought of what everyone would say about her if she backed out now. How they'd call her 'pathetic' and 'boring'. Or maybe it was just FOMO. She didn't want to feel left out; she wanted to be included, to be a part of something.

There was a train from Paddington to Salisbury in an hour. Rose leapt out of bed and headed straight to the shower. It wasn't until she was on the train, trying to find enough saliva in her mouth to swallow the two paracetamol she found by chance in her handbag, that she remembered she'd messaged Milo.

'Fuck's sake,' she muttered under her breath, opening the message.

Yep, he'd seen it and not replied.

That was it. This was his final chance and he'd blown it. No more. Rose was done. She wouldn't block him because then he'd realise she cared. She just plugged in her headphones, and took a nap until she got to Salisbury.

Fran was waiting for her at the station, smoking a cigarette while leaning against a silver Volvo. Rose was relieved.

'Thank you so much, Fran,' she said, rushing to hug her.

Fran barely moved, her body limp as Rose wrapped her arms around it.

'Sure,' she replied, with as little vocal effort as possible. 'There's no space in the boot so you'll have to put your bag on your lap.'

'No problem,' replied Rose, as chirpily as she could.

She shuffled into the back seat, which was loaded up with Ikea bags filled with booze, clothes and food.

'How come you brought so much stuff?' asked Rose.

Fran scoffed. 'The packing list. Did you even read it?'

'Oh right, yeah, yeah, of course.'

Lizzie appeared out of nowhere and bundled in next to her, giving Rose a hug with one hand while the other stayed firmly inside a newly opened bag of Haribo.

'Hi, babe!'

'Hey, Lizzie.'

'You excited?'

'Very.' Rose smiled so hard it hurt her cheeks.

They pulled into a field where four other cars were parked. A bright-red Mini (Pippa's), a bright-blue Toyota (Grace's), a white Mercedes (Pippa's mum, Nikki) and a black Tesla (Jessie's) that looked so obnoxious in a countryside field Rose found herself imagining how it might feel to smash the windows with a baseball bat.

'Guess we know where the party is,' said Lizzie, gesturing towards a pair of giant penis-shaped balloons that had been tied around the gate into the property.

Rose let out a feeble laugh.

'Lighten up, Petal,' said Fran, smirking because she knew how much Rose hated that nickname. It was what the older girls called her when she'd arrived in Year 7. She'd walked past them in the hallway in her first week when one of them asked her what her name was. When she replied 'Rose' they all burst out laughing. 'Adorable,' someone said. 'We'll call you Petal.' Somehow, Fran and co got wind of this and so, for much of Rose's teenage life, she was known as 'Petal'.

The women gathered up their items from the car, with

Rose taking a very heavy Ikea bag containing what felt like three large Smirnoff bottles given to her by Fran.

They walked down a pebble-covered path before the house came into view. It was unlike anything Rose had ever seen before. With turrets coming out of the top, brickwork that looked like it was from the seventeenth century, and an actual moat circling it, this was a home from a fairy tale.

'Holy shit,' she muttered.

'Have you not been to Pippa's country house before?' asked Lizzie, so shocked it was like she'd just asked if Rose didn't have a second foot.

'No,' she replied. Pippa always used to invite a select group of people down to the house at weekends. They'd dress up and post pictures on Facebook, which Rose would trawl through every Monday morning, seething in envy. Pippa's mother used to be a model in her early twenties and then devoted herself to her children – five of them to be precise. Despite Ver de Veux & Partners being well known, there had always been a rumour at school that Pippa's father was secretly part of the Mafia. But they always said that about wildly wealthy people. There had to be a darkness attached to them. Mostly because there almost always was, Mafia or not.

As they neared what might just have been the most absurd hen do venue in the history of all hen dos, Rose was suddenly struck by the fact they had each paid £250 to attend a party inside a manor owned by a billionaire. What exactly all this money was going towards was unclear to anyone except the bridesmaids. Though, as they walked over a curved wooden bridge, Rose noticed that small penis-shaped lanterns had been neatly placed on either side, running all the way up a pebbled path to the front door. Maybe penis-shaped lanterns came at a high premium.

All of them were startled by the voice of Jessie suddenly bellowing from inside.

'Quick! You're already late. Come in! Come on!'

Rose's headache was getting worse. She had asked Lizzie for some ibuprofen in the car and she had said no, explaining she had only packed two tablets for herself for tomorrow morning. There was no point asking Fran.

As the three women went inside, the status of the home they had entered came into full view. In front of them was a staircase that must have been at least two metres wide; it snaked off into two separate staircases on either side. Penis-shaped cushions had been carefully positioned on the staircase, each of them with Pippa's fiancé's face printed on them. Rose pictured them ending up in landfill, or in a dusty cupboard that would be forgotten about until one curious guest decided to open it, prompting an avalanche of penis-shaped soft furnishing to tumble down.

To the right of the staircase was a giant placard with photographs of each of the hens' faces stuck together to indicate their room allocations. Rose breathed a sigh of relief when she saw she was sharing with Lizzie and not with Fran or Jessie, or any of Pippa's university friends she didn't know.

They had used a photograph of Rose taken from the

leavers' party in the sixth form. God, she looked terrible, she thought, staring back at her teenage, fake-tanned face. Her collarbones were jutting out, arms slim and frail, hanging by her side in a bright-blue dress from Mango that was too big for her, even though it was a size six.

None of them ate much back then, particularly not in the run-up to the leavers' party. Rose never considered herself as someone with an eating disorder. Even when she did try to stick her fingers down her throat, she told herself it was because everyone else did it and she wanted to fit in. Not because she actually wanted to throw up. It never worked, anyway. Rose would just end up gagging and spitting balls of saliva into the toilet bowl.

Seeing the photos, though, was confronting. All of them looked so unwell. Fran, in particular, was so gaunt it looked like she hadn't eaten in weeks. Her cheeks were completely hollow, her body totally outsized by her lollipop head.

'Right, no time to drop your bags, I'm afraid,' said Jessie, hurrying them into the kitchen, where Nikki was tending to a cocktail jug filled with pink, sparkly liquid, swirling it around with a giant penis-shaped straw.

'Hi, girls!' she said waving. Nikki was wearing just a slim white vest top and tight jeans with 'TEAM BRIDE' written on the back in fuchsia lettering. Without a single wrinkle on her face, she could have easily passed for twenty-eight.

Everyone said their hellos before they were quickly ushered by Jessie into a bathroom (there were nine in the whole house) to get changed into their allocated 'drunk Pippa' outfit.

The bathroom Rose was chivvied into was covered in damask wallpaper. There was a landscape painting in a gold frame positioned above a standing bathtub. The scene was a cliffside beach, violent waves rolling onto the shore, where a man tended to a small boat by some rocks. Oils. Nineteenth century. She looked closer, sure it couldn't be real. It was signed M. Smith, which, if Rose was right, meant it was by Mortimer Smith and would be worth at least £20,000. And yet, this was surely just one artwork of many, in one bathroom of many.

The bathtub was one that Rose had only ever seen pictured in *Hives & Dives*. Freestanding, brass, with little gold feet on each of the four corners. It was a bath you could sink into, utterly and completely, stewing in scalding hot temperatures as every part of your skin absorbed the heat. Rose debated how much trouble she'd be in with Jessie for locking the door and getting into the bath, staying there for the duration of the weekend. Then she wondered if anyone would actually notice.

Once she had changed, Rose stared at herself in the mirror. There were dark, swollen bags forming under her eyes and she could swear that was a wrinkle near her nose. She applied all the make-up she had brought at once, even the gold eyeshadow.

Just before leaving the bathroom, she decided to check her phone one last time before turning it off.

There was a notification from Instagram: Milo had replied.

I'm great, thanks. You doing anything fun this weekend?

It was as if the message had been sent by someone

else. Zero acknowledgement of that night in the hotel suite.

It made no sense. Neither did the fact that she replied immediately. *Just at a hen do. Really busy. Have a good weekend*, she typed, pressing 'Send' before turning her phone off, stuffing it in her bag and heading back to the kitchen. Her heart felt like it was beating outside of her body.

Walking along the vast corridor, Rose could hear the gaggle of women in the kitchen and the eighties synth sounds of Madonna's 'Like a Virgin'. She paused and took a deep breath. God, she wished Luce was here.

'There you are!' shouted Jessie, who was standing in a line with the eight other hens. 'Go on the end here, Rose,' she said, handing her a mask with Pippa's face on it. 'Put that on. Now!'

Rose silently acquiesced as someone turned the music up.

She only knew Jessie, Fran, Lizzie and Grace. The others – Emma, Tessa, Ruby and Nina – were Pippa's friends from Liverpool.

'Okay, ladies!' Jessie started clapping her hands over her head, her manic eyes trying to catch everyone else's. 'Pip is just around the corner. I want you all to start singing along. And put your masks on!'

'Shall we dance, too?' asked Ruby, in a tone that sounded completely earnest.

'Yes! Dance!' Jessie replied, mask now on, stepping from side to side in a pair of penis-shaped sunglasses that she kept pushing back up her nose. 'Like this please! Left, right. Left right.'

Rose couldn't see anything through her mask. The eye holes were minuscule; she could barely breathe. The cardboard pressed against her nose and the string pulled against her hair. She couldn't have a panic attack now. She closed her eyes and dug her fingernails into the sides of her thighs, continuing to sway from side to side as the sounds of 'Like a Virgin' became slow and zombie-like. The smell of cheap cardboard entered her nostrils with every pathetic inhalation she attempted.

Then came the sound of cheers and Rose knew this was her cue.

She jumped back to attention, and started whooping in unison with her fellow drunk Pippas, her voice reverberating against the cardboard in front of her. Bodies were moving in her vicinity and Rose could hear Pippa laughing. She took this as a sign that she could now take the mask off and felt the air rush into her lungs. She sighed and rushed over to Pippa with the other hens to coo in the way she was expected to.

Jessie had allowed for exactly fifteen minutes of mingling before she was standing on a stool, clapping her hands in the air and shushing everybody.

'Right, everyone. Please can I have your attention?' She smiled knowingly, with an expression that both acknowledged her dominance and commanded submission.

'It's almost time for the first activity of the day. If you haven't already, please help yourself to a glass of Buck's Fizz; there are jugs dotted across the living room. I say glass, I mean a plastic cup. Sorry to all the eco-warriors out there, all the glasses in this house are crystal, ha!'

A simmering chuckle passed across the room.

'Once you've done that, please meet me in the conservatory. See you shortly!'

Rose was pouring herself a plastic cup of Buck's Fizz from one of the jugs laid out on the marble countertop. The drink might calm her down, she thought, as she quickly sank the entire cup before pouring herself another one.

'Steady on, mate!' boomed a new voice from behind her.

Rose turned around to find herself staring at a man's bare chest. She looked up to find the face it belonged to, startled that a man had inveigled his way into this environment. He had a slick, clean face. Blond hair that had been gelled back and a glistening torso that must have been covered in oil.

'Who are you?' she asked.

'Not sure I'm supposed to tell you,' he said grinning at her, all bug-eyed as he looked her up and down. Rose felt hyper aware that she wasn't wearing a bra. She'd flung on the green T-shirt in such a rush, and her breasts weren't really large enough to warrant one anyway.

'Johnny!' snapped Jessie, stomping up behind the half-naked man.

'What?' He turned around, bemused, pouring himself a glass of Buck's Fizz.

'You're not meant to be here,' she whispered. 'Go back into the barn like we discussed.'

Johnny groaned. 'I was just talking to . . .' He turned to look at Rose, eyebrows raised. But before she could respond, Jessie had Johnny by the bicep and was leading him out of the room like an owner with a naughty puppy.

The first game was a secret one. Each of the hens had been given an individual dare to complete at some point during the party, but nobody knew what anyone else's dare was. If you guessed that somebody had said or done something as a dare, you would win a shot of the 'really expensive tequila'. Everyone picked theirs out of a hat. Rose's made her heart sink the second she read it.

'Perform a striptease at random and straddle the bride while singing the lyrics to "It's Raining Men".' It was the kind of thing Rose would never do drunk or sober even if it was just in front of Luce. She would tackle it later, she resolved, when people were more drunk. Or maybe by then everyone would have forgotten about the dares altogether. She poured herself another Buck's Fizz.

The next few hours passed mercifully quickly. There was a pub quiz where all of the questions were about Pippa's various sexual encounters – 'When did she meet "cone penis"?', 'Who could only come if she called him "big daddy"?' This was coupled with a series of anagrams of names of the people she'd slept with, featuring clues such as 'locked her in his bedroom to "protect his documents" when he woke up and forced her to climb out of the window' and 'got a nosebleed when he went down on her because he was a ketamine addict'.

Nikki seemed unfazed, laughing along at each of the sexual escapades that emerged through the course of the game. She would get on well with Lola. The next game was 'pin the penis', where every hen had to put a paper penis onto a life-size photograph of Mike – whoever was closest won the tequila shot. Although it seemed like everyone was made to do a tequila shot anyway, regardless of how successfully they pinned the penis.

Rose found herself slowly feeling more comfortable as the day progressed. This was probably helped by the Buck's Fizz and that they went straight from game to game, meaning there was almost no time left for idle conversation with strangers (and people she didn't like) in between.

Slowly, it transpired what people's 'dares' were. Lizzie started to reply to people exclusively in song. They all guessed that one pretty quickly. Ruby did the worm out of nowhere in the middle of the living-room floor – that was also quite an obvious one. And during the 'pin the penis' game, Fran began to moan and soon broke into a full *When Harry Met Sally*-style orgasm. It took the room a while to work out what was going on. Grace was about to call 999 when Fran, sensing this, adjusted her wails to sound less pained. 'Don't call 999,' Rose said. 'I think this is her dare.' Fran, whose head was tilted back by this point, stopped moaning suddenly. 'Thanks, Petal, way to spoil the fun.'

'Here's your shot, Rose!' said Jessie, handing her the tequila.

'Thanks,' she replied, knocking it back and slamming the shot glass down onto the marble table, staring defiantly at Fran, who stared furiously back at her.

As each dare passed, Rose became acutely aware that hers was by far the most daring.

Grace's dare was to text Mike from Pippa's phone with quotes from *The Devil Wears Prada*. She had a strict script to follow.

I need ten or fifteen skirts from Calvin Klein, the first message began.

So do I, Mike replied to much fanfare.

'Oh, he's good!' chimed Ruby.

Then: *Please bore someone else with your questions, and make sure we have Pier 59 at 8 a.m. tomorrow.*

Another reply: *What?*

Remind Jocelyn I need to see a few of those satchels that Marc is doing in the pony, and then tell Simone I'll take Jackie if Maggie isn't available.

Are you on acid again?

Everyone looked at Nikki. 'Oh, I don't mind!' she said, laughing.

Did Demarchelier confirm?

By this point, Mike had worked it out. '*The Devil Wears Prada*! Dammit.'

Everyone in the group was very pleased with him for getting this right.

'Who else hasn't done their dare yet?' asked Grace when hers was wrapped up.

'Obviously Rose hasn't done hers yet,' scoffed Fran.

'Go on, Rose. Do yours!' shouted Lizzie from the other side of the room.

She sighed. 'Okay, Pip, go and sit over there,' she said, pointing to the brown leather armchair.

There was music playing faintly in the background, although Rose couldn't tell from where. It would have to do. She could just get this over with quickly. As Pippa sat down and Rose faced her, she could hear a furious cacophony of whispers forming behind her. She was sweating. Someone had changed the music and turned it up to top volume. 'It's Raining Men' by Geri Halliwell filled the room. Jessie, who must've come up with the dare, gave her an encouraging thumbs up. This would be fine.

Rose started to sway her hips from left to right, lifting her hands up and moving them around Pippa's neck. She could see from Pippa's expression that this was uncomfortable for them both, so Rose turned around, and tried very hard to look down at the floor instead of directly at the women in front of her as she bent down and wiggled her bum in Pippa's face.

This was mortifying; just a few more seconds.

'You gotta take something off!' shouted Jessie.

This was true. It wasn't just a lap dance: it was a striptease.

Rose started to peel her green T-shirt up, suddenly very aware of the chill surrounding her stomach and the fact that she couldn't remember the last time she'd done a sit-up. Pippa couldn't look directly at her, but neither could Rose, instead fixing her gaze on a spot behind Pippa on the wall where yet another nineteenth-century landscape was hanging. She tried to think about how much something like that would cost as she pretended to pull her top over her head.

'Take it off!' shouted Fran.

Rose looked up. 'I'm not wearing a bra.'

'That's fine!'

But Rose was adamant. She kept her T-shirt on and after a few more agonising seconds of terrible teasing and dancing, took a bow. Most of the girls cheered.

'Always so timid,' said Fran to the others.

Pippa's university friends were harmless by comparison. They faded into the background when juxtaposed with Fran, Grace and Lizzie, who were constantly talking over one another, exchanging anecdotes at a volume that seemed to drown out everything else in the room.

They were midway through playing 'Mr and Mrs', Jessie playing a video of Mike answering how Pippa liked to take her coffee in the morning, when Tessa yelped 'Holy shit!' Jessie shot her a look of pure rage as she paused the clip.

'Christ, Tessa, what is it?' she asked.

Tessa was lost for words, her hands holding a phone, eyes glued to the screen. 'I'm just, I'm just . . .'

Rose looked closer. It was her phone.

'Oh for God's sake,' said Jessie. 'Is this part of your dare?'

'Tessa, why have you got my phone?' Rose asked quietly, careful not to make too much of a fuss as she quickly rushed over to her.

Tessa moved away so Rose couldn't take it from her.

'Sorry, this is your phone?' she asked, eyebrows raised.

'Yes, please give it back,' Rose replied, suddenly very aware this woman was a total stranger.

'Ah well, you see my dare was to grab someone else's phone and send a message to Mike from it telling him we were all snogging the strippers and I was just about to do it on Instagram and then I saw—'

'Tessa!' Rose shot her a look, pleading.

Tessa's eyes met Rose's and her expression changed. A tacit understanding was forming.

'You don't know what this is about,' Rose whispered.

Tessa smiled and then nodded. 'Sorry, guys. False alarm – Mike is private on Insta so, Rose, you actually can't message him – as you were.'

Had everyone in the room been a little more sober, they would not have let this slide. Thankfully, everyone was drunk, including Nikki. Rose snatched her phone back and immediately put a passcode on it, astonished at her own stupidity.

Tessa crouched down on the sofa beside Rose.

'I want that story later, please,' she whispered.

Rose's stomach flipped as she nodded, trying to think about how much she would have seen, and how much she would have to tell her.

By the end of 'Mr and Mrs', Rose was feeling drunk. Pippa kept getting the answers right to every question – her and Mike answered the exact same way when they were asked about how they met (behind the Portaloos at Glastonbury when they both skipped the queue to pee in the bushes) and their first kiss (a few minutes after they'd each had a wee). It meant the hens had been drinking shots of Jägerbombs every few minutes for the past hour. Rose had pretended to drink hers by fake swallowing and then quickly spitting it out into the empty mug she'd placed in front of her for that exact purpose – but Fran had spotted her.

'Rose, you can't spit it out!' she said loud enough so that the entire room heard.

'I just really hate Jäger,' Rose replied, helplessly, looking around the room trying to find eye contact with someone else who also hated Jäger. No one looked up.

Fran handed her the mug back and demanded Rose drink it. She obliged, the sweet liquor lingering on the sides of her throat.

By the evening, Rose had taken to smoking as often as she could to get a break from the activities inside. Amazingly, this was something that Jessie permitted. Lizzie and Ruby were often outside, too, both smoking roll-ups that they were more than happy to offer Rose. Instead of smoking on the estate's grounds, they'd chosen a small balcony off one of the guest bedrooms. It was removed: silent, peaceful and less intimidating. In the evening light, the vast acres of land surrounding Pippa's home were in full view. Rose looked out onto a vegetable patch on one side, and what appeared to be a rose garden on the other, while Lizzie and Ruby mostly gossiped about the other hens. Rose didn't need to say anything to learn, within a matter of five minutes, that Jessie was sleeping with her boss. 'You'd think she'd be a little less uptight,' laughed Lizzie. They continued to talk about the other girls in the group but Rose had zoned out.

Instead, her eyes and ears remained fixed on the world beneath the balcony. There were hedges that had been perfectly trimmed to represent every possible geometrical shape possible, even a hexagon. Further on, if she really stretched her eyes she could just make out the cool blue shape of a pool, enclosed by more hedges.

'It's pretty wild, isn't it?' said Lizzie, her head peeking over her shoulder, cigarette dangling to the right as ash stained the tiles on the balcony floor.

'I had no idea it was like this,' Rose replied.

'She really never invited you when we were at school?' Lizzie asked.

Rose shook her head, inhaling the dregs of her cigarette. 'We weren't that close.'

Lizzie hunched her shoulders and blew smoke out. 'I kind of thought we were all as close as each other.'

What a privilege, Rose thought, to be so safely cocooned in your own bubble that you think everyone else is just as content as you are.

When they went back into the kitchen to top up their drinks, they saw the backs of two naked men huddled around a sink. On closer inspection, it seemed both had ties around their waists. They turned around when they heard footsteps, revealing mini aprons.

'Johnny,' said Rose, nodding at the one on the right.

'Hello,' he smiled, politely.

'You two know each other?' Lizzie asked.

'GIRLS!!!! GET YOUR TIGHT ARSES BACK HERE RIGGHHHHHT NOOWWWW!!' Jessie's orders had become increasingly screeched as she drank more.

All three women turned and started to walk back to the conservatory.

'Seriously, Rose, how do you know the butler in the buff?' asked Lizzie.

'I don't. He was just friendly earlier.'

'He's hot! I'm jealous.'

'I'm sure you'll get every opportunity to ogle at him in a minute.'

'Hope so,' Lizzie said, rubbing her hands together.

'FINALLY! OKAY, ARE WE READY?' Jessie was standing on the sofa again, holding her phone. She tapped something and then Nelly's 'Hot in Herre' started to play from hidden speakers.

Sniggers emerged around the room as everyone realised what was about to happen.

In swaggered Johnny and the other man Rose had just seen in the kitchen.

Everyone was whooping and cheering. Rose just watched – until Johnny caught her eye, raising an eyebrow when he noticed she wasn't clapping. On impulse, she relented, giving him what he wanted. Her whoop was quiet and pathetic but Johnny smiled.

'He is seriously eye-fucking you,' whispered Lizzie.

Rose laughed and shook her head.

The girls had to surround Johnny and his colleague, if you could call him that, in a semicircle. Both men looked almost identical. They introduced themselves and it transpired that Johnny and Jamie were twin brothers from Newcastle. Johnny enjoyed 'cooking pasta and going to the gym', Jamie enjoyed 'lifting weights and licking pussy'.

'Is stripping a family business?' slurred Nikki, who had not stopped twirling her hair around her fingers since the two men arrived.

'You could say that,' Johnny said and winked at her, prompting a fit of giggles.

Pippa sighed. 'I'm sorry about my mother,' she said.

'Don't be, we love a MILF!' replied Jamie.

'A MILF! Golly, I've always wanted to be one of those,' swooned Nikki.

Each of the men had the same grooves in the corners of their shoulders, the same firm, protruding pecs, and the same bulging arms. If Rose squinted slightly, they looked like legs of ham, primed for a honey glaze.

The men gave each of the women a shot of tequila and introduced the first game: body parts, which was as straightforward as it sounded. Everyone had to say their name and the part of someone else's body they would most like to lick.

Johnny went first. 'Boobs,' he said, grinning.

Jamie said 'pussy', unsurprisingly. Most of the women said 'abs', 'arse', or 'dick'. Nikki said 'left butt cheek', reaching her hands out and squeezing the air to demonstrate. Rose said 'arms'.

This, it transpired, was a very good choice, because the next round of the game was to lick that body part of the person next to you.

Rose was relieved that she was standing next to Lizzie, and Emma licked Rose's stomach, her tongue slimy and warm. Rose licked Lizzie's arm, wondering what part of marriage compelled women to binge drink with strangers and lick parts of each other's bodies.

The ones who had said 'dick' or 'pussy' were permitted to lick the crotch area of the person standing next to them over their clothing. This was all very well and good until it got to Ruby, who was fidgeting furiously. She was standing next to Jamie.

Johnny licked Jamie's chest and then it was his turn. He turned to Ruby, mouth agape with hunger. She said nothing as this man proceeded to bend down, put his hands on her thighs, and moved his head underneath her dress.

Jessie was cheering and the other girls joined in. Ruby looked completely paralysed, her mouth slightly open with eyes glued to the floor.

When he removed his head, Johnny gave Ruby a kiss on the cheek and turned back to face the semicircle of women, all of whom were laughing and cheering as he took a bow.

'I only kissed her knickers, calm down,' he said, noticing Rose's silence.

The games became increasingly uncomfortable. Rose had never been to a hen do and had nothing to compare it to. During another cigarette break, Grace, who had been to a few hens, even admitted it wasn't supposed to be this full on. 'The butlers in the buff are meant to just top up our drinks and get the mood going,' she said. Still, everyone seemed to be enjoying themselves apart from Rose and Ruby, who hadn't said anything since the first game.

There was only one game that Rose enjoyed. The women were split into teams and given a series of riddles to solve. They were all sex-related, but it was the least X-rated game of the bunch.

'You stick your poles inside me. You tie me down to get me up. I get wet before you do. What am I?' asked Jamie.

'Tent!' Rose shouted. She kept getting the answers right, which meant she kept choosing who had to drink a shot. She gave the first one to Fran and then, not wanting to risk someone bitching about her later, decided to spread them evenly between the group. Eventually, Johnny and Jamie began to sigh when she kept getting the answers right. So Rose stopped guessing, even though she knew the answer to every single riddle that followed.

Finally, there was just one game left. They were allocated a twenty-minute break before it began.

Rose had managed to sober up since 'Mr and Mrs', having got away with drinking sparkling water masquerading as a G&T for the last few hours.

'Cigarette?' asked Lizzie, waving her green bag of tobacco in Rose's face.

'God, yes. Do we have time?' Rose replied.

Lizzie looked over at Jessie, who appeared to be babysitting Nikki, who was counting Jamie's abs.

'Yes, I think we're fine,' said Lizzie, heading towards the balcony.

The grounds looked eery in the dark. Rose couldn't remember the last time she'd looked out of a window and saw nothing but pitch black. It made everything seem vaster, more threatening. Like if you stepped outside, the night would swallow you whole.

'What time is it?' Rose asked Lizzie.

'Fuck knows. This has been going on for hours.'

'Grace said hens aren't usually like this.'

Lizzie laughed. 'It's a hen do. Of course it's supposed to be like this.'

'Jamie and Johnny just seem a bit much.'

'Well, probably because they both want to fuck you,' Lizzie said, making Os with her smoke.

'I hope not.'

'What do you mean?'

'I don't want to fuck either of them.'

'So don't.'

'Yeah,' Rose nodded.

'I'd fuck one of them,' Lizzie said. 'Maybe both, actually.'

'Which one?'

'Either to be honest. It's been so long since I had someone pump me.'

Rose laughed. 'Pump you?'

'Yeah, you know. Just really fuck you. Throw you around. Wrap your legs around them. Put their hand on your throat, choking you until you come all over them. Ugh. God, I'm getting horny just thinking about it.'

Rose felt her face flush.

'Oh, I know what I wanted to ask you about,' Lizzie continued, relighting her cigarette. 'What was the deal with your phone?'

'What do you mean?'

'You know, when Tessa grabbed it and then gave it back to you, like she'd seen a naked selfie or something.'

Rose paused, deliberating how to handle this.

'It was nothing,' she replied. 'I just don't like people looking through my phone.'

'Was it a naked selfie?' Lizzie asked, eyes wide.

Rose decided it was best to nod and smile.

'Ha, love that for you. Right, let's go flirt with some naked butlers.'

'Okay, ladies,' boomed Johnny, looking around the room, eyes fixing on Rose when she entered.

'Now, we've been keeping things pretty tame around

here so far,' he laughed. 'But it's time to take things up a notch!'

Everyone cheered, their voices loose and encouraging.

'First off, I want all of you to drink a shot of tequila,' added Johnny.

Jamie came around with a bottle, pouring shots into the mini shot cups everyone had been told to keep near them at all times. Rose shuddered when she saw Jamie wink at Ruby as he topped up her cup.

'Okay! So this game is called sex positions,' said Johnny. More cheering. Rose felt something shifting around deep inside her stomach.

'Jamie here is going to wear a blindfold and we're going to spin him around until he points to someone. Whoever he points to will then be given the name of a sex position by me – and, don't worry, we have illustrations where necessary,' he laughed. 'That person will then need to whisper the name of the position to Jamie and get into the sex position with him as quickly as possible. Whoever guesses the name of the sex position first, gets . . .'

'Let me guess, a shot?' asked Fran.

Johnny stopped and smiled at her. 'Yes!'

Jessie shot Fran a look, prompting Fran to roll her eyes. Maybe she wasn't enjoying herself either.

Tessa, Jessie and Lizzie were chosen first. Spooning. Missionary. Reverse Cowgirl. Jamie slapped Lizzie's bum when she walked off; she blew him a kiss in return.

It was nauseating to watch. No one seemed to find it odd that a man nobody knew was pretending to aggressively fuck each of them. Nikki was cheering the names of each woman like she was on the sidelines of a school netball match.

The last person to be chosen was Fran. Rose sighed with relief.

Fran nodded when she was told the position as if she'd been given an instruction from a colleague. She whispered it to Jamie and he bit his lower lip, let out a quiet moan and pulled Fran into him by her hips, pushing her down onto the sofa beneath him. Fran's body softened as Jamie lifted her torso so that she was on all fours. He was kneeling behind her, hands firmly positioned on either side of her pelvis as he rammed into her with a ferocity he had spared the others. It was like all the testosterone that had slowly been building throughout the day had erupted at a singular moment. His performance was elevated, too, by beastly grunts and groans.

Fran was facing the group. At first, she was smiling, weakly, trying to play along. Then as Jamie became more animated, the smile faded, Fran's mouth falling to a neutral position. Her eyes squinted whenever Jamie slammed his body into hers, jolting her further forward a little more each time, her hands losing their grip on the sofa underneath her.

Everyone except Rose and Ruby was shouting her name, cheering them both on. Finally Grace called out, 'Doggy!' and Jamie stopped. Fran's gaze was fixed on a spot behind Rose. Her shoulders drooped as Jamie stepped off the sofa, removing his hands and allowing her body to flop down like a slinky.

'Good job, love,' Jamie said, lightly tapping her bum.

* * *

By dinner, everyone had started to sober up. The mood was still light, the cutlery penis-shaped. They were all allocated time to shower and change into their black tie dresses because, thankfully, there were no more activities. Now they could just eat and enjoy, although there had been whispers of a stripper coming later. They were served dinner by regular waiters in regular clothes – the catering company was local, friends of Nikki's.

The meal itself was fairly standard. There had been penis-shaped canapés, including cheese-filled pastries, and white wine spritzers to start. The main was either steak and chips, or tomato pasta for the veggies. And then buttered green beans on the side. They were basically eating from the kids' menu at Café Rouge. Jessie, who was vegan, had her own special penis-shaped canapés – pastries filled with avocado – and her main was a green salad with vegan cheese.

Conversation flitted between what Jessie ate on Christmas Day (mushroom roast) and if she brought her own food to dinner parties (yes, and she always offered it to everyone else too) to Tessa's new job at PWC and her awful boss ('She's in desperate need of a shag') and a drug ('A bit like if ketamine and MD had a lovechild') that Grace had tried last weekend. Nikki asked if she could get her some for a sixtieth birthday party; Grace promised to look into it.

Fran, meanwhile, was barely contributing, fixing her attention on her meal and little else. Ruby also seemed subdued. Rose couldn't stop looking at both of them, wondering if there would be an opportunity for her to ask if they were okay.

They would have undoubtedly been chirpier had Jamie and Johnny actually left. Jessie had politely tried to tell them to leave once the games had finished but Lizzie had begged them to stay. 'But we don't have enough seats for dinner,' Jessie protested, firmly, looking at Lizzie.

'Oh, that's fine! You boys can eat at the kitchen island while we sit in the dining room,' she said, winking at Jamie.

Rose had watched all of this unfold, hoping to see both men turn around and walk out the front door. Johnny's eyes kept flicking back to hers, apparently hoping Rose was thinking the opposite. Of all the women there, it baffled her that this guy would fixate on her. The one with the shortest legs, frizziest hair and by far the least interest in him. Maybe he saw her as a challenge.

From the dinner table, Rose could just about see the shadows of Johnny and Jamie across the courtyard that separated the formal dining room and the kitchen. Both had changed into grey tracksuit bottoms and white baggy T-shirts. Rose was almost certain Jamie would sleep with Lizzie. Maybe Johnny would too.

After the meal, the group dispersed and Rose went to the conservatory so she could look at her phone in private. She unlocked it and saw her messages with Milo. Rose gulped. There was a reply.

A hen do? Fun.

That was it. Why bother sending it at all?

Can we talk? she replied. She was fed up with the arbitrary back and forth.

'You okay, Rose?' a voice from around the corner arrived. It was Tessa. Of course, it was Tessa.

Her eyes lit up when she saw Rose was looking at her phone.

'Two guesses I know what this is about,' she said, smiling.

'You really don't,' Rose replied, stonily.

'Okay, okay, I don't. I can't believe I didn't realise it was your Instagram account. I just went straight to your inbox to DM Mike and my God, Rose. Come on. Tell me. Are you fucking Milo Jax?!'

'Shhh,' she replied, desperately. 'And no.'

'Okay.'

Tessa paused and tried again.

'Were you fucking Milo Jax?'

'No.'

'Okay. Do you want to fuck Milo Jax?'

'Tessa.'

'Yes, you're right. Silly question. Everyone wants to fuck Milo Jax.'

'Look, we really don't know each other. So I know you don't owe me anything. But I am begging you, please don't bring this up out there. You know what that group is like. I can't handle it. Not tonight.'

'I think you're overestimating how much people in that group give a shit about other people's lives,' Tessa scoffed.

'Good point.'

'But no, don't worry. I won't say anything.'

'Thank you.'

'On one condition.'

'Yes?'

'How big was his dick?'

'Why is everyone so obsessed with asking that question?'

'You can't be serious.'

'I don't know.'

'What?'

'I said I don't know.'

'But you slept with him?'

'Tessa, please.'

'It's a simple question.'

'Yes, I think so.'

'What do you mean, you think so?' Tessa laughed. 'It either goes in or it doesn't.'

'I was drunk.'

'They do say drunk sex is the best sex.'

'I don't think anyone says that.'

'Some of the best sex I've had I can't even remember.'

'That makes no sense.'

Tessa laughed again. 'How many people have you slept with, Rose?'

'Not many.'

'No shit. You just need to sleep with someone else and you'll feel better. A sexual palette cleanser. I'm sure one of the butlers would fuck you.'

'I'm going to go back inside now.'

'I actually just can't believe you fucked Milo Jax. I've never known anyone who has slept with a celebrity. They should put that on your gravestone or something. Aren't you going to reply to him?'

'No, I'm not.' And with that, Rose put her phone in her pocket and stormed out of the conservatory.

There was half a bottle of vodka waiting on the kitchen island alongside soda and lime cordial. She fixed herself a drink. It was 10.27 p.m. She only had to put up with this for another hour and a half until she could sneak off to bed. Midnight was generally the earliest acceptable bedtime at things like this.

Rose sat silently, vaguely listening while Pippa and Grace spoke about the complexities of planning a wedding. Grace had got married last year to a wealthy financier, so their weddings would be of a similar calibre, financially speaking, which Rose discovered quickly when she caught snippets of the conversation.

Grace's flowers had cost £8,000 because they were transported from a special garden in Spain. The invitations had cost £3,500 because they were hand-painted by an artist she'd found on Instagram. And the bespoke tablecloths that had been embroidered with their initials cost £4,500.

'Oh, I must have those!' said Pippa, taking down the name of the embroiderer.

It was easy enough to nod and smile every now and then to make them think Rose was listening.

Then she felt a hand on her shoulder and jumped.

'Whoa, easy girl,' said Johnny, towering over her.

'Why did you do that?' Rose snapped.

'I was saying your name and you didn't hear me, so I touched you on the shoulder. Relax.'

'I am relaxed.'

'Do you want to come and have a drink with me?'

Pippa and Grace hadn't turned around.

'No, thank you, I'm fine here.'

'Oh, come on, you're running empty,' he said, gesturing to her now nearly empty glass. She did want another drink, so she got up and followed Johnny into the empty kitchen.

Rose guessed that half the group were on the balcony smoking, a spot that felt less sacred now so many others had discovered it. And another half had piled into one of the bathrooms to do drugs. Rose never understood why people who did drugs always insisted on doing it in bathrooms. Even in a house like this, where the party was private and no one was going to kick you out for doing a few lines in the cubicle, why bother to sequester yourself away?

'Everyone's fucked off then?' Johnny said, pouring Rose a gin and tonic.

'Yeah, they're probably all huddled up around a bathtub somewhere,' Rose sighed.

'Why aren't you there?'

'I'm not interested.'

'You're different?'

Rose scoffed. 'Yeah. I'm not like other girls,' she said, mockingly.

'Is that so?' Johnny replied, evidently immune to sarcasm as he moved his body closer to hers, wrapping his arms around her waist.

For a split second, Rose considered sleeping with this man. It might help, she thought. It could be a way of shaking off the cobwebs of Milo, like Tessa said, even if it was just sex. A sexual palette cleanser. As Tessa pointed out, she hadn't had enough sexual experiences for a twenty-six-year-old woman anyway. Why not just fuck the butler in the buff? It would be a good story, something she could share over breakfast the next day while everyone hunched over the dining table with bagels and bacon. But before Rose had the chance to make a final decision, she felt Johnny's fingers already inside her.

'Fuck!' Rose shouted, pushing him off her.

'What?!' Johnny looked genuinely confused. 'Fucking hell, you lot are so frigid.'

Rose tried to say something but couldn't. She turned and walked as calmly as she could towards her bedroom, listening anxiously for footsteps behind her and grateful not to hear any. But as she got further away, it became harder to put one foot in front of the other, like there were sacks of flour beneath her feet she wasn't strong enough to lift. She collapsed onto something soft.

When Rose opened her eyes, she was lying on a bathroom floor, with a cold flannel on her forehead. The first thing she noticed was that it was light outside.

'You fainted,' said Fran, sitting in the empty bathtub opposite her, fully clothed and smoking. 'I found you on a rug in the corridor.'

'God,' Rose replied. 'I'm so sorry, Fran. I—'

'Don't apologise.'

'Thank you.'

'How do you feel now?' Fran still wasn't looking at her. She was gazing up at the ceiling, hand dangling out over the side of the bath, ash falling onto the wooden floor.

'A bit dizzy. But I think I'm okay. Do you have any water?'

'Yeah, here,' she said, passing her a half-empty bottle of water from Pret.

'What time is it?' she asked Fran.

'Just gone 6.30 a.m.,' she replied, biting her fingernails.

'God. How long have we been in here for?'

'A few hours,' she said.

'You've been in here the whole time?'

'Yes, Rose.'

Slowly, flashes of the hen started to come back to her.

'Are you okay?' Rose asked.

'What do you mean?'

'The butler. The game. It just felt, like . . .'

'Oh, right. Yeah, it was just a bit of banter.'

'Banter?'

'These things happen all the time, Rose.'

'What things?'

'Men like that using women as props. We're just sexual playthings to them. Cyborgs with vaginas ready to be fucked and discarded. It's fine. It really doesn't bother me. They're idiots.'

Rose stayed silent.

'Do you want to know the part that gets me?' Fran went on. 'It's that when they do these things, not one person says a fucking thing. When that bastard was pushing his semi-erect dick against me, I couldn't move. But no one, in a group full of women, no one tried to stop him. You know what you all did instead?'

Rose wanted to tell her that she had been desperate to do something. But that to do anything going against the grain in that group of girls was above her social capabilities. Still, she should have stopped him. Someone should have.

'You fucking laughed. All of you. You just laughed.'

'Fran, I'm so—'

'Go and get some sleep,' Fran replied, tapping the butt of her cigarette into the plughole.

'Okay, yeah. I will. Are you not going to come?'

'Nope.'

Rose decided it wasn't worth pressing her and walked the seven-minute journey through Pippa's vast mansion back to her room, where Lizzie was passed out in the bed, leaving the futon on the floor for her. Rose buried her body into the sleeping bag without taking off her make-up and closed her eyes.

TWO

The journey back to London took four hours when it should have taken two. Traffic was dreadful, and Fran had to keep stopping to use the toilet. Lizzie was sleeping in the front, her legs stretched out to the dashboard. Rose was in the back, her head leaning against the cool glass of the window. For the first hour, no one really spoke. Rose had only managed a couple of hours of sleep before Jessie rang a literal bell down the hallway to wake everyone up for breakfast. Fran said she slept for an hour.

Over breakfast, Rose learned that a stripper had arrived at around 2 a.m. and that he waved his flaccid penis around in front of Pippa's face like a helicopter propeller. At some point in the night, Nikki was walking around topless trying to get someone to teach her a dance routine from YouTube. And a lot of people overheard Jamie having a threesome with Emma and Nina, both of whom Rose had forgotten were even there. Apparently this was a major scandal because Nina had a long-term girlfriend and Emma was engaged.

Rose hadn't told anyone what Johnny had done. She was just relieved not to see him again in the morning.

They were about thirty minutes outside London when Lizzie rose from the dead.

'How long have I been asleep?' she said turning to Fran.

'Just the entire sodding journey.'

'Oh, sorry. I'm exhausted. Probably from all that shagging,' she said, winking at Fran, who did not wink back.

'You slept with someone?' asked Rose.

Lizzie laughed.

'I could hear them shagging from my room – that's why I went to sleep in the bath,' said Fran. 'You were absurdly loud. I felt like I was in there with you.'

'Oh, you should have been. It was fantastic.'

'Are you going to see him again?'

'Doubt it. He left straight after. But he was so complimentary. I have never been with someone like that. Made me feel really hot, you know. I realise how much shit I put up with from men who make me feel like an oompa loompa.'

'What did he say?'

'Just that he'd been staring at me all night. That he knew he wanted me the second he saw me. That he wanted to put his tongue all over my body.' She made an *mmm* sound.

Fran let out a weak laugh.

'This was Johnny?' asked Rose.

Lizzie and Fran were both laughing now.

'Yes, Johnny,' replied Lizzie, rolling her eyes as she turned to face Rose. 'Obviously.'

Fran dropped Rose off outside Archway station. 'You

good from here?' she said so flatly it was more of a statement than a question.

'Yep, thanks, Fran. Really. Bye, guys.'

'Bye, Rose, lovely to see you!' chirped Lizzie.

Fran stayed silent as Rose lugged herself and her bag out of the car, shutting the door as lightly as she could.

Once on the Tube, Rose slumped into her seat, the heaviness of her body overtaking her. Snippets from the previous evening came to her piece by piece. At every sight of Johnny's face, she felt his fingers stabbing inside her. She shuffled on her seat until the feeling went away. She wanted to listen to music but couldn't quite manage to get herself to reach for her headphones. She wanted to read the copy of the *Evening Standard* that was tucked neatly into the side next to her seat but couldn't send a signal from her brain to her hands to get it. And when the Tube got to Clapham Common, Rose couldn't lift her limbs. It was like all the strength in her body that such a motion would require had evaporated. So she stayed seated. Even when the Tube reached Morden, she stayed until it started moving again towards High Barnet.

Rose rode the entire Northern Line that afternoon. Twice.

*

By the time Monday morning rolled around, Rose was grateful. Even when her alarm went off at 6.30 a.m. Even when she dabbed concealer on various parts of her face and it somehow only highlighted the bags under her eyes.

Even when her body ached all over as she padded to the bathroom because she'd spent all of yesterday evening lying on the sofa, watching 'what I eat in a day' videos on YouTube. It was important to have somewhere she was supposed to be, a place where people were depending on her to show up. Because if it wasn't for the fact that there was a final planning meeting for the StandFirst launch party today, she probably would have called in sick.

Rose was pouring hot water into the cafètiere when a key sounded in the lock. For a split second, she completely forgot someone else lived in the flat and reached for a kitchen knife.

'Hello?' called Luce, surrounded by several Daunt Books totes and M&S bags.

'Hey!' Rose called from the kitchen, quickly putting the knife away.

'How are you then?' Luce asked robotically, walking to the kitchen.

'I'm okay, missed you at the hen.' Rose wrapped her arms around her oldest friend, noticing how much slimmer she felt. 'How have you been?'

'Oh yeah, great,' Luce scoffed.

'Sorry, I'm in a bit of a rush. Big meeting at work today.'

'Classic.'

'What does that mean?'

'You know there's a rumour going around that you shagged Milo Jax?'

'What?'

'Now I have your attention.'

'What do you mean there's a rumour? From who?'

'Is that why you ditched me on girls' night?'

'Was it Tessa?'

'Who?'

'I didn't ditch you. But I really have to go to work,' Rose replied, walking towards the front door.

'Rose. What the fuck? Are you serious? You actually slept with him?'

'If I did, would you suddenly take an interest in my life?'

'Are you kidding me? I've been trying to talk to you for weeks. You've just been so . . .'

'I'm sorry. But I've been dealing with a lot of stuff too, Luce.'

'Like what?'

Rose could feel her body stiffening in preparation to say his name. 'Milo.'

Luce laughed. 'Let me get this straight. I am dealing with a horrendous break-up yet again while you've been bonking one of the hottest men on the planet. And you're the one that's going through something? Are you high?'

Rose's whole body was vibrating now, her breath quickening. 'I can't remember what happened, Luce.'

'You mean you fucked him and you can't remember it?'

'No, I mean, yes. I guess—'

'Honestly, Rose. Do you know how many strangers I've woken up next to? The number of women that would murder puppies to have been in your position.'

'It's not like that.'

'I'm not sure you've had enough sex to make that judgement.'

'I really have to go.' Rose moved further out of the door, fighting back tears.

'Oh, come on, you know I didn't mean it like that,' Luce said, resting her hand on Rose's shoulder.

'Please just let me go to work,' she replied, her face hot and wet.

'Okay. We do need to talk though.'

Rose sighed, wiping her cheeks with the back of her hand. 'About what?'

'I have to up your rent.'

Rose turned around.

'Yeah, Mum wants to do a loft conversion,' Luce continued. 'I asked if she could find the money somewhere else but she's being pretty stubborn about it.'

This was too much for her to compute. 'How much?' Rose whimpered.

'A thousand a month.'

'That's double.'

'Yeah,' Luce said and shrugged.

'Do what you want,' Rose replied, slamming the door behind her.

Tears poured in abundance on the Tube, even when her eyes were closed. Rose wiped them away from underneath her sunglasses for the duration of the journey.

She'd pulled herself together by the time she arrived at the office, ready to play pretend and be distracted by literally anything. But just as she walked in, Oliver grabbed her by the arm and took her to one side.

'Finally. Right, there's been a problem.'

'What?'

'Milo Jax has gone completely AWOL.' Rose's stomach flipped. 'I need you to get him to come.'

'What, why?'

'If you ask him, he will come because he might want to sleep with you again.'

'I can't,' she replied.

'Yeah, look, I've heard gonorrhoea is rough. But please find a way to get him here.'

'Aren't you the one that's supposed to have all the contacts here?' she asked.

'Don't be a smartarse.'

'Fine. I'll email Joss again.'

'No. You need to message him.'

'I don't have his number.'

Oliver scoffed.

'I don't!'

'Okay, doll. Slide into his DMs then. Send a fucking owl. Whatever it is you do.'

'Oliver, can I ask you something?'

'If you ask me in less than twenty seconds, sure.'

'Why do you hate me so much?'

Oliver laughed. 'Hate you? Come on. Don't be such a main character.'

Rose paused, unsure whether there was any point proceeding.

'Okay, you don't hate me. Look, I don't mind – do whatever you need to do to feel important but—'

'To feel important? One report from me to Minnie and I can get you under HR supervision, Rose.'

Even though she knew Minnie would never do that, Rose said nothing.

'That's what I thought,' Oliver added. 'Now can you please just text your boyfriend? Thanks.'

Rose sat down at her desk and reluctantly opened her Instagram conversation with Milo, who had seen and ignored her *Can we talk?* message by the time she'd got back to London from the hen do. The only thing to do now was her job.

My boss would love you to come to the StandFirst launch on Thursday, she typed. *Have emailed Joss about it. Hopefully see you there.*

Casual. Professional. Fine. This was fine.

The office was quiet that afternoon. Oliver had gone out. The meeting wasn't for another two hours – Minnie was probably stress-walking in Regent's Park, which she often did before big meetings. And Annabelle was probably talking to one of her family friends at *MODE*, asking to borrow something from the fashion cupboard. Rose scrolled through Instagram, noticing the hens had shared photos from the weekend.

Pippa had shared a group picture of them all in their 'Drunk Pippa' outfits: *Best weekend ever. Love my hens xxxxx*. Grace had posted a photo of her and Pippa doing shots in the kitchen: *The most beautiful hen xx*, and Tessa had posted a few of the more drunken photos, including one of her and Lizzie grabbing each other's breasts while Rose was sitting on the sofa in the background, smiling awkwardly next to Pippa and Grace.

Fran had posted a photo of Jamie and Johnny posing with her, Lizzie and Pippa. In the photo, all of them were facing away from the camera, with both men standing next to each other, hands on hips, bums on full display. Lizzie's hand was hovering over Johnny's bum, Pippa's was just hovering in the air. Fran was the only one facing the camera, staring down the lens, smirking. *LOVED hanging out with these two at our gorgeous Pip's hen do this weekend*, read the caption. *We sure had a great time ;).*

Rose quickly drafted one final follow-up email for Joss. When she was done, her hands stayed firmly on the keyboard. Her breath was quickening, so she closed her eyes and tried to imagine she was somewhere else. The beach thing had stopped working a while ago. She tried a lake, which turned into a river. A calm, beautiful river. She was starting to pant. In and then out. In and then out.

'Are you okay, darling?' came Minnie's voice. Rose opened her eyes immediately, embarrassed.

'I'm fine. Sorry, I'm just finding it hard to breathe.'

Minnie rushed to her side and knelt down beside her, placing her hand on her arm. 'Okay, don't worry. Just take a deep breath, slowly. Inhale. Exhale. There you go.'

As Rose began to breathe normally, she turned to face her computer screen.

'No, no,' Minnie said. 'We're going for a walk. Come on.'

Rose had never really spent any time walking near the office. Why would she have, frankly, when all the nearby restaurants were £120 a head and the average diner was sixty-five? For a while, Rose and Minnie walked side by side in total silence. It all looked so inviting in the morning light. There were red-brick buildings with four storeys and bay windows, some had blue roofs. Elsewhere, there were plush cream townhouses, with steps leading up to the front door, plants lining either side and ivy covering the facade.

'How are you?' Minnie finally asked as they walked past an elderly couple carrying Liberty shopping bags.

'I'm okay,' sighed Rose. 'Sorry about that. It keeps happening lately. A sort of fainting thing. I think I must be anaemic or something.'

'Ah yes, anaemia,' she tutted. 'Why don't you tell me what's really going on?'

'What do you mean?'

'Rose. You're the best publicity assistant I've had in years. Diligent. Conscientious. And you didn't get here because your uncle went to Harrow with Jasper, or your mother once had an affair with the duke of wherever. That's rare.'

Rose laughed.

'Maybe if she had I'd be living in one of those houses,' she replied, pointing to an enormous townhouse that was all cast iron and sash windows.

'I know something has happened. Because ever since the Firehouse Awards, you've been different.'

'What do you mean?' Her heart was racing.

'Don't panic. I just mean that I've noticed some things. You seem . . .' Minnie paused. 'Dissociated.'

'Oh.' She was not expecting her to use that word.

'You just seem distant. And after walking into the office

and seeing you like that, I'm a little concerned. Do you see a therapist?'

'No.'

Rose had tried therapy after Richard left. She and Lola had used the same therapist, Chris, a middle-aged man that always wore odd socks. Rose would go in right after her mum and watch the clock for sixty minutes. She couldn't remember much from those sessions aside from being bored. But she could recall the musty scent of that room they sat in. How there were cobwebs creeping over every ceiling corner. How the lime-green sofa she sat on was sunken in the middle. How the room had no windows.

She only saw him for a few months before Lola told her they'd no longer be going there. Rose later found out this was because Chris kept asking her mother to go on a date.

'I think it could be worth trying it again,' said Minnie, after Rose explained how this had put her off therapy. 'I've been seeing the same therapist for twenty years. And we've only just started addressing the sister I don't talk to,' she said and laughed.

'How come?' asked Rose innocently.

'Oh, because we spent the first twenty years discussing the sister I do speak to.'

Rose smiled. 'I'm fine, really, Minnie. I'm sorry I worried you. It's just been a weird summer.'

'Do you ever speak to your father?'

'No. I don't even know where he lives.'

'But he sends you and your mother money still, right?'

'Yes. I don't know why. Maybe because he has so much. Maybe because he thinks charities are ponzi schemes. Maybe out of guilt for leaving us . . . I'm not sure.'

'You could always look at the bank statements to see where he's sending them from. If you'd like to know where he is, I mean.'

'I have thought about that.'

'But you haven't looked?'

'No. Not yet.' Rose paused. 'I'm not sure I want to know.'

'I understand that.'

They continued into Green Park, finding a sun-soaked path lined by lofty trees.

'Look, I know you've been working hard on the launch,' Minnie said. 'And I appreciate everything you've done for it. But if you don't want to come and work on the night, I will understand. Maybe it's best you take some time off instead.'

'No, no. I'll be there. I really don't need any time off.'

'Rose, do you enjoy what you do?'

'Yes.'

'Be honest.'

'Okay. I do enjoy it. I promise.' Rose took a deep breath. 'I just sometimes feel like the, erm . . .' She paused, feeling her chest tighten. 'Some of it is just a bit strange and I wonder if I'm maybe too . . . I don't know . . . sensitive to handle it?'

'What is it exactly that you find strange?'

'The celebrity stuff.'

'Go on.'

'Well, it's all of it. Isn't it? We only really sell magazines now because of them. What they said about their ex from five years ago in an interview or what they think of some political movement they pretend to be involved in. Or because they tell us what they put on their face every morning, or what their favourite pilates move is. I don't know why everyone cares so much.'

'You really think people would care about celebrities if we didn't tell them to?'

'Maybe not. Honestly, when I started here, it was all so . . .'

'Intoxicating?'

'Yes. But then you see what it's really like. And I guess, you see the humanity of it all. The illusion vanishes. And what's left behind is pretty hideous. It's hard to even look at it.'

'What do you mean?'

'We propel these people, talented people, sometimes, into stardom, right? We treat them like superior beings. Like they transcend humanity purely because they can, I don't know, sing to a tune or pretend to be someone they're not. But by doing that, we . . .' She paused, taking a breath. 'We give them a power they don't deserve. Power they haven't always earned. I guess, maybe that could be dangerous. Like, if someone wants to exploit that power. Sorry, I'm rambling.'

'What did Milo do, Rose? You can tell me.'

'Oh, no, no. He didn't do anything,' she said, shaking her head. 'I mean, other than just being a bit rude.'

'Are you sure?'

Telling Minnie meant admitting to something. Letting it out, whatever it was, knowing that once it had been released, it would mean relinquishing control. Then again, maybe she never had any in the first place. Maybe that was the problem.

'I can't remember what happened.'

'When you spent the night together?'

Rose turned to face Minnie, feeling the colour drain from her body. 'What?'

'Oh, come on, darling. It's obvious from the way your face turns into a raspberry every time someone mentions his name. A very sweet raspberry, might I add.'

'We . . . We had sex. Once.'

'Okay.'

Rose found herself tumbling into a diatribe against Milo. She told Minnie how he'd been the one to invite her to the afterparty. How he'd asked her to go to his house. How his house was strange and student-like. How ever since then, he'd treated her like a stranger. Or worse, a fan.

'I don't even like his music,' said Rose.

'So what's the part you don't remember?' Minnie asked.

'After he dropped me home.'

'Do you know if he came into the house with you?'

'I think he did. But . . .' She stopped, feeling her breath escape her. Rose kept her gaze fixed on the pavement and tried to think of something totally inane before she said the next bit so that she wouldn't cry. She pictured a hamburger.

'When I woke up, there was blood.'

'Right,' Minnie sighed. 'And did you report it?'

'Report what?'

'The rape, Rose. Did you report the rape?'

'Sorry? I never said . . .'

Rose had stopped walking, her limbs glued to the spot where she'd paused. There was a bench just ahead of them – Minnie took her hand and guided her to it.

'I'm sorry,' Minnie said, sitting down beside her. 'I don't want to use labels you don't feel comfortable using.'

'We had sex. Consensual sex.'

'Are you sure, Rose? Because there are things—'

'Look, I'm not even sure if there was a second time. Maybe the blood was from the first time. I just – I just can't remember. I was drunk. Very drunk.'

Minnie stayed silent.

'We had fun,' continued Rose, holding her head in her hands. 'I really like him. And I know everyone says that because he's Milo fucking Jax but—'

'Can I tell you a story?' asked Minnie, interrupting.

'Please.'

'When I was fifteen there was a guy at school I was obsessed with.'

Minnie had been married to Kyra for ten years.

'I didn't know you . . .' Rose began.

'Oh, this was before I came to my senses and realised I liked women,' Minnie said, anticipating what she was about to say. 'Anyway, he was a few years above me. One of the white boys. Gorgeous blond curly hair. There was a party one night at one of his friends' houses. My friends and I decided to crash it. But by the time we arrived, everyone was already hammered. So we played catch up, and drank as many shots of vodka as quickly as we could in the loo. To this day a bottle of Smirnoff makes me wince.' She shuddered.

'So this boy was there. Hugh. That was his name. Hugh Parks. I spent the entire evening trying to get his attention. I was relentlessly following him around. Dancing in front of him. You know how it is. Anyway he eventually did notice me, and somehow we ended up in a bedroom, sitting side by side on the bed, taking turns to drink from a bottle of something that tasted like petrol. But I pretended to like it. Out of nowhere, he starts kissing me. I was thrilled at first. But his hands started moving on to my thighs and up my skirt. He called me his "jungle queen", his "chocolate angel".'

'Jesus.'

'I'd never been with anyone before. In my family, sex wasn't talked about. We spoke about it at school. But I'd always found it all completely terrifying because it was all so . . . I don't know. Unknown, I suppose. My point is that I didn't stop him. I couldn't. I wanted to, and my God, the pain was excruciating. But the second his hand went onto my thigh, I froze. It was like something happened to my body and brain that just switched off. And do you want to know the strangest thing? The next morning, I couldn't remember any of it. It was like my brain had wiped the memory. Like it had never happened.'

'How did it come back to you?'

'Because these things never go away, Rose,' she said. 'It's like someone puts a plaster on them. And it's a heavy duty plaster, let me tell you. It's thick and tough and at some point you'll forget it's even there. It gets absorbed into your body and becomes a part of you. But the wound underneath, that part lingers. Even when you think it's gone. Even when you think everything is back to the way it was. It's still there, hiding under that plaster. Like a fucking parasite.'

Rose didn't know what to say. She couldn't imagine Minnie as a vulnerable teenager. To her, she was one of those women who'd always been strong. A leader. Someone nobody would dare take advantage of.

'Come on, let's head back for the meeting,' said Minnie. 'I don't know exactly what happened with Milo. And you don't have to tell me. But I do know that whatever it was, it has left a mark. And when the memory of how that mark happened comes back to you, I want you to call me. Okay?'

Rose nodded. 'I did try and ask him,' she said.

'When?'

'At a party recently. That night when I was with Clara, we went to a gig together and he was there.'

'And he didn't talk to you?'

'Not really, no.'

'Have you been in touch since?'

'A little.'

'Do you have his number?'

'No.'

'Cunt.'

* * *

After work, Rose tried to get the Tube from Oxford Circus but the station had been barricaded. This happened often. They'd close the Tubes in fear of overcrowding, which would ironically only create further overcrowding, often on the steps into the station. Sardines shuffling together trying to get home safely. The UK threat level had been 'severe' since the London Bridge attack, which, according to the BBC, meant that another terror attack was highly likely. Rose decided to wait it out in Zara.

Despite it still being 25 degrees outside, the shops were already getting their winter collections in. Halter-necks and denim mini skirts had been relegated to the back rooms. Up front it was all smocks, pinafores and brogues. Rose sighed. Summer was her season for clothes. Something about wrapping up and hiding yourself in layers pulled her deeper into her own head, as if she was hiding something. Dressing for summer was the opposite. She could just slip into a lightweight dress and move freely.

Rose walked straight past the rails of tunics to the back corner for the sale items. Here were the short skirts that grazed the thighs she wished didn't rub together. The flimsy threadbare vests that hung off her collarbones, revealing her shapeless upper body. It was the kind of thing Luna would look effortlessly gorgeous in. Rose hadn't planned on buying anything. But then she saw the flash of crimson peeking out from a mass of less interesting colours. It was a long, backless, and ever so slightly sheer, dress. The straps were delicate, like you'd barely be able to touch them without causing the whole dress to fall right off. Rose immediately took it to the changing room.

She unzipped it slowly, marvelling at the ease with which the flimsy fabric instantly dropped to either side. Rose hastily shuffled out of her jeans and unbuttoned her shirt, trying not to look at herself in the mirror. She was, as usual, wearing mismatched underwear: a black cotton bralette that was five years old, and pink knickers with 'Tuesday' written on them. She stepped into the dress and pulled it over her body. It felt snug over her hips, but looser as she reached her waist. The zip fastened all the way up – that was always reassuring.

Rose took a deep breath and turned to look at herself in the mirror. The dress did not fit properly. Because of the way it hugged her hips, she could see the exact outline of her thighs trying to burst out. Meanwhile, the straps were too tight and made her arms look like they, too, needed to burst free. Yet it was too loose on her waist. The crimson, which had once been seductive now appeared garish and uncouth. Rose looked like a rectangle.

She took the dress off as quickly as she could, wriggling her hips so that it collapsed onto the floor. It was then that she accidentally caught a view of herself. Her arms and thighs were a little red where the dress had tugged at them to try to make them smaller. The rest of her body was the same colour: pallid, sallow. Not quite white enough to be an English rose – her cheeks didn't flush in that way. A sort of muted milky, olive tone that was hard to pin down. Dimples scattered across her thighs, striped by stretch marks all the way up to her arse.

On the journey home, Rose drafted apology messages to Luce. She continued writing all the way up to the station until she'd realised there were now pages and pages of text in her Notes app. She had somehow charted their entire friendship, bringing in men, money, jealousy, privilege and everything in between. Rose stared at her magnum opus for a few seconds and then deleted all of it. *I miss you*, Rose wrote in WhatsApp, tapping 'Send' before she could hesitate. Luce read it immediately. Rose watched her screen intently until the 'Online' written beneath Luce's name disappeared, and no new message appeared.

Rose was prepared for a night at home alone. But when she walked through the front door, there was her housemate, sitting on the sofa, scrolling furiously through something on her phone with one hand, while the other was picking its way through a giant bag of sea salt Kettle chips.

'Hey,' Rose said, gently.

'Hi,' Luce replied, eyes still fixed on her screen.

'Can we talk?'

Luce continued to scroll.

'Luce?'

'You know he's seeing someone?'

'What?'

'Milo. There are photos of him on a yacht with Alice Miller.'

'That doesn't mean they're seeing each other,' Rose countered, surprised at her defensiveness.

'Look.' Luce turned the phone screen to face Rose. There were photographs of Milo reclining on the back of a very expensive-looking boat somewhere near Barcelona, where he'd just played a gig, his arms wrapped around a lithe, tanned body that could have belonged to a teenager.

Alice was a Swedish model with long blonde hair and 2.6 million Instagram followers.

'I don't know why you're showing this to me,' said Rose.

'She's an actor too,' Luce continued. 'In some new film directed by Scorsese. Think it's on Amazon Prime.' Neither Rose nor Luce had ever owned a streaming membership but had managed to gain access to every single one available courtesy of Luce's roster of exes, who were blissfully unaware of the streaming ring they'd both been running from south London.

'Okay, I'm going to go upstairs then. Let me know when you're ready to talk.'

'Talk about what?' Luce replied, just as Rose reached the bottom of the staircase.

'Well, I feel like we need to have a conversation about the rent and our friendship and—'

But before she could continue, Luce interrupted her: 'The rent is going up from next month. And I really don't care about the famous pop star you shagged, Rose. And, frankly, the guy probably fucks three different women every weekend. Maybe even every night. I'll bet there are at least four Alice Millers.'

Rose felt her breath quicken, becoming harder to draw. 'You're being . . . Luce, I can't . . .' She paused, eyes on the floor as she tried to collect herself. But by the time she looked up, Luce had already plugged her headphones in and was scrolling on her phone again.

The second Rose got back into her bedroom she closed the door behind her. She could have sworn the room was rotating, so she steadied herself against her bed's wooden frame until she allowed herself to slip down onto the floor, knees hunched to her chest, rubbing against damp cheeks. She gave herself some long, shaky breaths before opening her laptop, which lay beside her under a pile of unwashed clothes, and googling 'Scorsese Alice Miller'.

Alice Miller's film was not, in fact, showing on Amazon Prime but a new streaming service Rose had not heard of. As far as she was aware, no one Luce had slept with subscribed to it. Rose signed up to a seven-day free trial, entering her card details and setting a reminder in her phone to cancel it in six days' time.

God, Alice was pretty. The film opened with a sex scene – Rose watched as she wrapped her legs around a man's muscular torso, throwing her head back in pleasure as her fingers gripped his shoulders. She moaned like a porn star and Rose wondered if this was how she moaned when she was having sex with Milo. Just as the man was about to start going down on her, Rose's phone rang.

She paused the film.

'Clara, hey. I was wondering how you were. I'm sorry I haven't been in touch. Things have been so busy with the—'

'Rose,' Clara interjected in between sobs, 'please can you come and meet me? I didn't know who else to call. I'm sorry.'

'Of course,' she said, looking around the floor for her keys. 'Send me your location and I'll be there as quickly as I can.'

* * *

Rose had to double-check she had the right address. She was standing outside a bagel shop on Brick Lane with strip lighting. The Uber had taken forty-three minutes and cost £25, which was probably more than usual because it was 11.30 p.m. Despite the strange hour, there was a long queue outside the shop, mostly of lone bagel thrill-seekers, and a few gaggles of tipsy teens. Rose walked straight inside. Huddled in the corner underneath a not so inconspicuous pale pink fluffy hat and a matching jacket was Clara. All the external signs pointed to her identity, but when she lifted her face up to meet Rose's, it was clear that the person in front of her was only half there. Her eyes were sagging, her face entirely drained of life.

It didn't feel right to hug her. Rose sat down in the chair opposite and placed her hand on top of hers.

'Hey,' she whispered.

'Hey. Thank you for coming. It's one of the only places that stays open all night.'

'That's okay. You know, I love bagels. Such an underrated baked good.'

'They really are,' Clara replied, rubbing her eyes.

'Do you want to tell me what happened?'

Clara sighed. 'I do. I'm just . . .' She paused.

'It's okay. Take a deep breath. I get like this too sometimes when I'm upset. It's like the air is full of smog.'

Clara nodded, putting her hand on her chest and trying to breathe gently.

'So, we had an argument,' she began, looking at their hands.

'Did he hit you, Clara?'

'No. I actually think what happened was worse.'

'You can tell me. I won't judge you.'

'We were arguing. I can't even remember how it started. But he was accusing me of cheating on him again. I tried to tell him I never had. He was levelling insults at my career, telling me it was pathetic I made my living off photos of myself. Normally, when he goes on these rants, I just try to sit there and take it until he calms down. But this time I didn't. I made the mistake of bringing up his drinking. And that sparked something in him. I can't even remember what he said but he was screaming in my face. I ran into the bedroom and tried to lock the door. But it's one of those newbuild flats where you can quite easily unlock any door from the outside. Anyway, he got inside. He was shouting at me, telling me to stop crying. Calling me a baby. I just got into bed. But then he ripped the duvet off and grabbed me, bringing my body in to his.' Clara's hands held on to her arms to mimic his movements. 'It was like he was trying to soothe me, I guess? Like he suddenly felt guilty or something. So he held me, really tightly so that I couldn't move. I don't really remember how it happened but something about being constricted, or . . . I don't know. It was like my body went into a rage blackout. Something switched inside me and I just . . . it was like I was caged. And I needed to get free. And then . . .' She had started to cry again.

'What happened, Clara?'

'I hit him,' she whispered. 'On the arm. After he'd let me go. I think I was trying to push him away and then

I was just hitting his fucking arm, scratching him. Oh God.'

'Once?'

'No. I don't know. I think a few times. I left a mark.'

'Oh.'

'I know.'

'What did he do?'

'I can't really remember. It was like my body and brain went somewhere else for those few seconds. Then I realised what I was doing and just, I don't know, kept crying and crying until it hurt too much to keep going.'

'Where is he?'

'At the flat, I think. He keeps sending me photos of the marks on his arm. He's threatening to post them online. Oh God.'

Rose didn't know what else to say. She just kept squeezing Clara's hand, holding on to it tightly while she cried.

'Do you feel like you can walk away from this?' Rose finally asked.

'What do you mean?'

'The relationship. Do you think this might be the thing that helps you recognise it's time to end it? For good?'

Clara sighed. 'Yes. Probably. I don't know. It's not that simple.'

'I'm sure it isn't. But, Clara, fucking hell. This isn't okay for either of you. Something has to change.'

'What if he's been right this whole time, Rose?'

'What do you mean?'

'I mean, looking at it objectively. He has never hurt me.'

'Physically, maybe not. But Clara—'

'I have hurt him . . .' She had gone into action mode, her voice firmer and more authoritative. 'He has an actual physical mark, Rose, something to show for the pain I've caused him. He has evidence. Something substantial to show to someone who will immediately be saying, "Oh fuck, your girlfriend is a fucking lunatic, mate." I have memories, which means I have nothing.'

Rose looked at Clara's painfully thin hands, those tiny, childlike wrists.

'I'm not sure you're capable of physically harming someone three times your size.'

'But I hit him, Rose. Don't you see? I'm the problem. I am the . . .'

Rose got up then, walked over to Clara's chair, and wrapped both arms around her, stroking her hair.

Once she sat back down and Clara had managed to stop crying, she leaned into Rose and whispered. 'Can I tell you something mad?'

'Of course.'

'And please, look, I know how fucked up this is, okay? Believe me, I get it. But sometimes, I . . . I just wish he had hit me. Or at least tried to.'

'What do you mean?'

'Because then I'd have evidence too,' she whispered. 'A mark on my body to show the pain he has inflicted ever since I met him. Something to show people. So that they would believe me. Because fuck, Rose, if he posts that photo . . .' She started to hyperventilate.

'Clara, do you want to talk to someone about this?'

'No. I only want to talk to you.'

'Why?'

'Because I know you'll understand.'

'What do you mean?'

'You're kind, Rose. But you're far too kind to someone you don't really know. Too empathetic towards someone as broken as me. Most people don't care because they can't grasp the depth of what's happening. The only reason they do is if they're broken too.'

It was almost 2 a.m. by the time Rose got home. It came as no surprise that she couldn't sleep. Her mind was darting from Milo to Clara and back again. Would she leave him? Would he post those photos? What would happen to Clara's career if he did? Could Rose help her? Could Minnie?

It wasn't clear how or why she decided to hack into her mother's email, but at around 4.03 a.m. Rose found herself propping her laptop up over the top of her duvet, typing her birthday into the password space below Lola's email address and then staring at her inbox. She typed 'Richard' into the search bar so quickly, it was as if someone else was controlling the movement of her fingers. She held her breath as she scanned through the list of results and their subject lines. The majority were promotional emails from Zara. But then, there was one from 'noreply-contextual' – and in the subject line, a series of numbers next to the name 'Richard Franks'. There was a reference number at the top. His name again. A date. And then an address.

Richard Franks
3 Pine Square
London
NW1 82B

Rose closed the lid of her laptop. NW1? Primrose Hill? Her father had been living in fucking Primrose Hill this entire time?

She rang Lola. And when she didn't answer, because it was 4 a.m. and she would be fast asleep, she rang again. And again. She stopped after the fourteenth call and opened Instagram.

Milo?

Sent.

You can't ignore me forever.

Sent.

Hello? I know you can see my messages.

Rose knew he would be fast asleep. She knew he would think she'd lost her mind. She knew this was not enough to stop her.

I woke up bleeding. Did you know that?

Blood everywhere. It fucking hurt.

I can't remember what happened.

Milo.

If you have a human soul you will answer me.

I just found out my dad has been living in the same city as me this whole time.

Please.

He probably has a whole new family.

Don't do this.

I just need to know what happened and then it will be okay.

I won't report it.

Please.

Please.

Please.

And then, because she could no longer watch her own words watching her, she deleted the conversation. The next thing Rose did was open Safari and type: 'how to report a rape' into the search bar, her body electrified by what she was about to do.

The information that came up was too garbled to navigate through. Some websites suggested going to your local police station. Others advised calling 101 if it wasn't an emergency. But this felt like one. Rose called 999.

'999, which service do you need?'

'Hello. Hi.'

'Police, fire or ambulance?'

'I'm . . . I'm not sure.'

'Why are you calling us tonight, ma'am?'

'I think I was raped.'

'Sorry, you're cutting out. Could you repeat that?'

'I said I think I was raped. By Milo Jax.'

'Milo, who?'

'Milo Jax. The singer.'

'Sorry – you're cracking out . . .'

The voice on the other end of the phone was crackling but it didn't matter. Rose couldn't help herself.

'MILO JAX. I WAS RAPED BY MILO JAX. THE SINGER. I HAD SEX WITH HIM AND THEN HE

RAPED ME AND I BLED AND I CANNOT GET HOLD OF HIM.'

Rose felt her throat straining with agony as she realised she was screaming.

'Putting you through to the fire service now.'

Rose hung up and threw her phone across the bedroom, bringing the duvet up to her face so she could scream and scream and scream and scream.

THREE

The hairdresser's smelt like burnt rubber. A fan of Firehouse magazines had been spread out in front of Rose, some of them more than three years old with pages that had curled up at the corners. She decided to flick through a *MODE* magazine from December 2015.

Minnie had booked blow-dries for the entire team ahead of the launch that evening. It would be taking place at the Serpentine Gallery, a location Liz had somehow secured just one week previously. It was hot, possibly the hottest day of the year so far. Rose was fanning herself with the magazine as she winced at her hair being tugged and twisted from behind.

The morning after Rose had sent those messages to Milo, there had been a split second of bliss before she'd remembered what she'd done. The shame smothered her. As for Lola, Rose had apologised for calling so many times and said it was an accident. She'd been ignoring her mother's calls ever since. It was too much to handle before such a big work event. Luce, meanwhile, had been avoiding her.

When Rose arrived at the Serpentine, her coiffed hair

already starting to frizz from the humidity, she felt prepared. She was grateful to have been given a StandFirst T-shirt to wear instead of a dress and had paired it with a short black skirt and black pointed stilettos that pinched her toes. Liz had said the uniform would make it easier for guests to identify the staff, which she suspected was code for: 'So you don't all get distracted and start flirting with the celebrities and vice versa.'

On the tip sheet, which would be handed out to photographers on arrival, was a mix of up-and-coming actors, musicians, models and influencers. There were more names Rose recognised than usual, mostly because everyone on it was under thirty. There was the girl band who had won a popular talent show last year. The American child star who'd just been cast to play a superhero in a Marvel film. And a YouTuber with more than 100,000 subscribers who made videos about shopping on ASOS.

A nervous fizz filled the air as guests started to arrive. Joss had confirmed that Milo would perform two days ago. Rose had simply forwarded the email to Minnie and Annabelle; they could deal with the logistics. She had already identified a spot where a potential confrontation could take place; Milo had his own dressing room backstage that he'd be waiting in before his performance later. Given she was looking after him tonight, it would be completely reasonable for her to be in his dressing room before the performance, checking if he needed anything. She just had to get rid of Annabelle somehow. But that shouldn't be too difficult; she could just put her in front of another famous person.

'How will we know he's about to arrive?' Annabelle asked Rose.

'He will probably call me,' she said.

'Wow, okay. So do you have his number?'

'No.'

'Oh, of course he calls on No Caller ID. Okay. Yes, okay. That makes sense.'

With every Firehouse event, it was always the least important people that arrived first. This bought everyone a little time before the real work began. Rose and Annabelle smiled and said hello to each of the guests, checking their pieces of paper that had everyone's names and faces on them so they could alert the photographers to anyone they wanted to get in their coverage the next day. Rose hadn't told the team anything about what was going on with Clara. She figured she just wouldn't show up. Rose had been calling her every day since that night at the bagel shop – but she hadn't picked up once.

It was oppressively warm. While everyone was delighted to have clear skies, it meant there wasn't even the slightest bit of a breeze.

Given that the party was outside, it was significantly easier for people to sneak in. Thankfully, this was not Rose's job to monitor. The freelancers Liz had hired had been assigned this particularly taxing role. It had only happened a few times – and it was always the same people. One man called Phil who worked in tech and usually came along with his wife, Babs, and one or two friends. Another woman in her mid-fifties with purple hair called Jill who always insisted she was on the list.

Minnie would send around photographs of them ahead of every event.

So far, though, it was all invitees they'd expected aside from one woman who arrived in a see-through black dress. Rose and Annabelle watched as she stormed off, indignant that the freelancer on the door would not let her in.

The freelancer was nervously speaking into her walkie-talkie.

'No. Don't let her in,' said Liz's voice, firmly.

'Okay, but she seems really set on coming in. I think she will come back.'

'Let her. If she gives you any more trouble I'll come and help.' Liz was like a Rottweiler in these scenarios, a trained defender of Firehouse's cloistered, invite-only quarters.

Rose spotted Clara the second she arrived. The paparazzi crowded her car as she stepped out, getting as close to her as they physically could with their cameras. Dressed head to toe in a white feathered strapless gown, her clavicles protruding, she looked impeccable. Her hair had been styled in loose, glossy curls that resembled that classic Hollywood style. Her lips were bright red and puckered. Her skin bright and firm, like it had been massaged by one of those machines that says it will give you an instant face lift. She looked the best Rose had ever seen her. Rose waved as she tried to catch her eye. But Clara was still looking across the swarm of photographers, duly posing for all of them, taking her phone out and getting a selfie before walking over to Annabelle and Rose.

'Hey,' said Rose, reaching out to hug her.

'Hi, darling!' said Clara, leaning in to air-kiss her.

'How are . . .?' but before Rose could finish, Clara was gone.

'That was rude,' said Annabelle.

'I'm sure she just wants to get the reception over and done with so she can get ready for the runway,' said Rose, turning away from Annabelle so she wouldn't see how red her cheeks now felt.

She watched as Clara glided towards the line of official photographers waiting by the step and repeat. She greeted them much like she had greeted Rose: from afar, not touching her face to anyone else's.

And then something astonishing happened. Clara flashed her left hand to the photographers, splaying it near her face and smiling as her head fell back with laughter.

'Oh my God, she's engaged?' Annabelle said, watching the same scene as Rose in amazement.

Rose saw the glare of a giant diamond, glinting in the light.

'Oh,' said Rose, watching as Clara giggled.

Oliver was open-mouthed, walking over to Annabelle and Rose.

'Rose, is she engaged?' he asked urgently.

'This is the first I've heard of it,' she replied.

'A heads up would have been good. Fuck sake. I need to draw up a press release for this now. It will be a huge diary story.'

'That's good, I guess, right?' asked Annabelle.

'Yeah. It's great. Don't try to take credit for it, Rose.'

'Please, Oliver,' she replied.

'Please what?'

'I'm just popping to the loo,' Annabelle whispered.

Rose waited for her to disappear from earshot. This was her moment.

'I'm fed up with this bullshit,' she said.

'Excuse me?'

'You know what I mean.'

'No, I really don't. Please enlighten me.'

'Why are you like this with me? Is it because I'm better at my job than you?'

'Oh, give me a break.'

'You already get preferential treatment at work. I'm younger than you. Less senior. Less respected. And the Milo stuff. You just – you have no idea what you're talking about.'

'Okay.'

'It's . . . something happened. He is not a good person. In fact, I think he's actually a pretty awful person. The worst kind of person. And you really don't need to do this to me. I already hate myself. I already feel isolated. I already feel . . .' She paused, feeling her throat clogging up. She took a deep breath and looked up at Oliver, hoping for a glimmer of humanity.

'You really shouldn't be such a drama queen,' he replied.

'Can we please just get on?'

'Rose, for fuck's sake, drop it? We get on fine, okay? Whatever conflict you've decided we have does not exist.'

'What?'

'It's in your head, Rose. It's all in your head.' He was holding one finger up, twirling it around next to his ear, smiling with *Schadenfreude*. The grin started to extend beyond his face and suddenly his cheeks disappeared, leaving only teeth and eyes. Then it was just the teeth. *It's all in your head.* The words danced around her brain like the chorus of a song you've been singing all your life, except the volume had been turned up so high it was all you could hear, drowning out every passing thought. *It's all in your head. It's all in your head.*

The next thing Rose heard was Annabelle talking about Clara's engagement ring.

'Surely about £50,000? Right? I mean look at the size of the thing. My God. She has money, I know. But that's like capital M money. That's "my husband's name is on the side of a bank" money. Wow.'

Oliver was nowhere to be seen. Instead, there was just the flurry of passing bodies she and Annabelle smiled politely at. And there, getting smaller and smaller as she moved into the party, was Clara. Or at least another version of her, one that was a total stranger to Rose.

Minnie and Liz would be thrilled. News of the engagement meant at least one national news story for the following day. And Clara was the target market for StandFirst. It was a perfect piece of press.

After a few more actors had arrived, Annabelle started to get itchy.

'Why hasn't Milo turned up yet?' she asked.

'He will probably be late, Annabelle.'

'But how late?'

'Late enough.'

'God, I'm so excited to meet him.'

Rose sighed.

'What?'

'Nothing. Sorry.'

'Will you tell me what happened with you two?'

'Nothing happened. He's not someone you should spend any time worrying about. Trust me.'

Annabelle sighed dreamily. 'Oh, but I don't worry. I just love him. My friends couldn't believe I'd be meeting him tonight. I promised one of them I'd get him to send a happy birthday message.'

'Don't do that.'

'Okay.'

Another twenty minutes passed. More actors and musicians arrived, Rose had to stop Annabelle from asking each of them for selfies. Both of them had to keep placating Liz when Milo still hadn't arrived by 8.30 p.m. The fashion show was meant to start at 9 p.m. Milo was meant to go on stage at 9.30 p.m.

By 8.45 p.m., Liz had started to panic. As had Minnie.

'Rose, can I talk to you for a second, please?' she asked, pulling her away from Annabelle.

'Sure,' she said, knowing exactly what she was about to ask.

'Look, I'm really sorry to ask you this. But I can't get hold of Joss. Is there any chance you could send him a message to see where he is? If he doesn't show, it will be a disaster.'

'Okay. Let me message him now.'

'Thank you,' she sighed with relief, placing both hands on Rose's arms. 'I know this isn't easy for you.'

Rose walked away from the crowd and opened Instagram. She went to search for Milo in the search bar as she usually did. 'Mil . . .' she typed, as usually this would bring up his name with a blue tick. But nothing came up except for fan accounts. She typed his full name. Still nothing. She opened Google, searched 'Milo Jax Instagram'. The link to his profile came up. She clicked on it and the page redirected to Instagram. She knew what was about to happen, her stomach sinking slowly into the rest of her body as she saw it.

His profile picture. The number of posts. The number of followers. The number of people he followed. But where it usually said 'Follow', it said 'User Not Found'. Below, just white space with the words 'No Posts Yet'. Her phone fell to the floor.

It took a few minutes for Rose to pick up her phone and walk back over to Minnie.

'I don't think he's coming,' she said in a single breath.

Minnie's face fell.

'Oh God,' she said, turning around to look for Liz. 'Okay, erm, don't worry. This isn't your fault, it happens all the time. Let's go and find Oliver.'

She carried on talking but Rose couldn't hear anything. Minnie might as well have been speaking an entirely different language. After a few minutes, she couldn't really see her either. All she could see was a disfigured face, one that was becoming more and more contorted. The Francis Bacon face. And then everything went a little blurry. Minnie must have noticed something was wrong because she asked Rose to go and sit down.

Then Liz rushed in behind Minnie, shouting about something completely different and inaudible. There was some sort of other problem that meant Rose could turn around and start walking away without anyone noticing.

An hour or so later, Rose found herself alone in Hyde Park, sitting on a bench. She must have kicked the stilettos off along the way because they weren't on her feet. Nor were they anywhere in sight. The noise of the party had long ago drifted behind her. She hadn't meant to leave the party at all. But once she had emerged from it and started putting one foot in front of the other, she found it hard to stop. At some point, she started to run. Then she ran faster and faster until she had to sit down to regain her breath.

So Milo had blocked her. She now had no way of contacting him. He had committed to coming tonight and decided not to, for whatever reason. Because of course that's exactly what he could do. It's what he always had the power to do. Why had she ever thought differently?

Her whole body was shaking. The glassy water of the Serpentine stretched before her, reflecting the evening light. She should have known this would happen, the second Milo invited her into his world, she should have realised it was never an invitation at all. But a reminder that she would only ever be on the periphery of someone else's life. That she would only ever be turned away.

She was crying now. And she couldn't stop. Her mind drifted back to that night in his mews. To the dancing. The kissing. The sex. And then to that face below her. That unrecognisable morphed mash of colours and shapes. It was even more horrifying to look at now. Clearer, too. Slowly, it started to become more like a human face. On top of a human body that lay beneath her.

Then a new picture emerged. This time she was in her own bed and facing Milo, her body immobile from exhaustion and alcohol. His mouth was on hers but this time it felt wet and slippery, like it was trying to suffocate her. His hands were on her too, heavy like chains as they pushed themselves into the softness of her flesh. She was so tired.

Before Richard left, he used to let Rose sleep in bed with him on the few occasions Lola went away. They would listen to George Michael albums and lie silently together, his arms wrapped around her until she dozed off. She remembered trying to recreate that feeling with Milo; there was an urge to feel safe. But what she felt next was pain, an unfamiliar blow, like everything inside her was being forced out. Then it all went numb; neither sight nor sound was available. There was no pain any more, just a body relaxing into its own paralysis. Soon, she would be able to fall asleep. Any minute now.

In the park, Rose was on the move again. Her limbs were shaking, driving her forward. She reached the bridge overlooking the lake and climbed over the top of the short, pillared wall, so that she was sitting down on the edge, a black mass of water waiting beneath her dangling feet. She exhaled into the calm of the night, stretching out her arms. Finally, a breeze. It cooled her. The rushing sound of water and a familiar face, his hand reaching out for her. She smiled, breathing it all in.

PART IV

ONE

I was in a bad mood from the start of the evening. I had slept terribly the night before the party – mostly because Guy had ended things out of the blue. We were in the middle of watching an episode of *Friends*, the one where Ross gets married to Emily, when he started saying he'd been thinking about where this was going. I didn't say much. I just let him talk. He said something about needing to focus on work and being emotionally unavailable. By the time Monica had started shagging Chandler, Guy was gone. I couldn't eat anything all day after that. So I arrived at the Serpentine hungry and horny. A bad combination if you want to achieve anything that isn't eating or fucking. Unfortunately, there wouldn't be time for either.

The party was a total shitshow. Not only was there no performer because Milo had decided to go to the Seychelles with his new girlfriend but the seafood reception gave everyone food poisoning. I knew this was going to happen. I always told Minnie and Liz seafood was a wild idea. But nobody ever listens to Oliver. Except for Jasper. But that's only because he wants to exploit my publicity contacts. Or fuck me, possibly with his wife. Or maybe it was just his wife. Honestly, I'm not sure what's worse.

Anyway, the worst part was that, by the time the fashion show was due to start, people had already started filling the bathroom cubicles. There were queues forming outside but no one was moving. So people sort of just started being sick in the queue. They were snaking around the entire building, a proper vomit train. The smell was unbearable, like a cross between a toilet that wouldn't flush and a bin bag of rotting chicken carcasses. Even Jasper was purging what looked like entire prawns he must have swallowed whole. There's a rumour someone vomited on Kate Moss.

The only people who weren't sick were the women modelling in the show because they hadn't eaten anything – I told Minnie real people were worse than models. I hadn't either, of course, because of my allergies, and neither had Minnie or anyone on the press team because we never eat the guests' food.

Minnie handled it like a true pro, quietly calming everyone down and bringing buckets out from the kitchen for people to vomit when they couldn't get into the bathroom. Obviously, the fashion show didn't go ahead. Liz was oddly serene about the whole thing, almost like she was relieved the event could be cancelled. I'm pretty sure I saw her smoking a joint outside at one stage.

I was trying to placate the journalists we'd invited and asking them not to write about everything. But there was no point. The ones who weren't aggressively vomiting were taking surreptitious selfies of all the celebrities who were. Some of the influencers were filming themselves while retching. Minnie and I toyed with the idea of pretending this was all intentional: a way of introducing StandFirst as a brand so fresh and new you need to purge the old you out before you could be part of it. But we let that idea go.

It wasn't until much later that I thought about Rose. It was the first work event when I hadn't been watching her every move, looking over my shoulder as Minnie tended to her like she was a child prodigy. God, she was irritating. I knew she was better at the job than me from the moment she started. I mean, for fuck's sake, she worked at a private members' club and immediately got a job at Firehouse. Who does that? And then she somehow manages to wangle Milo Jax as her first major A-list talent? I've endured hours of meetings with that toad Joss and it had all come to nothing. Until Rose. It was impossible not to resent her.

I was supposed to be the favourite, the 6'5" office wunderkind who could just as easily get you on the phone to Madonna as Cher. Okay, maybe not Cher. But almost anyone else. So whenever I felt like I wasn't the next best thing, I guess I was a bit of an arsehole. Honestly, sometimes I think I was just trying to provoke her, to see her actually get really angry, or say what she was really thinking. She never did.

I can't remember who told me she'd slept with Milo – probably one of the circulation girls – but it didn't surprise me. She was exactly his type: young, thin, with a naivety that was almost virginal. There were always so many rumours flying around about his sex life: that his seduction trick was to play Toto's 'Africa'. That he got girls to peg him on the first date. That he was actually a woman. Of course I was jealous Rose slept with him. Who wouldn't be? I mean, have you seen that man? Fucking hell.

Anyway, after it happened, something about her changed. It was like she retreated even further inside herself. It was frustrating to watch. And I swear Minnie was favouring her even more. And so I just sort of got . . . nastier. I know, I know. How petulant for a grown man to stamp his feet the moment he's not the centre of attention any more. But dating in London is a binfire right now. I still haven't found anyone to take my spare room. I'm surviving on my overdraft. And I might actually have to move back into the Leyton flat with Dad and vile Cynthia unless Minnie finally promotes me. This job is all I have.

It must have been around 10 p.m. by the time I'd walked outside to have my secret nightly cigarette and inhale something that wasn't vomit or despair when I noticed a woman on the other side of the Serpentine, barely visible through the dark. It was hard to make out any identifying features, but then she started running and I could've sworn she wasn't wearing any shoes. It's not often that you see someone running barefoot in Hyde Park. As she moved closer, I spotted the glint of the silver StandFirst logo on her top under a streetlight. We really should have gone with the white like I'd suggested.

Rose was running quickly towards the bridge. Then suddenly she stopped. That's when I started to run myself. She had climbed onto the top of the barrier by the time I'd arrived. She was sitting down, feet hanging over the edge with her arms spread wide, almost as if she was about to take flight. Her eyes were closed; it looked like she was smiling.

I didn't even think about what to do. I just wrapped my arms around her and pulled her down onto the road. She screamed and kicked me. Her eyes were tightly shut, I'm not sure she even knew it was me. She was hysterical, like a possessed toddler. Or some kind of feral creature. It was terrifying, to be completely honest. They don't train you for this kind of thing in publicity. I kept holding her, squeezing her tightly so she couldn't wriggle away, waiting for her to calm down. Eventually she stopped fighting and just sort of collapsed into my arms, like a broken bird.

I sat there on the ground with her until a black cab drove past and stopped to check if we were all right. I told the driver what had happened and he suggested we take her to hospital. So that's what we did. The queue for A&E was hours long. I tried to negotiate with the nurse but she wasn't having any of it. We had to wait. The cabbie, Dave, stayed with us for hours. He was pretty fit, actually. I couldn't work out if he stayed because he was worried about Rose or because he wanted to sleep with me.

Either way, we chatted for hours until we were seen. Rose stayed asleep the entire time; I kept checking her pulse every few minutes. Minnie hadn't stopped calling all evening for updates; eventually, I suggested she contact someone in Rose's family.

Her mum showed up just as we came out from taking Rose to the doctor, who'd asked us to leave them in private. She looked fabulous, actually. Very out of sync given the circumstances. Head to toe in leopard-print pyjamas with feathered bits at the end. I wasn't sure how much to tell this wondrous woman what had happened, so I just said that Rose had also fallen victim to the food poisoning from the seafood reception and we decided to bring her here as a precaution.

Then someone else called Luce arrived. I presume Rose's mum called her because when she got there the two of them just hugged and cried a little. Luce kept apologising; I'm not sure why.

Eventually, the doctor came out with an update. He asked if we were friends or family, and I quickly asserted that I was just a colleague while her mum stood up and declared, 'I am her mother.' The doctor asked her to come with him and then they disappeared down one of the hospital's corridors.

Obviously, I wanted to know what was going on. But something about the look on the doctor's face told me not to pry. A part of me thought it might be best to leave and let them get on with things; Rose would probably be furious if she found out I was there. But I couldn't leave without an update. I needed to know she was going to be okay.

Her mum came out after about an hour. She thanked me over and over again and explained that Rose was fine. Because of me. I didn't really know what to say to that so I just smiled. She said everything was going to be okay and they were going to check Rose in to some sort of residential facility for a few weeks to recover. I didn't want to ask what she would be recovering from. It didn't even seem like her mum knew, in all honesty.

Of course, Minnie was more than understanding. She gave

Rose a two-month sabbatical. No one at Firehouse asked any questions – none of the senior team really knew who Rose was, anyway, and those who did probably just assumed she'd gone to the Priory or something. That kind of thing was normal for us. Jasper did ask after someone called Roisin once. But I never met anyone at Firehouse called Roisin.

PART V

November 2017

Rose's alarm goes off at 6.37 a.m., which, according to her sleep app, is the exact time in her circadian rhythm that she should get up. It's a delicate plinky sound that is supposed to soothe her. On her screen is an affirmation: 'You are heading in the right direction,' it reads. Rose opens another app on her phone and starts her five-minute morning meditation. She lies back down in her bed, closes her eyes, and listens to the sounds of someone called Tamsin talking about which parts of her body are waking up first.

Once it's over, she gets up to pour herself a large glass of water that she sprinkles green powder into, turning it into a swamp-like shade. It tastes disgusting but she holds her breath and finishes it fast as usual.

Next, she walks over to her bathroom and opens the cupboard, where jars of various vitamins line the shelf at her eye line. She goes from left to right, starting with one vitamin C and ending with two probiotics. Then she takes her medication: one tablet every morning at 7 a.m.

She wiggles into an activewear set Lola bought for her. A black sports bra with matching leggings; there is leopard print faded into the design but it's subtle. She opens her laptop to a YouTube tutorial for thirty minutes of yoga and begins her routine. She is getting much better at the tree pose already.

Once that's over, she has a cold shower. This is still not something she has got used to. She gets dressed quickly – black jeans and an oversized vintage shirt she found in Portobello Market – and makes breakfast, using the posh smoothie maker Luce bought her as a housewarming gift. Then she makes a cup of hot water and lemon and sits at her desk with her notebook and pen. She writes for thirty minutes, mostly about the dreams she had last night. Then she writes down three things she's grateful for that day: her green smoothie, the smell of her bedsheets in the morning and her activewear set.

Finally, she turns her phone off 'Do Not Disturb' mode. There is a message from Lola asking how she slept. And one from Oliver asking if she's still free for coffee on Saturday. Rose replies to both immediately: she slept well, and yes, she is. There are no other messages. She puts the phone in her pocket, plugs her headphones in and presses play on a playlist she found yesterday on a website about ayurvedic living.

She bundles up her coat, wraps a large grey scarf around her neck, puts her hat on and finally a pair of oval black sunglasses. Looking around for her keys, Rose smiles when she finds them placed neatly on the side by the door. She steps out of the house and takes a deep breath. The air is chilled but she is wearing enough clothes to shield her from it. There are mothers pushing prams, laughing and chatting idly. Birds are singing as they wake up with the day. A father holds his young daughter's hand, her backpack perched over his shoulders. And then there's a gentle gust of wind, one that rushes past as if moving right through her.

*

Extract from a newspaper article
Published 20 November 2017

A British musician has been accused of sexual assault during a three-year period, this newspaper can exclusively reveal. Four women have alleged they were raped between 2014 and 2017. The musician, who we cannot name, is believed to have made contact with each of the women via social media.

While the circumstances surrounding each case differ, there are striking similarities. The musician initially befriended each of the women, none of whom are in the public eye or known to one another, before inviting them to his home, where they had consensual sex. Hours later, they claim he raped them, either at his home or theirs. Alcohol was involved in all of the scenarios, with most of it provided by the musician. The testimonies have been corroborated by friends the women confided in at the time of the alleged crimes.

All of the women have told this newspaper that they felt compelled to report what had happened to them in light of the #MeToo movement.

The investigation is ongoing.

Acknowledgements

For whatever reason, I start thinking about the acknowledgements of a book very early on. This is true for books that I've written and books that I've read. In cases of the latter, the acknowledgements are usually the first thing I look at. I love to know who the author is close to, who inspires them and who helped bring their project to life. As for the reason, well, maybe I find it contextualizes the piece of work I'm about to consume or teaches me something about the publishing industry. Maybe I'm just nosy. Who knows?

Either way, I want to start by thanking you, reader, for being here and for paying attention to this book. At least enough attention to make it to the acknowledgements. *Gold Rush* is something I've wanted to write for a very long time and I will be forever grateful to anyone and everyone who engages with it. It means more to me than you'll ever know.

First up, I want to thank Michelle Kane. Your support has been truly life changing and I will be forever grateful to your unrelenting belief and grace throughout this process, even while you were taking time off. I would never have had the confidence to write this book had it not been for your encouragement. You saw something in me that took years for me to see in myself; thank you.

Next is an enormous thank you to Katie Bowden, whose thoughtful and considered edits took this story to where it needed to go. You knew exactly what I was trying to do with *Gold Rush* from the beginning and I'm so pleased we had the opportunity to work on it together.

That brings me onto marketing wizard, Olivia Marsden, and publicity pro Nicola Webb. Thank you both so much for your dedication and commitment to *Gold Rush*. Also, thank you Jo Thomson for designing the truly stunning cover and Martine Johanna for allowing us to use your gorgeous portrait. And to Eve Hutchings and the entire team at 4th Estate: thank you, thank you, thank you.

Josie Freedman and everyone at CAA, thank you for seeing the power and potential of this story, and for helping me realise it, too. I'm now convinced that all exciting Zoom meetings should take place in the back of taxis on the way to fashion shows.

My wonderful, patient and kind agent, Emma Leong, it's hard to know where to start. You've been such a vital part of my life ever since that Zoom meeting we had during lockdown. Thank you for pushing me to write this story and for holding my hand (figuratively and literally) throughout the entire process, professionally and personally. You are sunshine.

Speaking of sunshine, a big thank you to Emma-Louise Boynton for always being there for me during my moments of madness. Same goes for Ella McMahon, Lexi Allan,

Chloe Taylor Gee, Bethan Jones and the rest of the GADS. We're so lucky to have been in each other's lives for as long as we have; I never take it for granted.

To Allie Miller, Abi Binns, Katie Mackilligin-Ware, Lydia Cooper, Jess Hollingberry, Grace Brown, Ally Seward, Lucy Seward, Oenone Forbat and Elspeth Merry, thank you for being such loyal and loving friends to me throughout this process. I adore you all deeply.

Thank you to Patrick Smith and everyone at the *Independent* for your unwavering support, and for giving me the time and space to work on this book.

None of this novel would have come to fruition had it not been for my esteemed former colleagues at Condé Nast: Nicky Eaton, Richard Pickard and Harriet Robertson. What a dreamy first job I had; I owe so much of my career to all of you. Thank you.

Finally, onto my family. Thank you to Dad, Juliet and Asher. To my aunts, Natalie and Katie, and also my grand-parents, Carole, Derick, Nanou and our late Puppy. Thank you Stuie. Thank you Blanche (yes, she's my cat but she must be thanked).

And last but not least, thank you to my absolute force of a mother, Coco. You are everything to me and I wake up each morning feeling grateful to have you in my life not just as my mum but also as my best friend. You make my life sparkle.